NFUDU

NFUDU

Skirts, Ties & Taboos

OBY ALIGWEKWE

To Nkiru
Wishing you abundant love!!!

Oby
6-4-2078

Eclat Books

Cover design by Panagiotis Lampridis
Author Photo by Mina

Visit: www.nfudu.com

For Edna Ifeobu

1

NFUDU was born in Eastern Nigeria at a time when the British ruled its vast lands. She had the most delicate charm and spoke with a musical tone in her voice. Gentlemen were turned on by her soft demeanor, often brawling while vying for her attention. Her legs seemed to start from the tip of her toes and end far beyond her well-figured hips. Her skin was an olive-brown shade that glowed in the light and glistened like dew drops on leaves when she was wet. Her shoulders were broad but elegant. She walked with such stylish steps that everyone who saw her took a second glance. Often, her friends would tease, "Hian! Nekwa ukwu!" as they marveled over her rhythmic hip movements. They tilted their heads to get a look and twisted their lips in mock derision. This infuriated her as her steps were all natural – not put on by any means.

Everyone in the community saw Nfudu blossoming into a great beauty. Wealthy families lined up their most promising sons to win her affection. Her beauty was a standing discussion in her parent's home during house parties. Guests exchanged opinions about the most potential suitor for her. The frequent attention did not turn her haughty because she was not aware of the impact of her beauty.

"Papa, People always stare whenever I'm out." She would often confide in her father as a young girl when she grew weary of the frequent stares from men.

Her father, Chief Ibe did his best to assuage her concerns to ensure she maintained a healthy self-esteem. "It's because you're beautiful," was his usual response. This did nothing to ease her anxiety, but it always put a smile on her face.

-

With seventeen siblings in total, Nfudu was never bored with the endless entertainment coming from all corners of her home. Their parties were always a big affair. An invitation to the Ibe's for a bash provided a great source of pride for other youngsters. Bouncers were always on hand to rid the gatherings of unwanted guests and troublemakers.

One week after Emeka and Dike, Nfudu's twin brothers celebrated their seventeenth birthday, Nfudu kicked around a streamer, which one of the cleaners had probably missed. The extravagant parties thrown at the Ibe compound were starting to give her a headache and this small litter almost tipped the scale.

"Mama, Mama!" Nfudu called as she saw her mother about to pull out of the driveway.

"Eh? Nfudu!" responded her mother, wondering why she looked ready to burst.

"Mama, I can't stand it anymore. Look at this."

"You should speak with the cleaners."

"Mama, I don't think you understand. There's a bigger problem. Do we really need parties for every single occasion? It's getting ridiculous."

"I agree, but can we discuss this when I return?"

When her mother came back, she stomped into her room to discuss the issue of excessive partying. "Mama, a simple solution will be to combine birthdays…"

"My dear, I have also noticed that there is always too much going on around here. Yet, what you're suggesting is an excellent idea in theory, but in practice… it will increase competition among my husband's wives…"

"Then we should involve Papa."

"And stir up a hornet's nest? Your father will most likely agree with you as his *Ada*, his first daughter, but his other wives will grumble and make life difficult. Each one of them will want to celebrate their children's birthdays and anniversaries. Which will you choose over the other?" her mother concluded, raising both hands in defeat.

Nfudu adjusted her position on the bed to face her mother. "Mama! Are you saying we should leave things as they are?"

"That's not exactly what I mean. I'm saying that it won't be easy with these other women."

"I don't know how you handle sharing your husband with three other women. You're strong."

"Strong?" Mrs. Ibe shook her head in disagreement. "It's not been rosy. Did you hear what Mama Nkechi did last week, while you were still in Lagos? She crashed her two-year-old Mercedes Benz. Rumor has it that it was because she couldn't bear the thought that your father bought the most recent model for me."

"Don't tell me that!" Nfudu stared at her mother in disbelief. "I thought the driver ran into a cow. ...So she lied?"

"Of course she lied. Did you see any bruise on the driver? That same night, she pretended to forget that it was Mama Azuka's turn and forced her way into your father's room."

"Why?" asked Nfudu amused yet trying hard not to laugh.

"For the sole reason of demanding a brand new car. I have never seen such stupidity." She snapped her fingers and shrugged her shoulders in disdain.

"Ridiculous!" exclaimed Nfudu wide-eyed with shock. "How did Mama Azuka respond? Did she let her walk all over her?"

"Ahh. Nooo. Those two are cats and dogs. They rained abuses on each other, got into a physical fight, and almost stripped to their bare bottoms. It got so bad their children got involved – Nkechi pulled a knife and threatened to stab Azuka."

"What!" Nfudu screeched. She grabbed the sides of the bed and looked at her mother in disbelief. "Where was father when all this was going on?"

"I don't know… but he came back later after everything had died down and demanded to see both women. It was chaotic. You're lucky you weren't here."

"Mama, you people need to send Nkechi to military school to check her behavior. I've heard about other times she's acted with rage, and no one should have to tolerate this anymore. Oh! As for Papa, I blame him and all the men in this world that feel the need to punish their kin by having more than one wife. I pray he lives long enough to see all his children through the important moments in their lives, let alone deal with the competition among his women."

"My dear, pray harder because in reality most of these men die young and leave their wives and children to deal with the mess they created."

-

Chief Ibe was the highest ranking chief in Abasi. His title – Akajiora, carried certain unique privileges such as veto power to appoint and dethrone the ruling Igwe. He was one of the foremost engineers in his town and was credited with constructing the Nkume-Abasi highway – an accomplishment that gave him unbridled popularity – and established his reputation as the best building contractor east of the Niger. He was also a real estate Baron and owned at least a third of the commercial buildings in Nkume, where his family resided for a part of each year. He contributed to a lot of worthy causes in Abasi, Nkume and other neighboring towns. The church buildings where his family worshipped, as well as the Aferi market in Abasi were built with his contributions.

In Abasi, prestige was measured by material wealth, stature and the number of wives and children possessed by a man compared to his peers. Chief Ibe's wealth knew no bounds, and with four wives and eighteen children – who treated him like a god and feared the sound of his booming voice, broad shoulders and towering six foot six stature – he was not considered wanting in any category. His children were also never found wanting as they had everything they desired. With the opportunities they had to travel to exotic locations and acquire the best money could buy, they were seen as trendsetters among their peers who envied and made up legendary tales about them.

The Ibe compounds in both Nkume and Abasi were lavish. Each was a mirror image of the other. Both contained five duplexes, one for each of Chief Ibe's four wives and the fifth for Chief Ibe to entertain his guests – mostly dignitaries – who often visited from far and wide. Four bungalow style homes, located in the north end of each duplex were reserved as servants' quarters. Each was lined with magnificent entrances with beautiful stone sculptures that seemed to come to life if stared at long enough.

The gardens were immaculately kept by the gardener, Ene, who prided himself on being able to make any plant from any part of the world grow under his 'magical hands'. As a result, several unique flowers could be seen lining the compounds at all times of the year. He was often heard singing while he worked. Although he had never stepped outside the shores of Nigeria nor received any formal education, this small middle-aged man spoke impeccable English, and would often welcome guests with a small bow and a "Hello, how do you do?" On occasion, he would correct an unsuspecting servant, who dared to respond with "Fine. Thank you," and force him to respond with, "How do you do?" He called it 'Queens English'.

Nfudu's Mother, being the first wife of Chief Ibe had the most revered position of all the wives. She was seen as the mother of the household, so she and her children occupied the largest of the four duplexes. She was beautiful – a mirror image of Nfudu, although lighter in complexion and of a bigger build. She welcomed everyone with open arms – a philanthropist of sorts – well known for providing clothes for the needy, visiting the sick and engaging in various humanitarian activities in both Abasi and Nkume.

Being the *Ada*, Nfudu got the opportunity to render her opinion before any of her siblings. Though, she was often under immense pressure whenever she needed to battle with difficult life decisions for her family. This privilege enhanced her self-confidence and provided her immense freedom. She understood her role but didn't abuse the power associated with it.

Nfudu dreamt of a time when she could escape the pandemonium in her home to build a life of her own. Whenever the wives fought, it motivated her to fight harder to secure her departure. Most days, she studied without break, never taking her eyes off the vision of passing her exams. A-levels was her passport out of her home and into the school of her choice, the International Institute of Fashion in Paris. The school was highly reputable and offered an excellent curriculum. Most of the graduates from the Institute went on to become world-renowned fashion designers.

Nfudu always had an aptitude for fashion. She had been making clothes for herself and her friends from the day she finished her first beginner's sewing course. Making perfectly fitted clothes for different body types became her forte. She was always the best-dressed person in any group, so when news got around that she made a majority of her clothes herself, it was not long before her friends started sending in requests to have her custom make their own clothes. She enjoyed her new hobby and with her keen attention to detail, she was able to deliver every time and please her clientele. As the requests became more frequent than she could handle, she began to decline a good number of them so she could focus on her studies. Since she lived and breathed fashion, no one was surprised when she chose fashion as a career.

Chief Ibe raised his girls with a mindset that contradicted the general belief in Igbo land that the traditional role of a woman is to marry a successful man and help him succeed in his endeavors. He was often heard saying, "The girls in this family should study very hard oh. Making it in this man led world is not going to be easy if you don't obtain professional degrees first." Nfudu understood this mindset and worked for it to become her reality as she had no plans of depending on any man for her wellbeing. Chief Ibe was delighted that she had decided on a vocation she could succeed at, and as a result, he was fully supportive of her choice.

-

"Nfudu... Nfudu... Nfudu...," yelled Mrs. Ibe as Nfudu bade farewell to her friends Ngozi and Nneka who had come to visit. Before she could respond, her mother ran to hug her as she headed back into the compound. To Nfudu's astonishment, she threw both hands in the air and exclaimed, "You've been accepted!"

At first, Nfudu was unsure of what she was referring to. "Accepted… where? Take a deep breath, Mama," she said, amused by the theatrics.

"Where else? The International Institute of Fashion."

In that moment, Nfudu knelt on the hard cement floor, raised both hands into the sun-filled sky and muttered a prayer under her breath. She then sprang up, hugged her mother and ran screaming into the compound to announce the good news to the rest of her siblings.

"I can't wait to give Papa the wonderful news."

"Hmm. You're now a big girl. Please don't forget us when you start making your millions oh," her mother teased, as Nfudu reeled from excitement.

Nfudu dimmed her eyes and a frown spread across her face as she feigned annoyance at her mother's comment. "Ahh, Mama …that is not possible. I will never forget you or any other member of my family for that matter. …In fact, when I make my millions, I'll make sure you're the first to know."

"I know my dear. I was just teasing. I know what you're capable of and I pray that God will go with you, guide you, protect you and bring you back home safely at the end of your program."

"Ameeen!" Nfudu shouted, happily.

–

It was June of 1963. From the demonstrations in Tehran to the civil rights movements in the United States to the Apartheid movement in South Africa, it seemed like the turmoil in the world would never end. In Europe, the Second World War was long over but the effects and the ravages of the war meant that there was still a long road to recovery for the victims. Even though the thought of moving to Paris was an exciting one for Nfudu, she was wary of the situation on the other side of the world. Her parents were less concerned – they had secured her a hostel accommodation – which would protect her to a large extent from the issues on the streets. In Nigeria on the other hand, in response to the newly acquired independence, the country was beginning to move towards self-governance on a representative and increasingly federal basis. It was an exciting time to be Nigerian as opportunities were limitless for citizens. In her dreams, Nfudu envisioned returning after her studies, when she had hopefully made a name for herself.

Freshman classes at the International Institute of Fashion were scheduled to resume in January, which gave Nfudu only a few months to prepare. In the time she had left with her family, her siblings entertained her with stories related to the amazing adventure she was about to embark on. Each of the stories, though ludicrous, got Nfudu even more excited than she originally was. Afonwa, who Nfudu was closest to, couldn't wait for her turn to go after her own dreams. She began to work extraordinarily hard at school to make sure that in a few years, she too would get an opportunity such as Nfudu's. One evening, she came into Nfudu's room and sulkily sat next to her.

"Sister," said Afonwa, "I hope when you make it you'll send for me to live with you?"

"Of course!" responded Nfudu. "And we will have so much fun together. I'll also send you nice things from Paris as soon as I settle down...Ok?"

"Ok!" Afonwa was smiling from ear to ear as Nfudu gave her a long hug and wondered when she would really see Afonwa again. In a few years, she would be an adult and who knows where in the world she could be.

Nfudu's move was fast approaching and with each ounce of excitement, she felt an equal amount of trepidation at the thought of moving away from home for the very first time. The years she spent in the boarding house in Nkume and the two she spent completing her A-levels in Lagos – during which she came home every few months – did not count. In boarding house, her father or mother visited her every week even though the school rules permitted visiting only once a term. All the students in her school knew who her parents were, and they often called her attention to their arrival, before the matron got a chance to inform her of their visit.

Despite having traveled to Europe a few times in the past, Nfudu had never been to Paris. She hoped the city would offer her everything she dreamed of. Her parents were happy she was pursuing her dreams but wanted her to maintain a certain status quo. This, her father made very clear when she took his medication to his room during one of the last nights she spent at home.

"I make one request of you." Chief Ibe began in a harsh tone.

"What Papa?"

With a straight face, he said matter-of-factly, "The only thing I ask is that you don't bring home a white man. There will be many suitors waiting for you when you return. Just focus on your studies and remember that there is time for everything!"

Nfudu wanted to crawl under the bed and hide from the embarrassment. "Papa, please stop," she said. "Pleeease... I'm going to Paris to study not to chase after men." She hissed under her breath and looked in the direction of the door as she planned her escape. When she stood up to leave, she heard him say, "Where do you think you're going?"

"Nowhere..." She continued to look at the door and let her father's scolding fall on deaf ears.

"I'm just warning you ahead of time because Okudo's daughter returned after six years in America with a white man and a baby. It was such a disappointment for all the young men that were waiting for her hand in marriage, and an even bigger disappointment for her parents."

Nfudu was stunned by his words but knew not to respond when her father got self-righteous as it had never gotten her anywhere. In fact, it could get her a slap and had in the past. She became tightlipped and provided the best answers she could to ensure she left his presence in one piece. She hated these conversations about men and suitors, especially with her father, who seemed to bring it up any chance he got. She was twenty, and even though she had a little bit of experience with men, she did not want to discuss the topic at this level of intimacy with her parents, who she felt would not understand where she was coming from.

Nfudu had never gone the whole way with a man. The most she knew about intimate male-female relations were from the stories she heard from her friends, who hadn't had any intimate relations themselves and from that horrible nanny that got fired seven years ago. The closest contact she had ever had with a member of the opposite sex were the kisses she stole from Amadi behind the cherry bushes in her father's compound, whenever she pretended to accompany him to his car to give him a message for his sister, Ngozi. Amadi was only two years her senior but seemed so knowledgeable about such matters, which made her accord him a certain level of respect.

A few weeks before she was scheduled to leave for Paris, Nfudu visited Ngozi in her family home when Amadi was around. She always craved his company. When Ngozi left for the kitchen to cook with her older sister Edith, Nfudu was left alone in the small living room with Amadi. They kissed and caressed. "We can't afford to let your parents see us," Nfudu said.

"Don't worry. They traveled to Lome and won't be back until tomorrow."

"Ok. But Edith might see us."

"Don't worry about that. Let's go to my room for a moment. There's something I'd like to show you." He said, looking at Nfudu rather seductively.

"What?"

"It's a surprise. You'll like it. I promise."

"We have to hurry so I can join Ngoo and Edith in the kitchen."

Nfudu did not believe he had any valuable surprise for her. Besides she was concerned about what Edith would think of her if she was seen anywhere in the vicinity of Amadi's room. Still, she didn't know if it was her curiosity or her new quest for adventure – brought on by her move to Paris – that made her go against her better judgment.

He took her hand, walked her upstairs to his bedroom and immediately shut the door behind them. He then reached into his closet and pulled out a small satin box which he handed to her. She opened the box right away to reveal a beautiful gold necklace, with a round pendant and the letter N inscribed inside the circle.

"Wow!" she exclaimed. "This is stunning." She looked up at him with her beautiful doe-shaped eyes. Knowing that they had a unique way of always revealing what she was feeling at any moment, she darted her head to the right in characteristic fashion, to hide the allure in them.

"Yeah. I had it especially made for you."

"Thank you!" She took the necklace out of the box and handed it to him. "Please help me put it on," she responded with a yielding tone.

"Sure, especially when you ask in that voice." He held her shoulders and swiftly turned her back towards himself. As he placed the necklace on her, he gently caressed her neck. Without a moment's notice, she felt a thick bulge on her back that grew and pulsated the longer he stood behind her. She froze on the spot. When she recovered and tried to take her leave, he whispered, "I wish you didn't have to go," into her ears, but she pulled away from him, rushed out the door and flew down the stairs. She was feeling rather agitated when she joined her friend in the kitchen and was lucky to have arrived in time.

"I was just about to go searching for you. Where were you?" Ngozi asked.

"Oh," Nfudu replied. "I was having a discussion with Amadi..." She was happy she left Amadi's room when she did. She couldn't imagine her embarrassment if Edith or Ngozi had found her in an uncompromising position with him.

For many months after that intimate encounter with Amadi, Nfudu had recurring dreams about sex. She woke up several mornings, moaning from the sheer pleasure of it. One day, she hoped, she would find that man with whom she could enjoy the pleasurable activity that she could only dare to dream about. She also looked forward to spooning with her dream man until they both would fall asleep. But with her trip to Paris pending, Nfudu had no plans of being bogged down by Amadi and other potential suitors. She had other dreams that spanned far beyond getting hitched. First, she had to conquer the world.

2

PARIS was buzzing when Nfudu arrived in the fall. Many structures were still in a terrible state even with the significant efforts made under de Gaulle's leadership to rebuild France. Several sections of the city were still severely damaged. A number of churches were burnt to the ground and former historical sites looked abandoned. Parisians were still recovering from the ravaging effects of the war. Peasants and beggars roamed the back streets and touts were scattered along the sidewalks looking to make a quick buck.

At first, Nfudu was disappointed when she saw the dilapidated state of some areas of the city, but a look beyond the surface opened her eyes to how romantic and beautiful Paris really was. Ancient stone structures filled the landscape. Beautiful cafes lined the streets. Even more beautiful were the women she saw darting in and out of the boutiques she saw along the way. Black seemed to be the choice color for the couture houses. She stared for hours at the clothes through the windows and imagined when she would run her own empire. Sometimes, she went inside the couture houses to inquire about the designs and was often greeted with warmth. At times, with her limited French, she could not get past the pleasantries to discuss in detail.

The admission letter to the International Institute of Fashion stated the official language of study as English. Despite that, Nfudu planned to improve her French speaking skills to the level of fluency expected of a native speaker. As an aspiring fashion designer, she wanted to be able to function outside the confines of the school without the language barrier as a hindrance. She had a few months before school resumed to attend a French language class and add finesse to her speech.

-

During her second week in Paris, Nfudu registered for a class for newcomers with varying degrees of French language knowledge. The class was made up of about thirty students of all ages and from all walks of life. It had a good mix of nationalities – at least half of the attendees were international students – who had recently relocated to France to study. There were a couple of clergies, a few businessmen and some stay-at-home moms. The Assistant Tutor – Vanessa – provided extra lessons to any students needing additional help understanding some of the topics taught in class. A handful of the students were new or existing students at the International Institute of Fashion. During breaks, the old students shared their experiences – some good and some bad – but at least Nfudu got to know what to expect.

During break time one afternoon, Vanessa came up to Nfudu, with her hand stretched out for a handshake. "You speak excellent English."

"Thank you," replied Nfudu, giving Vanessa her hand in return.

"Have you ever lived outside Nigeria?"

Nfudu chuckled slightly before responding, "No I haven't but English is the national language in Nigeria."

"Interesting," said Vanessa. "I really ought to know more about the world around me. Each day I find out how little I know."

"Don't we all?" added Nfudu, with a knowing smile on her face.

Nfudu's mind lingered on Vanessa's sweet demeanor and attractiveness. She had long shiny black hair, well defined facial features and a rear that put Nfudu's African version to shame.

"What are you doing this evening?" Vanessa asked as Nfudu was about to leave.

Nfudu had not given her evening a thought before that moment. "Nothing really!" she said, regretting her words as soon as they came out from fear that Vanessa might find her too eager or worse still – needy.

"I'm seeing a movie tonight with a couple of friends. Would you like to join?"

"I wouldn't like to impose on you and your friends."

"It's no imposition. We can pick you up at eight. Put down your address here," said Vanessa pulling out a notepad and pen from her satchel and handing it to Nfudu.

Nfudu scribbled the address on the note pad and handed it to Vanessa.

"You're staying at the Décolletage hostel of the International Institute of Fashion?"

"Yes," answered Nfudu. "I'll be starting classes there next year."

"It's no accident that we're friends. I'll be attending the same school, in January."

Nfudu's smile widened when Vanessa referred to her as a friend. "Will you be staying at the hostel also?"

"Yes and no," Vanessa responded, tilting her head to the side. "I mean…, I hope. Father may want me to stay with some friends in town. They have a big place on Germaine Street but I'll prefer the hostel. It will keep me close to the action. Do you like living at the hostel?"

"Yes! So far it has exceeded my expectations. I like the cafes and I don't have to step outside the grounds to shop or even be entertained. Also, since students lodge there all year round I'm guaranteed company during the holidays."

"That sounds great. Father and my stepmother will never sanction my staying in the hostel for the holidays though."

"Oh, your parents are divorced?" Nfudu blurted out, but immediately realized her slip-up. "Sorry I didn't mean to be nosy."

"It's nothing to be ashamed of. They've been divorced for four years. I live with my father Javier and stepmother Juliette in Nice. For the past three years, I attended boarding school in London which is my family's second home. I took this tutoring job right after graduation."

"Does your father approve of you working?"

"Yes! It was his idea. He thinks it'll make me well rounded. Taking the tutoring job in Paris was an easy decision for me because my boyfriend Jeremy lives here."

-

Vanessa picked Nfudu at eight from the Décolletage hostel lobby. As she entered the back seat of the black Porsche driven by Jeremy, she was greeted by Jeremy's friend Stanley.

"Glad you could join us. Stanley just arrived from Milan for the weekend," chimed Vanessa. "You've met Jeremy."

"Yes. A few times during lunch breaks at the French classes. Hi guys."

"Hello," both replied in unison.

Nfudu immediately noticed Stanley's serious look and dark well-coiffed hair, which was a stark contrast from Jeremy's blonde one. They were exact opposites in appearance and demeanor. Jeremy was very friendly and always seemed to have his lips curved into a smile. His tall muscular frame was a little bit intimidating. It seemed to contradict his friendly nature and the tousled hairstyle he wore all the time.

At the Cinema, they were swiftly met by a worker who leads them to their seats. Jeremy slipped a franc note into her hand and a huge smile spread across her face. Any onlooker could tell she received a generous tip. In their row, Nfudu sat next to Stanley, on one end, while Vanessa and Jeremy sat beside them. Jeremy leaned forward and cranked his head in Stanley's direction. "Make sure Nfudu is comfortable."

"I sure will," he responded.

The movie 'Three Girls in Paris' was highly anticipated by women all over Europe and that night, being the opening, the Cinema was filled to the brim with women of all ages and sizes. There were a few men with bored looks on their faces.

From talking to Stanley for only a few minutes, Nfudu learned he was a third-year law student at the University of Milan, had been a friend of Jeremy's since childhood and was taking a short break from school before the grind of the winter session began.

"Vanessa tells me you're here to attend the International Institute of Fashion. Congratulations!" Stanley half yelled amidst the loud noise in the cinema.

"Thank you!" Nfudu replied, raising her voice to be heard amidst the chatter throughout the theatre. "It's always been my dream to be a fashion designer. What is your motivation for studying Law?"

"I come from a family of lawyers. My grandfather owned a successful law firm and my father and older brother are also lawyers."

"Wow! What a pedigree," marveled Nfudu as the opening scene for the movie flashed on the screen and they leaned into their seats to watch. There were moments of silence within the first hour as the story built up, and collective oohs and ahhs when the characters – three Danish girls got lost on their trip to Paris. An annoying gentleman talked during most of the movie. Laughter reverberated through the cinema the two hours they were there.

"That was amazing!" Jeremy said as the credits rolled on the screen. "I hope you enjoyed it?"

"Very much. I agree. It was amazing! This is the most fun I have had since being in the city," Nfudu said as she made her way out of their row. "Thank you so much!"

"You're welcome," chimed in Vanessa. "Would you like to join us for a cruise around the Orangerie tomorrow afternoon? It will be fun. That is if you don't have anything better to do."

"I would love to. I have heard about that cruise from the girls at the hostel, but haven't got the chance to go. I guess there are a lot of places I haven't seen."

"Great. We'll pick you after lunch," Stanley responded with a wry smile before she stepped out of the car.

-

The next day, they cruised around the Orangerie and down to the Tuileries Gardens. Throughout the day, Stanley opened every door for Nfudu and pulled out all her chairs, which made her giggle at every gesture. As she spent most of the day by his side, she got acquainted with the musky but sweet smell of his cologne. She also admired the blue blazer he paired with his crisp white t-shirt.

On entering the dining hall, Nfudu marveled at the dinner setting. Delicate petals from fresh fall blooms floated around in transparent glass bowls that were used as centerpieces for the tables. The table arrangement provided diners the opportunity to interact with each other. Outside the window, the Eiffel tower could be seen changing color every two seconds from yellow to blue to purple as they cruised by. This made their evening even more spectacular. By the time Jeremy dropped Nfudu back at her hostel, she crashed down on her bed, rather exhausted. As she settled down for the night she thought about the events of the day and laughed to herself, shaking her head. With any other company, she might not have had as much fun, she thought.

-

Nfudu sat at her desk and looked over some of the receipts she had accumulated recently. They were way over the budget she had set for herself. Tuition for the French classes was incredibly high. Between payment for the classes and her social activities, she found life in Paris very expensive. During her short stay at the hostel, she had made quite a few friends, who were willing to show her around and this had blown her cash to bits. She soon found that when asked to dinner to celebrate a friend's birthday at a nice restaurant, she was expected to pay for her own share of the meal and drinks. This was a far cry from what she was used to in Nigeria, where the celebrant is expected to foot the bill for their own occasion. After learning the hard way Nfudu, became selective with social invitations to avoid creating a dire financial situation for herself.

She did not plan to bother her parents about money since she wanted to be seen as mature and independent. The only option she had was to look for a job, although she knew her parents would frown against it. She perused newspapers for modeling jobs and applied for all she could find. Soon she was getting calls and attending auditions, but experienced a lot of rejection as a result of her fuller figure. Often, she was told by modeling agencies that she had the type of body most people would envy, but her buttocks were too full to fit into their client's clothes, not fit for the runway or even the fashion magazines.

One cold day in November as she walked away from yet another rejection, she pulled her jacket tighter and adjusted her hood to prevent the icy November air from piercing her chest. As she stopped to check her reflection in a glazed over window she felt two light taps on her shoulder, causing her to jump. She turned around and quickly calmed when she realized it was the interviewer from her last walk-in. The small man gave her a faint smile, offering an apology for startling her. "Bernie's is looking for a sales girl to man the storefront and I think you'll be right for the job. Is that something you'll consider?" Nfudu had frequented the beautiful shops she saw along the way but hadn't considered working in one of them. However, she saw the offer as a great opportunity – one she could tolerate.

"Definitely," she answered. "When do they need one by?"

"Immediately. Their sales girl quit unexpectedly and since Christmas season is around the corner. They're frantic to get a replacement. …Your French is good. Besides, you're very beautiful and pleasant. They'll be elated to have you."

"Thank you! I'll appreciate if you can arrange a meeting for me."

The Store Manager at Bernie's called Nfudu that evening to ask if she could resume in two days. She accepted the offer although it meant missing the last week of her French classes.

The following evening, she invited Vanessa and Marion – a second-year student of the International Institute of Fashion, who she met while staying at the hostel to celebrate her new job. They hung out in Nfudu's hostel room and enjoyed some Chinese dinner from the vendor across the street and drank a cheap bottle of wine Nfudu had picked up from the liquor store near the French class.

"This is the best Chinese food I've ever had," exclaimed Vanessa as she took a second helping of the chicken fried rice.

"Yeah," agreed Nfudu. "It's my go-to food."

"I may decide to stay in the hostel for this."

"That will be nice," agreed Marion. "We'll both be happy to have you."

"Thank you, Marion."

"Congratulations on your new job," said Vanessa. "We'll miss you at French classes. If you like, I can help you cover the curriculum you're going to miss…"

"Thanks. That will be awesome." Nfudu's French was almost as fluent as she needed it to be after years of learning the language in Nigeria, and almost six months of practice since arriving in Paris. She had all she needed to resume her life as a French speaker but was grateful she wouldn't be missing anything.

After saying goodbye to her guests she tidied up what was left of their dinner and then hopped into bed to get some rest. She needed to get up early the following morning to get ready for work. No matter how hard she tried, sleep seemed to elude her. She was both anxious and excited about the following day. Finally, just before the sun started peeking out behind the trees. Nfudu was able to fall asleep. Unfortunately, she only got a few hours of sleep causing her to wake up groggy and sleepy. She took a quick bath and popped gum in her mouth to stay awake for her orientation before the stores opening at nine o'clock.

-

Being a stickler for time, Nfudu arrived at Bernie's at the nick of time, eager to start her orientation. It was crowded with shoppers from all corners of the world looking for stylish clothing and timeless accessories. She looked around at the faces of the people in the store, trying to guess which one could belong to her new boss. Her Manager, Sophie welcomed her with a kiss on the cheeks and a "Bonjour!"

"Bonjour," Nfudu responded, pleased for the warm welcome. The friendliness the French exhibited towards complete strangers never ceased to surprise her. It always made her feel at ease.

Sophie did not waste a single minute. She dragged Nfudu through the store's departments – safety, human resources, and payroll – where she was made to complete compulsory documentation. Each step in the process was as exciting and as revealing as the one before. "Let me know if you have any questions," Sophie said as they retreated from the storage room in the basement level of the building.

"I was wondering if I need to focus on any particular areas out of everything I've heard this morning."

"It's a lot," agreed Sophie. "Other than the safety training and the instruction you're about to receive on the shop floor, you don't need to bother about much else. Our temps are required to go through the same steps as permanent employees because Management needs to ensure certain standards are maintained."

"Ok. That makes sense."

When they finally got to the shop floor at quarter to nine, customers had begun to line up in front of the glass doors. Sophie rushed through the remaining steps with Nfudu before she flung the doors open and said a cheery "bienvenue!" to the shoppers as they streamed into the store.

Work was hectic that first day. Shoppers came in record numbers, allowing barely any time in between for Nfudu to get a break. She developed a brand new respect for all the salespeople she had ever met in her life; she realized that life as a working girl was no picnic. A majority of the customers were women. A handful of men also came to buy Christmas presents for their wives or girlfriends. She could always tell when it was the latter when the men splurged without any consideration of the cost of the items. It offended her whenever she was certain that was the case, and she said a little prayer for her future husband to treat her everlastingly like a girlfriend. She would have to keep him on his toes to make that certain.

That first day went by so fast Nfudu didn't remember she barely had any sleep the night before. She was a favorite at the store. Everyone swooned over her charming smile and accent. She was also a natural at helping the customers pick out the right attires for their body types. Some of the men merely came by to get a better look at her. By the end of that day, she built enough excitement to overcome the distress she felt the first few hours of being on the shop floor. It helped that the pay was generous, and as a Bernie's employee, she was entitled to a fifteen percent discount on any items she purchased.

She worked up until Christmas Eve and when she received her final paycheck from Sophie, she felt a surge of emotion as Sophie hugged her for what might be the last time. "We will miss you a lot," said Sophie releasing Nfudu's grip to wipe a tear that was beginning to drip down the corner of her eyes. "Promise you'll return if you ever need a job? Don't be a stranger."

"I'll miss you all too," Nfudu replied. "I may come in to help on weekends and some evenings, but that will depend on my school schedule."

"I understand. Let me know what works for you. Au revoir."

"Au revoir!"

As she headed home, Nfudu realized the splendor of the Christmas season in Paris. It had a poetic charm that thrilled the most delicate of senses and made one wonder about the beautiful works of the Creator. She was thrilled about the soft white snow, the beautiful Christmas decorations that lined the streets, especially the ones on Balmain Street and the cheer on the faces of Parisians as they proclaimed "Joyeaux Noel!" to one another. All that made her forget about the cold wintry air that blew across her face as she made her way to the train station.

When she got into the train, she felt a deep sense of nostalgia sweep over her. Her eyes glazed over as she thought about what her siblings would be doing at that moment. Since Christmas was usually the most exciting time of the year in Chief Ibe's home, everyone cast all their troubles aside and enjoyed the beauty and magic of the season. She imagined the older kids would be home from boarding school and would have lined up their Christmas attires in readiness for church service on Christmas day. She would be glaringly absent. They would miss her, just as much as she missed them. She had been too busy since her arrival in Paris and hadn't kept in touch adequately with her family. As a result, she felt estranged from them and decided to call as soon as she got to the hostel.

Now back to the warm comfort of her room, Nfudu immediately called home. Her mother picked the phone. "I have been expecting your call all day my daughter. Where have you been? More importantly, how have you been?" Nfudu had always wondered how her mother always accurately guessed who was on the other end of a line. When she was younger, she thought her mother was psychic. Later she realized she may just have a strong intuition.

"Sorry, Ma. I just returned from work."

"Work? On Christmas Eve? I don't know why you insist on punishing yourself. I told you that you didn't need to work. Your father can provide all your needs."

"Mama, everyone works here. It's fine. Also, I got a lot of experience working at Bernie's and made a lot of great contacts. Some of the kids I work with have rich parents too, and they don't rely entirely on them. It gives them a sense of pride to be independent."

"Ehh? Ok. No problem. How have you been? Your father is here. He wants to speak with you. Afonwa and Dike are also here to speak with you."

"Hello, my dear." Chief Ibe's voice echoed across the phone lines. "What did I just hear? …That you're working? From now on, I'll like you to focus on your studies. I didn't send you to Paris to work. *Inugo?*"

"Yes, Sir. I have heard. Today was my last day. It was just for a few weeks before school starts in January. Like I told Mama, I gained a lot of valuable experience from it. How are you all? I hope you're taking your blood pressure medication."

"I am fine my dear. I never miss my medication. Thank you."

Afonwa had so much to tell Nfudu when her turn came to speak with her, half of which may have interested her in the past, but not anymore. She told her about how Amadi had moved to America to study Medicine, how her father's wives were getting along and all the crushes she's had since her sister left. By the time Nfudu was done speaking with everyone, she was so tired, she fell right into bed barely having any strength left to remove her makeup or put on her nightgown.

She woke up on Christmas morning, concerned that it would be the loneliest of Christmas'. Other than being so far away from home, her best friends were also gone – Vanessa was in Nice with her family, while Stanley was in Milan. She ate a quiet breakfast in her room and walked two miles with Marion and Adalicia to Notre-Dame for the Gregorian Mass. The mass was in French and the priest spoke so fast that even with her aptitude for French Nfudu found it hard to follow.

The three girls sat in the pews and listened to the sweet hymns sang by the adult choir, led by none other than France's Henri Sylvian.

After church, she and her friends walked around the city and ate lunch along the way from one of the street vendors lining the entrance to the Eiffel tower. Her feelings of loneliness soon vanished as the beautiful sites renewed her joy. It was then that she realized she would never get tired of Paris and for the first time since her arrival, she felt at home in another man's land. She decided to make the best of her current situation, which many would give their right hand for. Besides, she was now a grown woman and couldn't always expect to be with her family. She would turn twenty-one in June and soon enough her parents would be expecting her to marry and move away from home.

Vanessa arrived at the hostel two days before New Year. Nfudu was overjoyed about her decision to live at the hostel. Their relationship had blossomed into a sisterhood. They had so much in common. Both were twenty going on twenty-one, had similar family backgrounds, same taste in men and a love of fashion. That evening, Nfudu joined her for dinner with her parents, who had driven with her all the way from Nice. Classes at the International Institute of Fashion were scheduled to resume on the fourth of January, so the hostel was beginning to fill up with new students and returnees.

Nfudu sat politely at the table, so as not to give away the anxiety she felt at meeting Vanessa's parents for the first time. From her position, she couldn't help but notice the strikingly handsome man sitting across from her. Vanessa's father, Javier was a business magnate, who made his money trading jewelry in the mid-fifties and later expanded his business to include a sportswear line. He was well known as a shrewd businessman, who wouldn't take no for an answer. He came from French aristocracy – twelfth in line to the French throne. He never gave his heritage much thought and when confronted with it, he brushed it off and was once rumored to have said, "My chance of ever ascending the throne is as much as the chance that the entire country will be overtaken by Orangutans." He rarely used his title Marquis, but on occasion alluded to it during official engagements.

Javier exuded a certain sex appeal, had an impeccable physique, taut muscles in his six foot four frame, which was rare for a man in his early forties. He was rather irresistible and had a taste for gorgeous women. His current wife, Juliette was very beautiful and merely a few years older than his daughter. His ex-wife Brandy, who had since remarried and moved to Ireland with her second husband, was also a looker. They had Vanessa when Brandy was about Vanessa's age. Their divorce shocked everyone who knew them as they had been completely smitten with each other and a great example of young love. No one, except the two of them, knew what went wrong in their relationship. Javier was devastated when it first happened but later recovered after he met Juliette.

At dinner, they enjoyed a wonderful meal of roast lamb, herby potatoes and zesty spring greens. Juliette seemed to have her mind elsewhere and was a little disinterested in the topics at hand. Javier, on the other hand, was more forthcoming. He seemed livelier and particularly happy to meet his daughter's new girlfriend. He engaged Nfudu in conversation throughout dinner and in return, Nfudu was elated by his interest in her. "Why did you stray so far away from home?" he asked. "The weather in Nigeria is so beautiful and the country is going in such an amazing direction, with the discovery of oil and independence..."

"You're right," responded Nfudu. "I miss home terribly. I would have loved to be back in Nigeria with my family for Christmas enjoying the thirty-degree weather."

"Dad! Please don't remind her that she's far from home," said Vanessa tapping her father's hand playfully.

"Oh! I'm sorry," said Javier. An awkward silence followed, so Nfudu guessed he was searching for a way to remedy the situation.

She provided him some respite. "I'm very happy to be in Paris. I've loved it so far and made great friends. Who can complain about this unique opportunity to study fashion in a school that has been described as 'The best place to kick-start a fashion career.'? There's plenty of time to enjoy the beautiful weather back home... and to partake in the 'oil boom.'"

"You're brave to have gone so far away from home." Nfudu was surprised to hear Juliette comment.

"...Thank you," Nfudu muttered, smiling and nodding in agreement with Juliette's remark.

"I also schooled abroad – in America. It was scary at first because I had to leave my family and everything I knew for the first time. In the end, I got accustomed to it and made some lifelong friends and business contacts."

Nfudu realized she may have judged Juliette too soon. She wasn't nearly as reticent as she had initially observed. Having bagged a degree in Finance from Duke, she was also very intelligent. She rarely smiled, but when she did, a twinkle flashed in her eyes and the smile lingered for moments longer than usual making it impossible to doubt its sincerity.

Throughout dinner, Nfudu felt Javier's deep-set green eyes pierce through her whenever he addressed her. Those moments literally took her breath away. The ease with which he engaged her in conversation on different topics would have given an onlooker the impression that they had known each other all their lives. She dismissed his interest in her as natural and innocent, as any man would have acted similarly when meeting their daughter's friend for the first time. It would have been unusual to expect a different outcome, just because she found him attractive.

Javier was the most interesting man Nfudu had ever met. She imagined that if he weren't her friend's Dad, and not married, she would definitely date him – if he asked her. She never expected in a million years to feel that much attraction for a much older man and hoped that no one could read her mind and the dirty thoughts floating on its surface. The fear of being discovered made her shudder. She was still lost in thought when Javier asked, "Care for coffee?" looking directly at her.

"...Y-yes please," she stuttered. "But only if everyone else is having."

"We're all having. Don't worry about it."

When dinner was over, Javier drove Nfudu and Vanessa to the hostel. After he and Juliette bade the girl's goodnight, he told Vanessa,

"We'll be driving back to Nice very early in the morning. We need to be home before lunch. Call me at the hotel if you need anything. …Je t'aime!"

"Je t'aime aussi! Have a safe trip Dad." Vanessa responded, blowing two kisses, one each for him and Juliette.

Before falling asleep that night, Nfudu thought about Javier in ways she was not proud of. She imagined him holding her in his arms while she ran her hands through his hair. Chuckling, she said to herself, "I must be dreaming." She cautioned herself to keep her feelings for him a secret until it passed. Better still, until she met a man that would interest her as much as he did. She hoped that would be soon.

‒

On New Year's Eve, Stanley and Jeremy took the girls to Rex where a crowd was beginning to gather way ahead of midnight to usher in the New Year. It was a popular spot amongst Parisians, who typically ushered in the New Year in grand style. When the foursome first arrived at the venue, it was impossible to get a seat in a good spot, but they finally found suitable seats at the bar. Soon, the girls began to feel more comfortable and started to enjoy themselves. They were on the dance floor when the countdown for New Year was announced through the loudspeakers. Nfudu was startled from her deep conversation with Stanley when she heard the piercing "…Eight, Seven, Six…." Before she realized what was going on, Stanley drew her close and planted a firm kiss on her lips. He then glided his hand up her back and rested it at the nape of her neck. She was about to shove him off when she realized that everyone around them was engaged in varied forms of making out. Some were 'Frenching' while others were planting light kisses on each other and more still were loudly smacking their mouths together for the whole town to hear. Everyone, to Nfudu's surprise, was engaging in some sort of 'Kissolorgy' on the dance floor. Since Stanley's kiss was innocent enough, Nfudu got over her initial shock but stared in astonishment at the crowd when cheers of "Bonne Annee!" filled the air.

When the excitement finally died down, Stanley drew close to Nfudu and whispered in her ear, "Have you seen Jeremy and Vanessa anywhere?"

"No, I haven't!" Nfudu responded. "We should probably go look for them."

They found the pair in a lip-lock in a dark corner. Vanessa was easy to spot because of her short red sequined dress, which glimmered in the dark. Laughing off the fact that they had been discovered, Vanessa and Jeremy followed the other two back to the main venue. The group partied until the early hours of the morning until they were too tired to go on.

The following day, Stanley left for Milan after a quick visit to the hostel. Nfudu was still a little self-conscious about what occurred the night before. The kiss, although seemingly innocent, made her wonder if Stanley was developing romantic feelings for her. Of greater concern to her was his hand lingering on her back. In the end, she brushed it off imagining that he'd had a little too much to drink.

.

3

THE International Institute of Fashion was founded by Mayor Theodore Luxe, who made his fortune as an oil merchant. The Luxe family still owned fifty-five percent of the Institute, but for many years, were the sole owners until World War II – which had a profound effect on their finances. Since then, ownership has been expanded to include a couple of other affluent families. However, as the family still holds majority ownership, their influence could still be seen everywhere around the campus.

The Institute was everything Nfudu had imagined and more. It had a certain luxurious feel that could only be seen to be believed. From the architectural buildings – constructed over 3 decades ago to the romantic tree-lined streets – she knew she would never get bored with her surroundings. An entire building was allocated for the gymnasium, rumored to be the largest in Europe, with its Olympic sized swimming pool and state of the art equipment. The library was an edifice that spanned several floors and culminated in a penthouse used as an exhibit for the Fashion House of Luxe, a prestigious clothing line that catered for the wealthy and owned by Theodore's granddaughter.

The hostels were a walking distance, via a scenic route from the classrooms. Right outside the establishment was at least half a dozen restaurants and cafés as well as an old eighteenth-century church where many atrocities were committed against prisoners of war. Memorabilia representing those atrocities were preserved as historical artifacts in secure glass displays inside the church building. The grounds were converted into a beautiful garden, with a large stone structure in the centre. A chronicle of the timeline of the events that occurred in the church was outlined on a plaque. Many a tourist would read it and shudder in disbelief at the plight of their fellow humans.

Schooling in Paris was not an easy undertaking for Nfudu, since she had to deal with both language and cultural barriers. Even though she spoke fluent French, she soon found by expanding her horizon of friends and instructors that the French language had several dialects, which required additional effort at understanding. Also, since she had not mastered the accent, she experienced frequent side looks when she spoke in certain circles. This caused her slight embarrassment, which she soon learned to ignore, and dared anyone who had a problem with her accent to try speaking her native Igbo dialect.

Within a short period of time, she made a lot of friends, but that didn't stop her from missing her family. She often received letters and phone calls from home. Her younger siblings often asked when they would see her again, and this always brought tears to her eyes. But her parents were the worst. They worried about everything – if she ate well, if she was getting sick, her safety, her studies – and everything else in between. She constantly tried to reassure them that she was well able to take care of herself, but it took a lot of convincing for them to believe.

With her hectic school schedule, it soon became clear to Nfudu that she could not return to Bernie's to work on weekends as she had originally hoped. The Institute was well known to be thorough in its effort to churn out the best fashion students the world had ever seen. Past students could testify to the difficult schedule and the even more difficult faculty. It was once written about the faculty, "They love to break you and then rebuild you." Nfudu was aware that schooling at the institute would not be easy, but had faith in the rather stringent orientation she got from schooling in her home country.

Nfudu picked up the phone to call Sophie, but hesitated for a second. When she finally got the courage to dial her desk at Bernie's, Sophie picked at the first ring as if she had been expecting an important call. "Hello, Sophie speaking."

"It's me, Nfudu."

"Oh, Nfudu! It's so nice to hear from you. How are your classes going?"

"They're very hectic. I can barely find time for the least amount of leisure, let alone work…"

"Well, I'm glad you called to let me know. Don't beat yourself up about it. You should really just focus on school. I imagine it's very difficult."

"Thanks, Sophie, you're so sweet."

"Keep in touch and drop by anytime. You're always welcome. Remember, don't be a stranger."

"I won't," responded Nfudu. She was glad she was doing well financially and didn't need the job anymore. After classes started at the institute, she was able to cut down on social activities which, in the past, had depleted her funds. This was good news for her parents who were still adamant that she should not work.

-

The curriculum at the International Institute of Fashion included a requirement for students to take part in internships during the free time between terms. As the winter session drew to a close, Nfudu made significant effort to secure a spot in a suitable fashion house for a spring internship. She visited every fashion house on Balmain Street but got a negative response each time. She was either told she was too late, and all available spaces had been filled, or the house was not taking any new interns that year. She was exhausted from trying, so was beyond herself with excitement when Vanessa barged into her room a few days before the end of the first semester with a mischievous smile on her face. "What do you say about a two-week internship in London over Easter?" Vanessa asked.

"You don't mean it! How?" asked Nfudu. "Spill the beans!" She didn't want to be held in suspense for a second longer.

"OK…" said Vanessa, continuing to taunt her. "Dad secured an internship at the House of Eudora for the two of us. He ran into Lady Eudora at a party last weekend and she said it would be ok for us to intern there. …Would you like to …?"

"Are you kidding?" Nfudu took a long deep breath and paused for a moment to contain a little bit of her excitement. "This is a dream come true! Of course, I would love to participate. We can shop and visit all the beautiful sites. But, wait… where will we stay in London?"

"We can both lodge at Dad's guest house and be catered to by a housekeeper and a butler…"

"Wow! That's a far cry from how we live here in the hostel." Nfudu exclaimed, secretly more excited about the possibility that she would be seeing Vanessa's father nearly every day.

"Yeah!" agreed Vanessa. "It's also a great opportunity for us to make leaps in our career. Lady Eudora is one of the best fashion designers in the business."

"I agree. Everything about it sounds fantastic. I can't wait to tell Mother."

"Well, I'm glad you're on board. It will be lots of fun."

For Nfudu, it was a no-brainer because she loved London. She thought it was one of the most exciting cities in the world and was happy for an opportunity to work there. Having visited twice in the past with her family, she had noted it as one of those places she would visit over and over again during her lifetime. Besides that, she looked forward to escaping the drudgery of the fashion school to spend two weeks with Vanessa.

Lady Jeannette Eudora was a family friend, who owed Javier a favor for a 'big deed' he had done for her in the past. Vanessa did not know the nature of this deed but knew that it was a long-standing family discussion. Often, she heard her parents speaking in hushed tones whenever they discussed Jeannette when she was younger. Their secrecy made her even more curious to discover what they were hiding. When she got older, it occurred to her that it may not have been anything significant, but for some reason, they had chosen to keep the issue a secret from her.

-

Nfudu and Vanessa left for London on the Metro a day after classes ended for the first semester. A limousine picked them at the train station and took them to the Lodge. On arrival, the girls were welcomed with colorful desserts and bubbling champagne. Nfudu was escorted to her room by the caretaker, who avoided her gaze. Vanessa's room was next door to hers and each of the rooms was nicely decorated with beautiful Victorian furniture. Nfudu was drawn to the window, where a bouquet of fresh flowers in an array of spring colors was placed on a small table. Plopping down on the bed she caressed the plush blanket for some minutes when she had a moment alone. It was the softest blanket she had ever touched.

When Vanessa gave her a tour of the Lodge, Nfudu discovered that the rest of the guest lodge was just as beautiful as their rooms. There was an indoor swimming pool, with a lounge and a bar for guests to relax after their day's activities.

"This is beautiful." Nfudu muttered under her breath. "I wonder how we're going to get any work done in a place like this."

"Wait till you see the garden," said Vanessa. "It's heavenly. Dad spends most of his time there when he's around. During good weather, he could stay there all day working and meeting with clients."

Nfudu felt her heart beating faster than usual by the mere mention of her dad. "Is he joining us for the break?" she asked rather furtively to mask her interest.

"Yes, with Juliette. They're arriving the day before Easter. It's going to be a full house."

"The more the merrier!"

"I agree, and Juliette is a lot of fun. Let's get some dinner and go to bed. We have to be at the House of Eudora first thing tomorrow morning."

-

When Nfudu and Vanessa arrived at the House of Eudora the following day they were disappointed by the tasks they were assigned. They were devoid of the glitz and glamour the girls had expected. Their disappointment dissipated after supervisor explained the structure of their internship.

"In the first installment, you'll complete two weeks in the merchandising department," she said. "After that, you'll work with various levels of Arts and Design. At the end of each stage, you will be assigned a small project with a buddy. This will be assessed using three major criteria – quality, originality and creativity."

"When do we get a chance to work on the fashion floor?" Vanessa asked, unable to hide her disappointment.

"Not until the next two sessions." replied the supervisor. "It could happen faster depending on the circumstances, but I'll advise you to relax. You'll get there sooner than you know. Our interns usually have a good time and as long as they work hard, they receive adequate training to excel in their careers."

They spent their first day in the merchandising department, where they learned the practical aspects of buying, selling and advertising, through occupation with small tasks. The program, however, was more intense than Nfudu and Vanessa had expected. There were long periods of working on commercials and a few short ten minute breaks for coffee. Lunch was practically nonexistent. Cold sandwiches were passed around to the interns. It got a little bit tiring and monotonous, but Nfudu was able to see the big picture. She could relate what she learned to everything she had been taught about fashion merchandising at the Institute

Back at the Lodge, the girls met a surprise – Javier was waiting in the large Victorian living room. He rose to welcome them as they walked in and hugged his daughter tightly.

"Dad, you tricked me! I thought you were coming a little bit later."

"It wasn't my intention to trick you," responded Javier. "Juliette opted to spend Easter with her parents in Venice. Her Brother Donald is visiting from Australia and she hasn't seen him in five years. I decided to come early rather than spend the next few days alone in Nice."

Vanessa was a little disappointed that Juliette would not be joining them as she had become accustomed to holidays with her. She always found it easier to get away with luxury shopping whenever Juliette was around. "Well, I'll miss her. Nfudu and I were hoping to shop with her."

"You should be glad to have Nfudu with you on this trip then. By the way, I haven't given a proper welcome to Nfudu. How are you dear? How did your day go?" asked Javier as he approached her and planted a kiss on each cheek before holding her hands.

Nfudu's heart skipped a beat. She felt self-conscious being around Javier. "It went really well. Going by the progress we made today, I'm confident we'll meet our objectives for this segment."

"I'm glad to hear that. How many segments are there?"

"Four in total...the curriculum mandates four two week internship sessions over the course of our study. Thank you for giving me this opportunity. I do appreciate it."

"It's my pleasure."

While Javier spoke, she noticed the way his black golf shirt hugged his taut muscles. She swallowed when she recalled how his brown cotton pants hugged his buttocks when he turned his back earlier to hug Vanessa. Even though he was forty-one years old, he was the most handsome man Nfudu had ever seen. He was both seductive and irresistible, and his cologne made her a little giddy. She found herself wondering if her hair and makeup were intact and wishing she had taken some time to freshen up before leaving the fashion house. She held her breath while she waited for him to release her hands. When he finally did, her heart pounded in her chest as he still stood very close to her. She could not fathom how he could have such a profound effect on her and hoped both he and Vanessa hadn't noticed her unease. It was unlikely that they did because Vanessa cut through her reverie and continued chattering about the day's work and her disappointment at not having Juliette for Easter.

The trio later stepped out for dinner at the prestigious Ritz Restaurant on the South Bank of the River Thames. Nfudu held her slick permed hair in a tight bun that accentuated her facial features and highlighted her beautiful eyes. She wore a tight black midi dress that she had picked up the day before they left for London. She was saving the dress for a special occasion but decided that dinner that evening was special enough. It was important for her to look her best.

On their way to the restaurant, the chauffeur made a stop to pick a pack of cigarettes for Javier, who used to be a chain smoker. He recently moderated his smoking to only a few times a week at the demands of the family doctor due to concerns about the damage the cigarette smoke was doing to his lungs. "Care for one?" he asked.

"Sure," responded Nfudu. She took one stick from the pack and handed to Javier to light it for her. "I love the smell of cigarettes…" she said, but stopped mid-sentence as the smoke caught in her throat and she began to cough.

"But I don't think it agrees with you," Vanessa interjected while Javier patted her back.

"Is this your first attempt?" he asked.

"Yeah…and that will be my last. It smells great but tastes awful."

"Give that to me," Javier said. He took the cigarette from her and quenched the cinders on the ashtray as they pulled in front of the restaurant.

Dinner was pasta, made with a selection of local cheeses that melted in Nfudu's mouth. Vanessa sat next to Javier, and Nfudu sat across from them. Nfudu felt Javier's eyes pierce through her as he addressed her during their meal. She chewed slowly to avoid spilling her food and found herself fidgeting over the smallest things. Over and over again she verified in her mind which the appropriate cutlery was for the appropriate hand and then for the course before her. Javier shared stories about his business, his associates, and the state of the European economy. He was extremely passionate about those topics and to Nfudu's surprise, Vanessa was just as passionate about them as her responses matched his in fervor. She listened and nodded her head while they argued.

As beautiful music by the Beatles 'I Want to Hold Your Hands' played, Vanessa stopped mid-speech and sang along to the tune.

"I'm so sorry. Vanessa and I have been talking for so long; it just occurred to me you may not be interested in the same topics." Javier said to Nfudu.

"Quite the contrary. I loved listening to both your arguments. I was also fascinated by the dynamics of your relationship. You argue like equals, and I find that endearing. Quite different from the relationship I have with my Dad."

Javier nodded and smiled. "I have always encouraged her to discuss freely with me. We're very much alike and share the same interests which make it easy for us to get along."

"I noticed that. It's really cool."

"Thanks," replied Javier. "What's your relationship with your Dad like?"

"Normal… No offense, but it's nothing like what you have with your daughter. He's a great Dad – a great provider. We discuss current affairs, but never like equals. It's always clear who the parent is."

"Interestingly, I believe most father-daughter relationships are like that," added Javier.

"I'll like to order some dessert?" Vanessa interjected. "Is anyone else having?"

"None for me. I'm watching my figure."

"Me neither," added Javier.

By the time they got back to the lodge, they were drowsy from the wine. Nfudu headed straight to her room and slipped into her nightgown and then hurriedly slid under her plush beddings to reminisce about dinner. Her feelings for Javier were out of control. She hugged her pillow and daydreamed about him until she slipped into an actual dream. She was walking hand in hand with him by a church and as they passed the entrance, they looked through the wide open door and saw Vanessa and Juliette kneeling at the altar – praying. They dashed behind the church only to discover a beautiful garden that was hidden behind a wall. She was angry when she woke up just as she and Javier held themselves in a warm embrace behind the walls. She wished the dream had lasted long enough to satisfy the need that began to well up inside her. It had felt so real, and was both romantic and confusing; so much that she lay on her bed for several minutes and obsessed about the significance of the dream. For the first time, she wondered if Javier felt something in return for her.

Nfudu looked forward to seeing Javier at breakfast the following morning. She let her beautiful black tresses down and took a little more care in applying her makeup. However, on stepping into the living room she was disappointed when the butler informed her that Javier had left earlier to attend an urgent meeting and wouldn't be joining them for breakfast. He provided a chauffeur to drive her and Vanessa to work and then meet him later.

-

It was the day before Easter and the interns at the House of Eudora were permitted to leave early in honor of the Easter celebrations. After work, Nfudu and Vanessa met Javier at the café Deloroso on Oxford Street, where they got a bite to eat and then proceeded to explore the shops. At Harrods, Nfudu tried on a beautiful Givenchy dress – one she knew she couldn't afford on her student allowance. Javier caught a glimpse of her in the dress when she and Vanessa walked back and forth their stalls in the changing room, and thought it looked divine on her. Later, when he saw the same dress being hung up by their sales attendant, he made sure to ask the attendant to package the dress for check out. When Nfudu got to the payment counter, she was handed a Givenchy box. She gasped after she was told by the cashier that the gentleman she came in with had paid for the contents.

"You shouldn't have," she said to Javier when she and Vanessa joined him outside the doors.

"Why not? It looked beautiful on you. It would be a shame to leave it hanging on the rack rather than on you. Worse still, it could end up hanging on some other woman who wouldn't do it justice."

Nfudu smiled. "Thank you so much. I wasn't really going to buy it, but wasn't going to leave the store without trying it on."

The three of them stopped at Trafalgar square and ate hot dogs while they watched a group of teenagers perform a dance routine. It was late by the time they got back to the lodge. The girls unpacked their loot and compared their finds in Vanessa's room before Nfudu made her way to hers. That night, she had the same dream from the night before and yet again woke up at the very same point. "That is so weird," she muttered to herself as she tried desperately to fall back to sleep.

The next day – Easter Sunday, Vanessa went to see her father in his room. She stopped outside his door when she overheard him having an argument over the phone with someone she suspected to be Juliette.

"How can you be so inconsiderate? I expect much better from you…" she heard her father saying.

She knocked on his door and waited a few minutes before walking in.

"Happy Easter, Dad! Ready for church?" It was a family tradition to attend church service every Easter Sunday, but with Javier's sad and disheveled look, Vanessa knew that tradition would not be kept.

Javier shook his head. "No. I won't be able to make it to church. I'll need to get some sleep now and join you later for lunch. Please excuse me."

His countenance worried Vanessa. It occurred to her that the argument she just overhead could be more serious than she had imagined. Javier loved Juliette a lot, even though they argued furiously at times. It was usually about nothing and they always found a way to hash things out amicably. Juliette had a quick temper and often misunderstood her father's intentions as he did hers. The problem with her father was that he never spent enough time to understand his partner and often misinterpreted her free spirit to be nonchalance to the important issues he cared about.

Vanessa and Nfudu attended Mass at St Paul's Cathedral. After church, they had lunch with Javier in the formal dining room in the lodge. Lunch was a rack of lamb, spring vegetables, slow roasted potatoes and chutney. It was delicious but Nfudu couldn't help noticing that Javier was a little withdrawn. He barely spoke except when spoken to, or to address the server. It was obvious something was bothering him. When Vanessa told her about the argument she had overheard him having that morning with Juliette, she felt at ease knowing his mood had nothing to do with her.

After lunch, they sat in the living room to watch the brand new colored television that was delivered to the lodge the day before. There was a little more cheer from Javier when he announced, "I'll be leaving early tomorrow morning."

"So soon?" Vanessa asked.

"Yeah. Try to make the most of your internship. It was very kind of Jeanette to offer you this opportunity. I'll see you both when next I come to Paris."

He left early the next morning, even before Nfudu and Vanessa got out of bed.

-

During their second week in London, Vanessa and Nfudu worked, shopped and explored as many places as they could. Nfudu finally got the chance to meet Lady Jeanette Eudora on the last day of their internship. She fit the description of a quintessential beauty. Nfudu thought that her pictures – placed in strategic positions on the various floors of the fashion house – had done her no justice. She was beautiful in a waif-like sort of way, with long black shiny hair and high cheekbones on a slightly rounded face. She commanded a great presence about her and being a former model, carried herself with undisputed elegance.

When Vanessa and Nfudu entered her office, she had her head down as she was looking over their files. "Have a seat," she said. She nodded silently to herself for a few minutes before saying, "I have heard about the amazing work you both did here in the House of Eudora. I'll like to congratulate you for that."

"Thank you!" they said in unison.

"You're both welcome to complete your remaining three internships with us. We'll need at least three weeks' notice if you plan on returning in the summer because our spots fill up quickly. We've had so many interns over the years, but none have received as much commendation as you two."

"We really enjoyed our internship here and would like to return. Thank you so much for your offer," said Nfudu.

"You're welcome," responded Lady Eudora. "Do you have any questions for me and my team?"

"Yes, of course," Nfudu responded, before she and Vanessa barraged her with questions, ranging from when they could join the design group to references for their faculty at the institute. Lady Eudora answered all their questions and even asked for suggestions on how they could improve things in her organization. She listened patiently as Vanessa and Nfudu provided her with insights on how to improve things around the House of Eudora, especially the plight of the interns.

By the time they left Lady Eudora's office, Nfudu was in complete awe of her. She was glad to have someone really accomplished to look up to in the industry. However, through the question and answer session, she wished she could ask Lady Eudora only one thing – what secret of hers Vanessa's parents held so dear.

4

The second semester kicked off right after Nfudu and Vanessa arrived in Paris. It promised to be even more hectic than the first. Nevertheless, being their second time around, the girls were more than ready to tackle the tasks at hand as they were now more accustomed to their schedules. Also, the practical experience they got from their internship gave them the confidence boost they needed to face the barrage of lessons and projects the faculty heaped on them.

The spring weather was pleasant, not too cold and not too hot by any means. The air was nice and fresh and the skies were serene, although they held a threat of rain every now and then. The streets had come to life again, right after the winter thawing, and flowers were blooming with vibrant colors and alluring aromas. Cherry blossoms lined the streets of the Institute, with their tops meeting at the highest points, and creating a cheery and romantic image.

It was a wonderful time of the year to explore the city. Nfudu used the opportunity to visit some of the sites she was yet to see in the beautiful 'City of Light'. When she could make some time out of her busy schedule, she went to view the exhibits in the historic Louvre and hang out at the Tuileries Gardens, adjacent from the museum. She had passed through the gardens several times in the past few months and was always intrigued by the hustle and bustle of people, the minstrels playing music and couples in various romantic postures on the grounds.

Nfudu's busy schedule, however, did not deter her from thinking about Javier. It became her guilty pleasure. She welcomed every opportunity to discuss him with Vanessa and caught herself overdoing it a few times. She still marveled at how easy it had been for her to fall for him, as she had always imagined she could only fall for someone who loved her desperately in return. In the past, she had only entertained feelings for men who had a burning desire for her and had on some occasions developed soft spots for some even if they were not her type. In those days, she was unsure about what to look out for in relationships, so she had relied on the affection shown to her by others to guide not only how she gave, but also how she received affection. Things were much different this time. The way she felt about Javier contradicted everything she thought she once knew about love. She figured this must be what falling in love really meant – loving despite not knowing if the one you love, loved you back.

-

The curriculum in the first semester involved a lot of theory and only a small amount of practical work. Nfudu considered the theoretical work a little bit monotonous. One class she enjoyed was figure drawing because she could see herself emerge into a budding fashion designer during those two hour periods. She also enjoyed the pattern making for skirts, which soon evolved into pattern making for blouses in the second semester. Through them, she became well versed in creating patterns and sewing more complex skirts and blouses. The math and English classes were her least favorite. She found them tiresome. These were included in the curriculum to provide a background for developing skills in business and entrepreneurship. Even though she excelled in English in high school, she always struggled to make a passing grade in math.

In contrast to the first semester, a majority of the second semester courses contained a large practical content. This inclusion excited Nfudu who couldn't wait to make even more complex creations and show the whole world her talent. She dreamed of the time when she would become a well-known fashion designer – the best the world had ever seen. She studied hard on weekdays, and on weekends she tried to complete her assignments. The Institute organized lots of social activities and excursions. These she attended whenever she could.

One of the excursions took her to London, where she thought she saw Javier everywhere she looked – in the crowd at Piccadilly, at a shop in Westfield, and even once on the train. Thoughts of him engulfed her so much on that trip that she missed out on all the fun. Her feelings were so strong that they weighed her down, but she dared not mention it to anyone because she knew it was a taboo. When Vanessa came to her room one evening to announce, "I think Dad and Juliette may be going their separate ways," she received this news with mixed feelings.

"What happened?" Nfudu asked. "I thought they were great for each other." She thought it was terrible news, but felt relieved knowing that the feelings she harbored for Javier would soon lose its atrocious nature and become slightly acceptable.

"They're hardly compatible," responded Vanessa, shaking her head. "They found comfort in each other's hands when they were both going through a hard time. Dad met her when he was reeling in sadness from his divorce from mom, and Juliette… I don't know. At first, I thought she was unsuitable until I realized how much Dad loved her. I think she loved him too. "He'll be in Paris on Monday and I don't know how to face him alone. If you have time, can you join us for a meal?"

"No problem," responded Nfudu. "This is really sad news. I still don't understand how things turned sour, so fast." Nfudu was not going to miss meeting Javier for anything in the world – not even for her lectures – which she took rather seriously. She checked her schedule for Monday and was disappointed when she found out she had evening lectures that day, but that didn't deter her from making plans for dinner.

-

Javier came in on Sunday evening and asked to see Nfudu after he was informed by the hostel attendant that Vanessa was at the gym. As Nfudu approached him in the visitor's lobby she felt a little uneasy.

Not paying close attention to where she was going, she nearly tripped but caught herself quickly. She scolded herself, wondering if Javier had noticed her slip up. She had been wondering how one could feel so much for another without them being aware through some sort of telepathic influence. The knot she felt in her stomach dissipated when Javier kissed her cheeks, and she noticed he was looking a little disoriented. After that, there was a weird silence before he finally said, "I really needed to see you," in an awkward tone that made her wonder about his sobriety.

"What for?" asked Nfudu surprised by the emotion she heard in his voice and concerned that he wanted to pour out his heart to her. She wasn't prepared to listen to his problems – especially if they had anything to do with his marital problems with Juliette. She had her own emotional turmoil, which due to its nature, made her the worst person to have such discussions with.

"Emm..." Javier muttered.

"Vanessa and I were actually expecting you tomorrow. When the attendant told me you were here, I called the gym and left a message for her to come down."

"The thing is... I need to discuss something with you... just the two of us," he said staring forlornly into her eyes and pointing his forefinger at her.

The sadness in his expression filled Nfudu with a different type of emotion – one she couldn't understand. She was at a loss for words. It occurred to her that Javier needed to see her more than he needed to see Vanessa. She hated being kept in suspense and decided to dig a little deeper. "I'm not sure what you mean. Can you tell me a little more...?"

"How about you and I go for a spin after supper to discuss?"

"Sure we can."

Nfudu felt uneasy about excluding Vanessa because she could not trust herself to be alone with him. But she was curious about what he needed to discuss with her. If it was really about Juliette, she wondered why their discussion about the state of his marital life should be shrouded in such secrecy. It didn't make sense to her, so she figured it had to be about something else. What it was, her usually wild imagination could not figure out.

It wasn't long before Vanessa returned from the gym, and three of them went for supper at a quiet restaurant, outside of the hostel premises. Javier was quiet at dinner and so was Nfudu. Thoughts of how she could pull off a later meeting with him bogged her mind.

Vanessa did most of the talking. "I'm sorry about Juliette," she said in the maternal tone she reserved for times like that.

"It wasn't your fault," Javier responded. "It's been a while coming."

"Well, I hope everything gets resolved amicably. I feel caught in the middle."

"We're doing our best to avoid a nasty outcome. I'm letting her have everything she's asked for. There is no need to complicate matters since we don't share any living being – neither child nor dog."

"The whole thing really sucks,"

"Yes it does." agreed Javier.

"Where is Juliette right now?" Nfudu asked, in an attempt to change the direction of the discussion to a less depressing one.

"She's staying at her family home in Venice until the divorce is finalized."

"Well… I hope the both of you can get on with your lives soon."

"I hope so too," responded Javier, fixing his gaze on her. "Our discussion with the mediators yesterday went smoothly, so I'm optimistic."

Vanessa could see that her father was heartbroken and wished there was something she could do to improve the situation. However, she was happy he hadn't tried to keep it all bottled in. Pouring his heart out to her and Nfudu, in her mind was a great step towards mending his broken heart.

After dinner, Javier drove the girls to their hostel. He got out of the car and kissed both of them on the cheeks before wishing them good night. "I'll be leaving tomorrow morning."

"What's the rush? Can you stay one more day?" pleaded Vanessa.

"No… I have work in London."

Vanessa hugged him. "Everything will be all right," she said, in the same maternal tone with which she addressed him earlier that evening.

Javier returned that night to see Nfudu. They drove to a dark corner of the crowded car park of the Décolletage hostel. The apprehension Nfudu felt sitting so close to him caused her heart to beat faster. His cologne sifted through the car air-conditioning and hit her nostrils with every breath she took. That, combined with the smell of new leather numbed her senses. At the entrance of the parking lot, he placed his hand on her right thigh and took her hand. She shuddered and held her breath. He parked in a secluded corner, pulled her towards him, and planted a kiss on her quivering lips. After a few moments, he released her and gazed into her eyes for a few seconds before he kissed her again. While they kissed, he gently pushed her dress halfway up to reveal some of her inner thighs and groaned, "I love you! I have loved you from the first time I set my eyes on you. I haven't been able to think of much else…?"

Nfudu's heart pounded heavily in her chest as she was beyond herself with disbelief. Her heart wanted to say, "I love you too!" but her mind cautioned her to exercise some restraint. She was elated at the realization that he had loved her the entire time she had been pining for him. On the other hand, she was confused about the timing as it coincided with the breakdown of his marriage with Juliette. She had so many questions she wanted to ask him but was tongue tied and confused. As she was saying, "What about Juliette?" he asked, "Can you spend the night…?"

"That's why I need you to come with me," he continued. "I'll explain everything to you."

Even though she was head over heels in love with him, she found the will to say "No."

"You won't even consider it?" he asked in dismay. "Why?"

"I don't know…," responded Nfudu. "Because someone could find out… Because you're still married and any form of relationship with you at this point could backfire and hurt the people we care about the most." She was also worried about what Javier might have thought about her lack of resistance when he kissed her. It bothered her that he may think she was easy prey and end up losing all respect for her. The thought made her shudder and loosen herself from his grip rather abruptly.

"Is something wrong?" he asked.

"No..." she lied. "I had a sudden rush of blood to my head."

He turned off the car engine and wound down the windows to let in the cool night breeze. When he was done, he looked at her and marveled at the contours of her face which were subtly lit by the moonlit sky.

"I was hoping you'd come with me so we could talk about us," he said, looking down at her with weary eyes.

"Well... I don't want us both to lose our inhibitions and do something we would both regret..." She had barely completed her last statement before Javier pulled her close and kissed her the third time that evening. This time around, she let go of her inhibitions – the same one she was worried about a few moments back and kissed him passionately like her life depended on it. She was panting heavily by the time they let go of each other because a car pulled into the slot beside them. They waited for the occupants of the car to leave before they snuggled back into each other's arms. Nfudu held on tight with both hands, afraid that if she moved an inch she would lose him forever. That third kiss told Javier everything he needed to know about her feelings towards him.

They were silent for a while, just listening to the buzz of the nightlife a short distance away and the sound of each other's heartbeat. Javier broke the silence. "I know you have a lot of questions. Spending the night together will be a great opportunity to answer some of them off the bat, but I'll respect your decision. I'll never force you to do anything you're uncomfortable with."

Nfudu looked up into his eyes. It was the closest she had ever been to him. She noticed their deep green color and how he gazed back at her with a slow smile spreading across his lips. She wanted to kiss him again in that moment and even surrender herself to him. Instead, she dug her head into his chest and mumbled, "Thank you," in her singsong voice. "You can help me answer my questions over the phone though."

"OK, I'll call you as soon as I get home…try not to think too much." He sounded like a parent, which amused her as he had always spoken to her as an equal.

"You know me too well," she chuckled.

"Of course, I have observed you closely since we met. One can always tell when you're worrying, because of those furrow lines that appear on your forehead, the distant look in your eyes and the serious face…look, you're doing it right now," Javier teased as he gently rubbed her forehead with his thumb to release the frown lines.

"That's an awful thing to say," Nfudu said removing his hand playfully. "You shouldn't tease. I may create more furrow lines."

Later that night, Javier drove Nfudu back to the hostel and took care to stop in a discreet corner to avoid attracting the attention of passersby. When he hugged her, she darted her eyes in every direction to ensure Vanessa or anyone who she knew was nowhere in sight. As long as he was still married to Juliette, their love was a taboo. Still deep in thought, she heard Javier say, "I'll call you when I get to London, my love."

Beside herself with emotion, she mumbled, "Goodnight…" She liked how he called her "My love," and reckoned they had achieved a lot in one night. If nothing else, she knew that he felt exactly the same way she did.

Nfudu hardly slept a wink that night. She woke up several times to contemplate if what had occurred between her and Javier was real. The following morning, she saw a folded note that smelt very familiar under her door.

I meant what I said last night. Love J.S.

Even though she was feeling completely lethargic from lack of sleep, she soon began to make sense of her feelings as the words confirmed the reality of her situation. She could not figure out what her next steps should be. Being in love with a man who was twenty years her senior was a lot more than she had bargained for. She had been able to manage her feelings when it was her little secret. However, finding out that the object of her affection loved her back further disoriented her as she realized she was not emotionally equipped to handle her fantasy turning into a reality.

Javier phoned as soon as he arrived in London. Nfudu guessed he was the one and answered after the third ring as she didn't want to seem too eager. "Hello!"

"Hello dear. Are you Ok?" asked Javier concerned by the somber tone of her voice.

"I'm fine. It's just that I didn't get any sleep last night."

"Me neither. I was thinking about you the whole night. What was your reason…?"

"I'm heartbroken that I have to hide all this from Vanessa. I feel like I'm cheating on her. And, I'm worried about everything else…"

"What else?" asked Javier eager to address her concerns.

"A lot of things are bothering me. The fact that you're still married to Juliette is the biggest one. What will people think of us… and me in particular? They may think that I'm the reason for your divorce, and, Father would never approve our relationship."

"What should we do about this then?" asked Javier sounding upset. He understood her concerns but didn't share them. "Should we end this relationship now even before it starts? I'll agree to that only under one condition, if you can tell me in plain words that you don't feel the same way I do."

Nfudu let out a deep sigh and after an awkward silence that lasted a few seconds, but seemed like an hour, she responded.

"I can't deny my feelings for you, Javier. You must understand that I feel lost because of the roadblocks I sense along the way. I'm so scared…" she confided. "…I have been head over heels in love with you, but had to internalize all my thoughts and dreams because I didn't want anyone to get hurt."

"I didn't know that…" Javier said, beyond himself with excitement. Her words changed everything for him. He became motivated to do everything in his power to address her concerns and make her feel confident and safe. "I love you too my darling. I'll come to Paris next week to visit you. Please don't say anything about it to

Vanessa, because I don't plan on seeing her. At that time, I'll answer all your questions. Like I said before, your concerns are valid, but every single one of them can be addressed except for the part about your father." He lowered his voice to a whisper, "Call me whenever you want. I'll call you every day to make sure you're ok... I love you."

"See you next week. I love you too."

-

Nfudu found it difficult to focus on anything afterwards. Thoughts of Javier filled her mind every day. She slept and woke up thinking of him, barely getting enough sleep as she tossed and turned several times in bed before finally falling asleep each night. She kept replaying their first kiss over and over in her mind until she had mastered every touch, feeling, and movement. She lay in bed at times imagining what their first sexual experience would be like. The desire and accompanying emotion left her breathless.

Vanessa noticed the changes in Nfudu and followed her to her room one day after classes. "Are you ill?"

"No! Why?"

"You looked lost in class today and that got me worried. And, you hardly eat these days. What is the problem then?"

For a moment, Nfudu considered telling Vanessa the truth about what was bothering her but thought against it. She cautioned herself to be patient since the issue was not solely her concern. "I'm fine. I've just been tired from all the studying." That was the truth, although not entirely. At least she felt good about not telling an outright lie to her. She had no intention of bringing her in on her secret until the time was right, that is assuming her relationship with Javier survived – she hoped it would survive because she loved Javier with every fiber of her being. She thought their love was the most beautiful thing that had ever happened to her, and she didn't want to jeopardize it. She believed he was her one true love, and being a firm believer that each individual gets only one true love in their lifetime, she did not intend to let hers pass through her fingers. Following her confrontation with Vanessa, Nfudu went about her business walking on eggshells. Though she felt extremely guilty about it, she became even more determined to keep her date with Javier the coming week.

5

THE week she waited for Javier's visit was the longest week of Nfudu's life. She counted the days and the minutes leading to his arrival. Nervous, she jumped at the slightest provocation. This was worsened by the fact that she had not quite figured out how she would explain her coming weekend disappearance to Vanessa. As the day drew closer, she worried herself sick trying to come up with a story for Vanessa about her whereabouts.

Javier's chauffeur picked her from the hostel around six o'clock on Friday morning for the Hotel de Le Mercidien, a luxury nineteenth-century hotel, located near the Vesinet *banlieue* of Paris. During the one hour drive to the hotel, Nfudu took in the breathtaking views of the Vesinet neighborhood and marveled at the picturesque surroundings. The chauffeur, Romeo claimed to have firsthand knowledge about the vicinity, and he provided Nfudu with a brief history on the drive-through. This included detailed information about the notable families occupying the lavish mansions that sprawled across the landmark veiled by the beautiful tree-lined streets.

As they passed the Bassinet family mansion, Romeo told a chilling tale about Rory Bassinet. The younger Bassinet's wife had murdered her husband, so as to be with Joey – her husband's younger brother – whom she was in love with, and engaged in a secret affair for several years. Rory was charged with her husband's murder and dragged around in a trial that trumped any in the history of Le Vesinet *banlieue*. After she was pronounced guilty by the Judge on the basis of a guilty verdict delivered by an all-male jury, she shot herself in the head with a gun she had somehow managed to smuggle into the courtroom as she was being approached by the jailors. Since her death in the late twenties, it's been rumored that her ghost roamed the mansion after midnight, scaring the occupants and any visitors that dared stay there beyond the dead of night.

Romeo was forced to halt another gory tale as they pulled into the magnificent gold-plated gate of the Hotel de Le Mercidien, with its beautiful grounds and breathtaking view of the Spritztville Castle in the distance. Nfudu could not help noticing the wooded streets and the beautiful Lac de Mercidien, from which the hotel derived its name. A significant portion of the Lake was located within the hotel grounds and a beautiful garden surrounded its boundaries. At the north end of the garden, was a beautiful life-sized sculpture of a man and woman in a warm embrace, with fountains of water erupting from the point at which their bodies collided. This aroused Nfudu's senses as she felt a sudden urge and inhaled deeply to soak up the beauty of her surroundings. She realized the hotel was truly romantic – the perfect site for her first rendezvous with Javier.

While Romeo circled through the driveway, Nfudu was filled with trepidation. Her temperature rose as she couldn't wait to set her eyes on Javier. When the car pulled in front of the hotel lobby, she saw him standing behind the glass revolving doors with a bouquet of lovely yellow daffodils in his hand. He dashed through the door, opened the backseat, and let Nfudu out gently. Holding one hand firmly, he gave her a long sensual kiss and handed her the bouquet.

"This is for you."

"Thank you," Nfudu responded, kissing his left cheek. She brought the bouquet close to her face for a whiff. "Hmm," she purred. "It smells really wonderful. How did you know yellow was my favorite color?"

"I know everything there is to know about you," Javier whispered into her left ear right after he kissed her cheek. He then grabbed her wrist and immediately whisked her off to their suite on the thirteenth floor of the hotel. As soon as the door was shut behind them, he slipped his hands under her silk dress and plunged her back into the wall, being careful not to hurt her while her slender frame spasmed uncontrollably. She made no attempt to resist him as he progressed to squeeze her nipples with his middle and index finger, while she moaned and grabbed his shoulders to pull him towards her. Her heart thumped furiously and this increased his desire. He carried her carefully to the bed and softly maneuvered her knees to draw them apart while she writhed in pleasure and surrendered herself with reckless abandon. As they made love that night, she felt a sudden rush of blood to her head as her body quivered feverishly, until she clenched herself when the orgasm coursed through her. He kissed her tenderly and whispered "I love you" as he devoured her over and over again.

They held each other in a long warm embrace afterwards as he gently fondled her breasts and caressed the whole length of her exquisite body. She wished she could remain in his arms for as long as she possibly could and dared not speak for fear of spoiling the moment. They were both so captivated by each other. After staring into each other's eyes for what seemed like two whole minutes, Javier broke the silence. "Can we go again?"

"What?" Nfudu giggled and covered herself with the sheets. She was happy that he loved their lovemaking enough to crave more, but embarrassed by his forwardness. "That was mind-blowing," she said as she sneaked out of the sheets, trying hard to avoid Javier's stare. "I don't know what I thought it would be like, but I never imagined..."

"Me neither. It was amazing. You're amazing... and I love you!"

She crept up his chest and planted a kiss on his lips. "I love you too..." Nfudu felt that her friends, with whom she had discussed sexual liaisons, had not described the experience adequately. None had come close to what had just occurred. From their stories, some had hated it, while others had plainly detested the person they shared the experience with.

Javier pulled her on top of him and kissed her over and over again, while she chuckled uncontrollably. At his insistence, they showered together; taking turns to massage each other's back as the water trickled down their bodies. They were interrupted by a loud bang on the door. "It's the champagne I ordered over two hours ago," said Javier grabbing a towel to answer the door.

Nfudu stepped out after him and threw on a simple dress. "I'm starving," she announced. "Can we get something to eat?"

"Sure. We can go for a quick bite in one of the hotel restaurants...A quick one, because I want you all to myself this evening."

"Ok," she answered giggling.

They walked hand in hand to the elevator and stopped at the second floor. After their meal, they took a walk along one of the hotel gardens, past the Lac de Mercidien.

"I feel as if I have known you forever," Javier said, rubbing her hands in gentle strokes as they walked along the garden.

"Same here. We could be soul mates," responded Nfudu. "I barely remember a time when I didn't know you. Isn't that strange? It must be that we're meant to be together."

"When did you become so philosophical?"

"Since I met you," Nfudu tugged at his side in retaliation for his teasing.

He pulled her closer to himself. "Jokes aside, I wonder where you've been my whole life. I have felt that way from the very first time I met you."

"But you were with Juliette, so how could that be?"

"Juliette and I were already falling apart when we first met. It should have been pretty obvious to anyone that there was a problem in our marriage."

"That is one thing I have been curious about," said Nfudu stopping to face Javier, "How long have you and Juliette had issues? I won't forgive myself if it has anything to do with me."

"Nothing of the sort," Javier said, grasping her hand in his and looking her straight in the eyes. "Our issues started long before I met you. In the end, it was Juliette that called it quits – although I saw it coming. Leading to that, we did everything we could to keep our family together and we were both very good at hiding our differences."

"Does Vanessa know all this?"

"I doubt even Vanessa knew how serious our issues were... Juliette and Vanessa are very close, so in a way, I think Vanessa may have seen this coming but I doubt it."

"You need to tell her the truth."

"No, not now. It will devastate her. Besides I don't want to put her in a position where she has to take sides."

"Well... when it first happened, she told me she was stunned by the news. She knew you both argued, like most married couples, but was devastated that it had gone this far..." Nfudu could not finish her sentence. She shivered as the night air began to get chilly. Javier wrapped his hands around her. As their bodies merged, they kissed under the starlit skies until they were both startled by some noise in the bushes. "What is that?" asked Nfudu, scared out of her wits.

"Probably just a rabbit...we should retreat to our room soon and finish our discussion there."

As they headed back to their room, they heard a jazz band playing in the direction of the terrace and decided to join the party. There they saw over twenty hotel guests drinking and dancing. They ordered some champagne and later joined the other guests on the dance floor, and danced until their heads swooned "It must be the champagne," said Nfudu, stumbling on Javier's toe. As they were about to leave, she heard music by Johnnie Ray - *"Just Walking in the Rain."* They left right after dancing to that number, while the night was still young and a number of couples were still on the dance floor.

"It's been a long day," whispered Nfudu as they approached their suite.

"It could be an even longer night," responded Javier, as he whisked her off her feet and stepped into their suite at a little past midnight. Right on the centre of the bed, on a silver tray, she saw a lovely spread of macaroons, strawberries dipped in chocolate and an expensive bottle of red wine. Javier read the surprise in Nfudu's eyes. "I asked housekeeping to clean the room and have desserts delivered to refuel your energy after your romp." He searched her face for an expression, but it took her a minute to realize he was teasing her again. She loved his sense of humor – one of the first things that attracted her to him.

"That is so sweet of you. I needed a refill after all that dancing." She smiled wryly and was happy to deny him the pleasure of knowing that he had her in a corner with his comment."

The colors and the smells of the macaroons teased Nfudu's senses as she devoured them one after the other while sitting on Javier's lap. They fed each other the chocolate covered strawberries and planted kisses on each other's lips between bites.

"You have a sweet tooth!" teased Javier again as he watched Nfudu licking the chocolate off a strawberry. "And sweet lips."

"What a marvelous choice for treats," Nfudu said, smirking as she ignored his latter comment.

"Yes, sweetheart. I knew you would like it." Javier opened the bottle of wine and poured into the two tall glasses and toasted to their future together.

They cuddled in bed later that night and as they talked, Javier took her hand in his and squeezed it tightly. "I have a confession to make…" his voice trailed off to a whisper, "Please don't judge me,"

"Of course not."

"At Easter, I arrived a day earlier than planned because I wanted so desperately to see you. Don't get me wrong. As I told you earlier, Juliette and I were already having problems at that time and it was impossible to see any clear future for us."

"So why did you leave so abruptly?"

"When it became clear Juliette couldn't make it for Easter, I had to make up a reason to return to Nice. I was conflicted about my feelings for you and wanted to avoid raising any suspicions from Vanessa and the lodge staff by staying and potentially getting into an uncompromising situation. Besides I didn't know if you liked me in return."

"I was pining for you then. I barely slept thinking about you"

"Is that true?"

"No!" teased Nfudu covering her face in embarrassment with her hands.

They made love one more time that night and finally fell asleep in each other arms. Their chemistry was incomparable to anything either one of them had ever experienced. It was a wonder they were able to hide their feelings from each other for so long. Nfudu slept feeling content. Javier had answered a lot of her burning questions as she did his. She no longer had a shred of fear being with him and decided that night to give their relationship all she had.

By Eight the following morning, Javier was startled by the ringing alarm on his bedside. He groped desperately to put it on snooze to avoid waking her while she slept so peacefully beside him. His body had formed a habit of waking up early no matter what time he went to sleep, so he was already awake, for at least an hour. Staring at Nfudu sleeping next to him, Javier was unable to contain the joy he felt knowing she was his. He got up to make some calls in the living room, to avoid waking her. When he crept back into bed, he kissed her forehead, her cheeks, and her lips. She whimpered as he kissed one taut nipple, and before she could think of resisting him she surrendered herself to him.

She was embarrassed by the amount of sex they were having and looked away as Javier pleaded with her to partake of the delicious breakfast of waffles, fruits and coffee that was just delivered in the living room. He rolled the breakfast trolley to her side of the bed and helped her dish out a sizeable portion. "You're going to need a lot of energy because we have a lot planned for today."

"What are we doing?"

"We'll be going to a wine Cellar about two and half hours drive away in Epernay. There will be lots of drinking so you need a good breakfast to stomach the wine. We'll have lunch there."

"It's a little too early for me to eat, but I'll try my best."

They ate their breakfast in bed staring at the contours of each other's face, with their legs interlocked together.

"I wish this moment could last forever," muttered Nfudu. She wanted to ask where they would go from there but didn't want to seem too forward. She started worrying about the reality they were bound to face when they finally revealed their love to the world.

"You're starting to worry again," said Javier, noticing her forehead starting to crease. "What is it this time?"

"It's nothing," Nfudu lied. She didn't want to bother him with the negative thoughts that clouded her mind. These ranged from the age difference between them to the obvious racial bias they were most certainly going to face. The issues overwhelmed her, but she suppressed her thoughts and decided to live in the moment and enjoy his love for as long as she could. She considered herself a sensible girl, but in matters of love, she chose to act with reckless abandon because she was also a true romantic.

They first drove to Reims Cathedral and walked hand in hand enjoying the beautiful paintings and sculptures that lined the cathedral walls and ceilings. The gothic paintings were over a hundred years old and were in various forms of restoration as many of the artifacts were partially destroyed during World War II. They stopped at an altar where about half a dozen visitors were kneeling in prayer and joined them for a few minutes.

"What did you pray for?" asked Javier as he reached for Nfudu's hand to assist her from her kneeling position.

"I prayed that God should give us the strength to weather any storms that may come between us."

"I prayed for exactly the same thing, but I put it differently. I asked that you be made mine and only mine."

Nfudu chuckled. "I'm yours and only yours already so you may have wasted a prayer."

"Is your family religious?" asked Javier.

"To a large extent... and I mean that literally. My father has four wives and eighteen children." She searched his face as she anticipated shock, but to her surprise, he remained calm. "Each of the wives has responsibility for their children, including making sure they attend church regularly. He hardly attends church himself, but barks at anyone seen hanging around the compound during church service on Sundays."

"He sounds rather imposing."

"Oh yeah! It's worse when it's something to do with me because as the first child I'm expected to be infallible and a good example to my siblings and in the society in general."

Javier looked at Nfudu with genuine admiration. "That's a lot to expect from one person. You must feel extreme pressure."

"It's a lot," Nfudu agreed. "However, it comes with a lot of privileges, so I can't complain."

"It must be a culture shock for you, seeing how things are done in France. First and foremost, our families are not as large as yours and polygamy is frowned upon."

"Polygamy is only practiced by a handful of families in Nigeria. And yes, I did and still experience a culture shock in France. Mostly, I think it stems from being far away from home where I was treated like a celebrity. Here, I'm a different type of celebrity – I stick out like a sore thumb in a sea of white people."

"En route to Epernaaay…" They were interrupted by the tour guide as he bellowed to alert their group to join the tour bus. This was their cue to locate their car, which was parked two blocks outside the cathedral gates and drive behind the tour bus in the direction of Epernay. As they stepped outside the gates, they stopped to purchase artifacts ranging from miniature sculptures of past kings of France to the Last Supper.

"You're funny," said Javier laughing uncontrollably. "You stick out like a sore thumb?"

"That was an exaggeration." Nfudu was surprised by the ease with which she revealed herself to him. She had not been embarrassed to tell him that her long silky hair was the product of chemical straightening with a relaxer and that her natural hair was curly, luscious and thick. Though equally beautiful, the hair that grew from her scalp was harder to manage in its natural form, hence the perm. He assured her that he would have loved her still even if she was bald.

They had lunch at a wine cellar in Epernay, while a local connoisseur explained the process and method of winemaking. After tasting a variety of wines from different regions and eras, they participated in making a batch of wine. Nfudu learned so much about wine during the one and half hour lunch than she had ever had the privilege to learn in her whole life. After lunch, they took a tour of the vineyard, where they managed to find a corner to kiss as their heads swooned from all the wine they had consumed that afternoon.

"You have to tell me about your family, where you're from, your parents, and siblings, all of it. I want to hear all of it." Nfudu prodded.

"Of course, on our drive back to the hotel. That is if you don't sleep off along the way."

-

Their date that afternoon was perfect as it was outside of the public eye. It was carefully orchestrated by Javier since he considered it important to remain discreet until his divorce from Juliette was concluded. He and Juliette were no longer living as man and wife, but he thought it was in bad taste to be open with any liaisons until it was appropriate to do so.

On their drive back to the hotel, just as Javier had predicted, Nfudu slept during the entire ride. It was an easy prediction for him because they had both slept very late the night before and he had interrupted her sleep in the morning. While driving, he kept his eye on the road and at intervals watched as she slept with her head leaning on the car door. He marveled at how beautiful her face was and the way her chest heaved up and down with each breath she took. He drove as gently as possible to avoid waking her. On arrival at the hotel, he woke her up and she smiled shyly when she saw him looking down at her. "How long have you been watching me? Are we there yet?"

"Yes, Sleeping Beauty. We're here." They were both exhausted when they got to their suite, so they decided to eat in. Dinner was light – both of them were still heavy from the buffet lunch they had indulged in that afternoon. He told her about his family as they ate celery soup, roasted lamb chops and grilled vegetables. "My family is a small one, compared to yours. I am the younger of two children, my only sibling Janice, lives in Barcelona with her husband and five children. My parents live in Nice – thirty minutes by car from me. I see them as often as I can, almost every weekend. My dad is a retired army general, who fought in both World Wars, with lots of scars to show for it."

Nfudu listened intently, while she munched on her lamb chops and watched his facial expressions. She interrupted him when she heard scars. "Hmm! What type of scars?"

"A massive one. He lost his right ear and some of his right cheekbone during the last war. There's a deep hole where his ear used to be. He wears a prosthetic on that side of his face, so his scars are not visible to the public. It looks very natural. He's still an extremely handsome man, even with all that."

"Is he more handsome than you?" Nfudu asked, mischievously.

"I'll like to think that I'm more handsome," said Javier, bobbing his now tilted head up and down in an uncharacteristic show of arrogance that made Nfudu burst out into laughter. After he assumed a serious demeanor, he told her about his mother. She was one of the most interesting characters she had ever heard of. "Mother is a socialite," he said, "In the heyday of her beauty she turned heads wherever she went. She was engaged to be married at one point to the second in line to the king of France but later dumped him to be with my father, who was a young engineer at the time. Her whirlwind romance with the Prince was so well publicized, that when she broke off the engagement, there was a public uproar; it was almost too much for my young father at the time to bear. Both of them had to move out of France to start a family. They only moved back after the racket died down."

"Your Dad must have been quite a bloke for him to create such a commotion."

"I heard he was. Mostly, I think my mother fell for him because of his heart. They still love each other very much, just like it was yesterday."

They continued talking until they finally fell asleep. The following day they kissed each other goodbye as Javier headed to the airport to catch his flight to Nice. He wished he could have accompanied Nfudu on her ride to the hostel, but chose to avoid further exposure by letting Romeo chauffeur her alone.

When she got to her room, Nfudu first unpacked her clothes and winced as she jumped into her bed. She was both excited and exhausted as she reminisced about the events of the past two days. Her body ached and her insides felt raw from all the sex. A whole hour passed before she was able to take a little nap, but woke up to the sound of the phone ringing. It was Javier. "I miss you already," he said. "And wish I could spend every day with you."

"I miss you too."

"I'll be coming to Paris in two weeks. I'll see you and Vanessa then."

"Should we tell her when you visit?"

"I have no clue if I'll be ready then. All I know is that we cannot hold it off much longer."

"I agree." Nfudu hated the idea of continuing to keep her relationship with Javier a secret from his daughter.

"Okay darling, get some rest. We'll discuss later how and when to reveal everything to her. I don't think she'll take it well, so we need to be careful with our choice of words. She and Juliette are very close."

"I understand My Love. I will wait for your cue before I say anything to her. For the time being, I'll try my best to act like nothing is wrong."

In order to make her weekend escape, Nfudu told Vanessa that she was attending a field trip, for a course elective. Vanessa had readily believed her and not paid any attention to the details because she also had a busy weekend ahead of her. When Nfudu knocked on Vanessa's door, she was relieved to discover that she had company. Vanessa got up to give her a kiss on her cheeks. "You're absolutely glowing!" chirped Vanessa.

Nfudu's heart beat faster than usual as she feared the implication of Vanessa's words. She wondered if Vanessa knew where she had really been all this while. "How do you mean glowing?"

"You look a bit fresher. I don't know… you're just glowing."

It was then Nfudu realized that the guilt she felt from harboring an important secret made her read the wrong meaning into Vanessa's words. She shook away the feeling as she responded, "Uh? Thanks. You look great too. What have you been up to?"

"Not much," responded Vanessa, shaking her head to indicate her displeasure. "I was helping Jeremy decorate his new flat. It turned out to be quite a lot of work. He's promised to hire an interior decorator next time. I'm literally rolling my eyes in my head right now."

Nfudu chuckled. "That's funny. You've got your Dad's sense of humor…" Nfudu stopped mid-sentence as she realized talking about Javier could arouse unnecessary suspicion.

"You think so?"

"Not really," responded Nfudu eager to change the direction of their conversation as she turned her attention to Vanessa's guests.

6

NFUDU talked to Javier every day since their trip. She went into a panic any day she didn't hear from him and acted very miserably until she could speak with him again. He visited often during the semester and both of them managed to keep their relationship under wraps. She devised all types of methods to hide her relationship from Vanessa and make her interactions with Javier seem normal. Vanessa was kept out of the loop a couple of times when Javier came to Paris to visit Nfudu for a no-holds-barred time together. As their relationship progressed, Nfudu began to distance herself from Vanessa, which saddened her, even though Vanessa didn't seem to notice. All she knew was that in recent times, Nfudu looked severely melancholic when she thought no one was looking. She had made nothing of it since she knew her best friend was probably going through a lot as a result of being so far away from her family and trying to manage her school schedule, which had become more hectic as their program progressed.

A number of their friends had developed serious relationships – a couple of the girls had even gotten married. Therefore, Vanessa wondered if having a boyfriend would do Nfudu good and perhaps take her mind away from her family. She had often speculated about Nfudu's relationship with Stanley, who she thought would be a great match for her someday. On their way back from classes, Vanessa took the bait.

"How is Stanley?"

"He is fine. I presume…"

"Has he asked you?"

"Asked me what?" Nfudu was perplexed about the unexpected line of questioning.

"To be official," responded Vanessa. "I know he's nuts about you, but you know he's shy."

"Are you kidding?"

"Noo…"

Nfudu burst out laughing. "Nuts? You're kidding right?" She halted to grimace at Vanessa and placed the back of her hand on Vanessa's forehead to make sure she wasn't running a high temperature. "Stanley and I talk often and get along well, but I didn't think he was 'nuts' about me. I always thought he liked me as a friend… nothing more. Wait! Except for that kiss on New Year's Eve…." She lowered her voice to a whisper. "Could he think there's more than a friendship between us?"

"Well… maybe," responded Vanessa shrugging off Nfudu's protests.

"Nooo. It's only platonic," said Nfudu shaking her head gently.

"Okay," accepted Vanessa grudgingly. "If you say so… Are you interested in anybody I need to know about?"

Nfudu felt cornered. She wondered if Vanessa knew more than she was letting on but decided to play it cool. "Hmm… No. Not really."

"How do you mean not really? Is there someone or not?"

"No one!" responded Nfudu shaking her head.

"Okaay!" responded Vanessa, throwing both hands in the air. She decided to stop her questioning because the longer they talked, the farther Nfudu retreated into her shell. This frustrated Vanessa because until then, she thought they told each other everything.

Nfudu called Javier as soon as she got to her room, but was unable to reach him right away. When he finally picked the phone, he could hear the agitation in her voice, which got him agitated in return.

"I hope everything is all right."

"Not really. I almost gave up our secret," she said to him. "I just had a conversation with Vanessa, and it seems to me that she knows something. We have to tell her now."

"Not now," responded Javier emphatically.

"Why not?" retorted Nfudu. "I'm getting fed up with sneaking around. What's the worst that can happen if we tell her now?" They rarely disagreed, but Nfudu could not endure the guilt any longer and decided to put her foot down.

"Please calm down. The divorce has taken an unexpected turn. Juliette put forward a ton of demands that I don't think I'll be able to meet. It hurts because I want to finalize as quickly as possible to allow me to be with you the way I want."

"What kind of demands?"

"Financial ones. I don't want to bother you with the details, but that doesn't mean I'm going to let the woman I love suffer any longer. We can tell Vanessa over Christmas."

Christmas was only a little over a month away so Nfudu felt she could wait. "I'm sorry love. I feel frustrated at times that I can't help you speed things up. I see the toll this divorce is taking on you."

"It's not your fault. Don't worry about it. Everything will be all right in the end."

"I promise to do everything possible to prevent Vanessa from finding out before you're ready to speak with her. I love you!"

"I love you too!"

Javier continued to shower Nfudu with love as autumn progressed into winter. By Christmastime, the weather became extremely cold. Nfudu was grateful for her last shopping spree with Vanessa at the end of their summer internship In London. They had purchased items she never imagined were wearable items of clothing.

"It would never have occurred to me to pick up a muffler or toque if you hadn't insisted I'd need them for the winter season," said Nfudu to Vanessa as they disembarked their train in London, where they planned to spend their Christmas holidays.

"Isn't winter the coolest season? And I don't mean that literally. There are so many options for looking fashionable."

"Yeah!" agreed Nfudu. "I can also conveniently cover my hair with a hat during those bad hair days."

"Those days come more often than not this cold …cold winter," said Vanessa shivering as they entered the limousine waiting to take them to the lodge.

–

One of those cold winter nights, Vanessa left Javier and Nfudu by themselves in the living room so she could take a nap after a late lunch because she had felt a terrible headache earlier that afternoon. Unable to sleep, she tossed and turned around for what seemed like an hour before deciding to rejoin the party in the living room. When she didn't find Javier and Nfudu there, she stepped onto the porch overlooking the gardens to get some air. As she stepped down from the porch, she saw Nfudu and her dad in a tight embrace. Nfudu was backing her, while Javier was kissing Nfudu's neck, with both hands caressing her buttocks in a circular motion. Nfudu's hands were around his shoulders as she wriggled her body in response to Javier's advances.

When their hug culminated into a long sensual kiss, with both of them moaning uncontrollably, while devouring each other, Vanessa realized she had been frozen in the same spot for over ten minutes and retreated stealthily back to her room. It was then that it occurred to her that the connection between Nfudu and her Dad had morphed into a romantic one, with a life of its own. Still in shock, she paced back and forth several times, until her head started to pound furiously. She slid back into the bed and cried to wash away the plethora of emotions that coursed through her body. She tried very hard to define exactly what those emotions were as it always made her feel better to pinpoint exactly what she was feeling in every circumstance. In that moment, she felt shock, anger and depression. While she played with the words in her mind, it occurred to her that they formed the acronym SAD, which in return summarized everything she was feeling. "This must be the origin of word sad. How could I not have known that all along?"

she thought to herself, relieved by the respite this play with words provided after her traumatic experience.

Her little discovery did nothing to calm her nerves as so many thoughts continued to go through her mind as she lay in bed after taking yet another aspirin. Feeling infinitely sick to her stomach, she leaned over her bed, hoping to throw up all the lunch she ate that afternoon, but nothing came up. She was unsure as to how to confront both her father and Nfudu and wondered how long they had been deceiving her. She felt doubly betrayed by both of them and wondered if their affair was the cause of the split from Juliette until her head began to spin from the unanswered questions.

As Vanessa continued to work herself into a frenzy, it soon occurred to her that she had missed the signs, which had been everywhere. She remembered the beautiful Tiffany scarf she had seen in the trunk of her father's car during one of his visits, but later found around Nfudu's neck. She had made nothing of it at the time but remembered mentioning to Nfudu that she had just seen a similar scarf in Javier's car during his last visit. However, it was all now making sense as it occurred to her that Javier must have seen Nfudu during that same visit, but wondered how they pulled that off. She also recalled Nfudu's melancholic phase, which suddenly disappeared immediately after they set foot in London. The more she recalled the incidents of the past few months, the more she felt like a big fool. She finally fell asleep but woke up to Nfudu's knock on her door.

"How are you precious one?" asked Nfudu oblivious to the state of Vanessa's mind.

"I'm fine. Just need to rest a little bit more. Please let Dad know that I need to be excused from dinner."

"Oh no!" exclaimed Nfudu. "Get some rest then. I'll bring your dinner to you. It's a shame you'll miss the fondue the cook is preparing for dessert."

"Don't worry about that. Just ask the butler to get me some steamed vegetables and the cheesecake from last night if there's any left."

"Ok. Get better soon. I'll check on you later."

"No need for that," Vanessa responded. "I may go to sleep early, because of the aspirin," She just wanted to be left alone.

-

Free to enjoy each other's company as they pleased, Nfudu accepted Javier's offer to spend the night in his room. He gave the staff the rest of the night off after dinner was served to avoid arousing any suspicion. Their foreplay earlier that day left both of them in an extreme state of arousal and the happiest they had ever been as they made love all night. Javier taught her new positions to enhance arousal and the perfect way to position her hips for ultimate pleasure. Nfudu came over and over again that night as she put her newly acquired skills to use. Her screams would have been heard down the hallway, if not for the superior acoustics at the lodge.

"It's almost a year now…" stated Javier as he stared at Nfudu through the sliver of light coming through his curtains from the moonlit sky.

"Since what?" asked Nfudu.

"Pay attention to the times my dear. Since we started dating." He tickled her sides. "It's about time we tell Vanessa what's up."

"I agree."

"Tomorrow morning before we head out for Christmas shopping should be a perfect time. We can't hide this any longer. It may be better if you give her a hint before I have a go at it. What do you think?" asked Javier.

"I'm not so sure about the approach… but I'll give it a try. I feel like crap. Excuse my language."

"I've never heard such foul language from you," teased Javier. "It's probably those American novels I catch you reading at times…"

Nfudu slept restlessly and woke up to sweet kisses from Javier and music by Ray Charles and Betty Carter - '*Baby its Cold Outside*' on the stereo record player. She looked out the window and was surprised to see a snowstorm and signs of sunrise. Even though it was such a beautiful sight to behold especially while in the arms of the one she loved, she threw on her clothes in a hurry and quickly ran both hands through her hair. "I have to head back before Vanessa starts to wonder where I've gone. Besides I need to talk to her. Pray for me to come up with the right words." Javier gave her a kiss for luck before she dashed out of the room.

When she got to Vanessa's room, she was already bathed and dressed for the day. While Vanessa was adjusting her makeup on her vanity mirror, Nfudu sat on the bed. "You look more cheerful today. Have you got enough rest? How is the headache?"

"It's completely disappeared. How was your night?"

"Great. I'm glad you're feeling better. ...There's something I need to tell you. I have wanted to tell you for a long time. Please come over here," said Nfudu patting the space on the bed beside her.

Vanessa obliged Nfudu and sat on the bed, but ensured that she kept some distance between the two of them. An awkward silence passed between them before Vanessa chose to speak first. "I think I already know what you have to say... Then again, I could be wrong, because who knows what other things you're hiding from me."

"What do you mean?" asked Nfudu wide-eyed.

Vanessa had resolved the night before after she recovered from her shock that she would confront Javier and Nfudu about what she discovered. She did not want the state of affairs to ruin her Christmas any more than it had. "I saw you and Dad after lunch in the garden... kissing..." said Vanessa, looking Nfudu right in the eyes.

Nfudu looked away and adjusted herself uncomfortably on the bed. At a loss for words, she managed to say, "I didn't mean for you to find out this way. Javier and I discussed..."

"Wait a minute," interrupted Vanessa, uninterested in the explanation Nfudu had to offer. "How long has this been going on?"

Nfudu immediately regretted not having Javier present. She was having an incredibly difficult time and felt completely blindsided by Vanessa. "It's been a little over eight months."

"Eight months? You've been hiding this from me for eight months? Unbelievable! I trusted you... Ok so tell me, what are you doing with him, just fucking or are you lovers?"

Nfudu was smart enough to realize she wouldn't get anywhere with the conversation at the rate it was going. Vanessa was too furious to be rational in the moment. She sought desperately to leave her presence to alert Javier, so she excused herself abruptly and snuck into Javier's room. She was breathing heavily when she said, "She saw us in the garden yesterday, She's furious. I feel horrible."

"You should feel horrible," said Vanessa sarcastically as she walked in behind her. Javier reached for his robe and grabbed Nfudu's hand when she tried to leave the room on hearing Vanessa. Nfudu was sobbing, and Javier tried to console her. He had not intended to discuss their relationship with Nfudu present, but with the situation out of control, he felt he had no choice but to have the conversation with all three of them in the room.

"Dad, with all due respect, does Juliette know about your affair with Nfudu? Is Nfudu the real cause of your split? And has this really been going on for eight months behind my back? I am so hurt by your actions. I don't understand how two of the people that are closest to me can betray me in this way. You both have ruined my Christmas..."

Javier let Vanessa rant for five minutes, while Nfudu looked on in bewilderment, her chest panting heavily. When Vanessa was done, Javier held her and sat her on the settee in his bedroom. Looking into her eyes and holding her shoulders in a firm grip he said, "I swear that I never meant to hurt you or hide the relationship. I was incited to do so for this long because the divorce was taking longer than I expected. The divorce was already underway before Nfudu and I got together the first time... and no she's not the cause of my split with Juliette. You very well know that my problems with Juliette started long before I met Nfudu."

"...But why did you both deceive me for so long?" Vanessa asked choking on her words.

"Please forgive us. Nfudu wanted so badly to tell you, but I deterred her."

Vanessa did not know what to believe. She wasn't sure that she could trust her father and Nfudu any longer.

"Forgive you? Do I have any choice? You're my family."

"Nfudu is your family also."

"No, she isn't. I can choose not to forgive her."

"That's harsh my dear," retorted Javier.

Deciding she couldn't take anymore, Nfudu ran out of the room sobbing.

Vanessa left soon after, but with a parting message for her father, "I feel really weird about you sleeping with her. She is my age mate and best friend and I don't think it's appropriate." She shook her head gently, but couldn't shake off the thought that they could end up getting married, which would make Nfudu her stepmother. The thought made her shudder as she shut the door behind her.

-

The three of them had breakfast together but hardly spoke to one another. However, Nfudu was relieved that everything was out in the open and they could begin from then on to pick up the pieces of their lives after the betrayal. Breakfast was drearier than it should have been because they had to wait for the snow storm outside to peter out before heading out for their Christmas shopping. "Please call me when you're ready," Vanessa said to Javier as she pulled her chair to leave when she realized she couldn't sit with the two of them any longer.

Javier wasn't having it. "I'll like to see you in my study," he said to her.

They were in the study for close to two hours and by the time they finally emerged and joined Nfudu in the living room, they both looked ready to move on. To Nfudu's relief, Vanessa gave her a wry smile, creating hope for the survival of their friendship.

-

The rest of Christmas holiday, 1964 was uneventful. Nfudu, Javier and Vanessa spent the rest of their time in London getting to know each other all over again after the recent events that threatened to destroy the dynamics of their relationships. Vanessa and Nfudu barely spoke to each other the first few days after the incident, but later got back on talking terms after great effort on both sides.

During one of the evenings at the lodge, Javier revealed the mystery surrounding Jeannette Eudora to the girls.

"It's nothing bad, it's just that Jeannette will skin me alive if she found out I told you. You must never repeat it to anyone outside this room." He looked at both of them in turn as they nodded their agreement. "Ok," he continued "When we were a lot younger, about fourteen or so, Jeannette loved to act mysteriously. I'm sure you can still see a little bit of that trait in her."

"Sure…" replied Vanessa, nodding her head in agreement.

"Anyway, one day, her parents, who were well known London socialites, were having a party, where both our parents – mine and your mothers were invited. They decided to take us along, so we could play with Jeannette in her room, while the adults partied downstairs. It happened that Jeanette had a crush on this handsome pilot, her father's friend. When she revealed this to us, we dared her to go down the stairs, find the pilot, look him in the face and tell him 'Manny, I'll marry you. You and I will get married on an airplane'"

Javier paused for a second and heard screams of, "Continue, continue, why did you stop?"

"I just wanted to make sure you're listening."

"Of course we are," answered Nfudu impatiently.

"Ok!" continued Javier. "Jeannette took the dare and didn't even remember to ask for a wager. She found Manny close to the hallway, grabbed him by his arms and proceeded to yell amidst the sound of music playing in the background, 'Manny, I'll marry you. You and I will get married in an airplane.' While she was mouthing the last word, she realized the whole room had stopped to stare at her, and that the music had stopped incidentally when she started. She had blurted out all the words without realizing that the room was completely quiet. It all happened in one split second. It was such an embarrassment for her parents, who had the crème de la crème of London at the party, from royals to cardinals, to top military personnel. Jeannette was being groomed at the time for high society, so her parents were aptly disappointed by her charade."

"So what happened next?" asked Nfudu.

"The whole room roared with laughter. …Jeannette ran up her room sobbing and unable to look anybody in the eye."

"Did you and Vanessa's mom get in trouble afterwards?"

"No, not with our parents, but Jeannette's mother never invited us to another party after that, at least, not the children. You have to understand that they were the very strict aristocratic type."

"Wow! What a story. Lady Eudora was certainly naughty as hell," chimed Vanessa.

"Definitely very interesting," mused Nfudu. "She still ended up marrying well, so I presume her misdeeds didn't ruin her chances in society."

"I hope I have satisfied both your curiosities," said Javier, smiling mischievously at the girls and happy to have used that opportunity for all three of them to create a new bond, even though it was at Lady Eudora's expense.

"You certainly have," said Nfudu and Vanessa in unison.

-

During the rest of their stay in London, Nfudu and Vanessa completed the last phase of their internship at the House of Eudora. Lady Eudora was in attendance at the farewell ceremony that was held for them and some of the other interns. As she presented completion certificates to the girls, she gave them a handshake and an offer to pursue further opportunities at the fashion house after graduation from the International Institute of Fashion. She commended them for a job well done and offered to include their creative designs in her spring collection. They readily agreed. It was a unique opportunity for Nfudu and Vanessa to get recognition and make some royalties in the process.

They returned to school a day after New Year for the second semester of their second year at the International Institute of Fashion. Graduation from the school was slated for July. Both of them were clear on the direction they needed to take in their profession after graduation, thanks to the internship program they attended. Vanessa would be taking up a position as the Creative Director for a new brand Lady Eudora was creating for young adults. Nfudu was also offered a position, but she turned the offer down as she had other plans for her fashion career.

7

JAVIER and Juliette's divorce became final in February of 1965. This was right after Juliette eased her terms for settlement so she could pursue her future with a French Baron, to whom she was already engaged. The day after Javier received the good news, he drove nine long hours to Paris. Nfudu and Vanessa were ecstatic to see him. They took turns hugging and congratulating him. After they caught a late lunch together, Nfudu accompanied him for a ride around the city. They drove to Montmartre – the perfect location to relax and talk right before sunset, and parked before walking a considerable distance to the Sacre-Coeur Basilica on the highest point of Mont Martyr. When they left the solemn atmosphere in the sanctuary, they were immediately greeted by an impromptu street show.

"What would your father think of me?" asked Javier as the raucous began to die down from the street performance. Javier already knew what Nfudu's fears regarding her father were, but needed further clarification. A few months back, Nfudu had told him a story about how her older maternal cousin had been forbidden from marrying her fiancé because he was from a different state of origin. It hadn't mattered to her family that the state in question was a neighboring one, with the same language and culture as their home state. This worried Javier as he imagined how much more difficult it would be for him to be accepted by Nfudu's family, considering they were many cultures and a couple of decades apart.

Nfudu felt pensive. She guessed where Javier was going with his question. His divorce was finally over and he wanted to gauge the possibility of a future with her. "He'll definitely put up a fight," responded Nfudu nodding her head. "But, he'll have to give in if we're able to persist. It won't be easy, but... if we stay committed then he'll have no choice but to let us be."

"A friend of mine told me that the right thing to do is to ask your father for 'your hand in marriage' before asking you... Under the current circumstances, is it advisable for me to speak with him?"

"Hmm!" sighed Nfudu. "That's a tough call. I'm not sure the best way to handle this."

"It's obvious you're scared stiff of him and for good reason. He sounds like a tough guy."

"Yes! And a big one too," agreed Nfudu. "But I'm not scared of him alone. I would have to contend with some members of my extended family also. But you needn't worry. No matter what, you're my first love and I want you to be my last." She gave him a kiss on his lips, turning up his smile.

Nfudu had never mentioned Javier to her parents or any member of her family, other than Afonwa, who was surprised that she was dating a 'White Man'. "*Onye Ocha?*" Was Afonwa's response when Nfudu mentioned the fact to her, during a phone call to Nigeria when she felt she couldn't bear the secrecy any longer. Nfudu had regretted blurting out that information but warned Afonwa not to repeat it to anyone, especially their parents. She wanted to reveal the relationship when she felt the timing was right.

They walked hand in hand to one of the quaint cafes lining the street to grab a sandwich. Right after they took their seats, a waiter came by to take their orders. He eyed them mysteriously before handing them a menu. The waiter returned with Javier's order first, and Javier immediately asked him to take it back.

"*Pourquoi?*" The waiter asked looking genuinely surprised.

"Why?" responded Javier. "Because I'm with my lady and I expect her to be served first."

"I'm sorry." The waiter returned Javier's order to the kitchen and came back a few minutes later with Nfudu's order and a fresh one for Javier.

"That was too obvious… Did you see the angst on his face?" asked Javier.

"Yeah."

"I'm sorry he treated you that way."

"That's ok. I'm glad he corrected it right away. This is one of the storms we're going to have to weather. I never thought it would be smooth sailing."

They enjoyed the view and compared ideas on the latest fashion trends while they munched on their sandwiches.

"What about the age issue?" asked Javier as he took one big bite off his sandwich.

"They'll all have something to say about it I'm sure."

"And your age… Will your father think you're too young?"

"Noo. Girls from my place are usually married by the time they are eighteen. Any woman married after the age of twenty-five is considered an old maid. I would be considered very ripe for marriage. They're most likely going to be looking at the age difference."

"Did you just say you were ripe…? That's hysterical," said Javier laughing. "They also probably have someone in mind to marry you off to."

"Not one. I hear about three suitors, who they say I must meet whenever I return home."

"You're not going to meet them. Are you?" asked Javier visibly upset.

"No. I even dread the conversation with my parents. It's awful. How can I marry someone I don't know?"

"What about you. Does our age difference bother you?"

Nfudu laughed. "Not at all. I'm in love with you. I don't even see it."

They left the café at close to eight and spent the night in Javier's hotel. He left the following day for Nice, feeling freer and lighter than he had felt in a long time.

-

Nfudu and Vanessa were turning twenty-two that year – 1965. They had both bloomed into beautiful young women. Their friendship had changed over the years, from one where they partied and hung out with boys to a mutually beneficial adult relationship, which had survived a number of difficulties, the biggest being the revelation of Nfudu and Javier's affair. Vanessa finally forgave Nfudu after she understood she and Javier had an unbreakable bond – the kind that needed to be seen to be believed.

During her stay in Paris, Nfudu developed a strong network of friends and associates. She hoped to put this to good use when it was time to market her first collection, which she hoped to perfect over the coming months. The Monreaux Fashion House in London, the top and foremost fashion outfit had taken a sneak peek into her developing collection and provided her with feedback. They liked what they saw and offered her a job after graduation. The job came with a clause promising to liberate her when she was ready to branch out on her own. Nfudu kept that offer open. Javier encouraged her to consider it. He also offered to help with the publicity required to get her brand noticed and respected.

The International Institute of Fashion's courses on branding and entrepreneurship gave their students the technical knowledge required to set up and succeed in business. Also, its courses in business law equipped the students with legal knowledge for surviving in the world of business. Nfudu wanted to delve right into the business world after graduation. She had the appropriate backing in Paris and London but wanted to ensure her father had her back as well. She called him to discuss her future plans.

"Papa, you know I'm planning to return home for a year after graduation."

"I thought you'll be coming home for good. Why for a year?" asked Chief Ibe.

Nfudu paused for a minute before saying slowly, "I want to set up a fashion house in London before I move back to Nigeria."

"It sounds like you have thought out this plan of yours very well …but when are you planning to get married?"

Nfudu's blood boiled at his comment. While she was considering her response, Chief Ibe continued, "I'm waiting for an answer. You know you're 'ripe for marriage' and…"

Nfudu could not take it anymore. In the quietest and coolest tone she could muster, without being rude, she said, "Papa, Papa…"

"Yeees? Go oon."

"I don't know why you're always bothering me about marriage. I'm only twenty-three years old and people don't get married that early these days."

"Which days? You have to come home as soon as you can and make the choice of a man to marry. So many suitors are already lined up waiting for you so there is no need to waste time by opening up a fashion house in London. When you get married, you and your husband will decide which direction you need to take. There is no need delaying as 'time waits for no one' besides that, your siblings are all looking up to you."

Nfudu knew better than to try to win this argument with her father. It was an impossible task to accomplish. Either way, she would be left with a rotten feeling that would refuse to disappear for days on end and affect her ability to function. Trusting her better judgment, she responded, "I have heard you, Papa. Have a great day."

She was content with how she handled her father and wondered what he would think if he knew her plans were already set in stone and that she already had the 'perfect' suitor, with whom she could plan her future with.

During the rest of the semester, Nfudu did the best she could to make her plan of returning home after graduation possible. She worked hard to improve her final grades to impress her Dad. Mediocrity was not permitted amongst Chief Ibe's children, especially not from the *Ada*. Javier was disappointed when he learned she would be leaving for a year. However, he still supported her choice and agreed to visit her often during her one-year hiatus in Nigeria. Nfudu knew they would have obstacles to overcome as a result of the cultural and age barriers between them, but she tried not to worry about it. Her constant prayer was that her love for Javier – which she thought was irreplaceable not be obstructed by her families' beliefs.

-

Vanessa and Nfudu completed their studies at the International Institute of Fashion without any hitch. While in Paris, Nfudu perfected her French and even spoke with a Parisian accent. She was the second best graduating student in her class, an honor that entitled her to an opportunity to pursue a career as an instructor in the school and an opportunity to choose a lucrative role from one of the top four fashion houses that automatically received the results of her academic achievements from the Institute's administration.

"We are so proud of you!" said Mrs. Ibe excitedly as Nfudu gave her news of her results.

"Thank you, Mama. You know that my graduation is on the twenty-seventh of July. I hope you'll all be able to come."

"I'll come with your father. We wouldn't miss it for the world. This is a big achievement for our family. It calls for a big celebration. We're making plans for a big party when you return home."

"Ah Mama…" said Nfudu. She was worried her family would make a big spectacle of her.

"Oh yes! The party will serve as your reintroduction into society. We're inviting all the dignitaries from Abasi and its environs as well as their accomplished sons and daughters from all over the country. We're even inviting people from overseas. It will be the party of the year. Wait till you see all we have planned."

"Hmm…"

"What is the hmm about?"

"Nothing… Just wondering…"

"You don't need to wonder about anything. The party is well deserved. It's going to be a big party and we've hired the best party planner to ensure it is well executed. We're even already reviewing different options for 'Aso-ebi - uniforms' and excitedly waiting for your return in November."

"Ok, Ma… Mama, but what is the political climate like now. I have been hearing all kinds of things."

"Yes. It's very unstable right now. This independence seems to be more of a curse than a blessing to our people. Listen to the news it will tell you everything you need to know."

Nfudu tuned her radio to BBS shortly after and heard the announcer saying in a deep Nigerian accent.

... Nigeria's independence from Britain in 1960 gave the country exclusive powers in defense, foreign relations and fiscal policy. Political parties created as a vehicle for democracy deviated from the spirit of their formations and tended to reflect the structure of the three main ethnic groups in Nigeria - Hausa, Yoruba and Igbo, rather than the principles and ideologies for which those parties were formed. The Nigerian People's Congress represents Hausa and Fulani interests; the National Council of Nigerian Citizens represents the Igbo's and the rest of the Eastern Region and the Action Group represents the interest of the Yoruba's in the Western Region of Nigeria. The national elections worsened the ethnic and political tensions as widespread electoral fraud were alleged. This put the newly independent nation on a path...

She turned it off soon after and muttered under her breath, "same story every day." She wondered when her people would stop and appreciate all the wonders they were blessed with and stop focusing on the negative. That time may still come, she hoped.

Despite the tensions brewing in Nigeria, Nfudu's parents still managed to attend her graduation ceremony in Paris. It was held in the Grande Theater of the school and attended by thousands of graduands, current and past students of the Institute. When the graduating class marched up the stage to accept their diplomas, the crowd cheered as their wards were called. When it came to Nfudu's turn, her mother couldn't contain her excitement. She cheered with the rest of the crowd, while Chief Ibe looked on and nodded in his usual way in acknowledgement of a job well done. The moment she received her diploma was such an emotional one for Nfudu. She cried tears of joy.

The occasion was also a family reunion for Vanessa who had almost her entire family – Javier, her mother Brandy, Grandmother Margaret and stepmother Juliette in attendance. Juliette left immediately after the ceremony, so she was absent when Vanessa introduced her mother and grandmother to Nfudu. They both took turns to kiss her on both cheeks and acted like they had known her forever.

"Vanessa has told us so much about you. I must say she did you no justice. You're truly beautiful." Margaret gushed, while Brandy looked on and nodded in agreement.

"What are your plans for the future?" Brandy asked.

"Travel for a bit and later return to London to pursue my career in fashion."

"Very well. Good luck with everything," she responded, without any trace of resentment. Nfudu treaded with caution during the rest of their conversation. She was not sure if Brandy knew about her relationship with Javier.

As Vanessa walked with Nfudu to meet her parents, Nfudu whispered, "Does your mother know?"

"Know what?"

"About Javier and I..."

"Oh. Of course! But she doesn't care because she's completely moved on from my Dad. She specifically requested to meet you and I think both her and granny loved you. Don't worry," Vanessa assured her.

"My parents don't know about Javier so I'm going to try to keep them apart from yours. You know what I mean?" asked Nfudu searching Vanessa's face for absolute understanding.

"Sure!" responded Vanessa. "Dad also asked me to be careful not to reveal anything to your parents. ...I wonder how long you can keep your relationship from them. It seems unhealthy to me that you both cannot come out to the open with it. Mom and granny are both leaving today anyway, but Dad as you know is staying for a couple of days."

"It's my parent's first visit to Paris so they're spending five whole days. Even at that, they keep apologizing for the short visit because they haven't seen me in two whole years… Here they are." Nfudu said, stopping in front of her parents.

"You must be Vanessa. Nfudu constantly talks about you." Nfudu's mother said.

"How are you my dear?" asked Chief Ibe stretching his hand out for a handshake.

"Very well sir." Replied Vanessa in the tiniest voice Nfudu had ever heard.

-

Nfudu's parents stayed at the Ritz Carlton Paris Hotel at the recommendation of their travel agent. She had convinced them that the Ritz would provide the best proximity to Nfudu's school, as well as the sites they planned to visit while in Paris. They met Javier and Vanessa for dinner in one of the private suites of Restaurant Laperouse on the day following the graduation ceremony. Nfudu introduced Javier as Vanessa's Dad and Javier, charming as usual, struck up a deep intellectual conversation with Chief Ibe about world politics focusing on its effect on the political climate in Nigeria. Both Nfudu and Chief Ibe were impressed by Javier's depth of knowledge about Nigerian politics.

As their camaraderie developed over dinner, Nfudu wasn't surprised when Chief Ibe said to Javier, "You and Vanessa must visit Nigeria and make sure you stay with us when you do. I also want to extend an invitation to you for Nfudu's welcome back party in December. Please try to make it if you can.

"My wife and I are very grateful for how well you have taken care of our daughter. She told us everything – about the Internship program that you helped her secure as well as the lodging you provided for her in London. God bless you both. We would love an opportunity to reciprocate your kindness in any way we can."

Javier was touched by Chief Ibe's show of appreciation. "Nfudu is like family to us. There is no need to thank us. She's such an amazing and intelligent girl. It was a pleasure taking care of her."

Even though he and Chief Ibe had got along well, Javier thought he fit the description Nfudu had provided of him – tall, imposing and a little bit intimidating. The thought may have crossed his mind to broach the subject of his relationship with Nfudu with him, but the impressive nature of the man before him wouldn't allow him give it a second thought. Bringing up the topic would definitely have elicited a negative reaction and potentially ruin the beautiful occasion.

"I wish she could return home with us," continued Chief Ibe. "I do understand she needs to stay a little bit after graduation to sort out the required paperwork and other details."

"In the next few weeks she'll be heading to London with Vanessa to conclude agreements and strengthen relationships with her potential partners, in order to have a more secure platform when she returns," added Javier.

"No... No... No... No" retorted Chief Ibe shaking his head aggressively. "She won't be returning... at least not to stay. We have other plans for her in Nigeria..."

Nfudu was baffled at how the two most important men in her life were discussing her future right in front of her as if she wasn't there. She prayed Javier wouldn't say anymore. She had forgotten to warn Javier to avoid discussing her future plans as they were not hundred percent sanctioned by her Dad. She was relieved when Javier spoke the words: "I'm sure she will succeed wherever she is. We'll give her all the support she needs if she needs to return to Nigeria."

"That's right. That's right," agreed Chief Ibe nodding explicitly. "She also has to get married. She's not getting any younger you know."

Nfudu wanted to hide her head in shame, while all the others, including her mother and Javier, laughed at Chief Ibe's comments. Javier knew he would have some explaining to do later on. When she escorted Javier and Vanessa to their car that evening, she commended him for the way he handled the difficult conversation with her father. "I'm glad you handled that diplomatically," she said.

"Of course," responded Javier. "I didn't want to take any wild chances. Just to remove any doubt that may have cropped up in that pretty head of yours, we want you to remain here with us. I can't imagine you vanishing right after graduation. I won't be able to bear it."

"Well... I'm glad you didn't say that to my father."

"I wouldn't dare," he responded smiling.
"I love you!"
"I love you too. Good night."

The following day, Nfudu's parents returned to Nigeria on the same Lufthain flight they arrived in. A majority of the passengers on the flight were Nigerians returning home from a visit to Paris and other cities in Europe. There was tension in the first class lounge where they waited for check-in. The tension transferred to the plane where the trending discussion was the unrest in Nigeria and the fear that a civil war could erupt at any moment. The passengers discussed openly the possibility of sending their children to Europe or America to avoid the tumultuous political climate in hopes of reducing the potential ravages of war on their families if one became inevitable. The situation at home was chilling. The fear could be seen in their eyes as they disembarked the plane at the Lagos International Airport and headed to their various destinations.

On getting into town, Chief Ibe saw the tension first hand and he wondered if he was in the same country he left just a few days back. The radio and other media outlets carried news of the hostility and the danger the people from the Eastern Region of Nigeria, living in the Northern Region were experiencing in the hands of their Northern brothers. The Easterners were beginning to retaliate and the bloody clashes that ensued were leaving people dead by the numbers. It became obvious to the different factions that they could not cohabit in the same geographical zone and citizens held their breath waiting for a miracle to diffuse the tension, which had reached uncontrollable heights.

8

TENSIONS continued to brew in Nigeria. The populace, both at home and abroad became increasingly frustrated with the system which they felt had failed them. People with means stashed large amounts of foreign currency in soak away pits and underground safes. They sent their children in droves to Europe and America and built fortresses and safe houses to mitigate against dangers anticipated should a war ensue. Visa offices for Europe and America were bombarded by Nigerians, who hoped to escape pending doom. A majority of the visa requests were turned down, but this didn't stop the rejected many from trying to obtain visas from other less sought after destinations. Households stocked up on piles of food and other necessities, including firearms which became an essential commodity for defending one's self at a time like that. The reality was that the future was bleak.

The stories circulating in different circles were chilling enough to make even the stoic Chief Ibe cringe. For the first time in his life, he feared for his family. Several deadly riots were being reported all over the country which required the police and army to step in. The death toll was increasing daily, and rumors about beheadings in the North also turned out to be true and on the rise. Chief Ibe began to have serious misgivings regarding Nfudu's return to Nigeria because he doubted a quick and easy resolution to the rising conflict in the country. Two of his children, Emeka and Dike were already in College in London. He remained alert to respond in the nick of time in case he needed to send his entire family to the UK. His biggest fear was that his boys would be forcefully recruited to fight in a war he felt was unwarranted.

Two weeks before Nfudu was meant to leave for Nigeria, he made a final decision to allow her remain in Paris as the threat of a civil war was further heightened by news that the new Republic, the Republic of Biafra had been acknowledged by two more countries and strengthened its ties with the west. Biafra was ready to fight and had gained significant ground in the Eastern Region of Nigeria. Nfudu was also following the news very closely and had already made a decision not to return home when Chief Ibe called to break the news to her.

"The instability in this country is becoming too glaring to risk your return," said Chief Ibe regrettably. "I have started making plans to send your mothers and siblings out of the country."

"Don't worry Papa," responded Nfudu. "Even though I have looked forward to this return for so many months, I understand that it's not a wise decision to visit now. I haven't been home in three years and it's beginning to feel like a lifetime. I miss everyone. I hope it all gets resolved soon, even though I doubt it will."

"It's a sad time for our country."

"When will you send the family to the UK?"

"I'm still watching to see if any progress will be made with the peace talks. In a week, there is a meeting of Northern and Eastern leaders with the political parties that is being attended by delegates from Britain. We're all hoping the salient issues will be addressed in that meeting so our lives can begin to get back to normal."

"Please Papa, don't wait too long. I don't trust these people. Where is the family now?"

"In Nkume. It feels safer here."

"OK. Greet Mama and my brothers and sisters for me. I'm really - really scared, but I'll do my best to stay positive."

"Try my dear. Your mother asked me to inform you that the welcome party has been cancelled."

"That makes sense, but what about all the people we invited?"

"Don't worry about it. We have sent apologies to everyone."

Nfudu welcomed the news of not travelling back to Nigeria with mixed feelings. She felt nostalgic about home, but returning was no longer an exciting prospect for her as fear and trepidation had taken over. It did not help that the catastrophe in Nigeria was front page news on a daily basis in London. The major radio and television channels, the BBS and VOA carried news about Nigeria daily, in addition to massive amounts of propaganda, which only worsened the tension. She feared about the welfare of her family and wished she was near enough to help them cope and make crucial decisions at that difficult time. It was a trying time for all Nigerians. The situation fluctuated between times of hope when peace talks appeared to be achieving their stated purpose to times of despair when relations between the warring factions deteriorated.

With her plans to return home thwarted, Nfudu took up a position at the Creative Director at the House of Monreaux, while she continued to work on the first collection of her self-titled fashion brand – Nfudu's Couture. She spoke to her family on a daily basis and prayed for the situation at home to turn around. She relied on the support provided by her friends to stay afloat, and on her work to keep her mind off her problems.

A series of military coups followed the growing crisis in Nigeria and a full-blown war broke out in 1967. Though the war was long anticipated and talked about, the sudden manner in which it broke out surprised everyone, Chief Ibe included. He, like most Nigerians, was hoping it could be averted by all the peace efforts and the deals made by the different factions. He felt helpless and dejected because he had not acted fast enough to protect his family from danger. He abandoned their properties and home in Nkume and took his four wives, fifteen children and some servants on a journey to Abasi when federal troops invaded the beautiful port town. They headed to Abasi but were stranded along the way for three weeks as they avoided getting captured by the forces on a route that would typically have taken three hours to maneuver. It was a grueling three weeks during which they were forced into hiding several times when news about citing of federal troops spread amongst the other Biafran returnees. On their way, they witnessed a massacre which forced them into hiding in an underground water tank for a whole week. From there, they monitored the environs until they were cleared to continue their journey.

Nfudu's eyes were glued daily on her colored television for news about the war in her brand new North West London flat. She could not believe the extent of devastation that had befallen her beloved country Nigeria. Worse still, she had not spoken to her parents or siblings for three whole weeks since they fled Nkume. She tried desperately to call them, but to no avail. What she did not realize was that the phone lines in the Eastern region were completely dead. She went into an uncontrollable panic. Javier ran to her side to console her but was unsuccessful. She refused to eat or drink or be consoled. It was not until another four weeks that she got news from the Red Cross Committee where she had registered as a family member and countryman of people stuck in war torn Nigeria. She was filled with trepidation when the Red Cross delegate handed over a piece of paper to her. It was the same style of writing and with the same letterhead she had seen handed over to a couple of her Nigerian friends to report on the status of their families in Nigeria.

> *Chief Ibe and his four wives were able to escape Nkume, but with only thirteen of the fifteen children in their care. The family is still unable to determine the whereabouts of the two oldest children Afonwa and Ijere, who still remain missing after one month of arriving in Abasi town. Afonwa and Ijere were separated from the rest of their family members during a scuffle to escape an approaching set of gun-wielding soldiers at Anwa junction. Efforts are being made to locate and bring them home safely to the family. The rest of the family is safe in the moment in Abasi, even though there are threats of a looming invasion. As at now, except for a few shells hitting the home during an air raid two weeks ago, the family is doing well. Take heart and keep them in your prayers as you are in theirs…*

Nfudu let out a loud cry of distress over the plight of her family and her missing siblings. Still crying uncontrollably, she collapsed into

Javier's hands. Later that day, she heard the stories of other members of the Nigerian community in London and realized that her family situation could be considered tolerable. Some of her friends had lost entire family members, while others could not reach a single member of their family. Whole cities had been burned down and thousands were rendered homeless. No one had imagined that amount of devastation so soon. Nfudu was so depressed she was unable to continue working on her collection. On the advice of some of her close friends, she joined a group of sympathizers, called the War Mission, comprised of Nigerians, members of the international community and other local organizations that sympathize with the situation in Nigeria.

The War Mission worked with the international community and charitable organizations to help Nigerians in London cope with the situation at home. They assisted with communication and providing help for family members to escape the carnage at home. All escape efforts so far had been however thwarted, because federal troops blockaded all the borders, thereby making it too dangerous a venture. Non-citizens had long been removed from the country by their embassies, many weeks before the war broke out and as a result, it was difficult to sneak escapees into planes with foreign diplomats.

The War Mission provided counseling, which Nfudu found helpful in dealing with the helpless situation she found herself in. Javier attended with her, whenever he was in London. She deepened her involvement with the group by becoming an advocate and starting an initiative called "Dress for Nigeria." The initiative encouraged members to dress in Ankara, lace or George to show their support and in the process raise funds for the hapless victims of the war. As part of the initiative, men were asked to grow their beards while the women let their hair out of their wigs.

-

It was during one of the weekly war mission meetings that Nfudu met Ikechi, a handsome twenty-nine-year-old. He had recently arrived from Nigeria to set up an investment management business but got stuck in London as a result of the war. She had caught him staring at her from a corner of the room and was baffled by his refusal to look away even after their eyes met. He walked towards her, ignoring everyone in his path.

"Hello, I'm Ikechi," he said, extending his right hand for a handshake, his eyes still poring over her.

"Hi! ...Nfudu," she stuttered as she gave him her hand in return, puzzled by the stares from this handsome stranger.

He chuckled. "Sorry for staring at you. When I first saw you, I thought you were someone I knew, but in close contact, I now know it was a mistake. Beautiful name... What does it mean?"

"No worries. I make the same mistake sometimes. My name is short for Nfudunkem which means one who would never lack. My grandmother gave it to me."

"She did an awesome job there. How long have you been in London?"

"Almost three years. And you?"

"I come and go. Stuck here for now and God knows for how long. I came to check up on my business, and then go back to my other businesses in Nigeria, but I miscalculated this time around."

While he spoke, Nfudu marveled at his ebony skin, strong cheekbones and thick defined brows. She saw a small hint of a nipple through his grey t-shirt and swallowed hard. "You should be glad you're not caught in the war," she eventually managed to say.

"Absolutely, but a part of me feels grossly stranded. The only silver lining is that our head office is in Lagos, so I'm still able to communicate with my staff. Most of them, especially those from the east have fled from fear of repercussion though. Do you attend all the War Mission meetings?"

"Yes," responded Nfudu nodding. "I'm also planning to increase my participation. I'm a strong believer in everyone pitching in however little way they can to make a difference. ...I notice you're starting to grow your beard." She bent her head to one side to further examine his chin, which was showing signs of stubble.

"Is it that obvious?" asked Ikechi, rubbing his chin with his left index finger. "Yes, I'm participating in 'Dress for Nigeria'. I've gone two days without shaving. I see you're also participating." He looked at her from head to toe, using the opportunity to scrutinize her sculpted five feet seven inches figure in the mermaid style Ankara skirt and blouse she was wearing.

"Yes! I founded the initiative," said Nfudu, shrugging her shoulders. "I'm trying to be a good example."

They were interrupted by the voice of the host on the microphone. "Everyone should try to meet at least one new person this evening, so we can grow our brotherhood. You can find snacks and drinks in the north corner. Enjoy and continue the good effort."

When the announcement was over, Nfudu leaned towards Ikechi with her hand stretched out. "It was nice meeting you, but I have to return to my work here," she said.

"It was really nice meeting you too, Nfudu." Ikechi responded, in a warm resonant voice, holding her hand a second longer than normal. "Will you be attending Dan's anniversary party at the Rims nightclub?"

"I'm not sure yet, but just might."

"I'm looking forward to catching up with you there. I think it starts at eight o'clock," said Ikechi, pointing in her general direction as he retreated back into the crowd.

There was an instant connection between them, but something about him baffled Nfudu. During their farewell handshake, right before he enquired about Dan's party, she felt he had let his index finger slide down her palm seductively. His mischief had achieved its purpose, as she found herself thinking about him and making plans to attend the party that night for the sole purpose of seeing him. When she got home at six o'clock, she paid particular attention to her makeup and attire. Determined to show some skin, she put on a black skin-tight skirt and a black lace bodice that left very little to the imagination. He was fresh and exciting; so she hoped he would find her attractive and irresistible. She hoped to get to know him a little better, and perhaps quench a little bit of her curiosity and the fire that was beginning to burn inside her.

When she arrived at the party, she looked around to see if she could find Ikechi. Seconds passed into minutes and minutes into hours and Ikechi was nowhere to be seen. She was disappointed when he didn't show up by the time she was leaving at the end of the night, and couldn't believe she had spent so much energy trying to look good for him. Shuddering at the thought that she had been attracted enough to another man to risk jeopardizing her relationship with Javier, Nfudu convinced herself that Ikechi was a ladies' man and not worth her time and energy. In her mind, gazillion girls in Ikechi's lifetime had received the same handshake that made her go soft inside.

Even though her relationship with Javier was still as strong as when it first began, Nfudu still found herself hoping to see Ikechi during the weekly War Mission meetings. Several weeks passed without any sight of him. As weeks turned into months, she started to think less about him, and reckoned that it was all for the better as she was beginning to lose control of herself. She did not understand how she fell for his charm and thought it may be because of her current emotional state and the fact that her whole world was currently turned upside down. She also imagined that it could be as a result of the familiarity she felt being around him. He fit the image of the kind of man her father would like her to marry. Whatever it was, she decided it was a smart move to let him be.

9

THE Nigerian-Biafran war raged on for years, and created a significant amount of destruction in its path. Over a million people were reported to have lost their lives in what has been described the world over as a mass massacre of the innocent. The fighting was sustained through the assistance of allies – Great Britain and the Soviet Union provided support to Nigeria, while France provided covert support through its African colonies to Biafra. Nfudu continued her work at the War Mission. Her 'Dress for Nigeria' initiative raised over twenty thousand pounds. The money was put to good use immediately through collaborations with international humanitarian agencies that were confirmed to be providing needed relief to the most affected areas.

Several months passed before Nfudu set eyes on Ikechi again. At a Christmas party held by a friend of hers, she was with Javier when Ikechi walked up to her.

"Hello, stranger?" He said with a grin.

"Hello. Long time no see. Meet my boyfriend Javier," said Nfudu pointing in Javier's direction. Gesturing from Javier to Ikechi now, she said "Meet Ikechi. We met at the war mission some months ago."

The two men exchanged a firm handshake. Ikechi fidgeted on the spot. He was unprepared to meet Nfudu's boyfriend. Javier, oblivious to their connection kept the conversation going. They all chatted for a while about the wonderful things the War Mission was doing, before Ikechi's date joined them with two drinks in hand. She handed one to Ikechi.

"This is Amanda. She's one of my partners." Ikechi announced.

"Hi Amanda," greeted Nfudu, eyeing her furtively, wondering if they are really just partners. "Nice meeting you."

"Same here," responded Amanda.

They joined the rest of the party just as a toast was being delivered by the host.

Nfudu could not remember Ikechi being so striking. It occurred to her that she had not really taken a good look at him the first time they met. Despite his looks, she realized what made him so appealing. It was the manner in which he carried himself. Also, the unfamiliar look in his eyes always seemed to be searching for something deeper. She thought he was the most mysterious person she had ever met and darted her eyes across the room to see if she could find him. He found her before she did, standing next to the punch bowl while Javier was chatting with their host.

"I thought I'd never find a moment with you. Your man was guarding you so closely," he teased.

Nfudu laughed, her heart beating forcefully. "Like he should," she said hoping he didn't notice her nervousness. "How have you been? I barely recognized you. It's been months."

"Yeah and sorry I couldn't attend Dan's event. Were you able to make it?"

Nfudu grimaced to feign ignorance for a brief moment before responding, "Oh, yeah! I was there. You said you would come. Why didn't you?"

"You won't believe what happened on that day. I had a medical emergency right before I was supposed to leave for the party," he responded with a frown.

"What sort of emergency? Hope nothing too serious." Nfudu said with great anticipation.

"It was serious – a hernia. The pain was unbearable and I thought I was going to die. An ambulance took me to the hospital on a stretcher that night to get emergency surgery."

"Wow!" said Nfudu, wide-eyed. She felt bad for calling him all sorts of names for not showing up when the whole time he was fighting for his life. "Sorry, I didn't know."

"No worries. I really wanted to come to the party to see you. I also didn't have your phone number so I couldn't call you afterwards."

"Is that so?" said Nfudu with an amused grin.

"You don't believe me?"

"If you really wanted to see me you could have asked for me at the War Mission."

"I swear that I'm telling the truth. I thought about coming to the War Mission to look for you, but had to leave for Barcelona right after my surgery. I stayed there for a while to recuperate. The weather there is better, and it's much less polluted."

"Why Barcelona?"

"I have a business and an apartment there."

"I hear it's a beautiful city. I would love to visit sometime. Anyway, glad you're feeling better now." Nfudu marveled at how forthcoming he had been about his illness and the fact that he had wanted to see her. It made her heart flutter and she smiled unknowingly.

"I'll take you anytime you're ready. How long have you been seeing your boyfriend?" Ikechi queried interrupting her reverie.

"Well, a long time. Almost four years. I better go now, actually, before he starts wondering where I am. It was nice seeing you again"

"Take care of yourself," he said, a little disappointed she had to go so early.

"And you."

Nfudu found Javier a few minutes later. He had also been searching for her, apparently.

"Where have you been?" he asked.

"Around the place, chatting with some friends," responded Nfudu.

"I wanted to ask you for a dance. I hope you're up for it."

Nfudu was relieved to do anything to get her mind back into the swing of things. They danced until midnight before bidding farewell to their host. On the drive home, Nfudu deliberated her discussion with

Ikechi. He was forthright in a way that she found disarming. She didn't know if she would ever see him again, or if she wanted to. She reckoned that seeing him again would complicate her life. She loved Javier. He was her whole world and she did not want to jeopardize that for a fleeting fling.

–

On Christmas morning, Nfudu got the best Christmas gift anyone could have given her – news that Afonwa and Ijere had been found after being missing for three years. They had been captured by soldiers and held in a prisoner camp for two years before they escaped during a raid of their camp in a battle that saw some of their captors dead and others running for their lives. They hid with a dozen escapee prisoners in a church in Afikpo for six whole months, before finding their way home through help from some good Samaritans, who showed them a secret escape route. When they got to Abasi, they were both unrecognizable. Their flesh was practically inexistent – only skin and bones remained. Both suffered from severe malnutrition and there were obvious signs that they had endured brutal torture. Afonwa lost the hearing in her right ear and Ijere now walked with a slight limp. Stories of their ordeal broke Nfudu's heart and brought tears to her eyes.

"They're mere children," Nfudu complained to Javier, Vanessa and her fiancé of four months, David, who had come to the lodge to spend Christmas together. "I can't fathom the suffering they must have endured at the hands of their captors. I feel so sad and wish I could see them right now and hold them tight in my arms, and let them know that everything would be OK."

Javier left his seat to occupy the one next to hers. He held her in his arms and she started to sob. "I wonder when this war will be over. All I hear daily is news of more and more devastation."

"Let's thank God Afonwa and Ijere were found. I just hope they're getting adequate medical attention for their injuries," interjected Vanessa.

"I hope so too," responded Nfudu.

"Now, those tears should be replaced with tears of joy because they returned alive," continued Vanessa. "Imagine how you would have felt if it was otherwise."

"God Forbid!"

"Exactly my point…"

"Even though I'm overjoyed by their return, I'm still sad because some of my friends at the War Mission received horrible news about their families. Nevertheless, I have never heard happier news in a long time. We need to toast to this."

"I agree," said Javier standing up to retrieve a bottle of Dom Perignon from the wine cabinet. He opened it and toasted to Nfudu's family and all the people caught in the war-torn country of Nigeria.

David, who had been sitting quietly this whole time, spoke up.

"Let us know if there's anything we can do to help. I'm sure we can never fully understand how you feel about what's going on, but we're always here for you."

"Thank you so much, David," Nfudu whispered. David was always so sweet to her. At first, when Vanessa broke off her relationship with Jeremy, Nfudu thought she was making a mistake – she felt they were soul mates. Just a few weeks into dating David, Vanessa confided in her that David was the one. She couldn't agree more as David treated her like a queen and adored Nfudu like a sister. He was always a joy to have around. It was his idea to spend Christmas at the lodge as a show of solidarity for Nfudu and the pain she was going through.

-

New Year was very quiet, but a very happy one as the war finally ended in January of 1970. On the morning the news broke, Nfudu was in bed with Javier in her flat when they heard the calm and confident voice of the announcer on the radio.

The news has broken that the Biafran military leader Effiong, has just surrendered to the Nigerian Army. This is exactly one week after his predecessor fled into exile after an exhausting three years of civil war that resulted in millions….

The masses are jumping and shouting on the streets. There is a massive riot in Nkume as houses and cars are being torched.... We will notify you as soon as we know more...

Nfudu could not believe her ears. She held Javier tight and cried uncontrollably. Javier shed tears also – tears of joy and relief. It had been a turbulent three years, in which both of them had developed a strong bond. They hugged and kissed and cried some more, until Nfudu sprang out of bed and tried desperately to place a call home.

"The lines are still dead," she said, disappointed she was unable to get through.

"I expect that to be the case for a little while," said Javier. We need to be patient till things get back to normal. We'll try every day until we can reach your family. There may be more news at the War Mission."

"The meeting is tonight. I'll need you to come with me."

"I won't miss it for the world," Javier responded, reassuringly.

"I'll call Emeka and Dike to make sure they know what's going on."

Emeka and Dike had both heard the news. They too had tried to call home but to no avail. All three of them agreed to meet at the War Mission that night. Nfudu spent the rest of the morning contacting friends and family to see if anyone had heard from her family. She had not spoken to them since the war began. It was lucky that she had Emeka and Dike around. Otherwise, she would have gone crazy. All three of them sent messages home. They received a couple through the War Mission, but without any indication that their messages reached their family since the messages they received were always in third person.

–

The War Mission was filled to the brim with friends and well-wishers. People talked over each other; some were hugging and crying, while others clustered around the information desk seeking any word about their loved ones. Many were feared dead.

The Nigerian Ambassador was in attendance at the meeting and gave a heartfelt speech. "Despite all the existing issues, the news is still a cause for celebration. I urge all Nigerians here and the world over to remain calm and do whatever they can to help their country recover from the devastation it has been through. I thank all the friends and well wishers at the War Mission for helping their Nigerian brothers in London keep afloat. God bless you! Now is the time for healing. This will require a lot of patience and effort. Our government has promised that it will provide all the necessary support to help us all recover, but we must not rely on that, alone. I applaud the efforts of the War Mission and plead that those efforts continue until full recovery is achieved."

It was almost one month before Nfudu could speak to her family. The phone rang in Nfudu's flat early one morning and she picked it at the second ring.

"My child,' Chief Ibe's voice said. Nfudu's heart almost stopped. Her father's voice was still imposing, but much more subdued than she remembered.

'Papa... Papa...' Nfudu sobbed. "Where are you? How are you? What are you doing?"

"I'm fine. We're all fine and I'm here with your mother. We're calling from a business center in Asha. Our phone lines are yet to be restored. Hold on and speak with your mother."

"Nfudum..." The sound of her mother's voice was like sweet music to her ears. Although she was happy to hear it, she was heartbroken at the defeat that enveloped it.

"Mama... How are you? How is everybody? I have missed you so much."

"Everybody is fine my dear," Mrs. Ibe responded rather hurriedly. "We're more concerned about you. We can only talk for five minutes before they cut us off, so I'll come back tomorrow to call again. The line-up of people waiting their turn to speak to their loved ones is really long. How are Dike and Emeka?"

"I understand Mama. Dike and Emeka are fine. How are Afonwa and Ijere? Did you get any of my messages?"

"We got one in the beginning, but later, we heard all correspondence to Abasi was being intercepted by federal troops in Asha. Don't worry. We know you were thinking about us. I'm overjoyed we all came out of it intact. Afonwa is slowly recovering her hearing, but Ijere still walks with a limp. We'll have special shoes made for him when everything settles."

"Thank God everyone is fine. I'm doing fine and even better now that I've spoken to you. Give my love to everybody. I'll wait for your call tomorrow."

"Ok dear. Take care now,"

"You too Mama..."

Mrs. Ibe made the one hour trip by road to Asha the following day to speak to Nfudu again from the business centre. She repeated this process once a week for two months until their phone lines were restored. It was a while before Nfudu started to sense hope and healing in her voice and the voices of her siblings. She was happy knowing all members of her family were intact. Other families had suffered a worse fate and recovery was long coming. When they started asking when she would be returning home, she knew they were all starting to feel safe again.

In London, Nfudu and Javier's relationship continued to blossom. They were so close, they were often mistaken as a married couple because they dressed alike, acted alike and finished each other's sentences. Now that the war was over, Javier saw no reason in delaying asking her to marry him, especially as Nfudu – now twenty-six was mature enough to handle the idea. She was very progressive unlike many young women her age, so she barely talked about marriage especially after what she had to go through as a result of the war. Her efforts were mostly focused on being self-sufficient and developing a successful career than worrying about getting married. Sometimes she thought about Ikechi with a smile on her face but didn't know exactly what she felt for him. She didn't think it was possible to love two men at the same time and concluded that what she felt for Ikechi was passing – a fling or a crush that creates a burning desire and eventually simmers down once the initial excitement wears off.

-

Vanessa and David got married at Easter in a beautiful outdoor wedding, attended by only sixty guests – her closest friends and family. Nfudu served as her Maid of Honor and Javier walked her down the aisle, while a live band played a beautiful jazz number under the beautiful evening sky, by a small lake at the Crystal Event Center. The guests were treated to three courses, after which they danced the rest of the night. Cocktails were served from a well-stocked bar, where a third of the guests clustered after the first dance. At midnight, while the live band played light music in the background, Javier and Nfudu walked hand in hand by the lakeside, stopping at intervals to kiss and caress.

"This is the most beautiful wedding I have ever attended," Nfudu said, staring into Javier's eyes.

"And you're the most beautiful girl I've ever seen," responded Javier, unable to take his eyes off her.

"You're making me blush," Nfudu said, looking away from him.

"You...? Blush? Let me see." He pretended to inspect her face for a second and then in a swift motion, lifted her up her feet. She squealed with delight, and surrendered herself to him, while he planted his lips on hers.

The kiss lasted for at least five minutes before Nfudu shrieked, "Stop! What if someone sees us?"

"Who will see us? And if they see us, what does it matter?" he responded smiling mischievously.

They walked back to the rest of the party a short while later, aroused from their short encounter by the lake.

"Where were you?" scolded Vanessa. "We were about to cut the cake without you."

"We're here now," answered Javier, a naughty grin spreading across his face. He turned to wink at Nfudu. She looked away shamefacedly and giggled quietly.

"You love birds," Vanessa teased. I wonder what you both have been up to.

The party lasted until the morning, long after Vanessa and David left for their honeymoon to Peru. Before she left, she threw her bouquet to the single female crowd, but not before she positioned herself to ensure her best friend and confidant, Nfudu was the most likely recipient of the bouquet. Sure enough, Nfudu caught it. The crowd cheered for her, and as they did, she wondered for the first time, when her turn would come.

—

During the years she was stuck in London as a result of the war, Nfudu focused most of her energy on her work as Creative Director at the House of Monreaux and on her first collection. She made a lot of headway in the London fashion scene and gained recognition for her unique designs and simple, yet luxurious quality that she introduced to the Monreaux brand.

Her personal collection was to showcase at the London Fashion Show in August. She worked night and day to ensure its success. Her education at the International Institute of Fashion and her African background reflected so beautifully in her designs that after a sneak peek of her collection, the London Inquirer wrote:

"Nfudu's designs have a unique western flair and an exoticness that only her African origin and unique sense of style could have brought about. This is the new designer to watch out for."

This was the first of many public reviews Nfudu received for her work. It gave her the boost she needed to launch her business into the public domain. Her picture was intentionally left out of the article on the advice of her publicist, to create a mysterious air about her and entice the public. The plan was to reveal her picture at a future date to coincide with the first public view of her collection.

Vanessa was the first to call and congratulate her on the article in the Inquirer.

"That was a job well done."

"Thank you, sweetheart! How is married life going? Is it anything we imagined?"

"Even better. David is lovely. I couldn't have asked for a better man. You're next in line."

"Not necessarily," Nfudu responded still wary of any discussion about marriage.

"I'm serious! You just wait and see. Do you plan on visiting your family in Nigeria soon?"

"After showcasing the collection in August I have to make time out to visit. Christmas might be a good time. I pray things would have calmed down by then."

"Good luck, babe."

"You too... Thanks."

Nfudu hoped and prayed everything would go as planned, to make her return a reality. Friends and family continued to send her congratulatory messages, and for the first time in years, she felt her efforts had paid off. She continued to work hard to maintain the current momentum, with Javier always on her side.

10

NFUDU was rapidly winning popular acclaim in the fashion world. The publicity garnered from her earlier private viewings and the public reviews gave Nfudu's Couture – her self-titled designer brand – the boost it needed to compete with well-known brands like Channel and Yves Saint Laurent. It was a cut above the rest because Nfudu had a certain savoir-faire obtained from her ethnicity and educational background. Besides that, her worldly travels, which always provided an opportunity for escape from the humdrum of everyday life, gave her the opportunity to observe styles from all over the world. Over the years, she learnt to interpret fashion from one culture to the next. For one item in her collection, inspired by the Japanese Kimono, she created a timeless piece using batik and lace.

Despite the success achieved so far, Nfudu believed that her performance at that year's London Fashion Show would be a big determining factor for the success of her brand. As a result, she continued preparations right after Easter by fine-tuning and updating her designs over and over again. She arranged for models way ahead of time and took care of other logistics such as storage, hair, make-up and accommodation. A few months back, to prove she was self-sufficient, she rejected both Javier's and her father's offer to provide the seed funding required for making her debut collection a success. Instead, she turned to her friends for support, but this turned out to be inadequate.

"You should accept my offer to fund the entire project. Pay back whenever you're able." This was Javier's third attempt at offering Nfudu the needed funds.

"Ok. I accept," responded Nfudu without further hesitation. She had run out of time and options and was now willing to budge a little. "Thank you, darling. I'll pay back every cent as soon as I can."

"I thought you'd never accept. Now let's get to work. You hardly have any time left …the show is in two weeks." Javier was ecstatic. Having had the opportunity to view Nfudu's work first hand, he knew it was definitely worth investing in. Also, he admired her ability to focus. He had been around long enough to know that a mixture of such talent and work ethic was a great recipe for success.

They went to work right away to tie up all the loose ends. Javier went over all the vendors Nfudu had selected to make sure they were the best money could buy. He hired a licensing company to review her entire collection and provide feedback on their marketability. When the results came in, he assisted with changes to the collection. This took everything Nfudu had originally done to a different level of class and maturity. She was glad she had let him because she would never have been able to conceive everything all on her own even with her immense talent and education.

The models chosen for the catwalk comprised of different ethnicities – African, Asian and European descent and were made up of a combination of skinny to average sized girls – who would have been otherwise considered too heavy for the runway. The idea to use beauty in all shapes and sizes was conceived by Nfudu who got the inspiration from women in her home country Nigeria where beauty came in varied forms. In Nigeria, all girls, no matter their size, age, shape or skin color felt completely beautiful. Add a little makeup and a pretty dress and they would wriggle their waists in every direction to the ends of the earth. There, girls walked tall, with their shoulders held high and their busts and hips sticking out.

Backstage at the London Fashion Show, Nfudu panicked that the models wouldn't come out on time. One had a wardrobe malfunction minutes before her segment was about to begin.

As she frantically searched for a solution, she bumped into a chair. "Ouch!" she shrieked. "Can someone get Vanessa," she almost yelled at one of the assistants.

Vanessa helped coordinate the various aspects of the show. She was called upon when a model was late or when one was throwing a fit. She was also called when the air conditioning in their room malfunctioned. Each time, she pulled all possible strings to resolve the issue at hand, putting her mild nature and ability for handling difficult situations to use. When she heard Nfudu shriek, she left her station, where she was putting finishing touches on a model to come to her rescue.

"Don't worry babe," she said trying to assuage Nfudu's concerns. "It'll only be a few minutes."

In a matter of seconds, Vanessa was able to resolve the issue before the models were ushered down the runway.

Her segment featured two couture designs as a teaser and eleven of her ready to wear designs. Those were the favorite of shoppers, who ordered every single item in the collection and in numbers that made Nfudu marvel at the results. Although her models reflected immense variety, her team was able to coordinate the outfits to match each model. Their lips were smeared with a little rouge, while their hair was slicked with a deep side part and pulled to the back into a beautiful chignon. Nfudu looked beautiful in one of her figure-hugging designs. When she stepped out for a final bow on the runway, she received cheers from the crowd. Despite being a first-timer at the internationally acclaimed fashion event, Nfudu was able to pull a show stopper. The event turned out to be an incredible success for her and her team.

Javier watched in amazement from his front row seat. He was proud when he saw everything they had worked on for months come to fruition.

"The success of this event exceeded my wildest imaginations," said Nfudu to Javier and Vanessa, when they sat down to look at the numbers as they were being tallied by the accountant at the end of the show.

"Unbelievable!" agreed Javier, stretching his hands to give Nfudu a hug. "The crowd loved it. Not surprised by the sales."

"These shoppers represent the biggest department stores in London. I'm elated. My designs are going to be sold all over Europe. Thank you both so much for helping me realize this dream. I really don't know what I could have done without both of you."

"What do you mean?" asked Vanessa. "It was a fun experience and I learned a lot working on it. You don't need to thank us. We're your family. I need to leave both of you now. I have to meet with David. Let's try to catch up later for drinks. This is worth celebrating."

Nfudu gave Vanessa a big long hug and kisses on both cheeks. "See you later. I'll call you to let you know where to meet. Bring David if he's free."

Nfudu addressed the models. "Thank you and congratulations for a job well done."

Javier had come prepared with three bottles of champagne and some disposable cups. He distributed drinks to everyone.

"This is to our continued success," he said. Everyone raised their glasses and cheered and toasted to one another.

After everyone left, Javier and Nfudu stayed with the accountant to tidy up the rest of the paperwork.

They joined Vanessa and David later that evening to celebrate what Javier called "A great outing." As Javier spoke, Nfudu was too tired and elated to focus. She went into her head space and fantasized about the event and its highlights. She tried to devise strategies she could use to keep up the momentum while the ovation was still high. Javier touched her arm to help her regain her focus when he found she was too deep in thought to realize she was being questioned by David.

"So what are the next steps?" David repeated, amused that Nfudu got lost in her own world.

"I'm sorry. I was just going through that in my mind. I'm thinking of opening a shop in London or Paris, where I can sell my designs. I would also love to show at the Paris Couture Show or even the New York Fashion Week."

"Wow!" exclaimed David. "The sky is your limit."

-

Javier and Nfudu planned to spend the night at the lodge. Nfudu's flat was upside down from preparations for the show, with fabrics and gadgets strewn around, creating a pile. She wondered how she lived in that space the whole week.

"What do you think about becoming my business partner?" Nfudu asked Javier as they drove to the lodge. She had meant to ask him for a while but had been too anxious to do so, afraid that he may reject her proposal. There was also the fear that he might say yes when he would rather say no. This she felt was worse than the former. Either way, their relationship would be impacted.

Javier paused for a moment and then looked at her for a brief second before asking, "Are you sure that's what you want?"

"Yes, otherwise I wouldn't ask. Is it something you'll consider?"

"I thought you'd never ask. Of course, I would love to partner with you. I see your brand going places, and I would be honored to be a part of it." He squeezed her hand tightly.

"Thanks, love. I knew I could count on you," said Nfudu smiling at him and squeezing his hand in return. "I have thought about it for a while now, but wanted to wait for the show to be over before I asked you." She let go of his hand and kissed his face numerous times. When she caught the chauffeur watching from the rearview mirror, she restrained herself, and instead fondled his arms.

"On Monday, we can meet with my lawyer to work out the details. Because of my time commitment to my other businesses, I see myself being only a financial partner, but you know I'll always be there when you need me."

"That's more than I expected. I'm so excited we're in business together. Couldn't have asked for a better partner," she concluded shaking her head.

-

At the lodge, Nfudu and Javier took turns scrubbing each other's backs in the shower, gently washing away the stress from two weeks of non-stop activity. The water drizzled down their bare skin while they hugged, and rubbed each other's shoulders. Nfudu let her hand slide down Javier's spine, down to his buttocks. This caused his already bulging manhood to stiffen and push against her belly. She moaned and thrust her butt back and forth on his groin. With both hands on her thighs, he lifted her a few inches. Groaning, he pressed his body against hers and moved in a quick successive pattern until she squealed with pleasure. He carried her out of the shower, onto the bed, where they continued kissing and caressing. Lying naked, they stared into each other's eyes. "It's been so long since we've been together like this," said Nfudu, breaking the silence. "I've missed you so much."

"Shhh!" hushed Javier. He was unwilling to stop looking at the smile on her face and relishing the contentment in her eyes. When he heard her stomach rumble, he buzzed the butler to serve their dinner in bed, while they shared stories dating as far back to the first time they met. Javier regaled Nfudu with his version of the history of their relationship, while Nfudu told him about one of her exploits.

"There's something that happened one day on the metro as Vanessa and I headed back to the lodge from our internship. It was so annoying," she said with an eye roll.

"Go ahead. I'm all ears," said Javier, unconsciously positioning himself to match her relaxed posture.

"London was tough in those days. People – mostly visitors from other cities… I think, used to stare at me like I was a work of art. They acted like they'd never seen a brown skinned person in their entire life let alone been in a closed space with one. A little girl, accompanied by her mother, joined the Metro at Piccadilly and before they took the seat across from us, she pointed her index finger at me and screamed 'niggger'. It took a few seconds for what she said to sink in. When it finally did, I stood up from my seat, pointed at the kid, and with a faked and fierce evil facial gesture, I muttered *'Nnnei Nigger'*"

"What!" exclaimed Javier wide-eyed.

"Well, of course. She didn't understand I was just saying 'your mother is a nigger' but she suddenly burst into tears and grabbed her mother, who gave me quite a vicious stare, and shook her head unstoppably…" Nfudu shook her head in mock contempt to mimic the mother in her story.

Javier burst out laughing. When he recovered, he said to her, with tears in his eyes, "you must have scared the hell out of that kid."

"Yes. She thought I cast an evil spell on her. I hope her mother learnt a lesson. It's impossible for a kid to use such dirty language if they never once heard their mother using it."

"I agree," responded Javier, still amused. "They both deserved what they got that day. I'm proud of you sweetheart. You have come so far and achieved so much by not letting people like that get in your way. We need to toast to that." Javier was amazed at how Nfudu weathered all the odds to become a successful fashion designer in a world that was still so biased towards anyone that looked un-European.

"Thanks love. I consider myself blessed to have people like you, Vanessa and my family in my life. You're my support system."

"We're even more blessed to have you in our lives. Don't know what it would have been like without you in it."

"Aww!" Nfudu purred as she sipped on her champagne and giggled nonstop.

-

The London Fashion Show gave Nfudu's Couture so much exposure and accolade that magazines houses soon started calling to feature Nfudu and her brand in their magazines. Her work life became so hectic with so many requests for interviews and appearances. On Javier's advice, she hired a personal assistant to handle the growing demands on her time. Soon after, a publicist was added to the payroll to ensure that she portrayed the right public image. The publicist did a great job at weeding out unnecessary demands on Nfudu's time by choosing only the most beneficial appearances. Also, she helped ensure that any misunderstandings and issues with the press got resolved quietly to avoid tarnishing the image she had worked so hard to build. Two weeks after the London Fashion Show, Javier took Nfudu to Paris for a much-needed break. This was a carefully planned weekend, in which he hoped they could both relax at the Mirabelle Chateau, with nothing else to do but eat, sleep, swim and make love.

When they arrived at the Chateau early Friday morning, Nfudu was impressed by the surroundings and got a sudden feeling of déjà vu over their first meeting as lovers at the Hotel de Le Mercidien some years back.

"It seems like a lifetime away since that first romantic encounter," said Nfudu to Javier.

"I agree. So much has happened since then. You seem so much older now compared to the twenty-year-old I fell in love with. You were so 'wet behind the ears'."

"Stop!" Nfudu protested smiling. "I liked to think of myself back then as pretty mature so I disagree with you. You, on the other hand, have not changed one bit. You're still the beautiful man I grew up loving. I found comfort in your arms then and still do now."

Javier was touched by her words and stopped for a moment to look into her eyes. "I consider myself lucky to be your man and wouldn't have it any other way. I tell you how amazing you are all the time. But I haven't told you the whole story. You're the best thing that has ever happened to me. I place you next to God in my life."

"Awww!" cried Nfudu. "I always say to anyone that cares to listen that you're a gift from God – one I'm still unwrapping after so many years together."

"I love you."

"I love you too my darling."

That night they made love like it was their first time. Nfudu trembled in his arms as Javier brought her to new heights of pleasure. She had never felt this close to anyone and wanted that night to last forever. It was then she knew she didn't want to be with anyone else but him. She slept peacefully in his arms, while he stared at her beautiful face for a long time before finally falling asleep.

-

Javier treated Nfudu to a private candlelit dinner the following day. Their table was set by the quiet penthouse poolside and lined with a red satin tablecloth and a black velvet runner. Candles were placed in several sections of the pool. The lights were turned off to create an alluring and romantic feeling. Nfudu wore a lovely maroon colored dress, which flattered her figure so well that she moved with a fluid like motion. Javier ran his hands the entire length of her frame after she pulled it on to confirm there was a real person in there. Javier had bought it specifically for the occasion and convinced her to wear it that night on the guise that the Chateau owner, a bosom friend of his, was hosting an event in the penthouse. Nfudu had not made much of the dinner until she arrived at the venue and realized that other than the chateau staff strategically positioned in certain spots to attend to their demands, they were very much alone. Her jaw dropped when she saw the décor and the lighting. The light music playing in the background and the extra effort the hotel staff made with their uniforms – each had a red satin sash thrown across their necks – reminded her of something from the scene of a movie. As the music progressed from one song to the next, she recognized the recording as the collection of her favorite love songs, which she had gifted Javier a year after they started dating.

"I never knew you valued this recording, let alone…" she stopped mid-sentence to catch her breath.

"Let alone what?" asked Javier, looking at her adoringly.

"Let alone love it enough to play at what seems to be a carefully orchestrated dinner several years later." She searched his eyes for answers, her heart beating.

"I value anything you've ever given me," he responded with little expression.

Her heart beat even faster when she realized what the set up could mean, but she kept her composure as she did not want to be assumed presumptuous. Tugging at his arm, she whispered, "What is this? Javier, what is going on? I thought you said…"

"Be patient!" Javier responded and pulled out a seat for her. He gestured to a waiter to pour them both a glass of champagne. After one sip, he laid his glass on the table and fiddled with something in his breast pocket. Nfudu nearly fainted when Javier got on one knee, took her hands in his, looked deep into her dewy eyes, and asked: "Will you marry me?" Gently letting go of both her hands, he removed a small maroon colored satin box from the same breast pocket he had fiddled with earlier and presented a beautiful but mysterious looking five-carat red diamond engagement ring to her.

Nfudu's heart stopped the moment she set eyes on the ring. She gaped in astonishment and whispered: "I've never seen anything this stunning in my life."

"Will you marry me then?" Javier repeated after he realized that Nfudu was too dazed to respond.

Her face lit up and she nearly choked as she said, "Of course I'll marry you. I love you more than anything." With her beautiful ring on her finger, she assisted him from his kneeling position, kissed him, and whispered "I love you." When her legs couldn't carry her any longer, she almost buckled, but Javier caught her in time. They remained locked in an embrace. "This is the best moment of my life."

"And mine too…" responded Javier.

They kissed, ignoring the chateau staff, who were cheering and running helter-skelter preparing their table for a meal. "I wish this night would never end," Nfudu said to Javier when they finally unlocked from their embrace and toasted with more champagne.

After appetizers and a delicious dinner, they changed into their swimwear, dismissed the chateau staff and slid into the swimming pool. The rest of dinner was a blur to Nfudu as her head spun from everything, the proposal, the ring, the events of the past few months and the past six years when they first met.

"Remember the months we spent hiding our relationship from the whole world?" Javier asked as they hugged in the pool.

This was a sensitive topic for Nfudu, who knew that a big part of their world – her family, was yet to be invited into their relationship. She did not want to address it then and spoil the beautiful engagement, so she smiled and averted her eyes.

It seemed like Javier read her thoughts when he asked, "When do you think your family should know?"

Struggling to meet his gaze, she responded, "I'll deal with the issue of my parents when I see them in a few months. This matter needs to be addressed in person."

"But, shouldn't you give them a hint before you arrive. It might help with breaking the ice."

"Hmm… I don't think so. Not after everything they've been through. I can't predict the state of my father's health. It's better I avoid any surprises until I see them face to face. Some of my siblings already know about us, so it's not entirely a secret," Nfudu concluded, shrugging her shoulders.

"You know your family better than I do, so I'll leave how you reveal it to them up to you. Your trip is less than three months away. What is that compared to the six years we've been together? I have the feeling your father already knows but is waiting for you to confirm it."

Nfudu shook her head from side to side, and looked at Javier intently as she said, "I don't think so." She knew her father very well. If Chief Ibe had got wind of the fact that she was dating Javier, she would have heard of it and it would not have been pleasant. Revealing this to Javier would only upset him, so she kept mum since she was already working on a strategy to convince her father to accept her choice. Being that they were now engaged, she felt she had more to fight for and that gave her renewed strength.

"Now that we're engaged, it should be easier for you to broach the subject with him," Javier said as he slid a finger inside her bikini and caressed her softly. She moaned when she felt his touch and placed her hand on his now erect mound while they kissed. That was the cue they needed to head back to their room. On getting through the door, before Nfudu got the chance to keep her belongings on the settee, Javier carried her and placed her on his side of the bed. He removed her bikini, taking his time to look adoringly at her. What happened next took her breath away. He knelt across from her, grabbed her back with two hands and threw her to the center of the bed in one swift movement. She moaned excitedly as he made love to her until she screamed. Then, he gently moved her to the corner of the bed and continued with gentle and evenly timed strokes until they finally collapsed into each other's arms as they came in unison.

When they woke up the next morning, Nfudu felt a throbbing at the back of her head. "It must be the champagne," said Javier as he rocked her in his hands and helped her dress up. "Let's get something to eat. You might feel better afterwards."

The pair had brunch at the chateau's restaurant and left for London soon after. At the lobby, the chateau staff greeted them with "*Felicitations a vous.*" News of their engagement had spread around the chateau.

Vanessa and David received the news before Javier and Nfudu arrived in London. Javier had told them of his plans to ask Nfudu to marry him before leaving for Paris and later called to inform them after she said yes. Vanessa sent flowers and chocolate to Nfudu's flat. Nfudu's joy about the engagement was apparent as she hugged Vanessa when they met the following day for breakfast. At the House of Monreaux, her colleagues had a cake waiting for her when she arrived right before noon. Everyone marveled at her engagement ring. "When is the wedding?" was the question on everyone's tongue. At first, she was stunned as she wasn't prepared to answer any questions, let alone that of her marriage while her father's approval was still hanging in the balance. But, with careful thought, she responded to everyone in pretty much the same way. "We haven't discussed that yet, but it'll be sometime next year."

-

Nfudu had a lot to contend with career-wise before her trip to Nigeria, where she planned to open an ultra-modern fashion school – the only one of its type in Lagos. She spoke frequently with her partners in Nigeria to complete preliminary steps, including obtaining required licenses and selecting consulting firms for the different aspects of the school creation. On top of it all, Nfudu's Couture was making a big splash in London and eating up most of her waking time.

An exclusive viewing of her haute couture designs was provided to representatives of major department stores, select designers, fashion magazines and the crème de la crème in the London fashion scene. The apparels were made of the most delicate fabrics and were so exceptional, dignitaries travelled from all over Europe to view and order items from the collection. In anticipation of their growing orders, their production was outsourced to a factory in Florence to avoid clogging up their New York facility which was feared inadequate to handle the barrage of orders.

The full range of the haute designs was excluded from the London Fashion Show, to draw attention to the ready to wear collection, which having been successful created a wild anticipation for the haute couture designs. These successes created further buzz for Nfudu and news spread that she was the designer to watch out for. To enable her focus on her top priorities, Nfudu resigned her position at the House of Monreaux the week before she left for Nigeria.

"We saw this coming… so it doesn't come as a surprise to me," the Executive Director at the House of Monreaux said to Nfudu after reading her resignation letter. "I knew that with the success of your brand you'd have no time to attend to anything else. The years you have spent with us have been amazing for the Monreaux brand and we owe our fresh take on fashion to you."

"Thank you so much," replied Nfudu. "This place has been amazing for me and my career. I basically gave back what I was given. Everyone here is like family also. I'll miss you all."

"We'll miss you too. And… hey the relationship doesn't have to end here. We can still support each other."

"Definitely," responded Nfudu giving her a handshake.

She celebrated her resignation with the rest of the Monreaux team that afternoon and in the evening went out for drinks at the Brews night-club with Vanessa and David. While the music blared and couples danced, Nfudu sat at the bar and reminisced about the events of the past few months. When she was done with the past, she began to worry about the near future and became increasingly anxious about confronting her family about her love life.

11

NFUDU spoke with her family as often as her busy schedule would allow her. They were elated by her success. Chief Ibe, in particular, was happy he had let her follow her dreams, rather than forcing her to pursue a more 'practical' profession like medicine or law. He had not always been convinced that Nfudu should study fashion for higher education. However, after Barrister Madu, a good friend of his encouraged him to support Nfudu he decided to give it a try. It was Barrister Madu that introduced him to the International Institute of Fashion, where most of the world's top fashion designers studied their craft. Chief Ibe became convinced after he made extensive inquiries and discovered that fashion was an economically viable profession.

Nfudu remembered Barrister Madu with fondness and gratitude for helping sway her father's mind when she needed it the most. She recalled how he often sang her praises whenever he visited her family. He once said to Chief Ibe, "Michael, you know Nfudu is one of the most beautiful women I have ever seen? She is as beautiful as the most beautiful women in the world, like Sofia Lauren and Elizabeth Taylor." Nfudu remembered her father laughing hysterically at Barrister Madu's comment. He also often teased her and called her "Pretty babbby." When he was in the mood, he would sing, "Pretty babby, I love you more than my mama." The comments, coming from any person other than Barrister Madu would have freaked Nfudu or even Chief Ibe out. But, since Barrister Madu was such a good man and a well-loved friend of the family no one ever imagined any bad intentions behind his admiration for Nfudu.

Even though she had never considered herself beautiful, Nfudu decided to believe that she was, especially as no member of her family disputed Barrister Madu's claims. It boosted her confidence and helped shape her into the amazing woman she turned out to be. She wondered if Barrister Madu survived the civil war. If he did, she hoped to see him as soon as she arrived in Nigeria to elicit his help in convincing her father that Javier was a good choice for her.

Nfudu's homecoming was highly anticipated by her family. Preparations, however, were minimal compared to what it would have been had she returned right after graduation. As a result of the war recovery efforts, no big party awaited her. This did not mean that her family was any less happy to see her.

The week before her trip, Nfudu called Chief Ibe to test the waters by enquiring about Barrister Madu. "Papa, how about Barrister Madu?"

"My dear, he is no more," answered Chief Ibe half-choking on his words.

Nfudu understood what his words meant. Her voice was filled with emotion when she asked, "What do you mean he's no more?"

"The war took him while he fought bravely for his people. This happened early on, but I only found out a few months ago. It's a pity."

"Ooooh," cried Nfudu, devastated by the news she just heard. "He was such a nice man. Lovely fellow... I'm so sad. Papa, you must miss him so much. I'm sorry."

"My dear don't worry. I have accepted it as fate. This world is not a permanent place. The living will keep on living. What can we do?"

Nfudu could tell that her father was deeply hurt by the death of his friend. Feeling the goose bumps rise on her arm, she wondered how many more news of this nature she could take. She missed Barrister Madu already, so she couldn't imagine how her father was feeling. Much worse, she presumed. She tried to console him further. "Papa don't worry. I'll be home soon. Please use that to console yourself."

"Ok Nne, we're waiting for you. Safe travels."

"Thank you, Papa."

-

When Nfudu's flight landed in Lagos, she was immediately filled with emotion. She thought to herself, "I do not remember the soil being so red," as she stared at the grounds through the window of her business class seat. When she stepped out of the plane, the warm moist air hit her face like steam from a sauna, giving her a feeling of déjà vu and the full realization that she had really arrived.

The airport was too crowded for Nfudu's liking and she couldn't remember that much disorderliness amongst the people. The manner in which they conducted their affairs baffled her. They cut in line and stood too close to speak to one another. In queues, people practically placed their whole bodies on the person standing in front of them and breathed over their shoulders. This appalled her as she found herself saying, "Move! Move!" while she wriggled to create space between herself and the tall large breasted woman standing behind her. She received stares that seemed to imply she felt superior to everyone else around her. If she could read their mind, she knew they would be saying, "Who does she think she is?" She had only been gone for six years but felt a whole world of difference between the Nigeria she left behind and the one she now met. One thing she found refreshing was that no one seemed to take themselves too seriously. Everyone moved around happily and cheerfully, speaking at the top of their voices. It was hard to believe that these same people had recently been in the throes of a civil war.

Fibi, Nfudu's new assistant met her right outside the baggage area. She was holding a yellow card that spelt out Nfudu's name with a bold black marker. Nfudu walked straight to her, while an airport worker rolled her luggage in a trolley.

"Hello, Fibi, you have changed a lot. If not for the card, I wouldn't have recognized you at all. Look at you," said Nfudu moving around to look at Fibi from all angles, "You have blossomed into such a beautiful woman."

Fibi was a cousin to Chinyere – Nfudu's longtime friend. She was only fifteen when Nfudu left Nigeria six years back. Even though she was just a few years younger than Nfudu, then, it had seemed like they were ages apart, but not anymore. They could now pass as age mates – with Fibi's impeccable makeup and voluptuous figure that was so incredible to look at. Her dark shiny skin glowed and formed a beautiful contrast with her pure white teeth. She was about the same height as Nfudu, but her high towering heels made her seem much taller. Nfudu felt tiny standing next to her.

"Thank you ma," replied Fibi. "I knew it was you immediately I saw you. You haven't really changed, except that you look more glamorous than before." Fibi giggled shyly after she completed her sentence.

"Ooh thanks! It's so hot out here," said Nfudu, fanning herself with her passport. "Where is the driver?"

"He's right outside. Chinyere is in the car with him."

Nfudu eyebrows lifted with joy, realizing she was going to see Fibi's cousin, Chinyere, after so long.

Chinyere introduced the idea of hiring Fibi as an assistant, while Nfudu was in London. Nfudu had asked Chinyere to help schedule interviews for the position of an Assistant, and Chinyere had indicated that she had the perfect applicant. Nfudu remembered Fibi, and interviewed her over the phone from London. It worked out perfectly for both of them. Nfudu was able to save the time needed to interview and select the perfect candidate amongst several applicants. Fibi, on her own part needed the job and the remuneration that came with it.

Outside, Nfudu sighted Chinyere standing beside the passenger door of a blue Mercedes with a worried look on her face. She had been waiting for over an hour and was getting frantic. She did not see Nfudu when she stepped out of the airport and walk quietly behind her to tap her shoulders. Chinyere was startled, but immediately started to scream "Nfudu! Nfudu!" when she saw her. They hugged, swaying from side to side and at intervals stopped to look at one another in admiration before resuming their hugging. Chinyere, who was six feet tall, used to be slender when Nfudu left home. She had become much heavier and

Nfudu couldn't help but comment. "What is this Chi? Your husband is feeding you well ooo. You're now an *'orobo'*."

Chinyere laughed. "Don't mind him ooo. Since the first time we met, he insists I eat 'enough' because, according to him, African men like something to hold. Can you imagine?"

"That's hilarious. In London, being skinny is the rave. Anyway, you look gorgeous. More gorgeous than when you were *'kpelenge'*."

"That's what everyone says. Me sef, I like myself this way. I like the way my breast and my bum look in my clothes. When I enter somewhere, people respect me, because they know that someone just arrived," she concluded, moving her shoulders from side to side and turning her lips upwards.

"Ah, Chi, you've not changed. You won't kill me." Nfudu laughed, holding her sides. She realized they had been standing in front of the airport and talking for too long when a car started honking at them for their spot.

"Let's start going it's getting late." She said to Chinyere. They both scrambled into the back of the car, while Fibi sat in front with the driver.

"Good afternoon ma," the driver said looking at Nfudu through the rearview mirror.

"Sorry ma, I forgot to introduce. This is Tunji your driver. He's from Ondo state," said Fibi, turning to Nfudu. "He used to drive for my aunt. We still interviewed him like you asked and did all the background and reference checks."

"Ok," replied Nfudu. "Tunji, it's nice to meet you. How old are you?"

"Twenty-nine ma, but I will turn thirty this year."

"Do you have a family? Are you married? Do you have children?"

"No ma. There's a girl I want to marry, but she hasn't agreed." Nfudu tried to hold back a chuckle, but Fibi and Chinyere erupted in laughter. Tunji, joined them.

When she regained her composure, Chinyere added, "He's an excellent driver, don't worry. He drove my mother for five years until she moved back to the East. When you asked us to find a reliable driver for you, we started asking around for him. We were lucky to find him."

"That's nice," said Nfudu. "I'm glad everything worked out well. And I'm so lucky to have Fibi working for me. I'm excited to get started!"

"Ma, it's my pleasure," interjected Fibi. "I'm the one who should be excited, working alongside a successful fashion designer. Thank you so much for offering me the job. I'm extremely grateful."

"Enough excitement everyone," added Chinyere, waving her hand in characteristic fashion. "Where are we going tonight?"

"We can hang out at my hotel – have dinner or something. I'll need to get some rest. Tomorrow will be a busy day…"

Before Nfudu could finish the sentence Chinyere interrupted her, shaking her head and hands from side to side. "Eh eh. This is not London. This is Naija. Ok? We have to go somewhere and have fun please."

"Ok!" responded Nfudu feeling defeated. She was too weak to have an argument with Chinyere, whose strong personality she found adorable at times even though she could never win an argument with her. "You can decide where we go since I don't know my left from my right."

"Hmm! Now we're talking," said Chinyere triumphantly.

As Tunji drove to Nfudu's hotel, she proceeded to catch up on the latest gossip with Chinyere, who provided the lowdown on everything that happened since she was away. Most of it was terrifying, while others reminded her of old times and gave her an idea of what her long lost friends were doing.

"We will see some of them when we go out tonight," promised Chinyere.

"I really hope so," responded Nfudu. "It's been so long."

"That reminds me… Fibi, let's go over my schedule before we settle down for fun. First, I'll spend a few days in Lagos and then head to Abasi for a few days and then return to Lagos. I'll make one more trip to Abasi to spend Christmas with my family and leave soon after I get back to Lagos."

"Ok, Ma," responded Fibi, checking out the details on the notes she had so meticulously taken. "Would you like me to come with you when you travel to Abasi?"

"Yeah, sure. I'll be working all through. We'll make appropriate accommodation for you. Other than the family, my main priority is to complete all the preliminary work required to set up the Lagos Fashion School. This requires a lot of time and energy and even though we've covered a lot of the groundwork, a lot still needs to be done."

Tunji pulled to the front of the hotel lobby and helped Nfudu retrieve her luggage from the car trunk. Chinyere and Fibi escorted Nfudu to her room. After they helped her settle in, they left her to get a little rest but promised to meet later that night.

Nfudu met with Fibi and Chinyere at the Queen Victoria Nightclub in Ikoyi around ten o'clock that night. Chinyere brought her husband along with her and Fibi came with her boyfriend. Chinyere's husband was a tall burly man. Nfudu could tell right away why the couple got along. They wasted no time getting up and gyrating on the dance floor in perfect unison, leaving Fibi and Nfudu to stare at each other in amazement.

"Go ahead and dance if you want to," said Nfudu to Fibi. "Don't mind me. I'm famished so I'll order some food before I consider stepping out on the dance floor."

"Oh! You didn't eat at the hotel?"

"No. I wasn't hungry then."

"We'll also order something to eat. Don't worry about us. We come here all the time. The party usually doesn't start until eleven o'clock anyway, so we have plenty of time to chill. What would you like to eat?"

Fibi beckoned to a male waiter, passing drinks on the table next to them. The waiter took their orders and maneuvered past the couples frolicking to music by Fela. Nfudu bobbed her head and tapped her finger on her knee to the rhythm of the song, wishing she too could get up and dance. The lively crowd around her when the number played caused her to loosen up a bit. She was glad she accepted the offer to come out, because the experience she'd had so far, gave her the right amount of stimulation to take on the tasks she came to Nigeria to accomplish. She was impressed by how the women rocked the dance floor and could not recall people dancing like that six years back. Definitely not the few times she was able to sneak out to a nightclub with her friends back in the sixties. Something had changed, she thought as she watched a girl in a short frilly navy blue dress bend halfway, with both hands at the back of her head gyrating to the afro music that was playing. The girl was backing her partner, who was winding his waist from side to side in a very seductive manner with both hands holding the girl's hips as she moved. She could not believe the liberation these women around her enjoyed or the fun they all seemed to be having. It was terribly contagious and having caught it, she was determined to join in after her meal.

After munching on some chicken wings and chips, Nfudu excused herself from Fibi when she was asked to dance by the owner of the club, an oddly handsome man, who had been eyeing her since she was introduced by Chinyere's husband when they first arrived at the club. While they danced, they chatted at the top of their voices – the only way to be heard in the club.

"I'm surprised how resilient our people are. They seem to have recovered from the war because I don't see the impact anywhere I look," Nfudu said snapping her fingers and moving her head from side to side.

"You won't see much impact here in Lagos. Most of the damage was done in the East. It's a totally different story down there. It will take years for recovery to be complete."

Nfudu felt a sudden flood of emotion, which was apparent when she said, "Those are my people you know? I don't know what to expect. I'm so afraid."

"They're my people too," he said raising his eyebrows.

"Yeah. We're all the same, Hausa, Igbo…"

"Not in that sense…" he responded. "I mean…I was directly impacted."

"Are you from the East?" asked Nfudu baffled. Judging by his looks, she had assumed he was a northerner. He was slim built and had a dark complexion. When he was introduced to her, his name had been lost with the noise in the club.

"Yes. I'm Igbo. I knew you were too from your name. Nfudu! …right? I'm sure you don't remember mine."

"I'm sorry. Please repeat it."

"Nkemka." He brought his hand forward for a handshake."

"Ooh! So nice to meet you Nkemka. I was so hungry when I arrived and… the noise. I didn't hear your name when it was said."

"No worries. You're forgiven."

They danced for a little bit and he excused himself to attend to matters at the club, but not before extending another invitation to Nfudu to visit his club again before she left Nigeria. He gave her his number and asked that she call him if she needed anything during her visit. When Nfudu saw that her friends were still shaking their waists on the dance floor, she sat at the bar for a drink as she was beginning to feel the weight of her legs. Shortly after, she felt a hand on her shoulder but couldn't imagine who it was, even though she smelt a familiar scent. When she looked back, her jaw dropped when she realized it was Ikechi. A combination of the noise, her fatigue, and the glass of wine she just had made seeing Ikechi too much for her to handle. Her head swirled. She stood up to hug him and let out a loud gasp, "What are you doing here?"

"I should ask you the same question. You're the last person I expected to see here tonight. The last time I asked about you at the War Mission, you were a 'big time' London fashion designer who couldn't attend meetings any longer."

"Ahh! You make it sound like I abandoned my responsibilities," responded Nfudu, furrow lines appearing on her forehead. "I got so busy and couldn't breathe. But I still provided support for the programs."

"I was just teasing," he said smiling down at her. "I'm so happy to see you. I regretted not saving your phone number the last time we met. That boyfriend of yours… What's his name again?"

"Javier…"

"Yes, Javier. He was keeping tabs on you." He said with a small chuckle.

"That's not true. He's not like that."

"If you were mine, I'd keep tabs on you too. A man would be a fool not to protect his assets from predators. Don't you think?" He winked at Nfudu causing her to blush. "So why are you here? How long are you staying or are you back for good? It'll be nice to have you."

"I will be around for three weeks. I'm here to see my family and I also have a lot of business to transact. I and my partners are opening a fashion school here in Lagos."

"Wow! That's amazing. You've conquered Europe, now you want to conquer Nigeria. Congratulations! Let me know if there's anything we can do to help make it go more smoothly."

"Thank you so much. What have you been up to?"

"I moved back home right after the war. When I came back, I found that my businesses had suffered so much, mainly due to deserting. Most of our employees had to move to be with their families. Anyway, we have been able to slowly build things back and are in better shape now. I still come to London every three months or so because as you know I have a business there and in Barcelona. Enough shop talk. I want to know how you're doing." Ikechi pulled her in for another hug. Nfudu embraced the hug, happy to be in his arms. It felt completely innocent.

"I've had an unbelievable year. Most of it is in the news…" As she started to tell him how the past year had progressed, Chinyere came by with a glass of red wine in her hand and her husband on her side. She held tight onto her husband to avoiding tripping in the middle of the club. Nfudu made a quick introduction to Ikechi and after an exchange of phone numbers; she was ready to call it a night.

-

Nfudu thought of her run-in with Ikechi the entire drive to her hotel. She was so lost in thought but was shaken out of her reverie when Tunji swung her door open so she could come out of the car. She thanked him, discussed plans for the following day and bade him goodnight before retiring to the hotel lobby. When she reached her room and found that she had a message from Javier, it occurred to her that the entire time she discussed with Ikechi, she never mentioned the occasion of her engagement to Javier. Her engagement was the most important thing that had happened to her that entire year, so she asked herself, "How come I didn't even mention it once?" She felt guilty at the realization. It was too late to call Javier so she made the decision to call him the moment she woke up the in morning.

Javier picked the phone after two rings.

"Hello?" Javier's voice pelted through the phone line.

"Hi, Love," replied Nfudu. "I'm so sorry I missed your call yesterday. I went out with Fibi and came back so late. I didn't want to go anywhere, but they insisted. How are you?"

"I'm fine. I was worried when I didn't hear from you. You should have at least called when you arrived to let me know you were Ok."

"I'm sorry. I should have called you when I came in late last night. I thought you might be sleeping and didn't want to wake you. I didn't mean to be so inconsiderate."

"That's fine. I don't have a problem with you going out and staying late, but with the state of affairs in Nigeria, I was worried when I couldn't reach you," Javier confided. "How is everything else progressing? Is your Personal Assistant working out? And the driver situation – how is that going?"

"Fibi is a dream come true and they found me a driver already. His name is Tunji. So far, I have no problem with him. Today is loaded with activities, though. I have to look at some of the locations the real estate agents identified as well as meet with the consultants. I'll let you know how that goes. I have to go now. I love you!"

"I love you too darling. I feel better now I know you're ok. Have a great day."

"You too," Nfudu concluded, heaving a sigh of relief. She had never heard Javier so upset and it made her feel awful.

Tunji was at the hotel by eight o'clock to take her to a meeting with the real estate agents selected to help with finding a site for the school. There were three locations to see that day. Nfudu was ready long before he arrived. She was excited to get started on this journey she had dreamed about for so long. Prior to arriving in Nigeria, she had already started her search for a school location.

The real estate agents went to work to narrow down their search to a few options. Nfudu wanted construction to begin as soon as the right location was found, and before she returned to London.

Lagos was chosen as the location for the Fashion School because it made sense for her target market, which included fashion students from all over the country, who could afford to pay the tuition and living expenses. The city was a central hub and the war had destroyed most of the other regions that would have been suitable. It was a no-brainer that it would be the choice location and to consequently name the school the Lagos Fashion School.

The consulting firm of Arthur & Co was appointed to assist with designing the curriculum for the school and to assist with hiring top of class lecturers. Since the Nigerian business landscape was completely novel to Nfudu, she tried to get professional help in setting up the school to the standard she envisioned for it. The project was guzzling a lot of money, but her parents and Javier provided her with the seed funding required to get it started. They believed in her and because of her business acumen and past record, they knew they would make attractive returns on their investment. The funds they provided was enough to get her started, but she still needed additional investment to make the dream a reality.

While Nfudu was out and about with the real estate agents, Ikechi came by to assist her with her viewings.

"I'm starting to get worried that we won't find anything suitable in this city," Nfudu said exasperatedly as they left the second site.

"Don't give up hope," responded Ikechi. You still have one more option. If that fails, we can always look for other alternatives.

They drove to the third site at Ikeja in their respective cars, and it turned out to be an old site for a secondary school that expanded and moved to a new location on the Island.

"This is the perfect site," Ikechi said to Nfudu, to the agreement of everyone around. "It means there will be no need to perform any major construction. You're good to go!"

"It will need a lot of remodeling though to fit my vision, and a lot of work to make it habitable. We'll see," added Nfudu as she turned to address the real estate agents. "Thanks a lot for your help. I have a lot of thinking to do. I'll get back to you as soon as I make a decision."

"I really liked that last one," Nfudu said to Fibi, as they parted with the real estate agents. "You need to follow up with the real estate agents and the lawyer ASAP to write up an offer. Tell the lawyer to do everything possible to make sure our offer is considered. Make the lawyer understand that this is the one... we can't lose this site. Also, he has to act in a way that won't make us seem too eager. That will inflate the price."

"Ok, ma. I understand. I'll get them to start working on an offer today and present it tomorrow at the latest."

Nfudu and Ikechi headed to the Sunset restaurant in Ikoyi to grab a quick lunch before Ikechi returned to work.

"I'm so hungry," muttered Nfudu as they took their seats. The restaurant had a beautiful ambience and Nfudu was finally happy to catch a break since her arrival. "Last night at the club was something else. You know I almost didn't come."

"I can't even imagine that," responded Ikechi shaking his head and heaving a huge sigh of relief. "I was beyond myself when I saw you. At first, I thought my eyes were deceiving me until I saw those long legs crossed underneath the table."

Nfudu laughed. "I was surprised to see you too. Talk about a chance meeting. By the way, thank you for today. I feel better knowing I had a second opinion. The location was no doubt a perfect choice, but, you never know right?"

"No worries. I was happy to help. I got to spend a whole afternoon with you. How many people can boast of that?" Ikechi responded grinning as he poured her some wine. "Besides, we were meant to meet again. What were the chances that I would be in that same club at the same time that you were there?" Ikechi spoke with so much seriousness, Nfudu almost burst out laughing.

"You're cracking me up."

"Seriously...? I meant every word."

Nfudu's amusement subsided when she realized he was being serious. She immediately changed the topic to something less personal. "FYI, I'll be leaving for Abasi on Tuesday morning by road with Fibi. Tunji will be driving us."

"How long will you be staying? I'll be in Enugu for a friend's wedding on Friday. I don't mind driving the thirty minutes it takes to go from Enugu to Abasi to see you if it's ok with you."

"That would be nice. I'll be leaving the following Monday. I haven't been home in six years so I'll need to spend a little time with them. Please come if you can. It'll be nice to see a familiar face."

"That's a plan. I'm sure you've missed everyone."

"Definitely! I can't wait to see them and learn all they have been up to. I also missed the food, the weather, the fashion and the language…"

"I can only imagine. The war created a gap that will take a long time to be filled. It has made me realize even more the importance of family. Unfortunately for some, their families became more distant as a result of the experience and the losses endured. Brace yourself as you never know what you'll find."

Nfudu did not expect her family to remain the same after all these years. Due to the passage of time, most of her siblings had grown older and left home. Some were attending boarding schools and a couple of them were outside the country, pursuing higher education. Although she dreaded the changes, it was the need to reveal her engagement to Javier to her family that made her the most apprehensive about going home.

12

NFUDU left for Abasi on Tuesday morning with Tunji on the wheels and Fibi in tow. It was a seven-hour trip by road, but with the tolls, added up to an eight-hour journey. The long ride provided Nfudu with an excellent view of the countryside and an opportunity to buy all the staples – plantain, coconut, yams and fruits – she knew her mother would love. These filled the trunk of the SUV they were travelling in they were almost spilling out. Even though Fibi came along to keep the ball rolling on Nfudu's business transactions, she also provided needed company since Nfudu considered her to be more of a friend than an assistant.

Fibi had an excellent personality, which endeared her to people. Her witty nature and ability to see the best in others made her excellent company for Nfudu. She made every situation seem so easy and knew how to get practically everything done. Nfudu recalled her second night in Nigeria, when after a long day of hard work in her hotel suite, she realized she hadn't eaten anything for dinner by one o'clock in the morning. When she mentioned to Fibi – who was about to head home – that she was hungry, Fibi asked her what she would like to eat. Nfudu recalled her exact response.

"The question should be …what is available at this time of the night, without my having to leave this room?"

"Say whatever comes to your mind," Fibi had pressed.

"*Akara* and *akamu*," Nfudu had proposed, certain that Fibi would be unable to satisfy her biggest craving at that time, being that *Akara* and *akamu* was a breakfast food – best served hot.

"*Akara* and *akamu*," Fibi had confirmed, nodding her head. "I'll go with Tunji. We can get that from the night market at Maroku. There's a woman there who sells the exact same combination to night workers and watches. We'll see you soon."

To Nfudu's surprise, Fibi came back in thirty minutes with a steaming bowl of *akara* and *akamu*, grinning from ear to ear. Since then, Nfudu developed a new found respect for Fibi and concluded she could accomplish any task. She was the perfect personal assistant.

Nfudu woke up from her long snooze when Tunji stopped at a crowded bus station to use the washroom.

"Where are we?" she enquired.

"Benin. Tunji needs to use the toilet," responded Fibi "Do you need to go?"

"Actually yes, but let's wait a minute for Tunji to return…" Before Nfudu could finish her sentence, she spotted Tunji heading towards their direction. They took off in the direction of the toilets, with Nfudu pressing her legs together tightly and swaying from side to side. When she saw the queue in the only available female stall, she immediately groaned aloud and turned to see if there was another bathroom. Waiting their turn was out of the question. She looked at Fibi, who winked at her and gestured in the direction of the bushes. Nfudu thought the idea was ludicrous but saw no other way.

They eased themselves behind a hedge, taking turns to watch out for passersby. When they were done, Nfudu was unable to contain her embarrassment. She looked around to make sure no one saw them as they stumbled out of the bushes. They chuckled as they rinsed their hands with a bottle of water before climbing back into the SUV.

"That was quite an adventure. Wait…what if a snake had bitten us?" Nfudu asked realizing the danger she had just put herself in.

"Anything is possible," Fibi said laughing hysterically. "People do it all the time. I doubt there were any snakes in there."

"Ok. If you say so. It's been all work and no play since I arrived. I haven't had the chance to ask you about your family. How are they?"

Nfudu felt a little guilty she had shown little interest in Fibi's personal life especially after the recent state of affairs in the country.

"They're mostly fine ma."

"Why mostly?" asked Nfudu sensing something serious.

"My parents are fine …but …but one of my sisters died when a shell hit our home in Nkume." Tears streamed down Fibi's face and she raised her handkerchief to wipe her cheeks and the corners of her eyes.

"Ooooh!" exclaimed Nfudu, throwing her head back in her chair and sighing heavily. "I didn't know... I'm so sorry. Which of your sisters?"

Fibi was emotional by the time she mumbled, "Ifeacho…"

"Ifeacho? Oh my God? What kind of thing is this? She said grabbing her head. "Why didn't Chinyere tell me anything about it?"

"Hmm… Perhaps she just wanted to forget. That's not all," continued Fibi, her voice still racked in emotion, "We lost all our properties in Nkume and since my parents didn't diversify, it meant everything we owned. It devastated my whole family and affected our mother the most. She hardly speaks anymore and suffers nightmares."

"That's terrible," said Nfudu shaking her head. "I hope she's getting the help she needs."

"Sort of. She's been to two doctors and the diagnosis was post traumatic stress disorder. She rejected all her medicines and is relying on her faith and prayers, hoping for the day she will start to feel like herself again."

"Oh no," said Nfudu shaking her head. "She needs to take her medicine. God gave us doctors for a reason. I don't agree with her method. How is everyone else coping?"

"My father's friend gave us a small bungalow to live in until we get back on our feet.

They were interrupted by Tunji, who looked into the rearview mirror to announce, "We don dey reach Asaba. You go soon see Niger Bridge."

"Thank you Tunji," Fibi said.

"Ooh, it's so beautiful. I'm so amazed by it," marveled Nfudu, looking out the window. Her conversation with Fibi had upset her, so she was glad to change the subject of their discussion.

"They just finish am," continued Tunji. "They demolish am for war."

"I heard so," replied Nfudu. "I'm happy things are getting back to normal."

-

At six o'clock in the evening, they finally arrived in Abasi. As they drove through the streets Nfudu was shocked by the amount of devastation along the way. The rehabilitation efforts she saw in the other cities they drove by on the trip were completely nonexistent in Abasi.

"What is this world coming to? See my beautiful Abasi." Nfudu said wiping the tears that were streaming down her face. Fibi tried to console her but to no avail. "The whole place is gone. Look at the people. They look so miserable. God will punish the people responsible for this." She wound down her window to get a better view when she passed the site of the popular Aferi market – formerly a central meeting point for entertainment activities during Christmas and Easter holidays. The market structure was non-existent. It was leveled to the ground in a pile of debris. As if that was not enough, Nfudu found that the local church, where her grandmother worshipped was completely destroyed. She asked Tunji to drive into the compound so she could see the vicar, whose makeshift home provided temporary accommodation for his family of six.

When the Vicar told Nfudu the story of the devastation it was worse than she had imagined. "Whole families were wiped out, men were tortured, women and children were raped and captured. Many collapsed and died from hunger," said the vicar to Nfudu.

"This is wicked," responded Nfudu. "I'm determined to help in any way I can so please let me know what the most urgent need is. I'll be home for a few days so come by whenever you can."

The Vicar, a middle-aged man, who Nfudu remembered for his robust and talkative nature now stooped to walk when he escorted her to the door. "Thank you, my daughter. God will bless you for stopping by. I'll see you before you leave. Please greet your parents for me."

"Thank you, sir. God bless you too," responded Nfudu.

She was in a terrible mood when she left the church compound. As they drove into her father's palatial compound her mood brightened a little bit. Luckily, their compound was still intact. It had a few signs of neglect – the garden was not as meticulous as it used to be and the walls of some of the buildings had holes where enemy shells had hit them. She wondered where the gardener Ene, with his 'Queens English', was. It was easy to guess he was not around; otherwise, the garden would not have looked so unkempt.

Afonwa was the first to run out to greet her.

"Mama, Nfudu is here." She squealed. They had been preparing for her arrival for days and were starting to wonder where she had been because they had expected her to arrive two hours earlier. "We've been expecting you. Where have you been?" Afonwa asked with a naughty frown on her face.

"I stopped at a few places and also went to see the Vicar at Mama's church. How are you, my darling sister? I can't believe my eyes." They hugged as if their lives depended on it.

Soon, everyone ran out of the house to welcome Nfudu. Chief Ibe tugged at his wrapper and her mother jiggled from side to side as she ran with a big smile on her face to meet her and her entourage. Everyone spoke at random. Her mother held her in a long hug, crying, "Nfudum oo…"

"Woman you're not the only parent she has. Move aside let me welcome my child properly." It was only when Chief Ibe bellowed, did Mrs. Ibe let go of Nfudu.

Her siblings took turns hugging her. She could count eight in total and noticed how they had all grown. Ifeanyi now had a beard and moustache and her half-sister, Chineme had grown breasts. She was tall and looked so much like Nfudu. "Wow! Chineme, you're now so beautiful. I hope boys are not disturbing you," Nfudu teased, causing Chineme to hide her face in embarrassment. It was a struggle differentiating some of her younger half-siblings as they were much younger when she left home. She was amazed by how old her father looked. Her mother looked older too, but was still as strong as she remembered. "It's incredible what the passage of time and war could do," she thought to herself, sighing.

Her mother caught her sighing and asked, "My dear, what is it?"

"Nothing Mama... Where is Ijere?"

"He's running an errand and will be back soon."

"Ok. I can't wait to see him," she said, disappointed she had to wait a minute longer to see her beloved brother.

After Nfudu and her guests were settled in their rooms, Mrs. Ibe laid out a beautiful feast in the large dining room but refused to sit down with everyone. She kept going back and forth to the kitchen and asking Nfudu at intervals if she wanted one thing or the other. "I'm not eating Mama until you sit down with the rest of us."

"Eh eh! Don't worry about me. Start eating and I'll join you soon," insisted her mother, still running hastily between the dining room, the kitchen and the parlor. She settled down with the rest of the family a little while later. "Make sure you eat enough. You're too skinny for my liking. You look like you're about to break in two. You know our African men like their women big."

"Mamaaa! Allow me to settle first before you start talking about men. This is ironic, because, in London, it's the other way around. Men like their women very skinny, but I guess it's different strokes for different folks."

Mrs. Ibe, unwilling to give up on her quest to make Nfudu fat continued, "This is not London. You're now in Nigeria."

It was a fantastic meal. The aroma wafted through the dining hall. Steam was oozing from the dishes, making Nfudu's mouth water. There was a plethora of dishes, from *onugbu* soup to pepper soup and *jollof* rice. She didn't know what to leave out, so she ate a little bit of everything. The spread was consistent with the one she had dreamt about all the years she was away from home. She still considered her mother the best cook in the world.

Ijere walked into the dining room while they were eating. She stood up and hugged him tearfully. He was considerably thinner than she remembered but was grateful to God they hadn't lost him. After their meal, the whole family gathered in the massive living room to exchange stories of their exploits before, during and after the war. Nfudu shared stories of her success in the British fashion scene as well as her pet project in Lagos. She revealed all she saw in Abasi earlier in the day. "I am disappointed by the sluggishness of rehabilitation efforts here. Why isn't anything being done to speed things up?" Nfudu asked after she took the seat next to her father.

"Reconstruction requests have been proposed for a number of the structures that were destroyed. However, the funding required to start and complete them are not forthcoming." Chief Ibe responded, confirming Nfudu's fears.

"That is so sad. Something needs to be done about it. Our people have suffered enough." Nfudu said, and then remembered her favorite gardener. "What of Ene?"

There was a moment of silence as her parents and siblings shifted uncomfortably in their seats. Her mother was the first to speak up.

"Ene was captured by soldiers during a raid at Ngwa. No one has seen him since then. We speak to his family every now and then to see if there's any news of him, but none has surfaced yet. He's feared dead."

"Oh no! Poor Ene. No wonder…" Nfudu was starting to say but was interrupted by Chief Ibe.

"No wonder what?"

"The gardens," Nfudu responded, choking on her emotions. "When I saw them, I knew something was wrong. Ene would never have left them in the state they're in. I miss him so much."

"Such is life," responded Chief Ibe, looking down and nodding his head.

In that moment, it occurred to Nfudu that she hadn't spoken to Javier since her arrival. "I need to make an important call. Can I be excused?" She missed her Javier and wondered what he was doing in that moment.

"Go ahead," responded Chief Ibe. "The phone is still in the same position. I hope you remember your way around."

"Of course!" Nfudu couldn't believe the phone was still kept in the same position – in the hallway leading to her parents' bedroom.

"Hello, my darling. I miss you awfully," she heard Javier say on the other end.

"Me too. It's so overwhelming here. I want nothing more right now than to be in your arms," whispered Nfudu.

"You can't be doing worse than I am. I get up some nights grabbing the sheets, only to wake and realize you're not there."

"I dreamt of you last night and could swear when I woke up you were really there in person. When I woke up and realized it was only a dream, I felt so miserable. It took Fibi to drag me out of the room in the morning."

"Why are you whispering?"

Nfudu lowered her voice even further to respond in a wispy tone. "The phone is right here in the hallway. Anyone can walk by at any moment."

"Ok. I understand. Have you had the chance to discuss our relationship with your parents?"

"I'm planning to do that tomorrow," she responded with conviction.

"How is your family though? That's the most important thing."

"Ooh!" sighed Nfudu. "Everything is changed. Father looks more subdued than I remember. I feel so horrible to have left them for so long."

"It wasn't your fault. Let me know how the discussion goes tomorrow. Between you and me, no matter the outcome of your conversation, our relationship is still intact..." Javier stated, although half questioningly.

"If they object, we'll have to look for other ways around it. I love you!" Nfudu said, sensing the doubt in his tone and trying to reassure him.

"I love you more, darling. Have a good night."

"You too."

Nfudu went to bed that night, thinking about all she had encountered since her arrival in Nigeria. The experience was so overwhelming compared to her cozy life in London. Both lives were many worlds apart – they couldn't be successfully merged to achieve the synergy she so badly desired for her peace of mind. She felt a little lost being so far away from everything she now knew and desired, and worried all night about how she was going to tackle the tasks ahead of her. By the time Fibi came knocking at her door in the morning, Nfudu had barely gotten any sleep and asked to be left alone for another two hours.

It was eleven o'clock before Nfudu finally left her room. Her parents and two siblings were in the small living room adjoining the palatial dining room. She apologized profusely to her mother. "Mama, I'm so sorry I missed breakfast. Do you know this is the most rested I've felt since my trip? Fibi told me I had some visitors."

"No problem my dear," responded Mrs. Ibe. "I understand you needed to rest. We kept some breakfast for you. Don't worry about the visitors. I asked them to come back later."

"Thanks, Mama. I almost forgot to tell you. After breakfast, I'll like to go and visit Grandma and Aunty Adiba. From there, I'll go to the stream."

"Stream? Nobody goes there anymore. It's basically now used as a refuse dump. Things have changed," said her mother half aghast, half smiling. "Also, be careful where you stop. There have been several armed robberies these days."

"Is it that bad?" Questioned Nfudu pondering the issues her mother just raised.

"Yes it is!" added Chief Ibe. "Be careful. I don't want to tell any stories."

"Ok, Mama and Papa. Thanks."

–

Her first port of call was her grandmother's house, where every item was still in its usual position. It was as if no time had passed by. When she visited her aunts and uncles, six in total, each one wanted to outdo the other in dishing out delicacies. They could not take no for an answer. By the end of the day, Nfudu could barely move from the gluttony and exhaustion. When she came home she met a hoard of visitors that came to see her. She entertained and distributed gifts to all the guests. It was such a glorious experience for her, seeing everybody after so many years. She looked intently at each of their faces and was surprised at how some of them had changed so drastically, as if they had been ravaged by factors beyond their control.

Chief Ibe was still the strong, enigmatic man Nfudu had known her whole life. Even though he now looked leaner and more subdued, she still dared not cross him. When all the guests finally left, Nfudu decided to speak to her mother about Javier to soften the blow, before taking the matter to her father.

"Mama." Nfudu started after they sat in her room. "There's something you should know."

"Ok. I'm all ears. Before you start, should I hold my breath?"

"No." responded Nfudu, shaking her head, while retaining a serious stance. "I have a boyfriend. He's white."

"Do you love him?" her mother asked staring at her intently.

"Yes, Mama."

"Ok. Then we'll just have to plead with your father to understand."

"But Mama, that's not the only thing. This man is Javier, Vanessa's father."

"Heeey!" exclaimed her mother considerably agitated. With her face contorted, she took a few minutes to absorb what she had just heard before responding, "But he's old enough to... Anyway, after everything we've been through, we really ought to live our lives the way that makes us truly happy. My dear, If Javier is the man you want to spend the rest of your life with, I'll support you. My only worry is that your father will not see things the same way. Give me a chance to speak with him first."

Two hours later, Nfudu was summoned to her parent's room. Her mother was sitting at the edge of the bed with a sullen look on her face, while Chief Ibe had a scowl, which immediately disappeared when he saw her.

Chief Ibe was the first to speak, "Come and sit next to me." Nfudu sat next to him and after a few minutes of silence, he spoke again. "Your mother has just revealed something to me. I believe you know what I'm referring to. Can you tell me what is going on... in your own words?"

Nfudu outlined the history of her relationship with Javier and provided details on when they first met, when they first started dating, how much they loved each other and their eventual engagement. She kept her story as pure as possible, while Chief Ibe listened patiently. He barely interrupted, but he stopped her at intervals for clarification. But, when she said, "... and I love him," he yelled, "*Love gbakwa oku* – to hell with love."

His words sent instant shockwaves across the room. Mrs. Ibe jumped in her seat, while Nfudu, mouth agape stared at her father as he continued. "Over my dead body will my Ada marry a white man, let alone one old enough to be her father. You have to select one of the men that have been waiting for you to return, so they can ask for your hand in marriage. These are prestigious Abasi men that have everything you need – money, virility, looks, name it... You don't need to subject your life to this nonsense..."

"Ahhh... Papa Nfudu... eh!" Mrs. Ibe exclaimed. "Please don't say things like that. How can you say 'over your dead body'? With everything that has happened in the world recently, is the most important thing not to be alive? If this man loves her and treats her well, she should be allowed to be with him? Let discuss this some more ... please."

"Papa, Javier has treated me better than any man can," said Nfudu after she recovered from her initial shock at her father's reaction.

"Did you say better than any man? Does he treat you better than your own father?"

"Papa, I did not mean that. Please consider everything we just discussed."

"There is nothing to consider." responded chief Ibe shaking his head and tapping his right foot noisily on the terrazzo floor.

Nfudu knew it would be an exercise in futility to try to convince him any further at that point. She excused herself and left the room. Her mother followed her right behind.

"Mama, you know that despite Papa's objections, I'll still marry Javier. He's the only man I'll ever need."

"No." her mother responded in a firm, warning tone, waving her right index finger in the air. "You can't do that. It's not right. There will surely be repercussions. You need to be patient. Give him time to absorb the idea and I'll talk to him again. Maybe when you come back for Christmas there will be a change in him. You're no longer a child and should be able to marry whomever you choose as long as he is not a criminal."

That night, before she went to bed, Nfudu snuck out of her room to her parent's hallway to call Javier. She revealed the unpleasant news to him, but left out the gory details. He was devastated. Nfudu tried to console him despite her own emotional state. "Don't worry love. I knew this would happen and this is why I have dreaded the conversation for so long. Trust me he'll eventually turn around…"

"And if he doesn't?" Javier interjected.

"He will. I don't plan on marrying anyone else."

Before they hung up, they both confirmed their commitment to each other and agreed to a plan of action. Javier would speak to Chief Ibe at an opportune time to carry out the traditional rite of asking for his daughter's 'hand in marriage'.

13

CHIEF Ifejaku of Umuani was a well-respected engineer and one of the first in Eastern Nigeria to be accepted into the Royal College of Engineers. He was a well-known philanthropist who used his personal funds to provide essential commodities and infrastructure needed by the indigenes of Umuani to survive after the perilous war. His children – three in total – with the exception of Ikechi followed in his footsteps and became successful engineers. Ikechi had a penchant for finance and knew early on the route he wanted to take. After bagging a degree in banking and finance from Oxford University, he got an offer to work in the prestigious investment financing firm of Lynch & Breuer. He rejected that offer and instead moved back to Nigeria to set up a savings and loans on Broad Street. Following the remarkable success attained in that venture, he moved to London for a short stay, in order to set up an investment management company with his partners. It was during that stay that he met Nfudu at the War Mission when he attended one of their meetings with a bosom friend and client.

Ikechi never stopped thinking about Nfudu since their initial meeting and regretted not getting her contact information during that first encounter. When he asked about her at the War Mission, he was told she was in a serious relationship. This deterred him from jumping through hoops to find her, but when he saw her again at that Christmas party with Javier two years back, his feelings for her were reignited. However, he observed she was completely devoted to Javier. Just when he gave up on his dream of pursuing a romantic relationship with her, their chance encounter at the Victoria nightclub on the day Nfudu arrived in Lagos gave him renewed hope.

Ikechi wasn't sure what endeared him to Nfudu – her beauty, class or the fact that she seemed unattainable. Each of those forces was powerful enough for him to be enamored of her and want her as desperately as he did. After he met her at the Victoria nightclub and got the chance to hang out with her during her stay in Lagos, he became determined to do everything in his power to make her his woman. He began to pull out all the stops to win her affection but was heartbroken when she revealed to him the night before she travelled to Abasi that she was engaged to Javier. This stumped him for a second but forced him to reinforce his strategies to achieve his ultimate goal of winning her heart.

With all the problems clouding her senses on her trip home, Nfudu completely forgot Ikechi was coming until he called to inform her that he was on his way. She was glad to hear his voice as she desperately needed a release from the tense situation between her and her father. In the week Nfudu spent in Abasi, Chief Ibe introduced her to a number of suitors, all under different guises. Unbeknownst to him, Nfudu could always tell when the men were potential suitors because he provided their genealogy along with the introductions. She found his approach and hidden innuendos amusing, yet exhausting because all she wanted to do was enjoy her family and complete the work she had to do. Chief Ibe was furious with her for not finding any of the men worthy, and that was the cause of the tension between them.

"That's it, Papa. I'm not sitting through one more boring conversation with any man," Nfudu announced after Chief Ejemba's son left their home following hours of interrogation from him.

"Why are you being impossible?" Chief Ibe barked in return.

"I'm not trying to be impossible Papa. Did you see how he was questioning me? One would think I was in a job interview. Job interviews aren't even this disturbing."

"You should also have grilled him in return. That's the way it's done."

-

Ikechi arrived late in the evening. He had driven from Enugu right after the wedding reception, checked into a hotel in Asaba and headed straight for Nfudu's home. The directions to Chief Ibe's mansion had been easy to get on arriving in Abasi. Ikechi's tinted SUV drove into the compound as Nfudu was walking her friend Ngozi to her car. It circled the driveway once and stopped right beside them, leaving Nfudu and Ngozi wondering who could be behind those tinted windows. When Ikechi stepped out of the back seat, Nfudu let out a gasp and turned to Ngozi, whose face was filled with admiration. Ikechi's black tux was exquisitely cut and a perfect match for his suave personality. He paired it with a crisp white shirt and a silvery blue tie. Ngozi whispered to Nfudu. "He could easily have stepped out of the pages of a magazine."

"He looks better than ever," Nfudu responded before giving her a quick goodbye hug, so she could attend to Ikechi.

"Welcome to Abasi," Nfudu said when Ikechi reached out to give her a hug. He seemed taller than she remembered and wore an amazing scent that made her mouth water. "You look great. How was the wedding?"

"It would have been better if you had come with me," he responded playfully.

"You didn't ask," she said with an accusing tone.

"I didn't know you would have accepted. I guess I shot myself in the foot with this one," Ikechi joked, feigning defeat.

"It would have been tough for me to leave though. I had lots of family obligations. Come inside and meet my family."

Nfudu led him indoors, and into their large sitting room, where her father was relaxing with a keg of palm wine with her uncle. Ikechi walked up to Chief Ibe and introduced himself with both hands placed behind his back while he gave a small bow. "Good evening sir. My name is Ikechi Ifejaku."

Chief Ibe moved forward in his seat, looked up to inspect Ikechi's face before asking, "From where?"

"From Umuani village, but I reside in Lagos. I came to visit Nfudu."

"Oh Oh. Nfudu!" exclaimed Chief Ibe. "You didn't tell me you were expecting anybody. *Nna* welcome. Welcome my son. Find a seat for him." He beckoned to the houseboy, "Bring some refreshments... quickly. Please repeat your last name again."

"Ifejaku."

"And you say you're from Umuani?"

"Yes, Sir."

"Please come here for a minute," said Chief Ibe, beckoning with his right hand. "Are you Linus Ifejaku's son?"

"Yes, Sir. I'm his first son," replied Ikechi.

"Are you serious?"

"Yes, sir."

"Come... Come here and embrace me," said Chief Ibe as he stood and spread both hands out to give Ikechi an embrace. After the two men shared a long embrace, Chief Ibe said rather emotionally, "Your father and I were very good friends. The last time I saw him was in 1954. I remember because that was the year Chineme was born. We knew each other as young men, but went our separate ways – your father to attend higher institution in the UK and me to Nkume to start a business. What a small world." he concluded shaking his head in disbelief. "Where did you and Nfudu meet?" Chief Ibe continued unable to conceal his excitement.

"In London," replied Ikechi.

"London? Welcome my child."

The two of them chatted for another while until Ikechi excused himself and promised to visit again. He was relieved to finally have time to speak to Nfudu alone as she walked him to the car. "How have you been?" Ikechi asked.

"Not good," she responded shaking her head. "There's been serious tension between me and my Dad. I meet three suitors on average daily and I'm almost fainting from exhaustion. Can you believe one of the men told me he cannot allow his wife to work? Another one offered to buy me an island and there was one who didn't speak proper English." Ikechi laughed as Nfudu continued her rant. "This experience reminds me of why I fell in love with Javier. They were all eligible, all well to do, but were all lacking in something I couldn't place my finger on. So sorry for my rants."

Ikechi, who was laughing at first, became sullen after Nfudu mentioned Javier. Noticing he was no longer interested, Nfudu changed the topic.

"What are your plans? When are you returning to Lagos?"

"The day after tomorrow. You should come with me," replied Ikechi.

"I was actually planning to return to Lagos by air and send Tunji by road with Fibi."

"Why don't you join me? It'll be a nice ride."

"Hmm! That may not be a bad idea."

"That sounds like a plan," agreed Ikechi. "I'm looking forward to our trip. I'll call you tomorrow to confirm."

"Great. We should plan to leave very early in the morning though."

"Agreed."

"Have a good night."

"You too."

That evening, Chief Ibe had a certain cheer about him. He was in the best mood Nfudu had seen since she broke the news of her engagement with Javier. After Nfudu joined him in the living room, it was not long before he revealed the source of his happiness. "Ikechi is the kind of man you should consider marrying," said Chief Ibe. "Firstly, he is Igbo. Also, he is very handsome and cultured and comes from a well to do family. He would make a great husband... and his father is a verrry good man," Chief Ibe concluded nodding dramatically in very slow motion.

"Papa, I'm not surprised you think so. You see every young man as a potential suitor."

"No," responded Chief Ibe, shaking his head furiously this time, "There's something different about this one..."

"Anyway," interjected Nfudu eager to change the topic. "I'll be travelling back to Lagos by road with him. Tunji will drive Fibi."

"That's not a problem. Have you told your mother?"

"Yes, I told her before coming to you."

-

For the rest of her stay in Abasi, Nfudu avoided any further conversations about Javier with her father. On Friday morning, she and Ikechi set off for Lagos as early as five o' clock. They talked incessantly from the moment they got into the back seat of Ikechi's SUV. The more they talked, the more they found out how much they had in common with each other.

"I'm so glad I saw you that night at the club," Ikechi said to Nfudu, reaching out to hold her hands as soon as they got on the Niger Bridge.

"Me too. I was surprised to see you and I remember thinking, 'What are the chances?'" She felt tingles course through her body as Ikechi continued to hold her slender hands firmly in his. She was stunned by how he affected her and froze from fear she would expose her panic if she moved, even a tiny bit. When she regained her composure, she broke the silence.

"How is your family?"

"They're all doing well," replied Ikechi. "It's a small family, compared to yours. Just me, my parents and two younger brothers."

"Where do they live?"

"The youngest is in University in Wales, while my immediate younger brother lives in Lagos, with his new wife." Ikechi released her hand for the first time since he took it to reach in his right jacket pocket. He retrieved a photograph and showed it to Nfudu. "This is from their wedding two months ago."

"Oh!" Nfudu exclaimed. "She's so beautiful. What's her name?"

"Nkemakonam. My brother is Donald."

"Donald looks a little bit like you. But, he's more handsome," Nfudu teased, with an exaggerated serious expression on her face.

"Do you mean it?" asked Ikechi looking visibly upset. "You may think differently when you meet him in person."

"I was just kidding," Nfudu laughed, noticing how adorably boyish he looked when he was upset. "Okay, if you say so... You know you're quite the celebrity. You're very popular in the London fashion scene. Where do you see yourself going from here?" Before Nfudu could respond, Ikechi placed his head on her right shoulder and squeezed her hands playfully. It reminded her of the first time they met a few years back since she recognized the same feelings she had for him returning once again. She thought of gently removing his head using an appropriate guise, but decided against it. She liked being that close to him. He felt very familiar and she was beginning to feel tingly. The longer he held her hand, the more hopeless she felt in the situation. She hoped he didn't notice her excitement as she didn't want to encourage him to continue on the dangerous path they were both beginning to tread.

Moments later, he took his head off her shoulders and announced, "I hardly got any sleep last night."

"You can lie down for some sleep..." Before the last word was out of her mouth, Ikechi adjusted his legs to a more comfortable position, and placed his head on her thighs. Nfudu was shocked beyond belief by his interpretation of her suggestion for him to lie down. She hadn't intended for it to be an invitation to take up her personal space. Wondering if he always behaved that way or if it was a calculated effort on his part to seduce her, she sat still, thinking it would be bad manners to ask him to get up.

"I'm listening," said Ikechi, startling her after settling on her laps.

"Where were we?" asked Nfudu, clearing her throat and looking out the window in search of a breather as the SUV suddenly felt too small a space for all three of them, including his driver to be in.

"You were going to tell me about your future plans."

"Oh!" exclaimed Nfudu as she proceeded to tell him about her plans to expand her brand through participation in additional fashion shows as well as the plan to open a shop in London. While she spoke, she mustered the courage not to rub his temples as he looked so cute lying there in total surrender to her even though he hardly knew her. In her mind, avoiding further closeness was necessary for maintaining her loyalty to Javier, even though she had already crossed some boundaries. However, she was uncertain as to how to resist any further advances from Ikechi as she felt totally and unequivocally powerless towards him.

When she finally fell asleep, Nfudu thought about her present predicament – Her attraction to Ikechi, love for Javier, and the strain her father was putting on her engagement to Javier. She hoped the reaction she got from Ikechi's touch was just infatuation, fueled by the need to fill the gap created by the emotional turmoil she experienced since arriving in Abasi. Having concluded that what she felt for Ikechi the first time they met – a few years back – was nothing short of lust, she convinced herself that was the case.

For the rest of the trip, Nfudu tried to comport herself. When they approached Lagos, Ikechi woke up from his slumber and apologized for his weight on her legs. "No problem," replied Nfudu. "I slept for a long while myself. Do you know you snore like a truck driver."

"I didn't hear myself snoring. Are you sure?"

"Listen to yourself," responded Nfudu laughing. "How could you have heard yourself? You slept like a baby."

"Should we ask the driver which one of us was snoring?" Ikechi asked jokingly.

"No need for that," Nfudu responded giggling.

"Hey! Look, we're almost at your hotel," said Ikechi looking out the window. "Can I see you tomorrow? It will be a busy day for me, but I'll be free anytime from seven. Dinner?"

"Sure. Call me when you figure out a time."

Nfudu wanted to avoid seeing him for a while to allow time to sort out her feelings. However, she accepted his offer for dinner. She did not want it to seem like she was rejecting him, but planned to provide an excuse closer to the time. This approach, she hoped, would provide a soft refusal and hopefully erase some of the bad impression she already created by succumbing to his wiles during their road trip. It was obvious to her that she needed to curb her feelings for him if she wanted to remain worthy of Javier's love for her.

Despite her convictions, Nfudu couldn't help being infatuated with Ikechi and thinking constantly about him. She tried to distract herself to make the thoughts stop, but realized they had become so ingrained in her she wondered if Ikechi had charmed her. After several failed attempts to erase him from her mind, she made up an excuse to call him after she settled into bed.

"Hello, it's Nfudu," muttered Nfudu, when Ikechi picked up the phone.

"Of course I know it's you. How are you dear?"

"I'm fine. Just wanted to say thank you for everything. Your visit, the ride ..."

"You're welcome. I'm so happy you called. In fact, I was just thinking about you but didn't want to bother you. I think you may have charmed me."

Nfudu's head reeled from the words, "You charmed me." She was stunned he had described his feelings for her the exact way she had just imagined her feelings for him. "I wouldn't know how to charm you, even if I wanted to..." She responded half defensively.

"Are you sure?"

"Of course!"

They talked for almost an hour and would have talked for longer, but for the knock on her door. It was the switchboard personnel trying to make sure she was all right, because Javier had repeatedly tried to call her, but found her phone to be engaged. Nfudu ended her conversation with Ikechi and called Javier right back. She felt guilty for not calling him right after she returned from her trip.

"I have been calling for the past hour. I got worried," said Javier

"I'm sorry love. I was busy organizing my things and getting ready for bed and then... how are you?"

"Missing you and counting the days till you return."

She had never needed to lie to Javier about anything and felt bad about keeping things from him. It was clear to her that it would have done more harm than good to tell him she had been on the phone with Ikechi for the past hour. They had never spent this much time apart from each other and it was beginning to tell on both of them, particularly her. She wondered if it was possible to be in love with more than one man at the same time. The more she thought about it, the more she realized she couldn't be in love with Ikechi because she didn't know him enough.

The following day was business as usual for Nfudu. She visited the site of the fashion school to take photos and conceptualize the changes to be made to the existing structure. Also, she finalized arrangements for staffing, equipment and facilities with the Consultants from Arthur & Co. Lunch was solo in a quiet café in Ikeja, where she took some time to make a few calls to London to check up on her businesses as well as attempt to put out a few fires on that end. When she called to speak with Javier, she got his secretary instead. He had left a message for her earlier to indicate that they had found perfect locations for two stores in London.

A number of the tasks Nfudu needed to accomplish remained outstanding. She got a good dose of the uncertain nature of the business environment when an appointment to meet one of her 'big man' investors got cancelled and rescheduled twice. The disappointment didn't end at that, because on getting to the man's office for the third scheduled appointment, Nfudu was told by his secretary that he had just boarded a private jet to Greece and would be returning at an undetermined date. Such disappointments, coupled with the fact that the search for a proprietor had not yielded positive results kept Nfudu up at night and threatened her timing for return to London. Arthur & Co. had interviewed numerous candidates, but none had met her expectations, not only in terms of skills, but also in terms of devotion to her cause, which transcended profit making. While she was pondering the proprietor issue, Fibi walked into the cafe to take her for their next meeting. It suddenly occurred to her that Fibi could be the one she was looking for all along.

"Fibi, have you thought about applying for the role of proprietor for the fashion school?" asked Nfudu peering intently at her. "I think you'll be a great fit – you're smart, hardworking and your work ethics are better than that of anyone I've ever met."

Fibi was flattered by Nfudu's compliments.

"Thank you, Ma. I have thought about it, but I realized I don't have the right qualifications. That's why I haven't applied."

"That's true. We asked Arthur & Co. to shortlist only applicants with a university degree. What we hadn't considered was that the war set a lot of talented people back. When will you be starting your program in Unilag?"

"Next year Ma."

"Forward your CV to Arthur & Co. I'll have a word with them to interview you nevertheless. We may hire you as Assistant Proprietor to groom you for the role and allow time for you to obtain your degree. I need you to be my eyes and ears while I'm away."

"Thank you so much, Ma!" exclaimed Fibi curtseying a little. "This is a dream come true."

"I don't know when you'll stop calling me Ma. If you notice, we're almost the same age. You can call me Nfudu. The fact that I'm your employer doesn't mean I'm Lord over you."

"Ok, Ma... Nfudu." Fibi laughed as they stood up to head out for their meeting. "It will be hard for me to stop calling you that right away since I've gotten so used to calling you Ma."

"I know," replied Nfudu.

-

By the end of the day, Nfudu was worn out. She found that her busy day had helped her forget a little about Ikechi, Javier and all the conflicting thoughts that were messing with her head. Her desire for a good night's rest was thwarted when she got to her room and found an emotionally charged message from Ikechi on her answering machine. "Hey! Missed you today... Can't wait to see you..." Nfudu called back right away.

"Hello, Ikechi here."

"Hi... How was your day?"

"Great. I have a meeting in your hotel lounge this evening. Can you join me for dinner afterwards? ...Around seven?"

"Hmm..." Nfudu didn't know how she could get out of that request. She had convinced herself earlier to dodge any dinner requests from him, but her body, mind and soul ached to see him, so she threw all caution to the wind. "I'll meet you in the lobby by seven thirty; I just got in and have a few things to tidy up."

"That works for me. See you then."

Nfudu rushed to take a shower and throw on a simple black sheath dress that covered her knees. She had chosen that particular dress as she hoped to distract Ikechi from her looks. Unfortunately for her, the simplicity of her dress did nothing to conceal her beauty; rather, it made her stand out even more as her elegance shone through. She put her hair up in a high bun, applied light makeup and her favorite scent and headed out to meet him. Ikechi was speaking with a man and a woman she didn't recognize when she arrived at the hotel lobby. He noticed her right away and motioned for her to join them.

"You look amazing," Ikechi said to her.

"Thanks," replied Nfudu

"Meet my friends, Mr. and Mrs. Okoye. They're celebrating their first wedding anniversary tomorrow, here in Ikoyi,"

"Congratulations!" replied Nfudu, reaching out to shake both Mr. and Mrs. Okoye's hands. "I wish you many more years of bliss."

"Thank you," responded the couple in unison.

"I hope you two can come," added Mr. Okoye. "You make a very fine couple."

"We'll try," replied Nfudu blushing. She noticed Ikechi smiling from the corner of her eye.

After they bade each other goodbye, Ikechi held her hand and dragged her gently to the car park.

"Where are you taking me," Nfudu asked.

"To dinner."

"Where? I thought we were having dinner here."

"I changed my mind. I'm taking you to the Presidential Hotel for music from a live band and some roasted fish."

"That sounds like a good idea," said Nfudu nodding her head in agreement.

When they walked onto the outdoor patio of the Presidential Hotel, where the restaurant was located, they got numerous admiring stares. The lead singer of the live band sang their praises as they were being escorted to their seat by the patron. At first, Nfudu felt self-conscious, but finally settled down to enjoy herself.

"They seem to know you really well here," said Nfudu as she sipped her drink and looked at Ikechi across the table through her large drinking glass.

"I guess so," responded Ikechi. "They also do that for personal gain. They'll be expecting a large tip before we leave."

When the live band started playing a romantic number, 'Love Nwantiti', Ikechi held Nfudu's hands on the table and looked into her eyes. She looked at him for a moment and then looked away when she couldn't bear to look at him any longer.

"What are you thinking right now?" he asked.

Nfudu tried to return his gaze. "…I don't know."

"I'll tell you what I'm thinking. That I've never seen anyone as beautiful as you. That I'm falling so deep and if I don't take my time, I might be in for some massive heartbreak."

Nfudu swallowed hard and looked away again.

"I don't know what to say. You know I'm engaged to someone that I really love and respect. I can't betray him."

"If you weren't with him, could you see yourself with me?" asked Ikechi with an emotional undertone to his voice.

"Absolutely. That is something I have thought about. Also, it would have been the easiest and most familiar option, since my family would have accepted you fully – no questions asked." As soon as the words came out of her mouth, she regretted revealing so much of what she was feeling.

"Really?" he said, with a satisfied look in his face.

"Yeah…" responded Nfudu, her eyes averting his gaze. She realized she couldn't take back her initial blunder, but tried to neutralize the effect. "You can't fake the chemistry …not the sort between us. However, I'm engaged so this can't go any further than it already has."

"Hmm?" hummed Ikechi, gazing at her.

After sharing a plate of fish and chips, they danced on the crowded dance floor. Nfudu felt Ikechi's body rubbing against hers and his hands stroking her back. As she was contemplating how to create some space between them, she felt his lips on hers and before she knew it, he was kissing her passionately. She felt her knees buckle.

Unable to resist him, she let go of all her inhibitions and kissed him back. As her body trembled and melted in his arms, he slid his hands down her back and onto the mounds of her bum and then back to her waist and drew her closer to him. She allowed the kiss to linger. She was completely drowning in her own emotion with no will left to stop him.

By the time Nfudu got back to her room, she shook with fear and guilt. The kiss she had just shared with Ikechi lingered languorously on her lips. It reminded her of her indiscretion. She knew she had gone too far with him and felt guilty about Javier – her beautiful, loyal Javier. She couldn't help thinking that something had to be seriously wrong with her if she could fall this easily for someone else. To make matters worse she needed to call Javier in the morning to deliver not so pleasant news.

"That is horrible news," said Javier after Nfudu revealed to him she would need to spend another month in Nigeria to complete a number of outstanding tasks.

"I'm sorry my love. Things here are different. One can never predict accurately how long certain things will take.

"Christmas is in a week. I had planned to spend it in Abasi, but may now spend it in Lagos and spend New Year in Abasi."

"Ok. Take all the time you need. But, if you move the date of your return one more time, I'll have to come and get you myself. Understand?"

"Yes."

"I need to rush to a meeting now. We'll talk later. Love you..."

"Love you too."

Nfudu felt even guiltier after speaking with Javier. For the rest of that week, she avoided Ikechi to give herself room to think. Ikechi called her daily, sometimes several times a day. She enjoyed her long conversations with him but made it clear she couldn't see him for reasons that were so clear to both of them.

14

THE Lagos Fashion School, a dream Nfudu nurtured since stepping foot into the International Institute of Fashion, was modeled after the veteran establishment and was slowly becoming a reality. The school was structured to serve a dual purpose – to serve a humanitarian cause by providing annual scholarships to a number of deserving students with dire financial needs, and to be a lucrative business venture. Tuition was set to match the class of the school and its students – wards from high-earning families who could afford the high cost. Nfudu and her team of consultants worked day and night to achieve their target of registering the pioneer class of students within a year. The project was at a point where she could conveniently leave and monitor its progress from London.

After working so closely for several weeks, Fibi and Nfudu developed a tight bond – strong enough they began to see each other like sisters. Fibi observed Nfudu's relationship with Ikechi with great interest. It was obvious to her the two had a huge amount of chemistry but had her own concerns.

"It's very obvious Ikechi likes you, or even possibly loves you," Fibi said to Nfudu after Ikechi dropped them off at a restaurant for dinner.

Nfudu wasn't sure if Fibi's comment was meant as a statement or a question. "Oh no. We're just friends. He hasn't told me he loves me or anything. By the way, how is your training for the new role going?" asked Nfudu, eager to change the subject to a less intrusive topic.

"It's going great. A bit overwhelming though. But I'm trying to learn all I can before the grind begins."

An awkward silence followed, during which Fibi tried to avoid Nfudu's gaze.

"What is it?" asked Nfudu.

"Nothing..."

"You don't look like it's nothing?"

"Ok," replied Fibi. "It's Ikechi. It's obvious he adores you and would do anything in the world for you but I wonder if he's distracting you from your fiancé."

"Don't worry Fibi. I'm fine. Nothing can come between me and Javier."

"Just to let you know, Ikechi is either hopelessly in love with you or he's a world-class playboy. Either way, please be careful."

Nfudu knew Fibi was right – Ikechi would go to the ends of the earth to please her. This affirmation, coming from Fibi worsened her emotional turmoil, especially as her only weapon – intimate distance between herself and Ikechi – was slowly chipping away and becoming ineffective.

Fibi's opinion was a far cry from Chief Ibe's as Nfudu was soon to find out when she travelled to Abasi for New Year celebrations.

"How is Ikechi?" Chief Ibe asked, stopping Nfudu in her tracks. Nfudu wondered if he knew something and considered her answer carefully.

"I guess he's fine," she responded shrugging her shoulders.

"Well, I hope you give him a chance because he's better suited for you than ... what is that white man's name again?" Chief Ibe snapped his fingers as he tried to recall Javier's name and then gave up. Nfudu wasn't sure if her father gave up on purpose or if he had genuinely forgotten Javier's name. However, she was stunned by his bluntness and looked at him with annoyance. Before she could respond her father continued. "Ikechi is the right age for you and he's also from your ethnic group. You should consider him seriously."

"Papa," whined Nfudu when she finally found her voice. "Do you now want me to start chasing Ikechi? Is that what you're saying?"

"'*Mbakwa*' – not at all. That is not what I meant. I just want you to have an open mind."

Nfudu made no further attempts to convince Chief Ibe to accept Javier since he was completely biased towards him. Besides, she was falling more and more each day for Ikechi and saw no reason to fight her father until she was able to settle her own inner turmoil. She called Javier less frequently. At first, it was to conceal her guilt, but later, it became the norm as Ikechi began to fill the gap created as a result.

Javier missed her terribly. Unable to bear her absence any longer, he phoned to express his distress.

"I'm coming to see you," announced Javier after Nfudu picked the phone. "Oftentimes when I call, you don't pick the phone and you rarely return my calls anymore. What's going on?"

"Nothing," responded Nfudu defensively. "I'm so sorry love. I've been swamped, running up and down and travelling. It's really crazy down here. You need to see it to believe. There's no need to come all the way. I'll soon be home."

Nfudu loved Javier deeply and missed him. However, her burning desire for Ikechi and the surrounding pressure from everyone she knew numbed her feelings until she got to a point where she surrendered her will and unconsciously let her circumstances dictate her destiny.

‐

Her connection with Ikechi grew stronger in the few weeks she remained in Lagos. She relied heavily on him but continued to avoid any form of intimacy with him. Ikechi in return respected her space.

Two days before Nfudu was bound to return to London, she asked Ikechi over to her hotel for a light supper. When they finished their meal, they hung out at the hotel bar and chatted for a little while.

"Where do you see our relationship going?" asked Ikechi.

"Hmm!" sighed Nfudu. "This is a tough question. I need a moment to process it."

"Take your time."

Nfudu did not have an answer right away so she looked in the direction of the exit while Ikechi patiently waited for her to respond. After a moments silence, she looked at him and shook her head. "I don't know the answer. What I know is I've grown really fond of you. I know you wouldn't like to hear this but I'm engaged to be married."

Ikechi swiveled his chair back and forth, scratched his head and gave Nfudu a piercing gaze.

"I'll tell you what I think. You should call off your engagement with Javier." Before he could finish his statement, Nfudu shook her head and fidgeted in her chair. "Please let me finish," pleaded Ikechi. "You know how I feel about you. I'm in love with you and I'm sure you have no doubt about that."

Nfudu gazed back at him, unable to speak. She searched his eyes for any hint of hesitation. "I already knew that... I just didn't think you'd have the guts to confess it to me knowing..." Her eyes grew misty, and she choked on her words.

Ikechi took the glass of chardonnay from her hand, placed it on the bar and helped her get on her feet.

"How long have you known?" Ikechi asked when they got on the elevator on the way to her room.

"I don't know," responded Nfudu shaking her head and dabbing her nose with a tissue. She checked her image in the elevator twice and looked up to see Ikechi gazing down at her, half-smiling and half-curious. She giggled lightly and her voice trailed off to a whisper. "I don't know what you want me to do."

"For starters tell me how you feel about me." The elevator door opened in that moment and they walked in silence to the privacy of Nfudu's room. She walked to the window and stared into the distance. Ikechi came behind her and held her waist before turning her around in a swift movement to look in her face. Nfudu's heart beat wildly as she looked back at him. He bent and kissed her gently on the lips. "Come," Ikechi said, guiding her to sit on the edge of the bed. He knelt beside her, and slowly removed her shoes one after the other.

"Thank you," said Nfudu. "Exactly what I needed. My feet have been hurting all day."

Ikechi looked up and smiled at her.

"Let me massage them," he said, after holding Nfudu's gaze for a brief moment.

"Ok."

He got up and grabbed her lotion from the vanity table. When he returned to his kneeling position beside the bed, he rubbed her feet one after the other with firm strokes that made her squeal as he reached her tense spots. After the massage, he placed his head on her laps while she stroked his temples.

"You haven't told me," said Ikechi raising his head to look at her.

"Told you what?"

"How you really feel."

"You don't give up, do you? ...Well if you must know I'm afraid to confess that even to myself." Ikechi raised his head and scanned the room with his eyes. Her clothes were strewn all over the settee and her shoes and bags were all over the floor of her suite.

"I'm not a very tidy person," Nfudu said, easing herself up from the bed. "I was packing for my trip before you arrived and ..."

"Who cares if you're untidy," responded Ikechi as he helped her pick up her shoes and arrange them in a suitcase in a flawless pattern. He folded her shirts when he was done with her shoes.

"Thanks for your help" Nfudu said with a smile.

"You're welcome."

Nfudu excused herself to take a quick shower. She found that a nightly shower helped her relax and sleep better. Ikechi kept himself busy with the newspapers he found in the room. He chatted with her from across the bathroom door and though Nfudu struggled to participate, it gave her comfort to know he was still there. She felt completely at home with him.

"I'll miss you, you know," declared Nfudu as she stepped out of the shower adorned with a large white towel wrapped around her chest, and a smaller white one in a loose turban, over her head. Ikechi could not get over how pure and fresh she looked standing there.

"You are beautiful," he said, slurring his speech.

"Thank you," she responded with a smile.

He walked towards her after she settled in the vanity chair. She caught a glimpse of him in the mirror, and her heart skipped a beat.

"Hand it over," said Ikechi reaching for the bottle of argan oil she was holding. "I'll help with your back."

Before she could resist, Ikechi took the bottle from her, poured some of the oil into his hands and massaged her back. He progressed to her neck and then slowly proceeded to her chest and gave her towel a slight tug. Nfudu let out a gasp as she stared helplessly at both their images in the mirror. In another swift motion, Ikechi pulled out the vanity chair while Nfudu tried half-heartedly to adjust the towel that was barely covering any part of her chest and stood up to face him.

"I won't let you leave for London before I show you how deeply I've fallen for you," he whispered, while holding her in a tight embrace.

"What do we do now?" she asked. She was completely unsure of herself.

"Follow your heart..."

Nfudu's heart was beating furiously and Ikechi's words made her already weak knees buckle. He gently removed her towel to reveal her entire frame. He then bent to kiss one warm breast while holding the other firmly in his hands. Nfudu felt her pleasure growing and moaned as Ikechi moved from one breast to the other. The towel on her head dropped to reveal her long beautiful hair, which was still wet and smelt of coconuts. Ikechi locked her lips with his, carried her to the bed and made love to her ever so gently. It felt so wrong, but so right and she allowed herself to embrace the magic of that moment.

Afterwards, she slept in his arms. Thirty minutes later, she woke up with a jolt. "I feel so bad," she cried realizing what she had done.

"Why?"

"I feel like the biggest whore on the planet earth."

"What do you mean by that?"

"You shouldn't put yourself down that way. There's nothing whorish about what we've just done. If anything, it's strengthened my affection for you and there's no turning back now." There was awkward silence before he asked, "Would you like some company overnight?"

Nfudu thought about resisting for a second but later gave in. "Ok..." she responded. She felt she had nothing to lose. Besides, she was afraid to break the bond they had just created. She was exhausted from the adventures of the last three months but felt a new strength soar through her body – one she could not explain. Perhaps, it was the realization that she had finally broken through the uncertainty that clouded her relationship with Javier, in the wake of her relationship with Ikechi. The realization was so strong that after Ikechi turned out the lights, she crawled on top of him and said, "I love you too."

"I know...," he said tugging her sides mischievously. "I have loved you from the very first time I set my eyes on you. I thought then... and still think you're a Goddess. ...When did you realize?"

"Hmm...I don't know. It might have been infatuation at first, and then love after our drive to Lagos from Abasi." Nfudu was still unsure when her feelings for Ikechi turned to love because she also loved Javier at the same time although in a different way. Her love for Javier's was pure and gentle, but with Ikechi, she felt uninhibited and alive.

"I want us to be exclusive," said Ikechi out of the blue. "Will you break off your engagement with Javier?"

"I don't know... I can't."

"Why not? I'll like us to get married as soon as possible."

"You need to put yourself in my shoes..." responded Nfudu sighing.

Nfudu had fantasized about marrying Ikechi numerous times but felt pressured in that moment. A tight knot formed in her stomach as she grew anxious thinking about Javier and the fact that she could break his heart into a million pieces.

"I'll need some time though..."

"Ok," she gasped in response.

Ikechi snuck out very early in the morning, while Nfudu was still asleep. She was jolted from her sleep around eight o'clock, after barely two hours of sleep by Fibi's knock on the door. When she got up, she saw a note from Ikechi. It was etched on a page of the hotel notepad that he picked from her work desk.

I love you, please give us a chance.

She scurried to find a suitable hiding place for the note before running to get the door for Fibi.

"You're still in your robe!" exclaimed Fibi, surprised that Nfudu, who was a stickler for time, would be that far behind on schedule. Fibi had arranged for her to meet D.Y. Ibrahim, a politician, turned entrepreneur, who acquired a thirty percent interest in the Lagos Fashion School. Neither one of them had met him, but they had both spoken to him over the phone. He was recommended by Danjuma – his eldest son who was also Fibi's friend as being likely to have interest in investing in the School. "Thank God I came in early," continued Fibi. "Have you figured out what to wear?"

"My navy blue pantsuit. Help me get it out of the closet."

Nfudu ran into the bathroom to take a quick shower, while Fibi arranged her clothes and a pair of matching shoes and purse.

"Do you know that D.Y asked his secretary to clear his schedule just to make sure he gets to meet you before you leave for London tomorrow?" said Fibi as soon as Nfudu stepped out of the shower with her dark olive skin glistening from the wetness. She had barely taken any time to dry her arms.

"Oh! That's sweet of him. I better hurry then."

"Don't worry. We'll be there in time. His office is in V.I. That's only a ten minutes drive, although in rush hour I'll give it another twenty minutes. This is Lagos."

When Nfudu stepped into D.Y.'s office she was surprised to see an impeccably dressed man in his mid-fifties. She had expected a much older gentleman, because of his clout and accomplishments. He exuded so much charisma that when he stood up to greet and usher her to a seat in a posh area of his large office, she gazed at him in admiration.

"Congratulations on your achievements in the world of fashion… and now the fashion school," he said with a baritone.

"Thank you so much sir," responded Nfudu smiling.

"There are few women, who have achieved what you have," continued D.Y. as he shook his head lightly and pursed his lips. "But none at such a young age. You made a great choice in accepting me as a partner. Make sure you let me know if you need anything else to advance your business interests."

"I'm very grateful sir," responded Nfudu, curtseying a little. We're all honored to have you on board. You're a well-respected man in the society and you're also well loved by many. I can't imagine a better partnership."

"Thank you, my dear," responded D.Y. as a huge smile spread across his face. "I don't know where you get your information from, but I'll accept the compliments. I would have loved to take you to lunch, but I cancelled two meetings just to make sure I see you before your trip. As you can imagine I have a backlog."

"I can imagine sir. Thank you for the concession."

"Anytime, my dear." He stood up and extended a handshake to Nfudu. "It was a pleasure meeting you."

"It's my pleasure too," replied Nfudu, taking his hand.

"Have a safe trip." He said, after walking her to the door.

"Thank you, sir!"

Nfudu walked to the reception where Fibi had been waiting for the past forty-five minutes.

"How did it go?" asked Fibi searching Nfudu's expression.

"Really well." Her voice trailed to a whisper. "Is he not the most gorgeous thing?"

"From the looks of it. I've never met him in person. I've only seen him on TV."

-

From D.Y.'s office, Tunji drove them to the popular Balogun market to shop for fabrics. On arriving at the hotel after dusk, Ikechi was waiting for her in the lobby. They headed straight for her room, ignoring everyone they met on their way. As soon as the door closed behind them, he grabbed her waist and locked her lips in a kiss that lasted at least ten minutes until she was able to wrestle away from him.

"I need to complete my packing," she whined.

Ikechi pretended not to have heard her. "I told my father about you," he said.

"What did you tell him?" she asked, halting her packing and searching his face for immediate answers.

"That you're the love of my life. That I'm going to marry you. You don't want to hear the rest."

Nfudu smiled, clasping her hands together in front of her face before whispering, "So what did he say?"

"He was rather happy and remembers your father very well. He only asked one thing, though."

"What?"

"That I put you in the family way soon, so he can carry his grandchild within a year."

"What?" shrieked Nfudu. Her mouth was agape for a few seconds afterwards. When she recovered, she rolled her eyes and laughed as she responded, "He can't be serious."

"He was and he can't wait to meet you."

"That's nice," she responded smiling.

Later, when they made love, it was more passionate than the night before. Nfudu was so uninhibited that before she fell asleep, she whispered to Ikechi, "I don't know what it is about you that makes me act so irresponsibly."

"It's called love," responded Ikechi, grinning contentedly in the dark.

—

Nfudu's flight to London was completely uneventful, but her mind was in a constant state of turmoil. It was hard for her to fall asleep and when she finally did, she felt too restless and woke up at intervals to realize she was still mid-air. Pondering the changes she was about to make in her life, she reckoned that if they were making her feel as insecure and restless as she felt, then they may not be so good for her after all. She looked at the couple sitting next to her in the business class cabin and wished she could feel as carefree as they looked and not be burdened by the thoughts possessing her mind. Her greatest concern was about Javier, and how he might feel if she called off the engagement. Then again, she was not sure she wanted to end it with Javier as she had become so accustomed to him that the thought of a separation filled her with dread. She shuddered when she realized that if she wanted to stay with Javier, she needed to come clean about her indiscretions with Ikechi and hope Javier forgives her.

When the plane approached the tarmac, Nfudu brushed her hair and reapplied her makeup. She didn't want Javier to see the bags under her eyes and immediately detect something was wrong.

"You look a little different, glowing I must say," Javier said as he lifted her up off her feet when he saw her stepping out from baggage claims at Heathrow Airport.

"Really?" said Nfudu, touching both her cheeks with her hands as though to feel the warmth of the glow. It suddenly occurred to her that if she glowed, it was as a result of the fact that she had not pined and missed him like she should have because Ikechi made her every bit as happy as Javier had made her. Pangs of guilt coursed through her.

"I'm so happy to have my girl back. It was too difficult communicating with you while you were gone. I could not reach you for whole days at a time ..."

"I'm so sorry love. It was a little bit crazy down there."

"How are your parents and siblings?"

"They're all fine. A little bit shaken from the war but in high spirits."

–

Javier took Nfudu to her flat, which smelt musky after two months of not being lived in. He opened the windows in the living room to let in a little air and brewed some coffee, while she drew a bath. When the coffee was ready, he took a cup to her and placed it on the edge of the bathtub. She was completely covered in foam except for half of her breasts, from a quarter of her nipples up. Javier was immediately aroused despite the million thoughts he had running through his mind. After he rolled up his sleeves, he gently caressed her breasts in a circular motion. Nfudu let out a deep sigh. He stopped to take off his clothes and slide into the bath with her. Kneeling across from her, he kissed her lips. Nfudu thrust her body upwards to savor every bit of what he delivered.

"It's been two whole months," he whispered as he pulled her to her side, so she could face the tub, and back him. He caressed her neck and shoulders for a few minutes before he pressed his whole frame hard against hers. "I've missed you," said Javier after they both climaxed and sat facing each other with their legs intertwined and gently rinsing the bath gel off each other's body.

Javier had a lot on his mind but waited until he carefully wrapped Nfudu in a robe to address his main concern. "Has your Dad warmed up a little bit to the idea of you and me?"

"Father is still adamant," replied Nfudu, shivering from the cold. Javier drew her closer to keep her warm and she lingered there to hide the distress she felt in the moment. Her distress took a whole new proportion as she realized through their lovemaking that Javier could be the one and that Ikechi may have merely been an obsession. Either way, she felt deeply for both men and hated the fact that she had to choose. Given the choice, she would gladly have chosen both of them.

15

THE team signed a two-year rental lease agreement for each of the two store spaces for the Nfudu Stores. The first of the stores was located at a busy corner of Regent Street, while the other was in Carnaby. Both locations were a hit. They were conveniently situated near restaurants and movie theaters, had their own parking lots and sidewalks and were in neighborhoods highly frequented by tourists. The Regent shop was right beside the Regent Sewing Institute, run by Nfudu's friend and associate, Nadia, which made that location a magnet for fashion insiders and their wards.

With just a few months to go until the official opening in spring, the team went to work right away to purchase equipment and install furniture and fittings. They worked long and hard to complete the summer collection which was to be on display during the opening. There was also the work involved in selecting partnering designers and fashion houses. Detailed screenings were performed to arrive at the shortlist. Several rejection letters were carefully crafted so as to manage hurt feelings whenever a designer didn't make the list. For the ones that made it, additional effort was needed to coordinate their stock and ensure it complemented the offerings in the store. All these made the process to get the stores ready overwhelming for all concerned. Nfudu bore the brunt of the stress since she refused to delegate certain tasks. She insisted on hiring the six full-time employees needed for both store locations – four sales girls, four cashiers and two store managers on her own. This was to ensure each of her employees fit the image and culture she wanted to portray for the stores. This turned out to be a daunting process as she had to select from a pool of over a hundred applicants. Nadia often came by at lunch to assist her whenever she could. One cold afternoon in February while she and Nadia were reviewing some pieces from the collection, Nfudu wondered if she had bitten off more than she could chew when her heart skipped three beats and she leaned forward holding her chest to gasp for breath.

"Are you ok?" Nadia asked, rushing to Nfudu's side to give her a hand.

"I'm not sure," she replied reaching for a seat. "My heart skipped a couple of beats. This hasn't happened since I had pneumonia my first year in fashion school. Should I be concerned?"

"It's probably nothing," insisted Nadia. "Could be the late nights you've been keeping …or even your diet."

"I don't think so. During my trip, I ate mostly fresh organic meals. I even made concerted effort to not overeat."

"Anyway, take it easy and watch for any more signs."

"I sure will."

Two days after her discussion with Nadia, Nfudu realized her period was late. At first, she made nothing of it since she was pretty irregular. However, she did not fathom all the other symptoms she was experiencing – headaches, missing heartbeats and an occasional feeling of nausea. She went to see her family doctor right away as she couldn't wait to rule out any distressing possibilities.

"You're pregnant," announced the doctor after Nfudu had waited almost an hour to get the results of her blood test.

Nfudu felt the blood drain from her veins. "Pregnant? I was being very cautious. Wait…"

"From what I see," continued the doctor, "You're three weeks along."

"No way!" exclaimed Nfudu. "I couldn't be pregnant. First of all, I have two shop openings to worry about, and I'm not married. This cannot be."

"An unexpected pregnancy," nodded the doctor as he took notes on his pad.

"Yes, and I'm really disappointed in myself," Nfudu responded, nodding in return.

"You don't need to panic. There are a number of routes you can take. I'd like to review them with you and the father of the baby. Who is the father?"

"The father?" Nfudu asked darting her eyes across the room.

"Yes."

"Did you say I was three weeks along?"

"Yes …give or take a few days."

Nfudu knew this could only mean one thing – she could not be certain who between Ikechi and Javier was the father of her baby. This jolted her beyond imagination. When she looked up from the examination table, she saw the doctor looking expectantly at her. "You look like you just saw a ghost. Are you all right?"

"I'm not sure who the father is. It could be either my fiancé or this guy, who I met recently… It's a long story. I'm at a loss for words." She confessed in a sullen tone, shaking her head persistently.

"That complicates matters. Don't you think? Try to recall which of the two men is more likely than the other to be the father."

"I was intimate with both of them one day apart, about three weeks ago, so I couldn't say for sure. Is there any way of confirming which one of them it could be? I've heard of DNA testing in the United States. Does it really work?"

The doctor shook his head. "No. Not with fetal testing. DNA is still being experimented with. It will take a little while to be fully developed. I'll refer you to a gynecologist to help answer all your questions. She will also care for you and the baby should you decide to keep it."

"Should I decide? No…," protested Nfudu shaking her head. She would never consider aborting her baby. No matter how difficult her circumstances turned out to be, it wasn't a choice she could ever make.

From the doctor's office, she went straight to her flat, laid on her bed and cried the rest of the afternoon. She felt lethargic when she woke up and needed desperately to speak to someone but was too embarrassed to reach out to anyone. In her mind, sensible girls like her did not get into such messes – their lives are carefully planned and executed – with no room for damage or heartbreak. She regretted not listening to her mother's life-long advice to always date with her clothes on. The following day, she visited the gynecologist on the far end of town after calling in sick at the stores.

The gynecologist, Doctor Harriman, was a beautiful, dark-haired American, who immediately took to Nfudu when she saw her.

"Not knowing the father of the baby is a major issue," she told Nfudu after she expressed her concerns to her. "You'll have to wait until it's born before you can know for certain."

"So I was told by my family doctor …but I was hoping for better news from you."

"No, No," said Doctor Harriman shaking her head. "In fact, attempting to take blood from the fetus the way some doctors are doing now in Australia, may complicate the life of the child and I seriously advise against it. These tests are still being developed and are not yet in use in mainstream medicine. After the baby is born, we can test for paternity by swabbing the baby's cheek and comparing the swab with DNA samples from the alleged fathers."

"I'm so devastated that we can't do anything about it right now, because after the baby is born, with or without a DNA test, I'll be able to tell who the father is."

"How?" asked Dr. Harriman tilting her head in curiosity.

"How do I put this?" responded Nfudu, looking away in embarrassment. "The baby could either turn out to be brown skinned like me or mixed."

Dr. Harriman still seemed perplexed, so Nfudu decided to spell it out in black and white. "Javier is white, and Ikechi is brown."

"Oh… Well…" said Dr. Harriman shaking her head while taking her seat. "I guess this makes this matter even more complicated."

"How…?" Nfudu asked, furrow lines forming on her forehead. She couldn't imagine things getting worse than they already were.

"Well…A lot of my patients, who find themselves in this type of predicament usually don't have the issue of race mixed in. As a result, they don't need to report their indiscretion unless they choose to. In your case, you have no choice but to tell the possible fathers while you're still pregnant that the child you're carrying may not be theirs. You don't want them to find out after it's born. Do you know for certain which one of them you want to be with?"

"Yes." Nfudu lied. She wasn't exactly sure of the doctor's intention for asking but wanted to avoid provoking judgment from the wonderfully accommodating doctor.

"Very good. It's not my place to direct you, but if I were in your shoes, I would come out to the one and hope he forgives me. Accepting the baby afterwards may be a different matter. However, I think it's worth the gamble."

"I agree with your suggestion. I'll have to find a way to dig myself out of this mess. I'm so tired of trying to be strong." Nfudu muttered as she wiped the tears that were streaming down her face with the back of her hands.

Dr. Harriman reached for the box of tissues on the counter and handed to her. "You have to be strong," she said. "Avoid worrying excessively. It's terrible for your condition. Everything will turn out right in the end."

"Thank you."

Nfudu left the doctor's office feeling more dejected than when she entered. She realized that she didn't have the liberty to dilly-dally between Ikechi and Javier anymore. The pregnancy had forced her to own up and reveal more than she was ready to. Unable to bear it any longer, she called Javier in Nice to tell him she was pregnant, but left out the part about Ikechi. She planned to reveal that bit over the weekend when he would be in London. Javier was elated by the news, but couldn't understand why Nfudu sounded unhappy. The wait till the weekend was unbearable for her, and for the rest of the week, she worried herself sick thinking about her predicament and how she was going to approach him with the whole truth. Her misery was palpable – she was jumpy and cried at every given opportunity. Everyone around her – friends, associates and employees, noticed her mood. This prompted her to isolate herself, which only drove her far deeper into her head. By the time Javier arrived on Saturday she broke down as she told him the whole story about her affair with Ikechi and the fact that she could not say for certain who the father of her baby was.

Javier was shaken by the revelation. He paced his room with both hands on his head. At intervals, he squeezed hard as though to prevent a massive explosion. When he got tired of pacing, he sat and rocked his chair while staring into thin air. Fifteen minutes later, he finally spoke.

"So… what does this all mean?" he mumbled.

"I don't know." Nfudu sighed.

"How could you not know? You created this mess."

She was taken aback by his tone as he had never ever spoken to her this harshly in the past. She gathered some courage and knelt before him, leaning on the chair for support. "I'm so sorry Javier," she cried. "I didn't mean for this to happen. There was so much pressure from my father. I can't…"

"Pressure from your father?" His tone became more menacing as he stood up and poured himself some brandy. "We both knew he wouldn't approve of us before you travelled, but that wasn't going to stop us. Was it? You shouldn't blame this on him."

"Yes… it was my fault. I shouldn't have blamed Father. He didn't force Ikechi on me." Tears were rolling down her cheeks as she got up from her kneeling position to assume a more comfortable one, sitting on the edge of the bed.

Javier stood to stare out the window with his drink, but barely took a sip out of it.

"I don't understand how you could do this," he said shaking his head. "I loved you… I love you with every fiber of my being. Why would you do this to us?" Suddenly, he felt a heavy pang of grief as the room seemed to swirl all around him. He put his glass down and held his chest as he slowly made his way to his chair.

Nfudu ran to his side. "I'm so sorry Javier," she cried.

He looked at her for one brief moment. "You have destroyed everything we shared. Where do we go from here?"

At first, Nfudu was tongue tied, but finally she responded, "I still love you."

"Yeah," he said with a slow drawl. "But not enough to not sleep around behind my back? Please leave. I'll need some space to collect my thoughts."

His words hit her like a ton of bricks, but she still managed to speak. "I can't leave you by yourself. Not now."

"I need to be left alone," he insisted.

Her heart sank beyond its lowest depths. She had never been as ashamed as she felt in that moment. Before she left, she placed her engagement ring on the bedside table when Javier wasn't looking and snuck out the door. When she got to her flat, she drew herself a bath to wash away her shame and loneliness. The combination of the pain she saw in Javier's eyes and the guilt she felt knowing she drove him to such despair made it impossible for her to sleep that night. The following day, she went to work feeling extremely miserable. She called Javier at the lodge but couldn't reach him. When she got back to her flat, she was surprised to find him sitting at the bar looking rather disheveled and holding her ring towards her.

"I'm not ready for us to be over," he begged. "Let's forget everything that has gone wrong and start all over again. I'll take responsibility for the baby even if it ends up not being mine. I love you and will never stop loving you."

Javier's pleas broke her heart, but she was too weak to think or give him a definitive answer. She couldn't believe he was willing to accept her – faults and all – and wondered if Ikechi would be that accepting also. She still loved him, but her love for Ikechi was new and fresh and uninhibited.

They spent an emotional night together in her flat, talking about their future until they were both exhausted. Nfudu was engulfed with guilt and couldn't provide a definitive answer as to why she was unfaithful. By the time she got up the following morning Javier had left, without so much as a word about his whereabouts. This hurt her beyond her expectations. She imagined he went back to the lodge and called to make sure he was all right. He picked after several rings. "Hello..." he answered with an iciness that froze her entire being.

"Hi... I just wanted to make sure you were ok. I didn't know when you left."

"Sorry about that. I needed time to clear my head. I'll call you when I arrive in Nice later this afternoon."

"Ok. Talk later..." He hung up before she could finish her sentence. She felt rotten to the core, but she knew she deserved every bit of the treatment she received from him. She also felt a huge weight lifted off her shoulders because she no longer needed to continue with the deception.

He didn't call her that day as promised. One day turned into two days, and two days, into two weeks. By the third week, Nfudu decided to call him to break the wall of silence between them. After three rings, he answered, but stayed silent on his end. It was obvious he knew who was calling.

"It's Nfudu...

"I know."

"We need to talk."

"I don't think so. What about?"

"Should we leave things the way they are then?" she asked, frustrated.

"I don't know," responded Javier. "You made the choices that brought us here... I appreciate you calling me but I'll be honest with you. I feel cheated and unappreciated, so I'm walking away with my pride as I see no escape from this impasse."

Nfudu was stunned by his aloofness. It would have spelt relief for her, had she not known and loved Javier for so long. Instead, she was disappointed in herself and the circumstances she created – circumstances that got Javier to that point.

-

During Javier's disappearance, Nfudu spoke with Ikechi about her pregnancy but remained silent on the issue of her baby's paternity. Discussing that over the phone with Ikechi would lead to more tension in her life and she was determined to keep her focus on her health, her baby's well-being and her work – aspects of her life that suffered greatly as a result of the events of the past month. Ikechi provided the much needed emotional support, which brought them closer. They fell more and more in love with each other. He wanted to marry her as soon as possible and asked her permission to initiate traditional marriage rites with his family. Even though she had a lukewarm attitude towards matrimony, she felt it was necessary to legitimize the relationship with Ikechi and give it a stamp of authenticity for the sake of her baby.

"Ibe's residence. Who is speaking?" Nfudu heard her father's deep voice when she called to give her parents the good news.

"It's me. How are you, Papa? How is Mama?"

"I'm fine my dear and your mother is right here. You can speak with her after we're done."

"I have good news. Ikechi wants to ask you for my hand in marriage. He wants to start traditional rites right away. Isn't that great?"

"This is great news, my daughter. The best we've heard in a while. Congratulations my dear. We must celebrate your change of heart. I don't need to know what prompted it, but I'm happy it happened." Nfudu was tempted to tell him about her pregnancy but decided to wait until a later date. She didn't want to answer a barrage of questions, not with the paternity issue still weighing down on her.

"I don't know what led to this new development." Nfudu heard her mother's voice say. "I thought you were adamant about marrying Javier." Her voice was tainted with concern.

"It's a long story, Mama. Ikechi and I became close while I was in Nigeria. I'll tell you the whole story some other time. I don't want Papa to overhear."

Mrs. Ibe was slightly disturbed by the news. There was no doubt in her mind that Javier was good for Nfudu and she had been determined to convince her husband to accept him wholeheartedly. She was disappointed that all the work Nfudu had done standing up to her father and challenging him in a way that nobody else had ever dared had all gone to naught. She was certain her husband would have budged eventually. What she had not prepared for was the sudden change of heart by her daughter. With her husband right beside her, she resisted voicing her concern to Nfudu and decided to call her back at a less inopportune time. "Ok, my dear. I've heard what you said. I wish you the very best that marriage has to offer."

"Thank you, Mama."

"Eh heh." continued Chief Ibe after his wife handed him the phone. "You need to inform Ikechi that there are slight differences between our traditional marriage process and theirs. For a marriage to be considered legal in Abasi, the groom's family must meet with the bride's family and announce their intention in a formal '*iku-aka* – introduction' ceremony. Prior to that, the groom's family has a responsibility to send emissaries to the bride's hometown to investigate the family and confirm there are no obstacles, taboos or hereditary factors that would prohibit their son from marrying his intended."

"What type of hereditary factors Papa?"

"Madness and certain hereditary illnesses. Don't worry. There's nothing in your lineage that'll forbid you from marrying anyone you want. This same step will be carried out simultaneously by our family to make sure Ikechi is truly worthy of you. However, we'll wait until they make their intentions known before we carry out an investigation."

"Why?" asked Nfudu. "I would have thought that doing it simultaneously will help reduce back and forth."

"Eh eh," disagreed Chief Ibe. It's better for the groom to go first, because carrying out this investigation before the customary *Iku-aka* makes the bride's family seem too presumptuous. You don't want that to be the case."

"Ok, Papa."

"However, nothing stops either side from asking questions informally and acting on answers as they deem fit. I have no concerns about the Ifejaku's so I'll wait until they make their intentions known. Greet my future son-in-law for me."

"I will Papa. Take care."

Chief Ibe had no doubt everything would check out fine for Chief Ifejaku's son. Ikechi was the second son to be married in Chief Ifejaku's family, so if anything was wrong, it would have been detected in the marriage between Donald, Ikechi's younger brother and his young wife, Nkemakonam.

While their families made plans, Ikechi and Nfudu made other plans of their own. "You know we could bypass the traditional rites and marry in a customary court before you start showing," said Ikechi to Nfudu during a long distance phone call from Nigeria.

"No," she responded. "Left to me, I'll postpone everything until the baby arrives."

"That is not an option," asserted Ikechi. "Society is not as liberal-minded as you are. Besides, my family will frown at marrying a woman with a child, even if that child was mine."

Nfudu shuddered a bit.

"Ok. We'll take it one day at a time." She mustered the courage to say.

She wondered what Ikechi would think if he knew the child had a fifty-fifty chance of not being his. With Ikechi's deep traditional views on marriage top in her mind, Nfudu became more anxious about revealing the paternity fiasco to him.

"No. Seriously think about it," he continued.

"I will…"

The more Nfudu worried about how to handle her discussion with Ikechi, the more Javier's reaction came to mind. She worried that Ikechi would have a similar or even worse reaction. However, she had no intentions of coercing Javier to take her back as their relationship had become extremely strained – lines had been drawn in the sand and they rarely talked to each other, except to discuss business related matters. Nfudu missed their relationship. They had been friends as well as lovers and had become so accustomed to one another, it was too difficult to let go. Javier still loved and respected her and with time, he forgave her and decided to speak to her about the situation and offer his forgiveness. He took her to lunch at the trendy Chocolat restaurant on Oxford Street after a whole morning working together at the Carnaby store. After they were seated, he took her hands in his and looked straight into her eyes. "My dear, I know you're not promiscuous, so I haven't lost an ounce of respect for you because of …" He started to trail off.

"I'm so sorry Javier."

"I've had time to think about everything and realized I could not offer you the acceptance and the peace of mind that comes freely with marrying someone from your own race. I'll still be there if you need me, but will try to stay out of the way in your new relationship."

"Thank you. I've been too ashamed."

"Hey! Don't be. You're carrying a baby and I need you to feel your best from now on. I still love you and consider you a member of my family. When the baby arrives, I'll take full responsibility if it turns out to be mine."

"That is a big consolation. I'm sure you'll make a great father. How is Vanessa? I've tried so many times to reach her but she hasn't returned my calls."

"She's probably pissed at you. Give her time to nurse her disappointment. Don't forget that she was gearing up to act as maid of honor and be godmother to our baby – a baby that now has only a fifty-fifty chance of being mine. Sorry to bring that up now."

"That's fine. I understand. It must be difficult for her. I'll pay her a visit this weekend."

"You should. So, what are your plans with Ikechi? Are you getting married anytime soon?"

"That depends."

"On what? If you don't mind my asking."

"Well ...I haven't told him the baby may not be his," she said, lowering her tone and looking away.

"What are you waiting for?" Javier asked, searching her face keenly for a response.

"I don't know. I mean, he's different from you," she said unsure of herself for the first time in a long time.

"How?" asked Javier.

"Well, with you, I had the assurance that you'll accept the baby even if it turned out not to be yours. With Ikechi, I don't think he'll buy that idea." In that moment, Nfudu realized that the trust in her relationship with Ikechi had not caught up to the euphoria.

"But you can't avoid it forever. The sooner you let him know, the better for everyone. Don't you think?"

"I know. I wasn't going to leave it for much longer. He's coming in a week. I'll tell him then."

16

IKECHI'S upcoming trip to London filled Nfudu with trepidation. Their love so far was beautiful, but with the uncertainty surrounding her pregnancy threatening to put everything they worked for so far to test, she was concerned things may not go her way. He arrived on a frigid day in February. It was damp and grey with an annoying drizzle threatening to last the whole day. After he settled into his suite at the Ritz, where he planned to spend the next two weeks and transact business, he took a limousine to Nfudu's flat and buzzed her. She had been waiting for two hours. The *oha* soup she spent the better half of her morning preparing for him was already cold on the stove and needed to be heated up.

"What took you so long?" Nfudu asked as she hugged him at her flat's reception desk. "I thought you'd be here two hours ago."

"Sorry love. I made a few stops before I went to the hotel. How are you? You look lovely."

"Thanks, darling." She took his hands and walked in the direction of the staircase. "You should have let me pick you at the airport."

"No… No way," responded Ikechi shaking his head. "Not in your condition. I don't want anything to happen to the baby. I shouldn't even have agreed to take the stairs when there's an elevator."

"It's only six flights," responded Nfudu laughing. "Besides, it's good exercise for me and the baby. The doctor recommended it."

"Wait," said Ikechi grabbing her by the waist and rubbing her belly after they walked two flights. "I don't see any bump. You're not eating enough?" Nfudu held the railings for support and laughed.

"Oh my goodness, darling! It's not supposed to show until I'm way past the first trimester. Don't worry so much." She unlocked the door to her flat and ushered Ikechi in, while she trailed behind him.

"Very nice!" exclaimed Ikechi. "You've got incredible taste. This is one of the cushiest flats I've ever seen. I love the combination of white and grey. And, the furniture... It matches your personality. I should have planned to stay here."

"You still could. I'm sure the Ritz will issue you a refund..."

"No. I'll be meeting several business contacts. If I stay here, there'll be a serious invasion of your privacy. We should leave things as they are. What is this aroma?"

"Oh!" exclaimed Nfudu rising from the settee. "It's the *oha* soup I made for you. I hope I got it right. My first attempt. I'll get some for you." She dished a generous quantity into a serving dish and placed some water to boil on the kettle for the *garri*. When the *garri* was ready, she signaled Ikechi to the dining table which she had decorated with her best linen, some candles and a vase filled with fresh flowers. After she set some drinks and glasses on the table, she clung on to him. "I'm so happy you're here," she said. You've made me forget all my worries."

"What do you think you're doing?" asked Ikechi as Nfudu pulled a chair for herself at the table after she released her grip. "Come here," he said tapping his laps in two quick consecutive movements. Nfudu obliged and sat on him. He scooped a spoon of soup, tasted it and fed her with it. She giggled as the spoon touched her lips and almost spurted the soup all over Ikechi. "Don't be shy. Take, eat. You're my baby and soon you'll be a baby mummy. The soup tastes like the one my mother used to make. Are you sure it's your first attempt at *oha*?"

"Yes. I'm sure. I was on the phone with Mama for almost an hour going over the recipe, while it was on the stove. It was bloody hectic. I'm glad you like it because I forgot to include *ogili*."

"That stinky bean? It's a good thing you didn't include it. By the way, I'll like you to move into my hotel for the period. I don't want you out of my sight."

"Ok," she responded, eyeing him surreptitiously.

"Ok?" Ikechi grabbed her and hugged her tightly. "Just like that?"

"Yes. I want to spend every possible minute with you. I haven't seen you in so long. It's been excruciating." Nfudu was excited about the prospect of spending two whole weeks with him. It would give both of them the opportunity to make up for lost time. After lunch, she packed a few items into a small suitcase.

"Are you sure this is all you need?" asked Ikechi.

"Yes," nodded Nfudu. "I'll come home often to get a change of clothes. Your hotel is only ten minutes away."

After they settled into the Ritz, Nfudu and Ikechi cuddled up in the bed to get warm after they treated themselves to eggnog. "My back hurts," Ikechi complained after a little while.

"Where?" asked Nfudu.

"Here." Ikechi took her hand and placed it on the trapezius muscles in his upper back.

"Wait," she said and grabbed some argan oil from her suitcase, before climbing onto his back in a perpendicular pose to give him a gentle massage. First, she sprinkled the oil in small sections of his back. Then she rubbed it all in using an up and down motion, stopping at intervals to knead him with her elbow. Ikechi grunted whenever she hit a sore spot. His "ahhs!" increased in intensity after she slid down to his buttocks to massage his gluts and inner thighs. When he couldn't bear the excitement any longer, he turned swiftly onto his stomach, causing Nfudu to gasp when she saw the size of his bulge. He threw her on the bed as she squealed and wrapped her legs around him with ease. He kissed her while they moved in a rhythmic pattern that felt extremely erotic, but at the same time felt sweet and guilt free. When they finally came, they crumpled into each other's hands kissing and caressing for hours.

Eating some late night desserts, they looked into each other's eyes as though meeting for the first time. Nfudu shuddered when she remembered that she hadn't been completely honest with him. With a clouded expression, she said, "I need to tell you something," as she assumed a more sober position.

"I'm listening," responded Ikechi, puzzled by the sudden change in mood.

"What I'm about to tell you is very difficult…"

"What is it?" asked Ikechi, his brow furrowed.

"It's about Javier."

"What about him?"

"When I got back to London, he picked me at the airport and… one thing led to another and we sort of …I slept with him that night. You have to understand… I didn't have enough time to process my feelings…I have since sorted out my feelings and broken off our engagement…"

Tears streamed down her face as Ikechi's expression changed from loving to vicious in a matter of seconds. It was a look she had never seen before nor ever wanted to see again for as long as she lived. He stormed out of his suite before she could say another word. A few moments later, he stormed right back in and asked, "So this baby is not mine?" It was half statement half question.

"There's a fifty percent chance it's yours."

"Really? You expect me to accept fifty percent?" he said thumping his fist on his chest. "Look. I didn't bargain for this. Wait a minute. Have you even ended it with him?"

"Yes… completely. The only thing between us now is work."

Ikechi nodded his head while staring angrily at her as his chest heaved frantically. Nfudu had never seen him so furious.

"So what do you want to do?" he asked, backing away from her.

"I don't know…"

"Are you planning on keeping it?"

"I didn't think there were any other options," responded Nfudu shaking her head slightly.

"You can't be planning to keep a baby that you don't know who the father is," said Ikechi, glaring at her in astonishment.

"If you're talking about an abortion… that is something I could never do. I won't dream of it." Nfudu said glaring back at him as she gained strength for the mere reason that she needed to defend her unborn child. The fact that he considered an abortion a viable option for the baby even if it only had a tiny chance of being his was a big disappointment to her. She understood that being an African man, he feared the disgrace birthing another man's baby would bring him. However, she remained adamant about her decision.

"I'll rather raise the baby by myself than kill it before it had a chance to come into this world."

"Then you'll have to raise this baby by yourself. Count me out!"

The defective cog in their positions was that he wanted to keep her sans the baby, while she wanted to be accepted baby and all. With the communication completely broken, Nfudu walked out of Ikechi's suite, took a taxi from the lobby of the hotel and headed back to her flat. She felt lost for the next couple of days and teary eyed every second that went by. Each day, she hoped he would come around and see her own side of the issue but he neither visited nor called her. After trying to call him a couple of times, only to be hung up on, she decided to give him space to process his thoughts. Three nights later, he sent his chauffeur to pick her up from her flat. Throwing on a pair of jeans, she immediately headed out to meet him. Completely oblivious to why he wanted to see her, she braced herself for the worst – complete and utter rejection. Her thoughts drifted once again to her mother's rule for dating and she imagined her mother's disappointment if she were to learn about her present predicament.

Her thoughts drifted back to Ikechi. Just then, he opened the door to let her in. To her surprise, he had a smile on his face.

"I'm sorry my darling. I shouldn't have acted so rashly. Can you forgive me?" he said after he grabbed her and kissed her on the lips.

Nfudu smiled for the first time in days. "Yes..." she whispered. "I already forgave you."

He took the bottle of champagne that was sitting on the centre table, gently removed the foil wrapping around it, and once most of the pressure was off the cork, he used his thumb and forefinger to remove it from the bottle. Nfudu watched him admiringly as he poured two glasses, handed her one, and toasted to their baby. "I love you and still want to marry you."

"I love you too," she responded as she bent over and kissed his cheek.

"You need to know that I don't blame you for what happened. I pushed you to have sex with me while you were still engaged, so it's every bit my fault as it is yours."

She cuddled up in his arms and sobbed lightly when she realized that the depression she had suffered in the past few days had disappeared as fast as it came.

"I love you. I'm so sorry." She said, kissing him again.

"That's Ok. I forgot to tell you earlier that my family concluded their inquiries on yours and everything checked out, so we have the go-ahead to proceed with the rest of the marriage rites."

"That's great!" replied Nfudu. "It's all happening so fast."

"Yeah! Pretty soon you'll be my wife."

She returned to Ikechi's suite that night, only leaving to go to work and stop by her flat every few days to get a change of clothes. Ikechi spent most of his days working and attending business meetings. They spent every night together and whenever he could, he drove her to doctor's appointments. He also helped her with several aspects of her business and was not afraid to get his hands dirty in the process. This endeared her to him as she fell more and more in love with him every day. As his stay was drawing to a close, Nfudu was anxious about being left alone to fend for herself in London. She had become so accustomed to him it was hard for her to imagine life without him. On the day of his departure, she rode with him to the airport. While they were in line waiting for his turn to check in, she grabbed her stomach and winced. "What is it, my dear?" Ikechi asked, worried by the look on her face.

"Morning sickness maybe. It's funny that I only started feeling it recently. I thought it only happened during the first few weeks of pregnancy."

"You should get some rest and something to eat once you go home. Keep your doctor's number handy, ok?"

"Ok," nodded Nfudu.

"Take care of yourself and the baby."

When they parted, the chauffeur drove Nfudu straight to her flat, where she continued to feel sick to her stomach. Two nights after Ikechi left, she became violently ill, with stomach cramps and spotting that started in the morning as little dots. By evening, it had progressed to larger amounts. There seemed to be no other option for her but to pay Doctor Harriman a visit.

"It's pretty normal to have cramps while in your condition," Doctor Harriman assured her. "We have to watch closely to make sure the spotting doesn't increase. If it does you'll have to go on bed rest until the issue resolves. ...Here is some medication to calm you down. Take a break for the next few days until you feel a little bit better."

"Ok. I will."

That night, while she slept, Nfudu dreamt that she was dressed in a luxurious long velvety black evening dress to attend a formal occasion at an unknown location. When she walked into the function, all the other guests lined up on both sides of the room and stared at her. She was the 'belle of the ball' and soon she was ushered into a back room. While there, the man who she was ushered to meet gave her a seat, but before she knew what was going on, he grabbed her hand violently, hurting her in the process. She screamed at the top of her voice. Still screaming and clenching her fists, Nfudu woke up suddenly and only untensed when she realized it was a dream. Sweating profusely, she raised her head to turn her pillow to the dry side, but felt a sharp pang in her stomach and what felt like a warm gel all over her nightgown. When she looked down on the bed, she saw a dark red liquid smeared all over her plush white bed sheet. She let out a blood-curdling scream and immediately called Javier. Several minutes later, she was driven by the Royal British Ambulance to the emergency ward. Luckily for her, Doctor Harriman, was on standby to receive her.

After her examination, the doctor informed Nfudu, that she lost her two and half month pregnancy. Javier held her close and tried to comfort her as she sobbed uncontrollably. "I'll need to keep her under observation tonight to make sure she doesn't develop any complications," Doctor Harriman said to Javier. "I have given her medication to flush out her system and prevent infection. Overnight, we'll administer anti-anxiety medication through this IV." She pointed at the intravenous device attached to Nfudu's left hand.

Javier stayed with her until morning. He left to get a change of clothes and some food for her to eat. He returned when Doctor Harriman was just completing her discharge forms.

"You can't be by yourself in the next two days," advised Doctor Harriman. "Get a friend or family member to stay with you."

"Thank you, doctor," she responded wondering who she would ask.

Javier took her to his car and insisted she stayed at the lodge, so he could watch her closely. She spent the rest of the day with him at the lodge, mostly sleeping and moping around. The following day, he took her to her flat at her insistence. However, he refused to leave her by herself. He brought her meals, fed and bathed her.

Two days after the incident, Javier mustered the courage to tell Nfudu how he had been feeling. "I'm devastated about the baby. The loss isn't yours alone to bear. It's also mine."

Nfudu was shocked by his revelation. "I'm so sorry, Javier," she said with tears welling up in her eyes. "I have been selfish in not realizing you were also hurt."

"You're not selfish. What happened to you is bad. It's just that since I got over my initial hurt regarding you and Ikechi, I've been making plans for a new baby in my life. That dream is shattered now."

"I'm so sorry," Nfudu responded weakly. "Thank you... Thank you for taking care of me."

—

Ikechi groaned in pain when Nfudu called him in Nigeria to relay the terrible news to him. "This is terrible," he said. "How are you coping?"

"I don't know. I can neither eat nor sleep. When I finally fall asleep for a few seconds, I wake up with terrible nightmares. Javier is here to help."

"Why? Couldn't you have asked either one of your brothers to stay with you?"

"There was no time. Javier is still my 'in case of emergency person' so..."

"You'll need to change that," said Ikechi, clearly disappointed. "You were in a long-term relationship with this man. I'm not comfortable with him being this close to you and you know why."

Nfudu fought back tears, but her misery was still apparent. His tone was unbearable. "He slept in the guest bedroom last night," she said. "I can assure you that there is nothing between us. Besides, I'm too ill to even think about that. You should be happy I have someone to take care of me."

"Ok. Ok, my darling. I didn't mean to upset you. That won't be good for your condition right now. I love you. Please calm down. When is he leaving?"

"Tomorrow."

"Ok. I'll have to come back sooner than planned. Can't leave you alone like this. I love you."

"I love you too."

Nfudu fell into a deep depression afterwards. Nothing seemed to cheer her up as she had grown to love the baby inside her, and even picked names for it. She decided to push forward the formal opening of the stores for another month to give herself time to fully recover. She continued to work on her collection since it was the only thing that could make her smile, but began to look at it with a different eye. Constantly, she tweaked it to match her feelings and this gave it a superb creative edge. When she wasn't working, she spent most of her time in her flat. After sundown, she walked around her neighborhood in slacks for a good dose of the evening air. Vanessa forgave her for her past indiscretions and ran to her side. She pleaded with Nfudu to move in with her and David, but to no avail. However, she came by daily to visit her. During her visits, she brought home-cooked meals, which she watched Nfudu eat to make sure it didn't end up in the trash. Javier made it a point of duty to see her whenever he was in town. With all the attention she got from Javier and Vanessa, Nfudu gradually began to bounce back to her usual self. Within two weeks, she felt strong enough to return to full-time work. She paid a visit to

Doctor Harriman to get the go-ahead she needed before she could confidently return.

"I feel great," Nfudu told Doctor Harriman during her visit.

"I'm glad to hear that. This is the best you've looked in a long time," said the doctor nodding her head in agreement. "You're very young so it's easy to bounce back. Look, I still want you to take it easy because I'm still looking into potential causes for the miscarriage especially, as you hadn't presented any underlying health problems during your prenatal checkups. I'm concerned that we may have missed something."

"Ok," responded Nfudu nodding in agreement. "I'd try not to stress my body. Besides, I'll like to get pregnant soon after getting married, so… yes, it's important to find out the cause and make sure this situation doesn't repeat itself."

"How soon are you getting married?" asked Doctor Harriman stunned by Nfudu's resilience.

"Summer 1972. August preferably for the church wedding," Nfudu replied, crossing her fingers. "We're working towards that."

"Next year! Congratulations!" Doctor Harriman stood up to hug her on the examination table. "Who is the lucky guy? Is it Javier?" she asked with a curious expression on her face.

"No… the other one – Ikechi." Responded Nfudu embarrassed.

"Oh, I shouldn't have jumped to conclusions so fast. You're a lucky girl. Congratulations!"

"Thank you!"

Back in Nigeria, marriage rites continued between Nfudu and Ikechi's family. It was an exciting time for both of them. Since a lot of the activities were going on in Nfudu's absence, she relied on regular feedback provided by Ikechi to feel as though she was a part of the process. Other than their traditional marriage, they also had a church wedding to plan. That was the difficult part considering their plan to host it in Nigeria, where all their friends and family members could attend. This meant they needed adequate time for preparation if every detail was to be perfect.

Afonwa was selected to represent Nfudu in her role as bride given that Nfudu was to be absent for the *iku-aka*. She was the natural choice for the role being that she was the oldest female child in the household.

"Afonwa …Afonwa …Afooonwaaa," Mrs. Ibe yelled in the direction of Afonwa's room.

"Mama, I'm coming."

"I called you for a reason." Mrs. Ibe said when Afonwa finally appeared. "I want to do a role play, which will involve you acting as an oblivious bride, who just discovered that a handsome young man is interested in making her his bride."

"Me?" responded Afonwa, pointing one finger at her chest.

"Yes, you," responded her mother. "Afoo, Nfudu is not around and you're the oldest. This is what I'll need you to do…"

"Mama. I've been worried about this. I'm not the one getting married, so why should I suffer this embarrassment."

"It's not an embarrassment. It's an obligation."

"I don't agree. Nfudu should have been here then to fulfill it. Why am I always the one to be called upon when things get tough, while others just relax and enjoy the privilege of their birthright?"

"Ah! Afoo! Why do you speak like that?" replied her mother, snapping both fingers in derision. "You've enjoyed more than anybody in this household. Other than me and your Father, Nfudu and your elder brothers pamper you. Stop complaining. It will be a fun experience."

"No problem Mama. But someone has to tell me what exactly I need to do on that day so I don't disgrace everybody."

"It's like this: After Ikechi's Father informs your Father about a 'beautiful fruit' residing in his household, which they have come to pluck, your father will ask if you'll agree to be plucked. You should respond that you'll consider the proposal if your family does not find the groom wanting."

Afonwa begins to laugh. A piercing sound, so unlike her usual sarcastic chuckle. "That sounds worse than I imagined. I had no clue I would be expected to speak. Anyway, I'll take it like one of my acting projects, but no one should blame me if I burst into laughter in the middle of the process o…"

"Please try not to laugh," pleaded her mother, as she chuckled herself.

-

The Iku-aka ceremony in Abasi was flamboyant and befitting of the son of a chief. Ikechi's family arrived in time with a motorcade of ten cars and gifts over and beyond what was required by tradition. Chief Ibe, his wives and children were seated in their beautiful attires when they arrived in the grand parlor, where the ceremony took place.

While the ceremony was going on, Nfudu was beside herself with joy. She couldn't wait for it to be over so she could speak to her family and get the full details of the event. She called several times, without luck, because no one was available to pick the phone. When she called at the end of the day, her mother answered.

"Nfudu, you need to practice patience," scolded her mother. "The phone was ringing non-stop while we were still carrying out the ceremony and I knew it was you."

"Sorry, Mama. I thought it was ending around four. That's why I've been calling since then."

"Yes, I know we said four, but you have to make allowance for 'African Time'. Anyway, it went very well. Afonwa represented you so well. In fact, in her traditional attire, I thought she too may be overripe for marriage," Mrs. Ibe sighed deeply.

"Mamaaa, you've come again. Please leave Afonwa alone to finish growing before pushing her into marriage. I'm so happy everything went well. How are Ikechi's parents? Do you like them?"

"Your father and Ikechi's father knew each other long ago, but they pretended not to during the ceremony to avoid endangering tradition. It was rather funny to watch. His mother – your future mother in law – is a very nice woman. I don't think she'll give you any trouble. Thank God."

"Yes o. We thank God."

"It's not easy what went on here today. I'm just happy my *Ada* is getting married. Soon, I'll be counting my grandchildren. God has done it again…"

"So Mama, what are the next steps?"

"We have to make our own inquiries," responded her mother.

"How long will that take?"

"Nfudu, *Nwayo nwayo ka eji alacha ofe di oku* – Hot soups are to be eaten slowly'"

"Ok Mama," she agreed, trying not to sound too eager any longer.

For the rest of the day, Nfudu smiled as she went about her business. She called Ikechi as soon as she woke up the following morning. "I was just about to call you," said Ikechi once he heard Nfudu's voice. "But you beat me to it. Sorry I didn't call yesterday. It was almost midnight by the time we arrived in Umuani."

"That's fine. I wasn't expecting a call from you. How did it all go? Mama was happy with the outcome."

"The right word to describe it is phenomenal. Everyone had so much fun. And Afonwa…"

"What about her?" asked Nfudu.

"She looks exactly like you!" exclaimed Ikechi. "I almost fainted when she came out in her traditional attire. She played her role marvelously. I wish you were there in person though."

"Afonwa will be happy to hear she did a good job. One thing I don't understand is why we have to carry out all these time wasting traditions."

"I don't see it that way. It's a way for our people to solidify the bonds of marriage and, it's a lot of fun. You would have agreed with me if you had been there."

"I know. Anyway, now there's no need to rush." Nfudu's voice dropped as she remembered her miscarriage. "We could stick with the original date."

"I agree."

"I'm so excited," continued Nfudu allowing herself to snap out of the dreary mood she had suddenly fallen into. She was grateful Ikechi didn't enable her continue on that path and loved him even more for it. It was impossible to catch him dwelling on the negative and she was determined to coach herself to be like that too.

"I love you," Ikechi said, "and can't wait for you to be my partner in crime."

"Me too darling. I miss you. When are you coming?"

"As soon as we complete all the steps for our traditional marriage. I'll love to be there for the store openings."

"Great! Looking forward to having you there."

-

Nfudu found renewed strength from the mental break she took from her work as well as her burgeoning relationship with Ikechi. She focused her new found energy on her stores and was surprised at how far a little break could go in helping her think more clearly and creatively. Even though opening ceremonies for the stores was rescheduled to the second week in May, demand for Nfudu's designs soared. Her summer collection, which had been tweaked and re-tweaked after the original date was moved forward, sold out in a number of weeks. Sales exceeded expectations by a hundred percent. Additional staff had to be hired to improve the chances of delivering on time.

Despite all she already had to contend with, Nfudu made updates to the décor and started work on her fall/winter collection. It usually took her several months to conceptualize her designs and even a couple more months to move them from the drawing board to the production floor. Fall/ winter being her third collection since her acclaim as a fashion designer, she wanted to leave no stone unturned and sought for inspiration everywhere she went.

Her recent misadventures spiked a new consciousness in her, but her creativity needed an immediate boost which she hoped to find through her impending nuptials with Ikechi. Though still a year away, the anticipation gave her the lift she needed to function. She felt more relaxed than she had been in a long time. Also, she was in love, getting married and fulfilling her professional dreams – all at once. It was strange for her to envisage that just a few weeks back, she had been suffering from a deep depression, only to end up happier than she could ever imagine. Had a fortune teller told her then that she would recover from the sadness she felt then, she would have asked for a refund.

17

CHIEF Ibe started formal inquiries into Ikechi's family background right after the *iku-aka* at Abasi. He sent Odimegwu and Ajukwu – Nfudu's uncles – to Umuani to conduct a thorough investigation. They set out early one Saturday morning by road with Chief Ibe's driver and houseboy to carry out their mission. When they arrived in Umuani, they first visited the traditional ruler – Eze Nnozie at his palace.

After formal introductions, Odimegwu said to him, "We have come all the way from Abasi to inquire about the Ifejaku's. Their son Ikechi is seeking the hand of our beautiful daughter in marriage."

Before Odimegwu could finish his statement, Eze Nnozie lifted a large embroidered hand fan made from cowhide and fur with H.R.H. Eze Nnozie I of Umuani embossed with rawhide on both sides. It was a signal for Odimegwu to be silent and wait to be summoned before uttering another word. After what seemed like ten whole minutes, Eze Nnozie spoke in a slow dignified tone. At the sound of his voice, everyone in the throne room – including his wives and a number of village elders stopped all movement and listened intently as though their whole lives depended on it. "What household in Abasi do you speak of?" he asked pointing his fan menacingly at Odimegwu.

"Your Highness, we came on behalf of Chief Ibe, Akajiora I of Abasi," responded Odimegwu in a frightened tone. He was unwilling to volunteer more than Eze Nnozie had asked in the moment.

"Ok," he said nodding his head. "So what information do you seek about the Ifejakus?"

"Your Highness, as is the tradition of our land, we seek to confirm that there is nothing on this earth or in the land of the spirits that will render the Ifejaku's unbefitting to marry into our family. They – the Ifejakus have made their own inquiries about our family and have found us to be untainted. We have merely come to fulfill our own end of the bargain before we surrender our daughter Nfudu to them and merge our families forever."

While Odimegwu spoke, Eze Nnozie nodded his head continuously and only stopped nodding after Odimegwu uttered the last word. "I have heard your request. I'll need you to excuse us. We'll deliberate and get back to you." He beckoned to one of his lavishly clad bodyguards. "He'll escort you to the other room. You can rejoin us after we're done."

The deliberation didn't take long. Soon, Odimegwu and Ajukwu were called back into the court.

"Eh hem…" Eze Nnozie cleared his throat after they took their seats. "I have deliberated with the elders and there is nothing… absolutely nothing that should prevent your daughter… what is her name again?" He leaned forward and placed his fan at the back of his right ear to channel the response correctly.

"Nfudu." responded Ajukwu.

"That's right," nodded Eze Nnozie, "Nfudu. …As I was saying, nothing should prevent her from marrying our son Ikechi. Chief Ifejaku is one of the most prestigious sons of our land. He is well known in these parts for his philanthropic and humanitarian efforts. I encourage you to continue with your efforts to join your families. You will find no better match." He concluded by beating his fan on his chest in three successive movements.

"Thank you, your highness," echoed Odimegwu and Ajukwu.

"Don't thank only me. Thank the elders."

"Thank you, our elders."

Their mission in Umuani didn't end there. They drove through the village square, the Catholic Church on the major road and the town hall to make further inquiries. In each location, they selected random people and presented them with the same request they made earlier to Eze Nnozie. Each person they spoke to responded with nothing but immense praise for the Ifejakus. The following day, they appeared before Chief Ibe to present their findings. He was prepared to welcome them with kola nuts and palm wine as well as goat meat pepper soup and '*isiewu*-goat head'. Four elders from their family were also present to witness the occasion.

"Good day my elders," said Odimegwu, stooping before Chief Ibe and all the elders in the room for a customary pat on the back with their hand fans.

"Good day," they all responded.

Osita, the oldest man in the family stood up as far as his hunched shoulder would permit him. He poured some palm wine on the ground as a libation to the gods, before announcing the purpose of the meeting. When he finished, Odimegwu took the floor to present the results of their mission.

"We travelled to Umuani to carry out an important assignment. We met with Eze Nnozie and spoke to many indigenes of Umuani. There is nothing that should prohibit us from marrying any member of their family."

"Wait …wait," said Osita. "So mental illness does not run in the family?"

"Yes my elder," responded Odimegwu.

"And the family is freeborn?"

"Yes my elder," nodded Odimegwu.

"The gods are smiling on us today," declared Osita. He adjusted the wrapper on his waist and beckoned to the server to pour more palm wine in his gourd and offered more libations to the gods.

"Thank God," said Chief Ibe, throwing his hands in the air. "Thank God," echoed all the elders, repeating the same gesture. Turn by turn, their gourds were refilled with palm wine as they chattered and celebrated the good news for the rest of the evening. When the celebration was over, most of the men slurred their speech. Some staggered as they retreated to their homes. After they had all left, Chief Ibe called Nfudu's mother to give her the good news. She in turn called Nfudu immediately to inform her.

Nfudu was elated.

"Mama, do you know what this means?"

"I know...We can go ahead and complete all the remaining steps. I'm happy for you my dear. Your father is travelling to Accra this week. When he returns, we'll discuss how to proceed."

"Ok, Mama. Please greet everyone back home."

–

Chief Ibe continued marriage preparations. There was nothing prohibiting a well-constituted marriage between his daughter and Ikechi. He could not imagine a better match and was elated by the way everything turned out for their families. Anyone who cared to listen heard how proud he was of his daughter and the match that was soon to be made to unite his family with that of Chief Ifejaku. It was during one of those conversations that Chief Ibe discovered something he wasn't prepared for. During the short one hour flight from Lagos to Accra, he struck up a conversation with the gentleman sitting next to him in his first-class cabin. When the topic of their discussion shifted from business to family, Chief Ibe announced that his *Ada* was getting married to the first son of the prestigious Ifejaku family from Umuani. It took him a while to realize that his proclamation had elicited an odd silence from Doctor Robert, as the man called himself.

"Do you know the family?" Chief Ibe asked when he noticed the sudden cold demeanor from Doctor Robert.

"As a matter of fact, I do. I know the Ifejaku's very well," replied Doctor Robert, while he maintained his awkward stance.

"I sense a little hesitation from you. Is anything the matter?"

"Hmm," expressed Doctor Robert. "I really shouldn't say anything because this could come back to haunt me in a really bad way. You have to promise to maintain my anonymity if I tell you what the issue is. I will be in danger of losing my life if you mention my name. In fact, the only reason I feel obliged to utter one more word about this is because I believe everything happens for a reason. Revealing this secret to you may be the sole purpose of our meeting.

"The Ifejakus are '*osus* – Outcastes'"

"What did you say?" asked Chief Ibe Starry-eyed.

"You heard me clearly. Have you looked into their family background?"

"Yes," replied Chief Ibe, nodding fervently. "Everything came out clean. In fact, I was sure that would be the case because I have known Chief Ifejaku for a long time and never heard their family was *osu*."

"I'm not surprised you said that," responded Doctor Robert shaking his head.

For the rest of the flight, Doctor Robert provided Chief Ibe with names, numbers and addresses needed to confirm his story. When he got back to Abasi, Chief Ibe immediately sent for Odimegwu and Ajukwu. In his private chambers, they discussed the secret second mission needed to further investigate the status of the Ifejaku family. The second mission started from Umuani and ended in the neighboring town of Abor. It was in Abor that the two emissaries uncovered a carefully hidden conspiracy to conceal the *osu* status of the Ifejakus.

-

The caste system amongst the Igbo people is extremely segregative to whole generations of families. Its origin could be traced back to early traditional practices in which individuals sacrificed their freedom to various deities in exchange for protection from wars and famine. Descendants of those individuals continued to be identified as *osu* – outcast. Those tainted by that label are considered inferior and excluded from certain societal activities. This practice still persists and continues to wreak havoc in the marriage institution – the only part of Igbo life that keeps the *osu* tradition intact.

Chief Ibe was a very traditional man, who believed strongly in the segregation upheld by this caste system as were so many men of his stature. He was dumbfounded that his daughter was almost given away to be married to an *osu*, and made an urgent call to Nfudu in London.

"My daughter," he said after they exchanged pleasantries. "I have some bad news for you."

"What is it, Papa? Firstly, how bad is this news?"

"Very bad, my dear. Please make sure you're seated."

Nfudu couldn't imagine what could be so bad. Her heart sank into her chest.

"Did anyone die?"

"No. God forbid!" responded Chief Ibe, circling his head twice with his hands and then snapping his fingers.

Nfudu heaved a sigh of relief. "Then what is it, Papa? Please tell me. I don't like the suspense."

"It's Ikechi…"

"What happened to Ikechi?" she asked frantically.

"We performed another set of investigations after some important information came to light… "

"What information?" Nfudu interrupted her father before he could complete his sentence.

" *'Nwee ndidi* – be patient' let me finish….."

"Ok Papa," responded Nfudu, breathing heavily. She hoped it was nothing too terrible as she wasn't ready to handle any more problems.

Chief Ibe told her about the passenger he met on the flight to Accra and everything else that occurred afterwards.

"It was by an unexpected stroke of luck that we discovered they are *osus*!"

"What? How? How can they be freeborn one day and then *osu* the next?"

"I don't know," responded Chief Ibe. "I'm devastated. This will cause our family a whole lot of embarrassment. Your mother and I have told everyone we know about your pending marriage."

"Hey!" exclaimed Nfudu. "Why this trouble now? Just when I thought everything was well with my world… now, this."

Nfudu did not know what to make of the news she just received from her father. There was no doubt in her mind that he had done a thorough job to prove why she could not marry a man that up until a week or so ago was his top choice for her. She was aware of the *osu* tradition in Igbo land, but she had never imagined she would be so closely affected by it nor thought it would be a deal breaker for her.

"Is there nothing we can do, Papa?" She asked, devastated by the curveball life had just thrown her. "What do you mean?" Chief Ibe responded, irritated by her question. "Absolutely nothing can be done. I'm highly disappointed with the things I found out about that family. In fact, the problem is not only that they are *osus*, it's that they go to such great lengths to hide it. You simply cannot marry Ikechi. We have halted all marriage negotiations, returned the gifts received from his family at the *iku-aka* and informed our kith and kin about the unfortunate end to the marriage proposal."

Nfudu stopped listening to her father minutes into his tirade. She was contemplating her next line of action. Caste had never been a criterion for her in choosing a marriage partner, so she did not see how Ikechi being an *osu* should affect her relationship with him. She loved him and still wanted to marry him. They had gone through so much together and prevailed. The pregnancy, his initial reaction and eventual acceptance of the situation showed how much he loved her. She wondered if her father's opinion on Ikechi would have been different if he knew about the pregnancy – and if it was still viable. Her father's voice jolted her while she played these thoughts in her head.

"I want you to end all relations with that boy. Have you heard me? You can pick any man from Abasi and environs to marry. I can recommend a few to you. Besides, you'll have no problem meeting someone new with your beauty, wealth and brains."

"It's not that easy Papa."

"Well, we'll have to find a way out."

After she got off the phone with her father, Nfudu's first instinct was to call Ikechi, but decided against it. She was not brave enough to handle the topic at hand with him in that moment. Also, she wasn't sure he had heard this news, so she decided to wait for him to call her first. Unfortunately for her, the wait lasted three days. Furious, she decided to call him to hear his side of the story. She waited till it was seven o'clock in Lagos to ensure he was home from his office.

"Hello." He said.

"Hi, Ikechi. How are you doing?"

"Fine love," he responded "Been meaning to call you. It's been so crazy around here."

Nfudu was stunned by his oblivion. "It's been three days since I heard from you. I assumed you were avoiding me."

"Impossible!"

"Father gave me some very disturbing news. I was wondering if you had anything to say about it."

"What exactly did he say?"

Nfudu told him the news she got from her father, but left out details about how he found out. Ikechi listened intently.

"Are you aware your family is *osu*?"

Ikechi paused for a minute before responding.

"I don't understand what you're getting at. I'm not aware my family is anything of that sort. Do you think I'll hide such a thing from you?"

"I don't know. I've asked myself the same question and wondered why you hadn't confided in me about your family history. It's a betrayal of sorts to keep such vital information away from someone you want to marry, especially if that person is completely honest with you."

"Have you been completely honest?" he asked derisively.

"Why? What do you mean?" asked Nfudu. "The biggest issue I have ever had to contend with – that relating to our child's paternity – I discussed with you. I deserve the same level of honesty from you."

"I'm sorry darling. I didn't mean to say you haven't been honest. I was dazed by the news you just gave me."

"So do you know anything about it?"

"Absolutely not!" Ikechi replied vehemently.

"I'm confused. Then why did father say…"

"I'm confused too. Give me the chance to confirm this news with my father and get back to you."

Nfudu found Ikechi's response strange, so she called her father to clear her confusion.

"Papa, are you sure about Ikechi?"

"What do you mean by am I sure?"

"Have you discussed the findings with his family?"

"Yes. It was done right away. It's our tradition to return the gifts offered during the *iku-aka* in circumstances like this and our emissaries confirmed they were delivered to the right members of the Ifejaku family. Also, because *osus* are lower class, communications between our families have ceased. From now on we have to communicate through intermediaries. Does that answer your question?"

"Well, I spoke to Ikechi and he sounded surprised by the news, so I'm confused."

"You see!" exclaimed Chief Ibe. "This is why I say you cannot trust 'them'. These are people that have gone to great lengths to hide their status. I'm not surprised by his denial. Count your losses and move on from that man. This is my final warning."

Despite Chief Ibe's convictions, Nfudu mustered all the courage she could garner to ask the question that had been plaguing her mind for days.

"Papa, what will happen if I go ahead and marry Ikechi?"

"Nfudu?"

"Yes, Papa."

"Nfudu …Nfudu. How many times did I call you?"

"Three times Papa."

"OK. I want you to hold your ear and listen carefully. If you marry that man, not only will our whole family automatically become *osus*, terrible things could happen to you and your future children. Should I say more? In fact, continuing communication with their family can bring curses onto ours. Any interactions between the two families from henceforth will be carried out through representatives for both families. Your uncle Odimegwu and Ajukwu had to receive special cleansing for their role in these transactions."

Nfudu did not know what to make of everything she just heard. All she knew was that there was no way she would consider giving up Ikechi for such a meaningless traditional belief. She had heard about people who married *osus* doing very well in all areas of life. Yet, she didn't know how to challenge the status quo if Ikechi could not be counted on to help make the fight easier through his sudden avoidance of her. She forgave his silence because she could only imagine the shame and embarrassment he felt. It was obvious to her that he had lied about his knowledge of the situation. To allow him save face, she decided to give him as much time and space as he needed to recover, before proceeding with the difficult conversations she knew they needed to have.

It was later that Nfudu found out the truth about Ikechi's lineage. Her mother told her the painful story during an hour-long phone call from Nigeria. According to her, Ikechi's family members were not traditionally *osus*. Their bloodline became tainted when Ikechi's great Uncle Odunna, the 'black sheep' of their family insisted on marrying an *osu* after numerous pleas from his family not to. This incident, which occurred over twenty years ago succeeded in tainting the Ifejaku family for generations to come. For so many years, the family carefully hid this truth. Chief Ifejaku quietly paid off everyone armed with the information and in the position to reveal it to potential suitors for his children. He was rumored to have threatened assassination towards anyone who crossed him on the matter and to have actually carried out the threat a few times. Since only a few people in Umuani were aware of the Ifejaku's status, their family enjoyed a 'normal' existence – married whomever they pleased – sometimes refusing requests for marriage on the grounds that the respective families were *osu*.

18

CHRISTMAS of seventy-one was the loneliest Nfudu had ever spent – Javier was in France with his entire family, while Ikechi was in Lagos. Nonetheless, she welcomed her time alone and used the opportunity to focus on getting the stores ready for their formal opening in the New Year, after shifting her deadline twice in the past year. She was determined to satisfy her partners – who had been unhappy with the delays – but gave some consideration because of the personal challenges they knew she faced. They were also able to look the other way because of the stellar performance of the stores, her summer collection and the rave reviews her fall/winter collection was already garnering in the wake of the openings.

Nfudu was less optimistic about her strained relationship with her father. They hardly spoke any longer, and when they did, their conversation was odd at best as neither one of them wanted to address the 'elephant in the room'. Each knew where the other stood on the matter of Ikechi and treaded carefully to minimize the number of explosive episodes between them. Chief Ibe was adamant about what needed to be done and hoped Nfudu wouldn't be so foolish to go against the wishes of her entire family to marry Ikechi. Nfudu had her own convictions about the matter and felt those strongly.

"How is Javier?" Chief Ibe asked during one of his strained conversations with Nfudu.

"I guess he's fine."

"Please give our regards to him."

"Ok. Papa..." Nfudu could only imagine that her father would rather she married Javier than Ikechi at that point. This made her wonder if one taboo was now completely acceptable to him because it had been replaced by a detestable, less bearable one.

While her relationship with her father deteriorated, what she shared with Ikechi recovered after months of semi estrangement between them. Their communication had been sparse at first but became more frequent when they both realized they missed each other. They agreed to put their issues aside and retain their commitment to tie the knot. Their wedding was moved forward indefinitely with hopes that their families would soon sort out their differences. Their love grew stronger as Ikechi continuously wooed her with every trick in the book. He called her every day, sent her flowers and chocolates on almost a daily basis and surprised her every now and then with little blue boxes from Tiffany.

"I don't think this issue will ever be resolved between our families." Ikechi confided, during one of their phone conversations. "But I still have to marry you no matter what. To avoid the resentment we're bound to face, we'll have to avoid Nigeria and make either England or Barcelona our home. I'll be the best husband you could ever imagine and the best father to our children."

"Stop!" said Nfudu. Her eyes were filled with tears and her voice choked with emotion. "I'll never stop loving you. I'll marry you now and damn all the consequences, but I fear neither of us will be able to execute our grand plans without the support of our families. It will be hellish and lonely to be disowned by my father."

"I know and I don't want that for you. Believe me, that's the only part that breaks my heart. Maybe he'll come around someday."

"No he won't," said Nfudu persuasively. "I know father will never come around, so there's no point in waiting for him to do so."

"I'm glad we're on the same page I miss you terribly."

"I miss you too. Do you know what I wish I could do right now?"

"Get between the sheets?" asked Ikechi mischievously.

"No!" protested Nfudu giggling. "I just want to cuddle."

"I feel so bad we can't do that. We have to vow never to spend another Christmas apart. Unfortunately, I also won't be able to make it for your opening. My plans to be in London fell through at the last minute."

"Ohh!" whined Nfudu. "I was hoping you'll be here."

"Don't worry. I'll come before the end of March."

"I'll be waiting for you."

Having worked through the Christmas holidays up until New Year, Nfudu was able to achieve a lot. She finalized inventory for the stores, drew up records, trained and retrained staff and applied finishing touches to the décor. By New Year's Day, the shops were ready to go. Only a few items were outstanding, and these were expected to be completed at least two days before the opening ceremonies. Her entire team was indispensable at that time. They worked all hours of the day, and some forfeited their holiday time to help her achieve the dream of opening two weeks after New Year a reality. In return, Nfudu provided them with a generous Christmas bonus and a promise of additional time off when they got over their crunch.

The night before the opening, Nfudu fought off her anxiety by taking a nice long soothing bath and drinking some lemon and chamomile tea to calm her nerves. She settled into bed right after dinner, with a nice book and some aspirin, and dozed off soon after. In the morning, she felt refreshed and ready to take on the challenge. The first thing she did was to go to the Regent store for a quick evaluation of the venue and found everything to be in order. She added finishing touches to the décor and convened with her staff to provide them with final instructions. Pieces from the collection were perfectly displayed – some hung on mannequins – others were at the shop window – while a majority hung from racks by style and category. A good number of pieces were showcased by models, positioned in strategic areas in the store. They looked exquisite as they struck poses while avoiding interactions with anyone in order to create a real-life mannequin effect. The idea for the models was Vanessa's who argued they would give life to the clothes and make them show better. Nfudu thought it was an excellent idea and went as far as handpicking the models herself. She made sure they came in all shapes and sizes to show that her designs did not cater only to tall skinny girls – but to every woman.

It was a different story when she got to the Carnaby store. The catering company hired to provide refreshment at that location was late. She panicked, because Carnaby, being the larger of the two stores was expected to draw a larger crowd as well as attract bigger press coverage. She made a few calls to see if she could get another catering company to cover for them. Just as she was completing her negotiation with one, Gina came into her office.

"They're here," she said.

"Thank God," exclaimed Nfudu relieved she didn't need to go through the process of hiring another caterer at such short notice.

"What happened?" Nfudu asked the catering company's manager when she stepped into her office.

"We're really sorry," the manager pleaded. "I underestimated the amount of time the hors-d'oeuvres was going to take to be completed. I promise it won't happen again."

"No problem," said Nfudu gathering her things to leave. "Gina will brief you on how we want things." She hurried off the door to the parking lot and into her car and headed in the direction of her flat to get ready for the event.

Nfudu looked incredibly beautiful in one of her designs – a flirty emerald green midi dress. The dress highlighted her toned arms and beautiful shoulders in its halter style. Heads turned to catch a glimpse of her when she walked through the small path created by reporters as she walked into the Regent Street store.

"What is your vision for the store?" asked a member of the press after another asked, "What inspired you?" Before she could answer either one of them, another immaculately dressed reporter from the London Times asked, "What are your biggest wins, regrets and plans for the future?"

"I'm not sure which to answer first," Nfudu said smiling. "At this rate, I may have to get a double," she concluded jestingly, inviting laughter from the crowd. "Starting with the first, 'our' vision is to make

Nfudu Stores a 'one-stop fashion shop' for Londoners and all of Europe. Our clothes are made for everyone, and with the most delicate, yet durable fabrics sourced specifically to bring out the best in every single one of our clientele." She picked the hem of her dress on both sides and let it drop gently, creating a fluid movement, "The fabric for my dress was sourced from India. That's how far we're willing to go to get the best." As she was about to answer the second question, her publicist wriggled through the crowd to her side and led her through the horde of reporters towards the direction of the store. "Excuse me," Nfudu said, "There's plenty of time to answer all your questions during the media slot. Please bear with me." They all trailed after her as she made her way into the store.

Inside, everything was set up like she had instructed. The décor looked magnificent and her designs looked elegant in their placement all around the store and on the models. The entertainers moved the crowd with their comedy, while patrons – mostly society men and women – browsed the collection and drank champagne from tall glasses, while they listened to the main comedy act via the speakers in the ceiling. They shopped for every single piece in the collection. Staff struggled to keep up with the demand as it far exceeded their expectations. The outfits worn by the models sold out within an hour; so the cashiers had to create back orders for the excess. Nfudu's outfit was the first to be sold out and the lineup of orders created for the emerald green dress made it inescapably the most popular dress of the year.

"How do you feel today?"

"Are you ready…?"

Another horde of reporters bombarded Nfudu as she made her way out of her car in the parking lot of the Carnaby store. Since the two stores were opening on the same day, she programmed her arrival at each location to align with the time her guests of honor were scheduled to arrive. The press was made aware of that schedule. The photographers positioned themselves to get the perfect shot of her dress – which was already 'the talk of the town' by the time she was leaving Regent Street. After addressing the reporters outside, she stepped into the store and was overwhelmed by what she saw. Carnaby was brimming with patrons, photographers, models, friends, family and entertainers. She thought the event planner did an amazing job putting together all the pieces that culminated in the exquisite affair before her. Javier was at the event long before Nfudu arrived. He ran to her side when he saw her.

"Welcome to Carnaby," he said with a slow sensual smile cutting across his lips.

"Thank you. Look at all this!" she exclaimed. "I'm speechless." Nfudu was grateful Javier was able to pull himself out of work to be in London for the events. As a silent partner, he was under no obligation to help with the details, but he did it anyway.

"This is the first day of your whole life," he said.

"Don't make me ruin my makeup, Javier." She said, clasping her hands over her mouth and blinking twice.

They were joined by her brothers – Emeka and Dike – who since morning had been incredibly busy attending to patrons and helping move things along between the floor, cashiers, entertainers and the press. After they chatted for a few minutes, Javier took Nfudu's hand and guided her through the crowd to the V.I.P. section. There he introduced her to a variety of people – most notable amongst them being the Mayor of London – Mayor Greenwich – the Duke of Edinburgh, his beautiful wife and his niece, who was about Nfudu's age. His niece was stunningly beautiful, with deep red hair and startling green eyes. She introduced herself as Samantha.

The crowd quieted down when Mayor Greenwich presented the opening speech. He praised Nfudu, her talent and entrepreneurial spirit, and described her as "the best fashion find since Chanel," which invited cheers from the crowd. He lauded all members of Nfudu's organization for their loyalty and hard work.

"You have made all Londoners proud." He concluded his speech by saying.

"That was an amazing speech," whispered Samantha to Nfudu, as she clapped with the rest of the guests.

"I agree!" responded Nfudu. "I'm so glad he could make it. Just yesterday, we weren't sure if he could. He had to skip other engagements that were every bit as important as ours to be here."

"You're a lucky girl," quipped Samantha.

"Oh! And thank you also for coming. I really appreciate it."

"It's my pleasure. I heard so much about you from Javier and the press. You're pretty impressive I must say – and beautiful too."

"Thank you," responded Nfudu, blushing underneath her brown skin. "You're also gorgeous. If you don't mind my asking what do you do for a living?"

"Professional modeling. My entire body of work is in America."

"How come?"

"I moved there right after college on a modeling contract with the Cooper Agency and have lived there since then. I moved back to the UK just a couple of months ago."

"Are you happy with your move?"

"It's been really crazy. A real culture clash," explained Samantha, gesticulating with her hands and whipping her hair from side to side. "I forgot how different things were down here."

Javier walked stealthily behind them.

"It's time to meet some other guests," he said.

"Please excuse me, Samantha. It was nice meeting you," Nfudu said extending her hand for a handshake.

"Same here," she responded taking Nfudu's hand.

In a different section of the store, Javier introduced her to a shipping magnate and his wife, who were on vacation from Australia. He also introduced her to a few magazine editors and a couple of his friends from the worlds of showbiz before ushering her into her newly renovated office for a quick bite when she began to feel faint. Inside the office, Vanessa and Gina were hurriedly sorting pieces of her collection to move to the shop floor to replace items being sold out.

"I'll be back in ten," said Javier as he scurried off after Nfudu settled down to a few bites of hors-d'oeuvres. He returned a few minutes later to take her back to the party.

Seeing her friends and family at work, made Nfudu teary-eyed for the mere fact that they always came to her rescue. She was particularly pleased that Javier hadn't pulled out his partnership interest in her business like he had wanted to when he first found out about Ikechi. His intentions had not been malicious; rather, he wanted to give her space to pursue her new relationship as well as create room for his own healing. In the end, he let go of his hurt and agreed to leave things as they were. As a compromise, Nfudu provided him with additional interest in the stores and gave him right of first offer in any new stores to be opened under her brand in the future.

Party guests drank and socialized until long after Big Ben chimed at midnight. As soon as the last guest left at two o'clock in the morning, the cleaners got to work right away to remove the awful mess that was left. They rearranged each of the stores for business to resume by noon. A record number of shoppers were expected to swarm the shops after news of the event hits the papers in the morning. Nfudu left Carnaby around six o'clock in the morning and even though she was extremely tired, she couldn't imagine going to sleep without giving her mother a report. Mrs. Ibe was still a little groggy from sleep when she picked the phone. "I fell asleep after waiting so long for your call. How did it all go?"

"Mama, it couldn't have gone better."

"Oooh! That's very good." Mrs. Ibe exclaimed.

"My friends and my brothers rallied around for me on this one. You need to thank them."

"That is wonderful. Your father is still sleeping; otherwise, he would have loved a word with you. I'll give him the news. You should try to get some sleep now before you fall sick."

"Ok, Mama. Sorry for waking you."

"No problem. I was already up."

Nfudu slept around eight o'clock but set her alarm for ten as she needed to be at the Carnaby store by eleven in the morning. She had barely had an hour of sleep before Gina – the Store Manager at the Carnaby store – pressed the buzzer. "I have a terrible headache," complained Nfudu.

"It will go away as soon as you see this," responded Gina handing her a bunch of papers and chattering excitedly, "We did it! We made front page news."

"Wow!" exclaimed Nfudu as she saw her image on the cover of the British Voice and read the headline: *"Young designer Nfudu wows again."*

She was photographed in her beautiful green dress as she was stepping out of her limo in Carnaby. The article inside the paper described the events from the night before, results of her interview and several pictures of her guests and models wearing pieces of her collection. The article concluded its write-up with: "...*She was well known for her designs before the stores, but now she has become a household name and broken all barriers to success.*"

There was no longer any doubt in Nfudu's mind that the opening events were a success. Other than the press acknowledgments, numerous items from her collection were sold out. Enough was earned in one night to not only pay for the event but to reinvest in the business. It was now left to her team to deliver on the back orders received that day to reap the full financial benefits.

When she arrived at the stores at eleven prompt, Nfudu was surprised to see Javier helping her workers set up for business that day. His knowledge of business was invaluable at times like that. "I didn't expect you here this early," she said to him.

"I was up even earlier. I just left Regent Street. Everything is ready to go over there."

"That means I don't need to rush over there then. Thank you."

"You're welcome."

"Let's grab lunch tomorrow. It's been a while."

"Works for me."

That day was more hectic than any other Nfudu's staff had ever experienced at the stores. It was a miracle that none of them collapsed from lack of sleep the night before. Customers streamed in and out eager to try on items and interact with the staff and other visitors. Many of the visitors demanded to see Nfudu in person and she obliged a few. Many asked for her autograph and most marveled at how young she was. When the stores finally closed at eight, Javier drove Nfudu to her flat and headed to the Lodge.

They met for lunch the following day, feeling more rested than the day before.

"I'm so happy we were able to sneak out," said Nfudu. "Thank you, Javier."

"What for?" asked Javier raising his hands midway into the air

"For the help you selflessly provide all the time."

"Have you forgotten that I own part of the business? I want it to succeed by all means."

His words melted Nfudu's heart. As she was about to drift into one of her daydreams, Javier continued.

"The event was incredibly successful. I admire your visionary ideas and your ability to turn anything you touch into gold."

"Thank you," responded Nfudu, shifting uncomfortably in her seat. "Had you not been by my side to help execute them, those ideas would have gone down the drain."

"Don't flatter me. It was all you. I mostly stood by and watched."

"Don't underestimate yourself," she said emphatically.

"So what's next in the pipeline?"

"I was thinking about opening sister stores in Paris, Milan and Athens. Maybe sometime next year?"

"Won't that be biting off more than we can chew? I'm worried it may become too overwhelming. It is too much too soon."

"I don't think so," argued Nfudu. "The London stores are a big success. We need a presence in other high fashion destinations before other designers saturate the market with our concept. In fact, if we step in sooner, we could get the best possible locations, establish a loyal clientele and leverage the publicity we enjoy with our London stores to make the new ones a success."

"You sound so sure about this. Give me time to familiarize myself with the concept and get back to you. Let me inform you that if we're to do this, it will require a huge capital outlay and one or two additional partners to make it happen."

"I know."

"Let's table the issue and discuss when next I'm in London."

With the store openings out of the way, Nfudu shifted her focus to designing her spring/summer collection. Her staff worked diligently day and night to fulfill their back orders and manage the stores successfully. Visitors to the stores increased by over two hundred percent making it necessary to hire additional staff to cater to the constant flock of shoppers – a large majority of which were tourists from all over the world – The United States, Asia, Africa and Australia. She visited each store location at least thrice each week. While there, she interacted with the customers, who were always so excited to meet her. The feedback from the interactions influenced her designs and helped them evolve.

Three months after the formal opening, the profit from the stores soared by a whopping sixty percent from the past quarter. This impressive result was all Javier needed to make a decision about Nfudu's requests for expansion to international locations. He dropped by to see her at the Carnaby store during a stop in London.

"I've thought a lot about our discussion," he said. "You're one of the best business women alive today and I fully trust your instincts. We should go ahead with the new stores."

"Really?" Nfudu was wide-eyed with excitement. She got up from her seat and gave Javier a standing ovation before hugging him. "I knew you would come around. I've been so busy with the stores and haven't had time to think about anything else."

"Well. I didn't need too much convincing."

"Thank you for believing in me… I mean us."

"Congratulations! I have other businesses of my own to run, so I'll let you take the lead in getting this off the ground. Let me know where l can deliver the best value."

"Thanks love." The words were out of her mouth before she realized she had used a term of endearment to address him.

Javier pretended not to have noticed the slip. However, he could not erase the smirk on his face as it occurred to him that Nfudu's acumen, which made her extremely competent in making business decisions, did nothing for her when it came to personal relationships. "Why did she ruin our relationship to be with Ikechi? I, who loved her more than anyone else on this earth" he thought.

Nfudu did not notice the smirk, but she saw his change in mood. "Are you okay?"

"Sure. I'm fine. I'll need to run now though. Contact the real estate agent to start looking for stores in Paris, Athens and Milan.

Location is everything. Also, consider who we may ask to partner. Later, we can hash out the other details."

"Thank you," responded Nfudu, "I'm so grateful I have you on my side."

"You're the mastermind behind the success of the business. There's no need to thank me."

With so much more work to do on the international locations, Nfudu trusted she could still rely on Javier as a partner to get the ball rolling before other designers saturated the market with her winning concept. She was ecstatic that their relationship improved significantly. This, she owed to the opportunities they had to work together. The guilt she harbored after their breakup had slowly dissipated to make way for a respectable working relationship. They had been great as a couple, but as business partners, there was nothing they couldn't conquer together. Her heart now belonged to Ikechi, although their relationship was considered a taboo by her family. This threw a curveball in her joy; she wondered if she could truly ever be happy, or was just in the world to simply exist.

News about the London stores reached Lagos when the advertising campaign for the pioneer set of students for the Lagos Fashion School was just kicking off. The publicity garnered from their success, and the fact that Nfudu had become a household name helped spike student's interest. Applications exceeded the number of spaces available causing the admission team to devise creative means for selecting the most deserving – not just on the basis of submitted applications – but also on the results of their face-to-face interviews. With the first set of classes scheduled to resume in September, Nfudu worked very hard to fulfill competing demands in London, so she could make it to Lagos in time for the school opening.

19

"**MY** goodness! You tricked me. I thought your flight was tomorrow," Nfudu said, as she jumped on Ikechi in full view of the shop employees and customers when he walked into the Carnaby store.

"I wanted to surprise you." He kissed her on her mouth before gently putting her down. She dragged him into her office, closed the door behind them and threw him down on the settee, planting a long kiss on him. Gasping for breath, he lifted her up with both hands as she giggled mischievously.

"The store is huuuge. I'm so proud of you. Come here." He grabbed her for another hug.

"Let me show you around. I don't want the staff to start wondering if there's hanky-panky occurring behind these doors."

"They don't know who I am. So it doesn't matter."

"You're kidding! They would have figured out by now that you're my fiancé, who I was expecting tomorrow..." She grabbed his hand and dragged him out of her office. She introduced him to all the employees on the shop floor. While she gave him a tour of the entire store, she caught her staff whispering from the corner of her eye.

"You have some explaining to do," Nfudu said to Ikechi. "What made you decide to come in today? I was preparing for your arrival tomorrow."

"I wanted to surprise you."

"But, how did you know where to find me? What if I wasn't here? I could have been at Regent Street or my flat?"

Ikechi laughed at her insinuations.

"I've spoken to you every day for the past three months. Your whereabouts at this time of the day on a Wednesday was a very easy guess for me. If I hadn't seen you here, I would have gone to your flat and waited until you returned. I always carry your key with me."

"Well, it was a pleasant surprise. I'm not complaining. Bring more surprises like this my way and you and I will work out just fine. I love you."

"I love you too, dear. From the accounts I heard from you, the stores are a hit. What you didn't tell me was how beautiful the décor was. The locations are also impressive. I'm really proud of you."

"Thank you, sweetie. I'm so happy to see you."

"Me too. I thought I was going to die if I spent one more day away from you."

—

The lovebirds headed straight to Nfudu's flat. On their way, they completely avoided the topics they so clearly needed to discuss and dived into enjoying each other's company. Seconds after stepping into Nfudu's bedroom, Ikechi picked her up and threw her on the bed. He then swiftly took off her shoes and pulled her clothes off before pulling his trousers and slowly unbuttoning his shirt, all the while staring at her as she looked at him in awe. After his shirt came off, he straddled her, and gave her a quick kiss on the mouth before he rested his taut body on hers. He was gentle at first, but slowly he increased his frequency until they both came together in perfect sync before collapsing feverishly in each other's arms. For the next few minutes, they kissed and caressed, while Nfudu reflected on how far they had come in the last one and half years. She smiled unconsciously, unaware that he was looking down at her.

"Wow!" exclaimed Ikechi. "I've been waiting to do that for months. What are you smiling about?"

"I wasn't smiling…" Nfudu responded, abashed and thinking about how much chemistry they shared. It had been unaltered by their time apart. While these thoughts were going through her mind, he grasped her by the waist and flipped her so that she straddled him on bended knees. He took a good long look at her, lifted his torso upwards and locked her into a kiss that culminated into another round of lovemaking that lasted another twenty minutes and left both of them panting in the end.

Ikechi was the first to recover.

"I want to take you to Barcelona for a couple of days."

"Sounds nice," responded Nfudu, "But I doubt there's time for a holiday. I just settled into business at the stores."

"Trust me, I don't think there could be a better time for one."

"When do you have in mind?"

"Next week."

"Next week? Wow! That's too soon. I have so much to do at the store. And the fashion school... they won't be able to reach me when they need to if I suddenly take off for days next week. It's a critical time for us."

"We can arrange for people to sit in for you in all areas of your business. You have the most amazing staff so I don't see any reason to worry at all. We need this time alone together to recuperate and plan our future together. Don't you think?"

"I agree. I'll have to double my speed this week to put everything in order before we leave. Can we sail and visit the beaches when we get there?"

"Coincidentally those two items are on my list," responded Ikechi.

"Wow! I can't wait. It's time I got back into the groove," she said excitedly.

"Yeah! You need to. You're turning into some type of workaholic," he responded with a smirk.

"I completely agree." Nfudu responded smiling. "I'm hungry. Let's order Chinese then I'll prepare a bath for you. I'm glad I get the chance to take care of you."

"Me too. It's great practice for when we finally get hitched."

Nfudu chuckled. "We've been practicing for a long time," she said.

Ikechi tended to his business out of Nfudu's office at the Carnaby Store, which gave her the moral support she so badly needed to cope with the amount of work she had to do. Due to their close proximity, he noticed that Nfudu and Javier were still extremely close. It made him furious when they spoke on the phone several times each day and for long periods of time. He also noticed that the staff adored Javier and spoke highly of him, which made him feel like an outsider. He confronted Nfudu about this when they returned to the flat on the second day.

"What was that with you and Javier? You remain too close to him."

"How do you mean? We're just partners. There's nothing even remotely romantic between us," responded Nfudu stunned by his accusations.

"You're constantly on the phone with him. I mean… how many times do you need to speak to one person in a day? And the staff…"

"What about the staff?"

"The way they talk about him. Like he's some god. They didn't know I was within earshot this afternoon as they went on and on about Javier and how he's made his mark in the business world…on and on. It was irritating."

"I'm sorry you feel that way. That has nothing to do with my relationship with him. They know him intimately. He's their boss. That's it. They only just met you, but have heard so much about you from the gossip mill. I'm sure they'll adore you even more than Javier when they get to know you. You have to be patient."

"Ok… Why do you have to talk for so long with him, though?"

"It's just business. We communicate as often as we need to, to address things that come up during the day. He's a partner in all of my businesses and this is a crucial period for us. All our business interests are going through the most critical phases of their existence. We only discuss work. I promise you that I don't view him as a romantic interest anymore."

"I know that, but what about him? Does he view you romantically?"

Nfudu was worn out by their conversation and reflected for a minute before she provided a response. "I don't think so. He's never given me the impression that he does since we broke up."

"You need to be careful. I know guys. He may still want you and yet pretend he has no feelings for you, while he waits for the right moment to pounce."

"No no," said Nfudu shaking her head. "I don't think so. You don't know him. If he had his way, he would give up his share of the business to avoid being caught up in anything awkward."

"Why don't you pay him off? Give him the option and sever relations with him. I can buy his share."

Nfudu did not think it was necessary to eject Javier from the business. She found him a very valuable partner and did not agree with Ikechi, so she decided to bite her tongue for the rest of the evening to avoid a massive quarrel. The argument left a sour taste in her mouth and they went to bed that night barely speaking to each other. The following day, Ikechi worked out of a hotel lounge, and subsequently reduced his appearance at the stores to short periods of time. He reckoned it was best to distance himself from things he didn't fully understand and from battles he knew he couldn't win. He hoped to address any outstanding issues with Nfudu after they were married.

-

Nfudu and Ikechi put their argument behind them as they headed off to Barcelona. He was particularly happy about his plan to propose to her on the trip. Even though he had asked her in so many ways to marry him, he had never done so through chivalry. The proposal initiated by the *iku-aka* ceremony, which had since been aborted could not be counted as valid anymore, since the process it was meant to usher in had been completely broken down by the failure of compromise. Ikechi did not consider himself a romantic, but he recognized a formal proposal to be an essential step forward in their relationship. In his viewpoint, chivalry was still very much alive and kicking and still expected by women everywhere.

To carry out his plan, Ikechi asked Gina to accompany him to Tiffany and together they picked the perfect engagement ring for

Nfudu. He then made arrangements with the hotel staff in Barcelona to place flowers, champagne and chocolate in their hotel room to create the right mood for him and his fiancée. Nfudu was completely oblivious of Ikechi's plans, which were initiated weeks before he arrived in London.

"What should I pack?" asked Nfudu the night before they were to leave, having left everything until the last minute.

"All the pretty spring clothes you have my darling." She and Ikechi had put their argument completely behind them.

"That means I'll need all the luggage bags I can find," Nfudu said giggling.

"No. Two bags will do. We're only spending four days…"

"Two bags? That should work since I expect to spend most of my time on the beach. I hear Barcelona has the most beautiful beaches."

"Pristine …pristine is the word."

Nfudu packed the prettiest clothes she could find for spring – elegant dresses, pretty scarves and shoes to match any occasion. Except for the few masterpieces she had acquired; either as gifts or purchase of heirlooms from the auctions she attended to support various worthy causes, she barely owned any jewelry. She also packed eight swimming suits as she figured she may need two per day.

–

The sleep Nfudu was able to squeeze in during the one hour flight from London to Barcelona was all she needed to rejuvenate her battered body. She barely slept the night before trying to complete outstanding work. When they arrived, she was woken by Ikechi.

"Darling we're here."

"Where?" she asked surprised.

"Barcelona," he responded with a sensuous smile.

"Don't tell me I slept the whole way."

"That's fine. I tried not to wake you up. You needed to rest to be able to function and stomach all I have planned for this trip. We have limited time here, so it would be a shame if we wasted our time sleeping rather than engaging in all the activities the beautiful city of Barcelona has to offer."

Nfudu took in the beautiful sights of buildings, dating from medieval times as they drove from the airport into the city of Barcelona. The Cathedral, the National Museum of Art and the various old churches were architectural marvels that kept her eyes transfixed to the road.

"I would definitely love to visit these sites if we have time. I love everything medieval. ...I think I may have existed in the medieval times," she concluded, dragging her words and nodding her head repeatedly.

"Really? Don't you have to believe in reincarnation to believe that?" teased Ikechi, happy she was excited about the city so far.

It was nine o'clock in the morning when they arrived at the hotel.

"I hope you're rested enough to embark on a morning swim with me," Ikechi said.

"Sure. I'm down for anything. I can't wait to start rocking one of my sexy bikinis." Nfudu said, moving her hips from side to side in a little dance.

"I have never seen you this happy," said Ikechi, retreating in amusement. "I have to take you on trips as often as possible. ...I always thought you were wonderful, but this whole new side beats me."

Nfudu laughed as she squeezed into her favorite swimwear – a red one-shouldered number made from a mixture of satin and lycra, with a chiffon cut-out on the waist that revealed part of her stomach and curvaceous hips. She had owned this piece for a long time and it looked good on her and hugged her beautiful figure in all the right places. Ikechi sat on the side of the bed and stared at her the whole time. As she threw a matching chiffon tunic over her swimsuit for cover-up, he pulled at the tunic and dragged her in between his legs and then began to caress her hips.

"Hey, stop!" Nfudu squealed as she squirmed in his hands. "Are you sure you want to get to the beach in one piece?"

Ikechi continued to caress her. "I can't keep my hands off you."

He succeeded in pulling off her tunic and the lone shoulder of her swimsuit as she tried to slide away from him, laughing flirtatiously the whole time. After he placed her on the massive bed, she pulled him down by his shoulders and kissed him passionately while he made love to her.

"I'll handcuff you to this bed for the remainder of your life," Ikechi exclaimed after he climaxed.

"What?" Nfudu asked, horrified.

"You heard me loud and clear, but we have to go now. I want to show you the sunset."

Nfudu threw on a hat and a pair of sunglasses and strutted past the hotel lobby, hand in hand with Ikechi and into the rented convertible he had waiting for them. It was a thirty-minute drive to the San Sebastia Beach. The ocean breeze swept across Nfudu's face and attempted to take her hat off her head. She held it with her right hand and with her left hand caressed Ikechi's lap as he drove at top speed along the highway.

"You want to get me into trouble N!" Ikechi mumbled as he throbbed from her touch. She looked at him and smiled mischievously, but continued to stroke his thighs back and forth, stopping at intervals to sweep the hair off her face or change the radio channels.

"N, you're getting me to a point, where it may be too dangerous for me to drive."

"Ok." Nfudu reluctantly pulled her hand away from him, but was shocked when he grabbed it and placed it back on his lap. She started to laugh when he firmly planted his hand over hers and start to mimic the back and forth motion she was making earlier.

"You're hilarious," Nfudu said and leaned sideways to kiss him. "I love you."

"I love you too sweetheart," responded Ikechi kissing her in return.

When they arrived at the beach, they took a ten-minute walk along the pristine golden brown sands, while a couple of beach hands helped set up a cabana for them. After they settled into their cabana they headed off for a swim. The currents were high so they stayed close to the shore and socialized with other beachgoers. Nfudu purchased matching green fiberglass bracelets for herself and Ikechi from a hawker. The whole time, Ikechi watched the sky for signs of the sunset.

As soon as he saw traces of orange on the horizon, he grabbed Nfudu by the hands and guided her to their cabana. He made sure to walk in first, while Nfudu tagged behind him. She was shocked to see beautiful yellow roses lining the ceiling and walls. In the corner, three Mariachi singers played a soulful tune on their Vihuelas. They serenaded her with a beautiful Spanish folklore *'Amor Ganado'* representing a story of love that had been through many challenges but prevailed in the end.

While she was tried to catch her breath and assess the situation, Ikechi took her hand, got down on one knee, and looked into her eyes.

"Sweetheart, I have loved you from the very first time I set my eyes on you. I was foolish not to have pursued you to the ends of the earth after I met you again and again, sometimes in unusual circumstances. When we found ourselves in each other's arms on that trip to Lagos I knew you were a true gem and realized the universe was pulling us together for a reason – that reason was that someday you'll be mine. I love you my N. Please will you overlook all my faults and marry me?"

Nfudu was in tears halfway through Ikechi's speech. She knelt before him, holding his bare shoulders and whispered delightfully.

"I will my love. I will."

The Mariachi singers cheered and played another tune – a joyful one this time as Ikechi slipped an exquisite cushion cut yellow diamond ring that glowed as if lit by an internal flame into her left middle finger. Her mouth was agape when she saw the ring. She looked at Ikechi and then back at the ring again, her mouth still agape. Ikechi got up and helped her to her feet, while a server poured champagne into their glasses and they toasted to their future together.

They drove back to the hotel before dark more in love than they had ever been.

"I can't believe what you just pulled off my darling," stated Nfudu, still in a daze about the proposal.

"You mean, for an African man?" responded Ikechi looking at her from the corner of his eye.

"Exactly my point!"

Ikechi laughed.

"African men are just as romantic as our European brothers. We just have other ways of showing it."

"Thanks to you I have proof of that now. You blew my mind away. I was literally shaking when I realized what you were about to do."

"It wasn't easy to pull off because you're so suspicious. The hotel staff was paid to help with most of it. They organized the singers, the cabana and the champagne."

"You got me. Thanks love."

"You're welcome, sweetie. You're worth it."

-

The celebration continued when they got back to the hotel, with more champagne and chocolate in the honeymoon suite. It was a beautifully laid out suite – the most luxurious in the hotel – Ikechi's idea.

"I had everything moved up here," Ikechi said as he led Nfudu into the seven hundred square feet suite with beautiful views of the entire city.

"Beautiful!" exclaimed Nfudu. "My things can stay down there. As far I'm concerned, if all we do for the rest of the weekend is lie in bed and make love, I'd be fine with it."

"I won't be," Ikechi joked, causing Nfudu to look at him wide-eyed. "I have other ideas. I promised this would be a trip to remember and we have plenty of time to make love."

"What are we doing tomorrow?"

"Sailing. It'll be lots of fun. Have you sailed before?"

"Not with my fiancé..," responded Nfudu giggling. She loved the sound of that word.

-

That night Nfudu made love to Ikechi without any inhibitions. She let him go to places she had never let him or any other man go before. He was completely hers and she was his. He promised her heaven on earth and in return, she affirmed her love for him over and over again.

"We have a long day tomorrow N so try to get some sleep."

"I wish it was that easy to fall asleep."

"Try ...just try," said Ikechi rubbing her back in vertical and circular movements until she finally slept like a baby in his arms. He ensured she was fast asleep before creeping out to the living room.

20

IKECHI was the first to wake up the following day. He did his best not to wake Nfudu. He tiptoed around their suite to get dressed and sneak out for some early morning errands. When Nfudu finally woke up at eleven, she saw a note he had left on her bedside.

Gone for an early morning jog. I'll return before you know it. Try to eat some food. We have a hectic day ahead of us.

Her eyes scanned the room for the food, and when she didn't find it, she took her search to the living room. There she saw a trolley with three silver platters, a jug of orange juice and some coffee in the center of the room. Inside the platters, she saw a delicious looking omelet in one, a fruit salad in the next, and an assortment of breads in the last. She ate ravenously thanking her stars Ikechi wasn't there to witness her lack of decorum.

Just as she was about to head back to bed, Ikechi came in panting. He gave her a hug and a long sensual kiss.

"I hope you're ready for our cruise. It's aboard the Girona-Costa cruise liner."

"Yes and I'm excited too! I even have the perfect outfit."

"Save your outfit for another occasion. I bought the perfect dress for you. Here…" Ikechi pulled out a beautiful Yves Saint Laurent dress from the suit bag he brought with him into the suite.

"Wow! This is beautiful." Nfudu exclaimed as she ran her hands over the dress – a short beige lace and satin dress with a small cape around the shoulders. The cape was embroidered with silk threads and tiny pearls that lined the edges. Each individual pearl was hand sewn in the most delicate pattern. Nfudu thought the dress was exquisite and marveled at Ikechi's taste. "I may have underestimated your taste in clothes. But won't I be overdressed for the cruise? Unless of course if the Queen of England will be attending."

"You never know. She may be attending. Be rest assured you won't be overdressed. Patrons of the Girona-Costa cruise liner dress to the nines. The ship only caters to the crème de la crème in society. It is rumored to be the official cruise liner of the Queen of Spain."

"A royal cruise? That sounds great."

"I've got matching shoes and a hat for you also. Come with me." He took her hand and led her to the living room, where two ladies in uniform were waiting with identical smiles on their faces. "These fine ladies are from the Sphinx salon, here in Barcelona. They'll help you get dressed. They'll also help with your hair and makeup. "Shoes and hat are in these boxes here," Ikechi said, pointing at two blue velvet boxes on the settee – one round – the other square.

Nfudu opened the square box to reveal a stunning beige satin stiletto. The round box contained an exquisite small tilted hat, the same shade as the pearls on her cape. It had some soft netting to veil the corners of her face and a little bit of her forehead.

"These are lovely How much time do I have to get dressed?"

"Thirty minutes max, so hurry and take a shower. The ship is leaving from Port Vell and sailing for three hours along the Barcelona River."

They showered together, taking turns to wash each other's backs. Ikechi exited first to get the door. As Nfudu was getting out, she heard a little commotion and people talking in hushed tones that quieted down as soon as she entered the living room with a towel wrapped around her chest.

"I heard noises," said Nfudu looking around to see if she could make out the source of the noise.

"It's nothing. Hurry and get dressed." Ikechi responded.

Nfudu stepped into her perfectly fitted dress and hurried into the living room to get her hair and makeup done. Her hair was sleeked back, parted on the side and pulled into a neat bun that rested at the top of her neck. Her hat was fastened to one side of her head. While she was getting her makeup done, she saw Ikechi in the mirror standing behind her, and looking handsome in a midnight blue tuxedo, with satin lapels. Her heart skipped a beat.

"Oh my God," she said. "You're so handsome. You're the most handsome man I've ever seen."

"Darling, don't tempt me right now. The only reason you're uttering this right now is because you know I can't do anything with you at the moment." Nfudu giggled and almost smeared the *kajal* on her dress.

"No. I mean it. You're sooo handsome," she cooed admiringly.

When the makeup artist was done applying rouge to her lips, Ikechi pulled out her chair, took her hand and pulled her to her feet. He twirled her around and let out a wolf-whistle, causing Nfudu to blush.

"No one can be more beautiful than my N. I would kiss you right now, but for that rouge on your lips. In fact, I may damn the consequences and do that." Ikechi bent Nfudu backwards a little bit and bent forward as if to kiss her. She playfully fought him off. Ignoring the "No, no!" from the makeup artist, he kissed her, but on her forehead and cheeks.

At the lobby, a limousine was waiting to take them to Port Vell. When they arrived at the port, they were ushered into the VIP section on the lower deck. A set of uniformed staff escorted them to a private room and left them alone.

"There's something you need to know," said Ikechi staring Nfudu in the eyes.

"Go on…" Nfudu nodded, urging him to continue.

"When I tell you what I'm about to say, I want you to think carefully about it and let me know with all honesty, from the bottom of your heart what you feel about it. No matter what answer you give, I'll like to assure you that we would still have a fun time today…"

Nfudu was visibly worried; she couldn't imagine what Ikechi needed to tell her. "I'm listening…"

"I planned a surprise wedding." Ikechi paused for his words to sink in before continuing. "Below this deck are fifty of our closest friends and family members, who have come from all over Europe to witness the occasion. I initiated this process weeks before my trip. Some of your staff and friends are in on it."

Nfudu's head spinned and she fell into a semi-trance.

"I need to sit."

"Sure," Ikechi replied helping her to a seat. While he looked on, Nfudu placed her hands on her legs and rubbed them in a back and forth motion while she recalled the events of the past two years of her life. There was her engagement to Javier, her love affair with Ikechi, the pregnancy, the miscarriage, the *osu* revelation and finally her conviction to stay with Ikechi. She remembered their engagement the day before and how happy he had made her. There was no doubt in her mind that she loved him enough to jump head first and face any consequences later. When she got out of her reflective state which lasted only five minutes, but to Ikechi seemed like a whole hour she looked up at him and muttered, "Erm…". Ikechi immediately placed a finger to his lips to hush her. He then knelt before her and leaned on her laps for support.

"Wait!" he said. "I don't want you to feel pressured for any reason. If you feel unable to commit to this, we could simply convert the surprise waiting downstairs into an engagement party."

"Let's do it."

"Which one? The wedding or the party?" Ikechi asked looking at her expectantly.

"Both," responded Nfudu her eyes glistening.

"Really?" Ikechi got up, lifted her and swung her around in the tiny room. Nfudu tugged at her dress and squealed with delight. He set her down after she became dizzy and begged him to stop.

"Just wondering," said Nfudu, "How did you pull this off?"

"Simple. I talked to Gi…" He stopped mid-sentence as he noticed the forlorn look on Nfudu's face. "What is it?" he asked.

"My dream wedding would have included my family, matching brides' maids and that something blue pinned to my dress." She pointed at a spot on her waist. "Not to mention something old from my grandmother or a great aunt. But..." she paused for a moment to shake her head.

"N, like I said earlier we can call this off..."

"No. Don't. The rules have never applied to me anyway. A marriage to the love of my life, on a luxury ship with fifty of our friends and family, sounds like something dreams are made of."

"That's my girl." Ikechi kissed her on the lips, not minding the rouge this time. "Come on let's go."

-

The upper deck where the wedding took place was beautifully decorated with white and light rose-colored linen. There were nine tables in total. Six of the tables were decorated with white, while three were decorated with rose colored linen. Beautiful flowers adorned the tables, the walls and the ceiling. The DJ played a soft tune, while guests stood around in groups chatting with cocktails in their hands. When Ikechi and Nfudu walked in, there was instant silence. All the guests stopped chattering as they marveled at the handsome couple. Some surrounded them and shook their hands to congratulate them. Nfudu could see who was there at a glance – there were Vanessa and David, Stanley, who Nfudu hadn't seen in ages, two friends from the International Institute of Fashion, a couple of celebrity fashion designers who were her friends, Nadia, some of her fashion industry acquaintances, Ikechi's friends and family who lived in London and other people who she could not recognize. She felt a little sad that there was no member of her family there, but refused to let it ruin the moment.

The DJ continued to play as the guests swarmed them with questions. Within the first thirty minutes of walking into the room, she thought she might wake up and realize it had all been a dream. She knew it was real after Vanessa walked up to her for a long hug and a congratulatory kiss. "I'm happy for you darling."

"Thank you. Were you in on this?"

"We all were. Ikechi contacted me when he came to London and I had no choice but to help him. You're my best friend and you're obviously happy with him, so why not?"

"What about Javier. Was he in too?"

"No, he wasn't. But he wasn't opposed to it either when I told him. Not sure why he couldn't make it. I'll leave you alone now so you can attend to your other guests. Congratulations!"

"Thanks, sweetie. Talk later."

The nuptials took place right after cocktails, on a small platform, with the guests looking on from their tables. A priest in a grey suit and white collar read their wedding vows and they said "I do" staring at each other affectionately. They exchanged rings and kissed amidst cheers from the crowd. After their first kiss, the crowd continued to cheer. Some banged their spoons on glasses to urge the newly married couple to entertain them with more kisses. Ikechi and Nfudu obliged and kissed over and over again. Before they had the wind knocked out of them, they were led to their table by the wedding planner - a celebrity planner, who Ikechi hired from London. Their table was one of the rose-colored ones and was strategically positioned in the center. To differentiate it from the rest, it had a crystal lampshade in the middle, with chandelier light bulbs with strobes and flashing lights that changed color every half minute. Dinner was served right after they were seated. Uniformed cruise personnel served the wedding guests from a selection of appetizers, entrées and dessert.

For their first dance, Ikechi chose Nfudu's favorite song "Love" by John Lennon. They held each other closely and swayed from side to side as they looked adoringly into each other's eyes. Their guests cheered. Many of them joined them on the dance floor. Some sprayed wads of fresh pound notes on their foreheads, their chest and shoulders. In no time, other guests followed suit after they learnt it was a traditional African practice. After their dance, Ikechi led Nfudu to their table, while their guests continued the celebration on the dance floor.

"I'll get it for you Mrs. Ifejaku." Ikechi teased as he pulled out her seat.

"Ahh!" exclaimed Nfudu. "It sounds so strange hearing that for the first time. I hope everyone else will get used to it."

"They will. If they can get used to saying Schumacher, then they can definitely say Ifejaku."

"You're hilarious my husband," said Nfudu looking at him seductively.

"What? What did I just hear you say?"

"My husband," Nfudu repeated, as they heard the jangle of glasses urging them to kiss. As they regaled the crowd with another kiss, the MC announced the cutting of the cake that had just been wheeled into the center of the room on a silver trolley. When Nfudu laid her eyes on the cake, she thought it was beautiful.

"And it tastes great too," Ikechi said when he saw her expression.

Each layer of the white three-tiered wedding cake was a different size and flavor. The patterns were flowers – rose for the base, daises for the middle and daffodils for the top. After cake, the guests danced until the MC announced that the ship had reached the dock.

Guests were led off the ship by the ushers. The wedding gifts were packed into a small truck. Nfudu and Ikechi bid the wedding guests goodbye and were driven back to their hotel in the limousine – which was now magnificently decorated with ribbons and flowers and a sign that said 'Just Married'. Inside were chilled refreshments and glasses for champagne. Ikechi poured some into their glasses and toasted.

"To a happy married life."

"Cheers," Nfudu responded, tired from the marathon. At that point, she realized what the past few hours signified – she was bound for the rest of her life to Ikechi. It also meant Ikechi was her family and that she now had fresh new battles to fight with her other family. Her brothers were absent at the wedding, not that she expected otherwise. Nevertheless, she decided to ask Ikechi.

"Did Dike and Emeka know about the wedding?"

"No. I didn't inform them, for obvious reasons. You know I love them, but I had to keep them in the dark about the surprises because I didn't want them to start a war."

"Hmm, I thought you guys got along great."

"Yes ...but as far as marrying you is concerned, I knew I would not have their support. They were fine with us dating, but would have thrown a fit if they knew we were getting hitched for good."

-

The morning after, Nfudu felt a pang of guilt when she thought about her father and the rest of her family. A shiver ran through her spine when she imagined what their reaction would be over the news of her marriage. The consequences were clear to her – disownment by her entire family. Even though she had been prepared for that, thinking about it broke her heart. She did not regret her decision, but wished things had been different.

News about the surprise wedding reached London the very same day it took place. Congratulatory messages and gifts were sent to Ikechi and Nfudu even though they still had another two days to spend in Barcelona. Nfudu's brothers also heard the news before Nfudu could call them the following day to inform them. She waited until late afternoon to dial their number. "Hello," answered Emeka.

"Hello," responded Nfudu. "There's something I want to tell..."

"We've heard," Emeka retorted. "It was all over the news. I guess you didn't know how much of a celebrity you were." Emeka concluded sarcastically.

"Really?" asked Nfudu, ignoring his tone. "What news sources exactly?"

"The usual. There are even pictures."

Nfudu pondered for a moment. Sadness filled her heart as she realized the possible implications.

"I regret that you and Dike couldn't come for the wedding. I'm really sorry and would have loved for you both to be there."

"We weren't informed and even if we were, we still wouldn't have come. I'm sure you understand."

"I do," she responded. "That's also why he didn't invite you."

"Wow!" Emeka exclaimed interrupting Nfudu mid-sentence. "Ikechi has finally manipulated you into marrying him. You know what father will do to you?"

"I know and I hope he will forgive me in good time. Please, no one must tell him. I need to inform him in my own time. We have to take his health into consideration."

"Well big sis. You should have thought of that before you made that move."

Nfudu's heart was heavy after she spoke to Emeka. When she went back to bed, she was glad Ikechi was not awake to witness the disappointment written all over her face. She snuggled close to him and stared at the contented look on his face while he slept. In that moment, she was convinced she had made the right decision, and it was up to her family to catch up to her level on the joy meter.

The next two days in Barcelona, Ikechi took Nfudu to see the old cathedral, the museums and the beach where he proposed to her. When they were not out scoping the sites or the restaurants, they stayed in bed and made love. When they were leaving, the hotel staff addressed Nfudu as Mrs. Ifejaku and she realized they had all been in on the surprise. Ikechi tipped them generously and promised to provide a glowing review when he returned to London.

In London, Ikechi had more surprises for Nfudu. He drove her to the driveway of a magnificent home in the prestigious Knightsworth neighborhood and presented her with the keys to the home.

"Here is your wedding present."

"Pardon?" asked Nfudu surprised and elated at the same time.

"I bought this home for us. Did you think we were going to live in your flat after we got married?"

"Noo …but I definitely didn't expect this. Thanks, darling. You're full of surprises." She hugged him with tears in her eyes – tears of joy – filled with the emotion that had built up and left her in a fragile state in that moment.

"You'll have to put your flat up for sale because you won't need it anymore. This house is big enough for us and all the children we're going to have," said Ikechi while he gave her a tour of the home. Nfudu was so excited about the home that she shelved discussing her flat to a later time. She had other ideas for the flat she had lived in for the past five years and it didn't include selling it.

"I love what I see. Thanks love.

After he took her on a tour of the six thousand square feet home, they were both exhausted driving to her flat. Nfudu knew she had a lot of work to do to fill the empty rooms and make the house look more like a home. "I'll have to hire an interior decorator."

"I think so. There's a lot of work to be done here. I didn't get any response from you about the fate of your flat."

"Oh, that …I'll still like to retain it so let me think about it a little bit."

"I don't understand why you need to think about it," asserted Ikechi, "It will be a waste to keep it, except if you want to rent it out for income. That has its own attendant problems. It can be time-consuming and extremely stressful dealing with tenants."

"I still think it's worth thinking about. I've lived there for five years. There's a lot of emotional attachment to it."

"Ok," responded Ikechi grudgingly, taking care to not agitate his new bride.

21

KNIGHTSWORTH Manor was ready for Nfudu and Ikechi to move into two weeks after the wedding. With eight bedrooms and three living rooms, the Manor was more house than Nfudu needed and definitely more work than she was willing to invest time into. An interior decorator was hired to work on the details, while she was consulted whenever strategic decisions needed to be made. It was expected that external work – such as the tennis court, the swimming pool and the pool bar – could go on for at least another month after they move in without interrupting the flow of activity in the main house.

Settling in at the Manor was a bit demanding for Nfudu. Not only was it far from her usual spots – her stores, grocery shopping, Oxford Street and church – it was difficult to navigate and get things done. However, she liked the prestige and privacy her new environment offered as well as the space she now had to accommodate domestic staff, including the chauffeur Ikechi provided for her. The manor also had a flower garden and a front lawn. Both, to Nfudu were such desirable aspects of a home, which she missed, living in her flat for so many years. Tending the garden helped her relax and the front lawn helped the ideas flow, especially as she watched the robins and collared doves perch on the silver birch and English oak trees in the lawn. Overall, the good outweighed the bad and she was pretty sure that soon the bad would become inconsequential.

Nfudu settled quickly into married life. Pleasing her new husband was the ultimate priority for her as this gave her joy and a feeling she was impacting another's life significantly – something she always wanted. Cooking was never her forte, so she hired a highly recommended African cooking coach to teach her how to prepare various traditional dishes that would appeal to her husband's taste buds. She practiced by attempting to make a new dish every night for Ikechi, who left for Nigeria on business two weeks after they moved into the manor. Consistent effort was made to perfect her craft before his return in three weeks. On the issue of her flat, there was a huge tug-of-war between her and Ikechi, before he finally agreed to let her keep it. This was a big win for Nfudu, who desperately wanted to retain some of her independence. She used it as a private office, which was especially useful whenever she needed zero interference to do her work.

The time and energy consumed by married life did nothing to help Nfudu escape the issues she faced with her family in Nigeria. News of their marriage got to her mother, the day after their wedding in Barcelona. Dike called to give their mother the full story, but asked her to conceal the news from their father, who had just been diagnosed with high blood pressure after a recent bout of malaria. Right away, Mrs. Ibe called Nfudu's flat in London, but was unable to reach her. She tried several times a day for two days. When they finally spoke she did her best to stay calm.

"My daughter, I've been trying to call you for three days now. Where have you been?"

"I'm sorry Mama. I was in Barcelona."

"Is it true then?"

"What exactly Mama?"

"That you married Ikechi?"

"Yes, Ma. I was going to call you."

Mrs. Ibe screamed, "Heeeyyy!" It was blood curdling and shrill. One that made Nfudu's heart sink to imagine she had hurt her mother that badly. She felt like she ripped her heart out but tried to calm her down. "Mama, please lower your voice. Is Papa there? Did you tell him?"

"No. Your father is very ill and he's downstairs right now so he can't hear me. I have no intentions of telling him because we have to resolve this matter before it gets to him.

"Listen, my daughter, you cannot stay married to that boy. You have to call it quits now to avoid the disaster that is sure to befall us. Your father must have explained the consequence of marrying an *osu* to you. Don't you understand?"

"He did. He explained everything to me."

"Good! So …are you too big to heed his warning?"

"Mama, I love Ikechi with my life. I had no other choice, but to marry him."

"Wait! Are you telling me that you love him enough to risk being disowned by your whole family, your whole clan?"

"I'm not saying that Mama. I'm hoping Papa and the rest of the family will to do away with this tradition. It's so archaic and just like the killing of twins it should be considered a crime against humanity."

"Hmm. Nfudu, there's nothing you and I can do about this issue now. Whether the caste system is done away with in the future or not, the fact still remains that while it's still part of our tradition, you stand to lose all your family ties if you don't obey. A word is enough for the wise."

The entire Ibe family struggled for several weeks to keep the news of Nfudu's wedding from Chief Ibe. What they hadn't accounted for was that Nfudu's celebrity status meant the news of her marriage would sooner or later become public knowledge and reach Chief Ibe when they least expected it. That was exactly what happened when Ejike – Chief Ibe's younger brother, who was based in Lagos, came to visit Chief Ibe and his family a few days after Nfudu had the heated discussion with her mother. Ejike marched into the living room where Chief Ibe was seated with three of his wives. He waved page six of the Lagos Life Magazine, where news of Nfudu's wedding was so elaborately reported, with a picture of the happy couple on the event of their marriage plastered on the entire page.

"Brother, how can you allow this to happen?" Ejike yelled.

"Ejike, calm down. What are you talking about?" asked Chief Ibe, visibly irritated.

"See," responded Ejike, bringing the magazine closer to him. He peered to read the contents, while the rest of the room occupants looked on, wondering what was going on.

"'*ebenebe egbuola*' – the unimaginable has happened." Nfudu's father wailed and immediately froze on the spot after he read the contents of the page. He then glared at everyone in the room and said, "I can't believe this!" and writhed uncomfortably in his chair. Mrs. Ibe ran to his side and took a look at the magazine to see what was eliciting such a reaction from him. When she realized what it was, she shook her head, eyed Ejike maliciously and muttered, "'*Anu ofia!*' – wild animal!" under her breath. Placing her right hand on her husband's shoulder, she urged him to calm down, but he was inconsolable. She was disappointed that Ejike had not exercised caution, knowing the condition of his brother's health. The cat had been let out of the bag and there was nothing she could do. She decided to continue to feign ignorance to avoid agitating her husband any further.

Chief Ibe continued to repeat, "This leaves us only one option," for a whole hour which made him sound delirious to everyone around him. Coupled with the wild stare in his eyes and his fragile state, he seemed to be suffering from some form of attack. The family doctor was called in to examine him.

When the doctor arrived, Mrs. Ibe took Ejike to the hallway and in a firm and angry tone said to him, "Delivering such news in the manner you did to your elder brother is tantamount to sending him to an early grave. How could you be so reckless?"

Ejike was quick to respond.

"How could I keep this sort of news from him? We have to act quickly to avoid tainting out family name."

"Look here. No one supports what my daughter did. All I'm saying is that we don't kill her father as a result. Some of us have known about this for days, but we've been waiting for the right time to tell him to avoid jeopardizing his health. Your brother is very sick. You can bear witness to it yourself."

"I see that now," responded Ejike apologetically, "He still needed to know sooner rather than later so he can take the necessary actions to avoid further damage to our family's reputation," he concluded brusquely.

"You're incorrigible!"

Their discussion was interrupted by the doctor when he joined them in the hallway.

"We'll need to admit Chief for at least two days for monitoring to make sure his condition doesn't deteriorate. Has this kind of thing ever happened to him?"

"No," Mrs. Ibe responded. "He just received some terrible news and since then he hasn't been himself."

"He's very delicate now," stressed the doctor. "Because of that, we have to avoid anything that will strain him. We also have to limit the number of people that can visit him while he's on admission to only his immediate family – his wives and children."

"Thank you, doctor."

Mrs. Ibe packed two bags for herself and her husband to take to the hospital. The first night, Chief Ibe was given sedatives to calm him. When he woke up the following morning, he seemed a bit calmer and ready to discuss more rationally.

"Mama Nfudu, we have to do something. I cannot afford to disown my precious Nfudu, but if she doesn't listen and end the marriage with that man immediately, she will leave us no other option."

"Papa Nfudu, please let's avoid having this discussion right now. The doctor…"

"I don't care what the doctor says. My house is on fire and my daughter is drowning and you dare to tell me what the doctor said."

"I'm sorry. I have tried to speak to her, but she doesn't seem to get the deeper implications of what she has done."

"What do you mean you have tried to speak with her? Are you saying that you've known all along?"

"Yes. I found out a few days ago and was waiting for when you felt better to tell you. I'm so mad at Ejike for telling you the way he did."

"You should have told me right away," retorted Chief Ibe. "It was irresponsible of you not to have told me as soon as you heard it. If it hadn't been for Ejike flashing that paper in my face, it would have been someone else. I hope you've learnt your lesson not to keep things from me."

"I have. I'm sorry."

"One of us needs to go to London to talk some sense into her. I won't be able to go in my state, so you may have to make an urgent trip to see her. I'm so heartbroken that my amazing *Ada* got us all entangled in this stupid mess." Chief Ibe, who had been fighting a tear suddenly broke down as he said, "I wonder where we went wrong in raising her. I hope she changes her mind to avoid the consequences of her actions. I would never advocate for divorce, but in this circumstance, it is absolutely necessary for her to leave him before this marriage results in a child, at which point it becomes too late for her to change her mind."

"Papa Nfudu, you need to rest now. I have heard you and will prepare to go to London. When I spoke to her a few days ago, she told me he was in Nigeria. Let's hope he won't be around when I get there."

When Chief Ibe got out of the hospital, he called Nfudu to hear her own side of the story.

"Nfudu what did you do?" Nfudu was surprised her father had already found out, and after hearing the manner in which he found out, she was completely devastated. She hadn't planned to keep him in the dark for long but wanted to handle communication in her own way.

"I'm sorry Papa about the way you found out. It's true. Ikechi and I are married now."

"You'll have to walk to the court and divorce him immediately."

"No Papa. I can't do that."

"It's an order!" barked Chief Ibe.

"Sorry, Papa. I didn't plan for things to happen this way. It's not my fault that the person I fell in love with is an *osu*. Remember that you, yourself even pushed me to be with him. One thing led to another and we fell in love with each other. How do you expect me to fall out of love with him so easily?"

"Nfudu my daughter. This is my final warning. Divorce Ikechi or you're disowned by your entire family, which means you'll lose all your privileges as *Ada*, lose your inheritance, as well as your 'chi – guardian angel'. Don't waste any more time or you will be stuck with this decision as soon as you bear a child for him."

"I knew about these implications before making my choice. I hope my family will change their mind towards this marriage. There are many religious movements working on abolishing this archaic culture of ours. I'm going to join those movements to ensure my children are not tainted by this abominable tradition."

Before Nfudu could finish, Chief Ibe hung up the phone. He was furious when he told Mrs. Ibe, "She has gone insane. The war, devastating as it was did not break our family but now, Chief Ifejaku's son and his wiles have torn my precious family and my heart apart."

"Hey, Papa Nfudu." Mrs. Ibe said with so much anguish of her own, "Please leave this matter alone for now. We have agreed that I'll visit Nfudu in London. I'll be leaving in a few weeks. Rest now as we continue to pray for an end to this nightmare."

-

Following the incident with Ejike, Chief Ibe was instructed by the family doctor to avoid stressful situations. Mrs. Ibe was asked to keep an eye on him. She constantly reminded him that besides Nfudu, he had seventeen other children to live for. That, she hoped would motivate him to remain strong in the circumstance they found themselves in. She continued making plans to visit Nfudu in London. There, she hoped to succeed in changing her mind and reverse the effects of the dastardly act she committed.

22

JAVIER did not attend Nfudu's wedding because he was facing a dilemma of his own. He sent his apologies and a congratulatory message to Nfudu when she returned from Barcelona. Ikechi had invited him, but had received a less than favorable response.

"I regarded Javier's rejection as a sign that he's still in love with you," Ikechi said to Nfudu during a phone call from Lagos.

"What rejection are you referring to?"

"With all the excitement I forgot to tell you that I personally invited Javier to the wedding. He rejected outright, and was particularly miffed when I told him it was a surprise."

"I had no clue," said Nfudu. "But, I don't believe your hypotheses that he turned the invitation down because he still loves me. I imagine he just felt awkward about attending our wedding… you know what I mean?"

"Well, I still think you need to take care around him. I don't trust him one bit."

"Darling, we've been through this before. Please leave it alone. I'm married to you. Isn't that reassuring enough?"

"It is, sweetheart, but until I figure out what his problem is you need to be careful. Enough about him. How are you coping by yourself in that large house?"

"I'm doing great. I miss you though. It would have been easier if you were here."

"Keep holding on. I'll be back soon."

-

Javier had never trusted Ikechi and it had nothing to do with the fact that he stole Nfudu from him. It was something he couldn't put his finger on that worried him the most about him. This was further worsened by the bizarre manner in which Nfudu miscarried right after spending time in Ikechi's company. He had gotten to love the unborn child and had made plans to be a father for the second time in the event of the child's birth. All hopes for that came crashing down when he heard the sad news about the miscarriage. He could not understand how that could have happened since Nfudu was a healthy woman who previously had not shown signs of any problems. Believing Ikechi may have driven her too hard or worse still stressed her beyond what her fragile pregnant frame could bear, he blamed Ikechi for the incident. Since Javier didn't want to leave his suspicions unfounded, he decided to find answers and some closure by paying a visit to Dr. Harriman. When he got there, the doctor led him straight to her office.

"Have a seat," Dr. Harriman said, pointing to the settee by the window. "You sounded concerned over the phone."

"Yes. I was devastated by the occurrence and was wondering if strenuous activity could have caused it," he asked, averting his eyes.

"If you mean rigorous sex, the answer is yes and no. It depends," she responded shaking her head slowly from side to side.

"On what if I may ask?"

"Rigorous sex can hurt a growing fetus if the mother has underlying health issues. However, studies have shown that women who have regular sex during pregnancy have a better chance of carrying their child to term. Nfudu falls into the latter category."

"What could have caused her miscarriage then? I agree that she seemed healthy enough."

"I ran a lot of tests to check a variety of things, including genetic abnormalities and they all turned out negative. Some are still with the lab. When these are released, we'll know more."

"Which ones are outstanding?"

"I'm not at liberty to reveal that information because of patient-client confidentiality. If you'll like to discuss her case further, you'll have to obtain a signed release permitting you to access her medical information on her behalf."

"No. That won't be necessary."

"All I can tell you is that the additional tests will throw more light into her condition. This is necessary if she is to avoid a similar incident in future."

Javier decided to probe further. "Nfudu was too devastated at the time to look into the cause. She attributed it to the stress she went through as a result of not knowing the paternity of her child. There could be more to this story. Perhaps he abused her. Is that possible?"

"Anything is possible. We normally look for signs of physical abuse when things like that happen and there was none in her case. Now that she's had some time to heal, I can meet with her again to find out if she can recall anything that can help with this investigation."

"I agree," responded Javier. "I doubt if she'll reveal anything to me so it's best you talk to her."

The meeting with Dr. Harriman did nothing to quell Javier's suspicions. It was while he was dealing with that, that Ikechi sprung an invitation to the wedding on him. They had argued about the surprise element of the wedding and concluded their discussion by Javier declining the invitation. Their argument had left Javier terribly agitated, so he decided to pay Vanessa a visit to express his concerns.

"I don't think Nfudu should marry Ikechi. We should put a stop to it," said Javier to Vanessa, unable to hide his distress.

"Why?" asked Vanessa, shocked that her father could think of taking such an extreme measure. "Don't tell me you're still in love with Nfudu. I thought you had moved on from her."

"Of course I still love her. Stopping the wedding has nothing to do with that. I just don't trust that guy!"

"Dad, please let them be. If they want to be together, nothing will stop them. Any action you take at this point will be seen as an act of rebellion and you could just be written off as a jealous lover."

"Well then, since I have no proof that he abused her, I'm better off keeping my opinion to myself."

"You think he abused her?" asked Vanessa, aghast.

"I thought so, but Dr. Harriman says there's no proof that he did. I'll rest my case."

"But Dad, you know you can't go around accusing people. Promise me you'll let it go."

"Ok. I promise."

Javier was convinced to let it go. However, he was adamant about not participating in the wedding celebrations.

-

Several weeks after the wedding, Javier was surprised when Doctor Harriman invited him for an urgent meeting at her clinic. When he entered her office, he realized he was not the sole invitee because Nfudu was sitting in the settee in Doctor Harriman's office, with her hands clasped together on her stomach as she rocked back and forth. She looked at him once and then looked away, while Doctor Harriman watched the two of them with interest.

"Is everything ok?" Javier asked, taking the seat next to Nfudu.

Before Nfudu could respond, Dr. Harriman opened the conversation. "I invited Nfudu to see me because I have pertinent information that I needed to disclose to her about her miscarriage. I also invited you because you were listed as the father in her prenatal records."

Javier looked at Nfudu and back at the doctor. "Ok. Go on..." he said.

"I already talked to Nfudu before you came in. I'll just repeat everything I told her. Now, what I'm about to tell you could make you cringe but bear with me until you hear the whole story."

"We're listening."

"When I saw Nfudu in the emergency during her miscarriage, I was suspicious that something had gone horribly wrong with her. I asked for some vials of the fetal remains, mostly blood and lymphocytes to be analyzed in the laboratory to help throw light into the cause. Mind you, this is normal procedure in our hospital when healthy mothers miscarry out of the blue. The main purpose of this test is to determine if there are any structural issues in the fetal DNA that could have led to its mortality."

"I'm getting worried," Javier said. "Did the tests show anything? I'm sorry. I can't bear the suspense any longer."

"No, there was nothing wrong with her. The DNA test checked out fine, but our lab scientists found something in her blood that was not natural and shouldn't have been there."

Javier looked at Nfudu who looked morose as her lips quivered. He held her hand in his and urged Dr. Harriman to continue.

"We found high concentrations of an abortifacient drug in her fetal sample. I asked her just before you came in if she tried to abort her baby and she said no. If she did, there's no need for her to panic since abortion has been legal in this part of the world since 1967. However, she said she would rather die than kill her baby and I believe her. The question now is if she didn't do it to herself, who did?"

Javier stared at the doctor in astonishment when the implication of what she just revealed dawned on him. His shock made him reticent until he was jolted back to reality by Nfudu's hysterical sobs. "I wouldn't dream of such a thing. How did the drug get into me?"

"I don't know," responded Dr. Harriman. "This is what we now have to find out. I suspect foul play. ...A criminal offense. This was a carefully orchestrated crime and whoever did this had the help of a medical practitioner or an errant pharmaceutical employee. The particular substance we found in your blood is only available by subscription."

"I don't know anyone that would want to harm me," insisted Nfudu.

Javier looked at her in astonishment. "I've heard enough. I wish I had trusted my instincts and stopped that wedding." He turned to face Nfudu. "I know you're devastated my dear, but I'll have to speak the truth now. Whether you want to admit it or not, it is clear to me that the culprit in this case is Ikechi. He was the only person with the motive and the opportunity to administer the said drug to you."

"How can you be sure?" asked Nfudu, staring at Javier in surprise. A part of her wanted to defend Ikechi, but something about the whole scenario made her shudder.

"I don't want to get ahead of myself, but I'm pretty sure Ikechi did this to you."

Nfudu sighed heavily. Feeling faint, she laid her head on the settee as she processed the information she just received. She couldn't believe she was the victim of such treachery, delivered possibly by the person she trusted the most in the world with her life – her husband.

"Look at the facts, my dear. Who else could have done this to you?" Javier asked.

When no answer came from Nfudu, Doctor Harriman continued.

"Because, this is a case of murder and attempted murder – Nfudu could have died in the process because of the concentration of the drug in her system, the hospital has to report this matter to the police. Any suspects will have to stand before a judge to have their fate decided. But, because you're a high profile patient, I'll give you the chance to decide if you want this matter dragged to the courts or not."

Nfudu was silent, so Javier answered for her. He spoke slowly.

"We will definitely like to see the culprit pay for their crime, but she will have to make the final call. Let's get back to you on that."

"Ok. She looks pale. You should take her somewhere safe to get some rest. Let me know what you decide in two days. Please take good care of her. She's suffered a lot.

"One more thing, we performed a paternity test with the fetal sample and the blood sample I collected from you…" she pointed at Javier, "During your last visit. The result of the test showed that the child was yours."

Nfudu broke down once again and started sobbing. She was inconsolable and leaned on Javier for support.

"I'm so sorry Javier."

Javier's eyes were filled with tears.

"I'm sorry too. I should have been there for you more. Should have never left your side. Oh my God. I'm heartbroken." Nfudu held and hugged him to ease his pain. She cried on his shoulder for a few minutes before they left the doctor's office. They did not utter a word to each other until after they stepped into Javier's car. He sat for a few minutes looking at the road ahead of him before putting the key in the ignition and turning it on. "I don't know what to say. What will you do now?"

"I don't know," said Nfudu, her head bent to one side. "I just want to go home."

On their drive to Knightsworth Manor, she tried to recall the events leading to her miscarriage. All fingers pointed to Ikechi and even though she wanted to give him the benefit of doubt, he was the only person that had complete physical access to her right before her miscarriage. And as for a motive, she saw one in Ikechi's reaction when she told him the baby may not be his. This made her shudder uncontrollably. Javier noticed and pulled her towards him. "You're shivering," he said. "I hope you're not about to fall sick. You've got to be strong now."

"I'm ok" responded Nfudu. "I just remembered Ikechi's initial reaction when I first told him the baby could be yours."

"Not good, I imagine."

"Right, but he later seemed to have embraced the situation. If he did this, then he's a really good actor. The care he pretended to show afterwards must have been just a farce. He wanted an opportunity to hurt the baby. Is that possible?" she concluded, looking forlornly at Javier.

"It seems to me you still have doubts. Think carefully now, who else could it have been? I want you to figure this out sooner rather than later because you could be in immediate danger."

Nfudu pulled herself away from Javier's embrace as they neared the manor.

"I spent two whole weeks leading to the miscarriage with him in his hotel room. He brought all my meals and acted like he cared, but the whole time he was slowly killing my baby."

"I'm glad you've figured that out."

"I have no doubt Ikechi did this to me. If it's proven to be true, I want him to pay for taking the life of an innocent. Oh, Javier," she sobbed, throwing her arms around him. "My own innocent child."

"Actually mine and yours," added Javier. "Have you decided if you want to press charges?"

"Do I have to decide now?"

"Not right now, but you have only two days according to Dr. Harriman. An advantage of reporting it is that all the evidence would be examined to prove within reasonable doubt whether he's innocent or guilty. You would want to know for sure if it's Ikechi, wouldn't you?"

"Of course… but the press?"

"We'll get the publicist involved. I'll also speak with Dr. Harriman to let her know we need to be as discrete as possible," Javier assured her.

-

"Good idea!" exclaimed Dr. Harriman after Nfudu informed her about her decision to report the crime to the authorities. "I'm very pleased with your decision. Our Victim's Support Unit will do their best to minimize any exposure to the public."

"Thank you, Doctor," Nfudu responded. She was sure of herself for the first time in days.

"I hope you're protecting yourself from Ikechi right now. You need to keep as much distance as possible from him until the investigation is concluded to avoid being further manipulated by him."

"He's out of town right now and not due back until another two weeks. I'm making arrangements to move out of the home I currently share with him."

"Awesome! Hopefully, we can make sufficient progress with the investigation before he returns. I'll hate to see you in harm's way."

-

Nfudu relied more and more on Javier as the days went by as she was shaken to her core and couldn't believe Ikechi's betrayal. Her eyes were frequently red from nonstop crying and she barely left the house. She would never have believed Ikechi had that much evil inside of him had she not experienced it directly. Even worse was that she chose him over Javier and even went against the wishes of her family. Whenever she remembered her plan to carry his babies against her parents' wishes and how that would have sealed the deal with her family, she shuddered. She was that close to becoming an irretrievable *osu* and being disowned forever.

Craving her own space, she moved out of Knightsworth Manor and into a hotel near her flat, until she could figure out a more permanent arrangement. Her new accommodation separated her not only from Ikechi but from everything she currently knew – she had judged her environment, the people in it and her circumstances incorrectly. She needed time to think, retrace her steps and figure out where she had gone wrong and which direction she needed to go. Whenever she felt completely lost, she picked up her phone to call Ikechi to hear his own side of the story until remembered the advice from the police investigators to avoid any contact with him until the matter was resolved.

Javier was happy that the matter had been brought to the open. The recent turn of events made him realize why he felt Ikechi couldn't be trusted. It was his opinion that Ikechi was extremely possessive and manipulative of Nfudu. When Nfudu suffered the miscarriage, he suspected it could have been caused by a physical altercation between her and Ikechi – one that was serious enough to cause her to lose the baby. Never in his wildest dreams had he expected Nfudu to be in as much danger as she turned out to be in. He still loved her, and wanted her to be safe by all means.

Stanley also ran to Nfudu's side. They hadn't seen each other since the wedding in Barcelona – which Vanessa had invited him to. He always liked Nfudu but never really made his intentions known. When he learnt that Nfudu was dating Javier, he lost all hope and later settled into a remarkable friendship with her. However, when he heard she was getting married to someone other than Javier, he was disappointed in himself for having given up so easily. Vanessa informed him about Nfudu's struggles, so he decided to visit her when he was in London. He surprised her at the Carnaby store. Nfudu jumped out of her seat when he walked into her office.

"How did you know where to find me?" she asked smiling for the first time in days.

"Vanessa. She thought you might be here."

After a long hug, she broke into tears. "Sorry," she apologized. "I do this so often these days."

"I quite understand. No need to apologize. The store is beautiful. You've done marvelously well."

"Thank you. I'm so happy to see you." She said, breaking away from him and wiping the tears from her eyes.

"Same here. I hope you're not too busy to catch a late lunch."

"Not at all. I haven't even eaten all day."

"Great, because I know just the place."

They walked down to Luigi Ristorante at the corner of Oxford Street for some pasta and light wine.

"How is Jeremy? You two must still keep in touch."

"Yeah! We're still very close friends. He's married and moved to Australia with his family."

"Wow! That's nice. She is a lucky woman. Jeremy is so sweet."

"I agree," said Stanley. "Now to the reason I came to see you today. Vanessa told me what you've been through recently."

"Oh that!" exclaimed Nfudu, "How much did she tell you?"

"A lot. Actually …everything. You need to consider getting a restraining order against Ikechi. From what I heard about the investigation, all fingers seem to be pointing to him."

"That's true. The laboratory has been able to isolate the specific drug that was used. It's a very potent one that works within forty-eight hours after it's been administered. I spent two days prior to the miscarriage with him and no one else. Also, a connection has been made with the pharmacy where the drug was obtained, although the investigators are still looking for accomplices. I wonder if there are any though."

"There must be. He couldn't have carried that out alone."

"I agree," she responded nodding.

"You have all the information you need. What are you waiting for then?"

"I don't know," responded Nfudu shaking her head and looking at Stanley intently. She couldn't believe that she hadn't asked herself that same question. "It has been too overwhelming to think beyond living day today."

Stanley watched as she twirled her spaghetti endlessly around her fork. He reached across the table and held her wrist to catch her attention.

"You can be completely free you know?"

"How do you mean?" asked Nfudu.

Stanley handed her a business card for a family lawyer.

"She's amazing. Talk to her about annulling the marriage. Family law is not my specialty, but I believe you can get your marriage annulled easily on the basis of extreme cruelty."

"Thanks, Stanley. That's exactly what it is."

They moved on to a more pleasant topic while they finished their lunch. "I'll see you when next I come to London. Stay safe and call the lawyer ASAP. She'll be expecting your call."

Nfudu filed for a restraining order against Ikechi the following day and called the lawyer to proceed with an annulment of her three month marriage to him. She was surprised by how easy the process of obtaining the restraining order was. As for the annulment, the lawyer told her she could finalize one in just a matter of weeks.

Ikechi was arrested by policemen from the Criminals Investigations Department of the New Scotland Yard when he arrived in London a week before he was scheduled to return. He was oblivious to the investigation and nearly lost his mind when his calls to Nfudu remained unreturned. Since the investigation and the events that brought it about were only known by a close group of friends, he was not aware of the issue at hand. When he didn't hear from Nfudu, he became infuriated and imagined that only one thing and one person – Javier – could have caused her to desert him. He feared that she may have reignited her relationship with Javier and left him in the cold. The obsession he had with Javier did not allow him consider other possibilities as to why Nfudu suddenly disappeared from his life.

Ikechi's nightmare when he was driven to Scotland Yard slowly became real when the police read him his rights and fed him a restraining order. It was not until they started questioning him that he realized why he was in custody. He was allowed to make a phone call to his lawyer, who came by to bail him, but not before he had been thoroughly grilled by the police. After he got to Knightsworth Manor and discovered that it had not been lived in for days, he realized his marriage as he knew it was over. Ikechi called Nfudu at the store and she picked up right away without realizing it was him.

"Hello," Ikechi spoke first.

"Hi," said Nfudu fighting back the intense anxiety that swept her entire being after hearing his voice for the first time in two weeks. "Where are you?"

"I just came into London. I was arrested at the airport and detained at the New Scotland Yard for hours. I tried several times to call you, but you didn't answer my calls. You should have at least called to tell me what was going on. What is all this about?"

"There's a restraining order barring you from contacting me. As much as I'll like to hear your own side of the story, I shouldn't speak with you now."

"Are you crazy?" Ikechi's voice reverberated across the phone lines. "How can you..."

Nfudu hung up before he could pelt more insults on her. Her heart rate increased and she restrained herself from ringing him and yelling insults at him. The experience left her so frustrated. It was not what she had expected from an initial interaction with him. Even though she hadn't expected him to confess and plead for forgiveness, she had hoped he would outrightly deny the allegations leveled against him. His attempt to gaslight her opened her eyes to who he really was. Unfortunately for him, that technique no longer had any power over her.

Ikechi's return filled Nfudu with trepidation. She was torn about how to proceed with the charges against him. On one hand, she wanted him to pay for his sins, while on the other, she did not want him to end up in jail. Mostly, she just wanted the nightmare to end. On his part, Ikechi continued to deny the allegations and even blatantly refused to grant Nfudu an annulment. He hired himself an outstanding lawyer – who made a reputation as a shark in criminal law before entering private practice to create a formidable defense against her.

"We have to make a deal with him," Nfudu's family lawyer advised after a demanding day in court.

"What sort of deal do you have in mind?"

"We'll offer him a 'no fuss' annulment in exchange for dropping the criminal charges. In essence, you're going to free him, if he would free you in return."

"I like that," agreed Nfudu. "Let's see what he says. I need my life back."

They called Ikechi's attorney to present the offer to him and he promised to discuss with his client and get back to them. In less than twenty minutes, Ikechi's attorney called back.

"I have spoken to my client and presented the offer," he said. "He's prepared to take his chances in criminal court and will under no circumstances grant the annulment as he believes he is innocent."

Nfudu felt as though someone had given her a kick in the stomach. "What do we do now?" she asked her lawyer.

"Nothing much. You just have to pursue the criminal case and pray you obtain enough evidence to convict him. That's the only thing that'll guarantee your freedom."

-

Weeks later, additional evidence was discovered by the prosecuting attorney to connect Ikechi with the criminal case. The evidence was overwhelming enough that when it was presented, Ikechi's lawyer convinced him to accept Nfudu's offer, or risk getting convicted if he allowed the case go before a judge. The annulment came exactly two weeks after both sides agreed to settle in what Nfudu's lawyer described as one of the most bizarre cases she had ever handled. This was an amazing victory for Nfudu. A few days after the annulment, she found out from friends that Ikechi was overheard saying, "The whore aborts her baby and blames me." According to her sources, he had planned to drag her around in court, until the Judge dismissed her case for lack of evidence.

Nfudu learnt that her father was sick again when she called to give her parents news of her annulment. She told them everything that occurred since she met Ikechi including the poisoning incident; the miscarriage and how it affected her life; the investigation and its results; and, the annulment of their marriage. Details about the paternity of the child were omitted as that would have caused a different set of problems for her. Her father would have thought she was immoral and her mother would have gone on a rant about how she thought she raised her better. Her parents were stunned by the news, particularly because they had been in the dark about the pregnancy. Despite that, they were ecstatic her relationship with Ikechi had been severed. Luckily for Nfudu, her father did not say "I told you so." But had he said it, Nfudu felt she would have deserved it. All he could mutter was, "All evil deeds stink. They can be covered up for a while but will always get discovered in the end."

Her mother added, "What a horrible year you've had. Married and then not married; in love and then suddenly in limbo; feeling alive and safe and then suddenly in fear of your life. '*Tufiakwa* – God forbid'. Even though Ikechi went scot-free, he must certainly meet his downfall."

"Mama, please don't curse him," Nfudu pleaded.

"'*Ogini* – what'?" responded her mother. "'*Ife emelu na nzuzo ga aputalili n'ife*' – Nothing is hidden under the sun." Nfudu was happy to have her parent's love again. She resolved to do everything in her power to make them proud of her once more.

"My daughter, come home and rest," continued her mother.

"Mama, I'll come, but not now. I can take care of myself in London and will see you folks when I visit Nigeria in November for the opening of the Lagos Fashion School. I pray Papa will be well enough to attend the event with the rest of the family."

Mrs. Ibe had a lot of questions still for Nfudu but reserved them for when she could speak to her alone. She called her the following day when she was sure Chief Ibe was not around.

"My dear, how is Javier?"

"Javier is fine. He's a wonderful friend to me. He basically carried me through all this drama."

"Any chance of getting back with him?"

"No Mama. He's been dating recently," she responded despondently.

"Oh! No problem. You can always find somebody else. When you come home, there will be lots of suitors waiting for you. I promise you."

"Mama, ...that is the least of my problems right now. I have a long road to recovery and won't worry about suitors just yet. I miss my work. I'll put all my focus in it."

"No problem, my dear. My biggest concern is your health, especially after the miscarriage. Em... I wanted to ask if you can still bear children. Hmm... and if you can, I hope you're not in the family way."

Nfudu laughed lightly when she realized her mother wanted to confirm she wasn't pregnant with Ikechi's child.

"Mamaaa," she called, "You are so hilarious. No, I'm not pregnant. As for being able to bear children, I asked the gynecologist the same question and she assured me the miscarriage did not affect my reproductive ability."

Mrs. Ibe heaved a sigh of relief.

"That makes me very happy. I'll relay this information to your father, just as I received it. My daughter, goodnight."

Nfudu's parents hosted a thanksgiving service the following Sunday to thank God for delivering their daughter from the hands of the evil one. It was well attended and they offered a sacrifice to rebuild the sections of the church that were destroyed during the war. Chief Ibe felt there was no sacrifice too much to offer in return for what God had done for them. His health improved significantly in the following weeks and he started to get back to his old self again.

-

Nfudu had her property moved out of her Knightsworth home into her flat. Her building security was informed to pay particular attention not to let certain individuals in. As she settled into her flat, she began to focus again on her work and efforts to repair her broken relationships. The most affected was her relationship with Emeka and Dike, who assured her that they never stopped loving her even though they were disappointed by her choices. They spent some nights at her flat after she moved back in to provide her a sense of safety before she felt confident enough to live by herself again.

23

IN no time, it became the craze for couture designers to open stores for their ready to wear collections to the general public who could afford their designs but had no time or patience to order custom-made outfits. The timing corresponded with the Equal Rights Amendment to the United States Constitution that proposed banning discrimination based on sex. Since the amendment was passed by the Senate, there has been a drastic shift in the demand for women's fashion, because more and more women became increasingly engaged in the workforce. This new breed of women was able to afford their own clothing and was constantly looking for options to that effect. This created more incentive for designers to tap into the ready to wear market. Armed with this knowledge, Nfudu and Javier intensified plans for opening the Paris, Athens and Milan stores. It was an exciting prospect, which they looked forward to as the next step in the expansion of Nfudu's business.

Lady Jeannette Eudora and T.Y Ibrahim joined the bandwagon as investors for the three new Nfudu Stores, ending the search for partners for that venture. Together, they provided enough capital outlay to cover the balance needed to make the new stores a reality. Javier didn't need to do a whole lot of convincing when he pitched the concept to Lady Eudora – she'd had her own first-hand witness of the performance of the London stores. In addition, she had a huge amount of respect for Nfudu and her achievements.

Getting T.Y Ibrahim on board was easy. He accepted the offer the moment it was pitched to him.

"I am certain that investing with Nfudu will guarantee a return on my investment. Besides, this is my opportunity to obtain the international diversification I've been seeking to expand my business empire." He said, with complete conviction.

With funding for the project resolved, Javier and Nfudu continued discussions with their real estate agents in each of the three locations to identify the appropriate sites for the stores. Each of the agents was tasked with identifying at least three options from which they could make their final selections when they visited each of the cities.

With too many conflicting priorities, Nfudu was forced to rely more heavily on her team to get things done. Gina's role as store manager also accorded her the position of a logistics coordinator and human resources administrator. She was organized, meticulous and selfless in her approach, which made her Nfudu's first choice whenever she had too much on her plate. "Gina," Nfudu called, stalling Gina as she passed her office. "Please coordinate with the real estate agents in Paris, Athens and Milan. Figure out a good time over the next couple of weeks for Javier and me to view the properties and book travel for us."

"Of course," responded Gina in her usual cheerful tone. "Would you prefer to go by air or train?"

"Not quite thought of it. Javier might have a preference, but frankly, he's too busy to be bothered by such details."

"Yes," Gina agreed. "I know what he'll prefer. I booked a flight two weeks ago to Rome for him and Samantha and he made his preferred mode of transportation clear to me then."

"Really?" asked Nfudu with complete despondency.

"Yeah! They just returned from Rome two days ago."

"I knew they were seeing each other," confessed Nfudu. "But I didn't know they were this serious."

"Apparently they are. They've travelled a couple of other times in each other's company. Should I book any leisure activities?"

"No. None whatsoever," Nfudu said shaking her head. "It's going to be strictly business. What I hope to achieve on this trip is to commit to sites and sign contracts to secure our choices."

"No problem. I'll get to work right away."

"Thank you." Nfudu was a little miffed. Not at Gina or anyone in particular. She hadn't expected Javier to be alone forever. However, she also hadn't prepared her mind for what the future held for the two of them. Part of her hoped they would get back together, but his being in a relationship destroyed that prospect.

-

The London stores continued to experience a sales boom. The high demand for ready to wear designs brought in huge profits for Nfudu and her partners. These pioneer stores remained her pride and joy as they were the bedrock for the international stores they were about to launch. Their winning business model would be used to operate the new stores – partnering designers would have sections assigned to them and profit from sales would be split in an agreed upon formula. In addition, each designer was required to pay a fixed amount for rent and a portion of the overhead incurred monthly. This arrangement worked so well in London that the London Times acknowledged Nfudu in an article:

"…*This business model was made popular by Nfudu Ibe – London based fashion designer and businesswoman. It requires a trusted partner with the wherewithal to set up a boutique with employees and other requirements as well as the power to draw a loyal customer base to their business to take responsibility for the other areas which the partners do not want to be bothered with. It results in a win-win situation for all involved.…*"

The launch for the international stores was targeted for scattered periods in the following year. Nfudu planned to expand her offerings of designers to include local designers from each location – a move she hoped would increase loyalty for her brand from shoppers in each of the three locations – Paris, Milan and Athens and eventually from the whole of Europe. The selection process for designer-partners had been ongoing for months and most of the spots were filled before even a guarantee of investment capital was made. Nfudu selected designers that complemented her brand and everything she stood for as a person to make for very cohesive business relationships.

With logistics and partners sorted out, getting good sites for the stores became of paramount importance. Javier and Nfudu set out on their trip early on Monday morning for their first port of call – Paris. They sat next to each other on the hour-long flight. She recalled the last time she and Javier were together on a plane and remembered how good they were together.

"Hey, I'm so glad you were able to make it. It would have been too much for me to handle all alone," said Nfudu.

"Choosing a location is one of the most important decisions we can make for the stores, so I wouldn't have missed this opportunity for the world. You know what they say, 'Location …Location …Location.' That is the driver of economic prosperity."

"That's quite intellectual. What happened to you?" teased Nfudu.

Flattered by her words, Javier turned the lens on Nfudu.

"Was it?" he asked. "Must be all those business articles you keep in the office. I've been reading them and they're messing with my mind."

"C'mon! You've always been intellectual," she said matter of factly.

"Thanks for noting that, but on a serious note," said Javier, "It's a very busy time of year for me. However, I didn't want to leave this all to you as 'two good heads are always better than one'. Don't you agree?"

"Actually I do."

For Nfudu, the trip was a welcome break from the hustle and bustle that typified her normal life and an opportunity to bond with Javier after the events of the past few months and the heartbreak she caused him. She still loved him, but being that he had a serious girlfriend, she was just content for an opportunity to connect with him as a friend and business partner.

Paris at that time of year had slowed in activity as Parisians were winding down for the summer. They had begun to move out in droves to their summer hideouts and vacations spots in the South of France. Several businesses were already closed. A majority of the people roaming the streets and swarming the shopping malls were tourists or owners of businesses that catered to tourists. It was safe to say that tourists owned Paris during the summer months.

"I have never really understood the nature of Parisians and the deference given to their summer," said Nfudu as they drove around the city to view the sites. "It's the only place I've ever been to, where local businesses are shut in the summer to allow the business owners some time to enjoy themselves."

"I adore that about them," responded Javier. "Life is short and people should really take the time to enjoy their hard earned money."

"That's true." Nfudu agreed. "I love that they do not take their leisure time for granted," she said as she scanned through the various pastries displayed behind the glass in a patisserie. "For Paris, we must choose a site in an area that is frequently visited by tourists, otherwise we may lose a lot of sales in the summer."

"Voila!" exclaimed Javier. "You've hit the nail on the head. Do you know what this means?"

"No. You tell me."

"We don't have to look any further."

The legendary Champs-Concorde Avenue was chosen as the new Paris home for Nfudu Stores. This choice out of three possible locations was hands down the best. It offered the right proportion of glamour and accessibility required by the Nfudu Store customer. It also had a romantic feel to it as a result of its proximity to the Elysee Palace, with its wonderful history and beautiful stone structures. Driving to their hotel after meeting with their agents, Nfudu and Javier went past many familiar spots they had visited when Nfudu was a student in Paris.

"I haven't been to Paris since my graduation," she said. "Everything looks just the same."

"Except for the Tour Montparnasse over there," said Javier pointing ahead to the tallest building for miles.

"Yeah! That is definitely a change, but other than that everything else seems frozen in time. Oh, I love Paris."

Dinner was at the penthouse of their hotel, with its beautiful view of the city. From their position, they could see the Eiffel Tower changing color at the stroke of the minute. "I just got off the phone with Samantha," announced Javier as they looked through the menu. "She'll be joining us in Milan tomorrow."

Nfudu's heart stopped for a moment. She wondered why Javier would ruin such a beautiful moment with news of Samantha. Thanks to the forewarning she received from Gina the day she asked her to book their flights, she recovered almost instantaneously.

"That'll be nice," she said feigning indifference. "It's great that I'll have someone to shop with."

An awkward silence passed between them during which Nfudu decided to face up to her concerns.

"You know I only found out recently that you and Samantha were dating."

"I thought you were aware. Anyway, we started dating close to two months ago, so it's pretty recent."

"...So you were you dating when I met her at the shop opening?"

"Hmm, yes and no," responded Javier. He was reluctant to broach the subject of his dating life. "There was no definition then. We had only just started seeing each other."

"Well, she's lovely."

"Thank you. Let's toast to our success at finding the perfect Paris location."

"Ok!" smiled Nfudu as she hesitantly raised her glass in the air. "Cheers."

They spent the night in Paris and left for Milan the following morning. Milan was expected to be a little bit trickier than Paris as Javier and Nfudu were less familiar with the city. To make sure they had enough time to make the right selection, they planned to spend two whole days, which they hoped would also leave ample time for shopping and sightseeing. Nfudu was a bit pensive about Samantha joining them. She hoped it wouldn't be awkward for the three of them.

Javier and Nfudu went to work as soon as they arrived in Milan. They viewed all three locations on their first day, but had to revisit all three of them again on the second day before they could arrive at a consensus.

"This is brutal," confessed Javier to Nfudu as they stepped into the hotel for a quick lunch, before heading out for a final viewing of their selected location – a store space in the Duomo fashion district.

"I know," responded Nfudu. "Every single one of the locations could have been the one, but I think we made the right choice. It was great to have narrowed it down to the most likely location to be visited by the Queen of England if she's in Milan, otherwise, we could still be searching."

"Exactly my sentiments. Do you now see why I tell everyone who cares to listen that you're the smartest person I know?" said Javier as he pulled her close without warning and gave her a hug. She giggled and pulled away awkwardly, amidst stares from passersby.

Right after their final viewing, they drove to the landlord's office to sign the lease and close the deal on what both of them agreed was one of the toughest business decisions they had ever made.

With only one evening left to go, Samantha was happy that Nfudu finally found time to shop with her. The two women giggled as they ran from shop to shop in a frenzy when they realized they only had a few hours to get all they needed. When the shops finally closed, they stopped at a quaint street side café in a quiet corner of the Duomo district to get some food. "Wow!" Samantha said, while she plopped into her seat. "I thought I was going to collapse out there."

"I thought so too," responded Nfudu. "You were crazy. It was so hilarious the way you almost pushed that woman down to grab that red pair of shoes. One would have thought your whole life depended on it."

Samantha laughed as she remembered her attempt to reach a pair of shoes while a voice from the loudspeaker was announcing that the store would close in fifteen minutes.

"Oh yeah!" she nodded in agreement. "My life did depend on it. I've been looking for shoes like that everywhere. I'm glad I found them though. Did you get everything you needed?"

"Not quite, but I'll be back in Milan soon enough. Then I'll have plenty of time to shop."

Samantha nodded in agreement and looked down at the menu to order.

"This menu is in Italian!" Samantha exclaimed. "We need a waiter who can speak English." She beckoned to one of the waiters. "Inglese?" she said. The waiter responded, "si im venire," and walked off. A few minutes later, they were assigned a friendly lad, who knew only a few words of English. Since they were starving, they settled for pizza that had toppings with names they couldn't pronounce.

"How is your modeling career going?" Nfudu asked.

"Very well actually. It's a bit different in the UK, but there is no place like home." As Samantha spoke, she moved her long red hair from side to side in a very sensual gesture. She was unmistakably beautiful and with a personality such as hers, Nfudu understood why Javier fell for her. "If I was a man," Nfudu thought to herself, "I too would have fallen for her."

"It was so much fun shopping with you," Nfudu said, aloud this time. "You sound more intelligent than most models I've met in my course of work. ...Don't get me wrong, it's not that I don't think models are intelligent, it's just that your vernacular is quite rich, which makes me wonder..."

Samantha threw her head back in laughter.

"I get that a lot," she continued still amused. "What a lot of people don't know about me is that I have a master's degree in economics. So yes! I use a lot of vocabulary that is not expected of models. Besides, my family consists of intellectuals. Dad and two elder brothers are doctors."

"That's an impressive family background." Nfudu was a little surprised to hear that Samantha had a lot going for her. She had secretly hoped that was not the case, so as to make the competition less stiff.

"That's nothing really. ...Enough about me, though. Tell me, how did you become such a successful businesswoman?"

"I don't consider myself that much of a success yet, but I'll get there. You're not doing badly yourself." Nfudu proceeded to give Samantha a brief history of her life, starting from when she interned with Lady Jeannette up until the present.

"Amazing!" responded Samantha. "It helps that you always knew what you wanted to do from the scratch. I like that."

The more Nfudu and Samantha spoke, the more they realized how much they had in common. Each had a strong admiration for what the other had achieved. The one thing that was off limits was Javier. Both women avoided discussing him because they both knew they were in love with the same man. After their meal, they rushed back to the hotel. Samantha went straight to meet Javier, who was stunned by her account of her evening. It appeared the two women got along.

"I'm so sorry love. We took so long," Samantha said to him.

"Don't worry about it. I had dinner and caught up on the news of the week while I waited for you to return. I'm glad you had a good time."

"It was more than a good time. It was a blast." Samantha said with both hands flailing in the air.

"Great." Responded Javier, secretly hoping her relationship with Nfudu would not be detrimental to their budding relationship. Samantha was his first serious girlfriend since his break up with Nfudu, and they were extremely compatible. Javier still loved Nfudu and had forgiven her, but couldn't envisage a relationship with her; it still hurt him to remember his heartbreak when she destroyed what they had.

In her room, Nfudu reminisced about her meeting with Samantha. It reminded her of how much she missed Javier, but was happy he had found love again. Samantha seemed to make him happy, which helped lessen the guilt she still felt as a result of the way she ended their once beautiful relationship. She wished them well and hoped she would eventually be able to settle down in a relationship with someone, who was perfect for her. For the time being, she planned to focus on her own recovery, so when she finally met that person she would feel whole.

Samantha left for London the following morning, while Javier and Nfudu flew to Athens for the last leg of their trip. After their experience from the past few days, their decision-making skills were enormously sharpened by the time they had to decide on a store location in Athens. They knew what to look out for and swiftly decided on a store along the Ermou – the main shopping street in Athens. It spanned almost two kilometers and was lined with shops that promoted many top designers. Antique churches occupied the little squares off the street. All these made the Ermou a tourist magnet and the perfect location for the store.

That evening, they toasted to their efforts and walked along the Ermou looking at the shops and stopping occasionally in the squares for some sightseeing.

"Samantha told me you two got along really well," Javier said.

"That's right. You would think we knew each other from the past."

"That's exactly how she described it. Do you want to try one of these ram kebabs?" Javier asked when they got to the barbecue stand at end of the road.

"It does smell great. That reminds me, I hardly ate at lunch," she responded rubbing her stomach sideways.

"Two," he said to the barbecue vendor with two fingers up.

"What about drinks?" the vendor asked with an accent Nfudu couldn't detect.

"None at all. We'll get some gelato on our way back," Javier concluded nodding in Nfudu's direction.

Nfudu nodded back in agreement.

That night, Nfudu felt more relaxed than she had been in a long time. She discussed at length with Javier – not only about business but also about politics – a topic she was beginning to show increased interest in.

When they returned to London the following morning, a team was set up to oversee all the logistics required to get the stores up and running. Plans were created right away to help them execute their vision. The plans addressed important details such as the requirement for staff sourced for each location to be comprised of at least ninety percent of its citizens. This was to ensure that the Nfudu brand benefited the communities in which they did business. Also, to ensure corporate responsibility, the business structure allowed for a portion of the profit from the stores to be used to engage in projects to benefit the communities.

When Nfudu got to her flat, she found numerous messages on her answering machine. Ten of those messages were from Ikechi, pleading for Nfudu to call him in every single one of them. One was from Nfudu's attorney advising her that Ikechi had been trying to reach her. The attorney advised Nfudu to be careful as Ikechi was no longer barred by the restraining order against him since she dropped the criminal charges. Nfudu wished things had turned out differently for her and Ikechi. After denying several pleas for a meeting with him in the past, because she was furious, she now felt it was time to reconsider. With the passage of time, she no longer felt angry about the situation – but experienced a different set of emotions even more damaging than anger – a lowered self-esteem and a reluctance to fully trust again. A meeting with him was an opportunity to get the closure she so badly craved, so she requested her attorney to set up a supervised meeting.

24

NFUDU met Ikechi at a busy restaurant at the corner of Beer Street, a quiet street often frequented by tourists because of its modest restaurants and proximity to shopping. Nfudu chose this spot – a public space at the advice of her attorney. She arrived at the restaurant a few minutes before Ikechi and ordered some coffee while she waited for him to show up. When she saw him through the window as he drove into the restaurant's parking lot, her feelings of anger consumed her once again. She contemplated leaving when her heart started beating erratically. Her stomach churned as she looked around furtively for potential escape routes.

When Ikechi stepped inside, he spotted Nfudu where she was seated with her dark oversized Dior shades that shielded most of her face. Walking slowly, he took the seat across from her. After exchanging pleasantries, much like strangers, they looked at each other for an awkward moment before Nfudu broke the ice.

"How have you been?" She spoke icily.

"I can't really say…. Disoriented, to say the least," replied Ikechi, looking up for a brief moment in hesitation and then returning her stare as she searched his face for answers.

Frustrated by his hesitation, Nfudu moved the subject to the purpose of their meeting.

"You invited me here to speak," she said tapping the table nervously with her middle finger. "I'd like to hear what you have to say."

Ikechi was stunned by her brusqueness, but he decided to ignore it. Referring to her sunglasses, he asked, "Are you going to leave those on the entire time?"

Nfudu gently removed them and placed on the table.

"Certainly not," she responded, ticked by Ikechi's mysterious vibes. A trait she once admired in him, but not anymore. "Ok. Why did you want to see me?" He was skirting around the issue and she was running out of patience. She picked her shades from the table and placed them back on her face, which made him realize she meant business.

"I'm still confused to this day about the crimes I was accused of," he said. "One day, I was on my way home to see my brand new wife and the next I was arrested for something I know nothing about. I didn't do those things. Javier must have concocted those lies to win you back."

Nfudu was stunned by his allegations and the manner in which he delivered it. Before she could figure out the right words to say to him, he delivered more accusations.

"I'm disappointed by how you treated me – ignoring my calls, taking a restraining order against me and moving out of our marital home – without giving me a chance to tell my side of the story."

"I believe that's why I'm here, to hear your side of the story," said Nfudu irritated, but trying hard not to show it. She looked him straight in the eyes when she spoke. "Now tell me, did you or did you not do it?"

"I just told you," responded Ikechi angrily, pounding the table with his fists in the process. "I can't believe you'd imagine I can do such a thing."

Nfudu was disappointed by his outburst. Embarrassed, she looked around at the other diners, and when she realized no one was paying attention to their table she heaved a sigh of relief. Her attorney had warned her to expect him to deny the allegations and attempt to blame her. It was typical psychotic behavior – an inability to take responsibility for one's actions. What bothered her most was his complete lack of emotion – except for anger.

"But the evidence against you was overwhelming and why did you not at any point during the investigation or your arrest call me to deny any of them?" asked Nfudu trying hard to maintain her composure. She saw through his charade and wondered why it took her so long to see him for who he was. "I have more questions for you, but I'm afraid you'll flat out deny everything."

"If that's how you feel then why are we here?"

"I don't know!" shrieked Nfudu, gesturing with her hands and shaking her head in disgust. Ikechi was taken aback by her outburst. "I'll ask one more thing. Did you know your family was *osu*... wait and did you ever love me?"

Ikechi, appalled by her allegations about his caste glared at her menacingly.

"How dare you refer to me as *osu*," he yelled, thumping his fist on his chest and standing up to leave. "Why do you have to be so dim?" he muttered under his breath and stormed out of the restaurant.

Nfudu sat there stunned for a few minutes. So many thoughts flashed through her head. She had come to the meeting hoping Ikechi would apologize for his deeds and ask for forgiveness. However, he left her feeling confused and certain that no aspect of their relationship was salvageable. Also, she found it strange that he had found the *osu* comment far more damaging than the allegations surrounding her miscarriage despite the fact that she had stuck by him and turned her back on her whole family after discovering he was an *osu*. In hindsight, she felt foolish for making such sacrifices for someone only for them to betray her the way he did.

"Little wonder he called me dim." She said to herself.

With the way she felt after her meeting with Ikechi, Nfudu was glad Javier was coming to London, so she could vent to him. She decided to complete her work for the day from her flat and asked Javier to meet her there to review some partner contracts for the international stores. When they settled down in the mini office Nfudu created from a portion of her living room, she told him about her encounter with Ikechi earlier that day. She ended up collapsing in his arms. "People must think I'm really foolish."

Shocked by her assessment of herself, Javier reassured her.

"No one would think that," he said. "Whoever does neither loved nor married Ikechi. He completely manipulated you. Nobody has the right to judge you until they have walked a mile in your shoes. By the way, you're not dim."

"I felt a little dim though."

Javier let out a loud sigh and adjusted his position to look straight into her dewy eyes.

"Listen, dear. Even though I completely understand why you needed to hear him out, I would have advised you against it and written it off as an exercise in futility. Ikechi, from all indications, exhibits the character traits of a psychopath. The mere fact that he goes around alleging that I orchestrated all this mess shows he's mentally not right. If I were you, I'll avoid any further contact with him, especially not in private as there is no telling what he's capable of."

"I don't plan on seeing him again."

By the time they were able to settle down to their work, it was late. They worked all night to make sure they included the necessary amendments to the contracts as they were to be submitted to their lawyer in the morning. It was three o'clock by the time they finished. "You can have my bed," Nfudu said to Javier.

"No thanks. I'll rather sleep on the settee. That will guarantee that I wake up in time for the marathon awaiting us tomorrow."

"There's also the guest bedroom."

"Thanks. You should get some sleep too. Don't worry about me."

Neither of them felt there was any harm in spending the night together as long as they respected each other's space. In the light of his relationship with Samantha which was getting more serious by the day, Nfudu accepted that all that could exist between she and Javier was friendship and didn't expect anything more than that.

Very early in the morning, even before Nfudu got up, Javier headed off to his lodge to bath and get dressed. They had a hectic day ahead of them that required going back and forth to lawyers offices and meeting with their partners and representatives. Their meetings lasted from morning till late afternoon, which was longer than both of them had expected. Javier was scheduled to return to Nice that evening but needed to conclude some work at Regent Street before driving to the train station.

"We need to hurry," said Javier to Nfudu. "The last train to Nice is leaving at five and I have to be home tonight. We're having dinner with Sammy's parents."

"No problem. You can append your signature to your section and I'll make sure all the amendments are made before I send them for printing."

"That's a great solution. I knew I could count on you."

"Whatever it takes to make both our lives easy," she responded smiling tenderly at him.

When they arrived at the store, they made a quick dash for Nfudu's office. However, seated right at the reception was Ikechi with a poignant look on his face. The look became dour when he saw Javier, but he barely glanced at him. As Nfudu was about to ask Ikechi to give her a minute to finish with Javier, Ikechi stood up and headed in the direction of Nfudu's office with them. Javier was astonished by Ikechi's belligerence.

"She'll be with you in a few minutes. I need to catch a train in thirty." Javier pleaded, gesturing in the direction of the seat Ikechi was occupying at the reception a minute earlier.

Ikechi ignored him and continued in the direction of Nfudu's office. "Excuse me?" he said to Javier and edged his way through the door at the same time that Javier was about to enter the office. Their shoulders brushed and Ikechi muttered an obscenity under his breath.

"What did you say?" asked Javier.

"Do you really want to know?" asked Ikechi, standing menacingly within inches of Javier's face. Before Javier could respond, Ikechi punched him on the right side of his face.

Javier retaliated by punching him on the nose. As some blood trickled down Ikechi's right nostril, he grabbed Javier's neck in a sudden chokehold. Nfudu screamed in terror as Ikechi tightened his hold on Javier's neck and pushed him fiercely against the door casing.

Javier tried to free himself from Ikechi's clutch, all to no avail. A streak of blood ran down the corner of Javier's right eye where Ikechi had punched him earlier. Nfudu tugged at Ikechi's jacket to pull him away from Javier, but he refused to budge and became even more menacing. One of the shop employees dialed 999 and the rest of the employees and customers ran to the scene. A bulky male customer gave Ikechi a powerful kick in his guts from behind, which made Ikechi howl in torment and race towards his attacker, but not before he pushed Javier forcefully to the ground. Javier was unconscious; Nfudu ran to his side trying desperately to resuscitate him. At the sound of a police siren and an ambulance, Ikechi abandoned his target and ran out of the store. He got into his car and zoomed off in the direction of the traffic.

Javier regained consciousness before the ambulance arrived. Nfudu watched as the paramedics wheeled him into the ambulance. She insisted on riding with him to the hospital. On their way, she spoke to him non-stop at the advice of the paramedics to ensure he didn't shift back into unconsciousness. While he was being carted into the emergency unit, Nfudu whispered in his ears, "You'll be all right my love. I'm so sorry." Javier squeezed her hand tightly to let her know he was ok. She leaned over and kissed him on the forehead. Fifteen minutes later, the doctor came out to inform her that he would need further examination in a different section of the hospital, where he would need to be admitted overnight or longer, depending on the results of his tests.

Nfudu held his hand while he was wheeled into a private room. "Do you know where Ikechi is at the moment?" he asked.

"No'" replied Nfudu. "He left before the police and the ambulance arrived. Don't worry, he's nowhere near you."

"I'm not worried about me," he said agitatedly. "It's you I'm worried about."

"Let's just take this one day at a time. We'll figure out what to do about Ikechi when you get out of here." Nfudu felt extremely guilty for inviting Ikechi into their lives. Had she not met with him the day before, he may not have had the guts to come near her, especially after his recent experience with the law.

After all the tests were done, it turned out that Javier did not suffer internal damage to his organs. According to the doctor, his blackout was as a result of the blow he suffered to his head. He also informed them that he notified the police about the visit. This was a customary procedure for injuries sustained from assault. After the policemen took their statements, they confirmed that their account corroborated the ones they obtained from witnesses at the scene of the fight. They were provided with two options by the police – to charge the attacker with assault, or let him go free and potentially hurt another individual. Javier did not want to make any rash decisions in his current state, but called his lawyer to get a protective order for himself and Nfudu. He spent the night at the hospital and was discharged the following day with a ton of medication to manage the pain and bruises from the attack.

Vanessa and Samantha were waiting at the lodge when Javier and Nfudu got there. Nfudu notified them of the assault the day before, and they arrived within minutes of each other. Samantha came from Nice, while Vanessa flew in from Paris where she was attending a business conference. Javier's face was covered with bruises. His right eye and his lips had turned a bluish black color and were so swollen he found it hard to speak or see anything through that eye.

"I can't believe this," moaned Vanessa when she first set her eyes on Javier. "Is Ikechi an animal?"

Samantha shook her head in disbelief.

"What could you have done to him to make him act so crazy? Is he mad?"

"He could be. He's definitely deranged," responded Javier, wincing as Samantha, helped him with his drink.

"I'm sorry love," said Samantha. "He's got to pay for this. We need to get a restraining order against this guy."

"Thank God," said Javier. "The doctor assured us that the injuries are external, which means they will heal in due time. I've asked the lawyer to get a protective order. The hearing is on the 25th. However, I have a temporary restraining order against him."

"Good," agreed Vanessa. "From the version Nfudu gave me, he attacked you first. That makes him the villain in this case. Am I right?"

"He completely caught me unawares. I recall asking him for a moment with Nfudu to finish our work, so I could catch my train on time. Before I knew what was going on, I felt a blow to the side of my head and a hand around my neck. Blood was dripping down my eye and all I could think about was a way to get away from his brute grip before it killed me. That was the last I remembered until the paramedics arrived. It all happened in a split second."

"He could have killed you," said Vanessa, shuddering. "I hate him for what he did to you."

Nfudu, who had been silent all this while, finally spoke.

"We have to press charges. He can't go scot-free this time."

"I agree," nodded Samantha. "The alternative is not an option." She looked at Vanessa, who also nodded her head in agreement.

-

Javier returned to Nice with Samantha to recuperate for a few days. Nfudu was left with a chunk of the unfinished work they had tried so hard to complete the day Ikechi showed up. Even though she was overwhelmed, she felt slightly relieved when Javier called her at the office.

"Hello," Nfudu said when she picked up her phone reluctantly at almost close of work.

"I'm calling to see if I can lend a helping hand somehow."

Javier's voice sounded like sweet music to her soul. "You should be resting," she said. "I'm actually doing ok. I got some help from the legal team so we're good to go."

"Excellent. Feel free to call me whenever you need help. I'm only taking time off to heal my injuries."

"I'm happy you're in high spirits already. What's your final decision about Ikechi? Do you want to press charges?"

"That's the only one way to go. We owe it to ourselves and the society to follow due process and ensure he gets what he deserves."

"I'm fine with any decision you take on the matter. I agree that he doesn't deserve any more chances to run rampage in the society."

-

The doorman approached Nfudu in a rather unusual manner when she returned to her flat that evening.

"Miss," he said. "I haven't seen you in two days."

"Uh huh," replied Nfudu. "I've been coming in later than usual. Any problem?"

"No Miss....I mean yes. Three nights ago we had an incident with Ike..." The doorman scratched his head as he was unable to remember Ikechi's name.

"You mean Ikechi?" asked Nfudu.

"Yes yes," nodded the doorman. "He came looking for you and since you asked us to never let him in, we refused. He got really mad and threatened to hurt me. As I was calling the building security he left. I was off duty the next day and I've been looking for you to ask that you be careful."

Nfudu was frightened by the report. She realized Ikechi had come to see her the same day he walked out on her in the restaurant after referring to her as dim. Still lost in thought, she heard the doorman say, "I hope you're fine miss."

"I'm fine. Thank you. You did a good job by not letting him in. From now on, under no circumstances should you allow him anywhere near here."

"Ok, Miss."

When she got into her flat, she plopped into the first seat she could find and thanked her stars that she had changed her locks just two weeks back. Her first instinct was to call Javier to tell him what she had just heard, but thought against it as she did not want to upset him any further. She got up and checked her doors and windows over and over again to make sure they were locked. In her panic, she considered going to a friend's house to sleep until she remembered Ikechi was still in police custody. His bail hearing was set to take place the following day, so she felt safe for at least that night.

-

The night the doorman kicked Ikechi out of the building, he had come to apologize to Nfudu for walking away from their meeting and calling her dim. He also hoped to further persuade her about his innocence and hopefully rekindle their romance. However, when he discovered that Nfudu had left instructions barring access to him, he became enraged. His rage turned to mad fury when he spotted Javier's car in the parking lot in front of the building. He retreated to his own car and waited several hours for Javier to leave, but Javier never left that night.

Ikechi stayed in his car all night. When he saw Javier leave Nfudu's building very early in the morning, he concluded they were seeing each other again. This discovery made his blood boil. He went home, took a shower, got some sleep and waited till when he thought Nfudu would be at the Carnaby store. When he got there, he was directed to Regent Street by Nfudu's staff. On arriving at the Regent Street store, he waited a couple of hours for Nfudu to arrive. When he saw her with Javier, he lost all control and attacked at the slightest provocation. Completely lost and confused after the attack, he ran to a friend's house, but with a warrant out for his arrest, his friend advised him to turn himself in to avoid piling additional charges on himself. He took his friend's advice and had been in custody at the New Scotland Yard pending his bail hearing.

The prosecutor upgraded Ikechi's charge from assault to attempted murder after he learnt from the police reports that he had strangled Javier to the point of unconsciousness. Because of the seriousness of the new charge, Ikechi was denied bail. Earlier in the week, he had been infuriated by news from his lawyer that his bail, if granted would restrict him from leaving the UK before a trial was concluded. Unbeknownst to him, he had bigger fish to fry. It never occurred to him that he would be faced with a scenario in which he would be refused bail. He cried when he realized his position – he was facing a murder trial – his reputation was severely damaged and his businesses were suffering tremendously. His life as he knew it was over.

Nfudu's lawyer called to tell her about Ikechi's situation.

"Now you have absolutely nothing to worry about as he's not going to come looking for you or Javier. I just spoke to his lawyer and he's distressed about his position. There's no way he can get out of this one now. The burden of proof now lies on him to prove that the day he assaulted Javier, there was no intent to murder him. His best bet at this point is to plead guilty and ask for leniency."

"Oh no!" Nfudu exclaimed. "This is tough…. I don't know what to say."

"He could have killed the guy."

"I agree, but I don't think he intended to."

"Whether he intended to or not, he put a fellow human beings life in jeopardy."

"I agree," responded Nfudu. "So what do we do now?"

"There really isn't much you can do except show up when you're called to testify. Other than that, you should just wait to see what happens next."

"I don't think you understand where I'm coming from. Is there a way we can reduce the charge to assault? Attempted murder seems a little too much. The guy could be locked up for a decade if found guilty and I don't want his blood on my hands."

"It's hard for me to believe the compassion you're showing towards him especially knowing how much he's disrupted your life."

"I know," responded Nfudu. "But that doesn't give me the right to disrupt his permanently."

"I must say you have a point there. There are ways you can help him. It starts with Javier and his lawyer."

—

Nfudu's struggles were multipronged. She felt herself plunge into unexpected sadness over Ikechi's condition. It was hard for her to believe she could still have that much compassion for him. Other than that, the publicity nightmare she and Javier faced following the assault also brought her down. She woke up one morning to the newspaper headline:

"Jealous Ex Attacks in This Bizarre Love Triangle."

The story told how Ikechi, Nfudu's ex attacked her lover/ fiancée at one of her retail shops, leaving him half dead and fighting for his life in a London hospital.

To control the damage, Nfudu called her publicist to ask for help.

"Hello," the publicist responded.

"Hello, have you seen the London Inquirer?" asked Nfudu, upset.

"Yes, I was just about to call you."

"I need your help to shut it down right away. The details are highly exaggerated. Javier is my ex-fiancé, not my lover and he has a serious girlfriend. This thrash could potentially ruin their relationship. Also, he is not nearly dead. I'm confused."

"I understand. I'll contact the Editor in Chief right away. They'll either need to retract their story or issue an apology, whichever they see fit."

"Thank you. If addressed successfully, that ought to be the starting point for shutting up the other media outlets that are following suit and ripping their claws into us."

"I agree. We'll address all of them, one by one."

The publicist went to work right away to ensure that the news was retracted and re-reported in a less embarrassing and more factual manner. She used the opportunity to put the popular slogan, "There's no such thing as bad publicity" to work for Nfudu by gaining her good publicity alongside the bad as she brought her history, struggles and accomplishments, including the new Paris, Milan and Athens stores to light in the refined report. The scandal garnered sympathy from some – while others sneered at the notion that Nfudu, with her business prowess and celebrity could not manage her private life effectively. As opinions were exchanged all over Europe and curiosity over her personal life grew, curiosity about her brand increased exponentially. Demand for her designs quadrupled and visitors to her stores doubled over the course of a few weeks. The irony of it all was that while the incident increased the mystery around her for some, others – the majority began to see her as human, not superhuman as was assumed by many as a result of her amazing accomplishments.

"Thank you... thank you... thank you," Nfudu told her publicist when she visited her at the Carnaby store. "Thank you for a job well done."

"No problem. It's not over yet. The trial, depending on how it goes can undo everything we've just achieved so we need to be cautious going forward."

"I agree. I feel a knot in my stomach when I think about the trial. I don't know if I can handle it."

"Talk to Javier. He might listen to you."

In a matter of weeks, the excitement over Nfudu's private life was replaced with even more exciting news about the senator who kidnapped his three children and fled to South America after the courts denied him custody. Nfudu heaved a huge sigh of relief and continued to work with her publicist to avoid further slips and ensure they maintained the momentum gathered so far for the sake of her business. The experience and the embarrassment it caused her and her establishment toughened Nfudu beyond her imagination. She realized she wasn't infallible and as a result, she permitted herself the same benefit of doubt she was already used to giving everybody else around her when they acted less than optimally.

25

JAVIER remained in Nice under Samantha's watchful care. Nfudu decided to pay him a surprise visit.

"Hello..." Nfudu's voice could be heard as she came down the hallway where Javier was seated with a pen in his hand and some papers scattered on the table in front of him. He looked rather serious as he stared at Nfudu in surprise. "How is the patient doing?"

"Nfudu..." Javier muttered as a broad smile spread across his face. After days of being cooped up in his home, he was obviously happy to see her. He got up and gave her a kiss on both cheeks and their customary third on the forehead before saying, "I'm so glad to see you. I Didn't know you were coming?"

"I wanted to surprise you, so I asked Samantha to keep it a secret. Thank God you're fully recovered," Nfudu said as she held his chin and moved it gently from side to side to review all the angles of his face. Standing that close to him, she felt a pang in her chest as she lowered her hand. "You've healed perfectly," she breathed. "No scars or bruises ...Wonderful!"

"Come over here." Javier took her hand and led her to the seat next to his. "How have you been?"

"The stress is unbearable. At times, I feel as though I can't get enough air to breathe."

"That's not good at all. Is there anything I can do to make it easier?"

"No…." Nfudu protested looking away to hide the tears that were starting to well up in her eyes after she had blinked twice to dry them. "I'm here to see if there's anything I can do to make it easier for you, not the other way around, so enough about me. How are you doing?"

"Sammy is taking excellent care of me, so I have no complaints." In that moment, Samantha walked into the room with a plate of hors-d'oeuvres and placed it on the side table between them.

"What would you like to drink?" asked Samantha

"Soda will do," responded Nfudu. "I have a slight headache. Do you have any painkillers?"

"Sure. I'll get some aspirin for you."

"Thank you."

Samantha got her a glass of soda and a bottle of aspirin on a silver tray and placed it beside the plate of hors-d'oeuvres. She then stood behind Javier and massaged his shoulders. Nfudu took a bite out of one of the hors-d'oeuvres.

"Ohh! It tastes heavenly," she said. "Did you make this Samantha?"

"No. The chef did. I'll be in charge of dinner. You can judge my cooking skills then." They all looked at one another and smiled. "How is the London circle? We haven't been anywhere in three whole weeks."

"It's definitely the same. A new scandal each week. Has the lawyer informed you that the trial is scheduled for the 31st of June?"

"She did," answered Javier. "But I wasn't expecting it to be so soon. I really am not ready for what I think it might entail. This craziness has taken a big toll on me, my work and my family life." Samantha gave Nfudu a quizzical look as Javier continued. "I'm not looking forward to being dragged around by the courts. And I'm dreading the publicity nightmare that is bound to arise."

Nfudu wasn't sure what Samantha's look meant, but she could only imagine that she wanted to change the direction of the conversation to happier topics, but she saw no way to remedy the situation at that point.

"I don't think you need to worry too much about publicity," she said. "We'll try our best to control the outcome."

"How do you hope to achieve that?" asked Javier.

"I'll say we work closely with our publicist. She has done wonders so far. I trust her. About your other concern, I'm sure we can talk to the lawyer to see if you can avoid being present at the trial. I don't know how possible that is, but because he attacked you in front of everyone it will be easy to convict him in your absence."

An uncomfortable silence followed during which Javier crossed his legs and bobbed his head back and forth. Samantha released his shoulders and snuggled up next to him. Nfudu felt a bit confused, but managed to find a different topic to diffuse the sullen atmosphere. "I would love to take a walk in the garden. It must be beautiful at this time of the year."

"Definitely. That should take our minds off things," said Javier.

-

The garden was superbly kept with the help of a local gardener. Nfudu had walked through it several times during her first and only visit to Nice, while she and Javier were dating, so she knew every corner of it. The multicolored roses and lilies gave off their best scents and colors at that time of the year. There were lilacs, pinks and purples and the white rose bush, Samantha's addition, was in full bloom. Samantha excused herself to prepare dinner, while Javier and Nfudu walked the entire length and breadth of the garden. In the beginning, they both entertained an awkward silence as neither one of them wanted to address the elephant in the room, until Javier spoke up.

"Of late, Sammy has been asking a lot of questions about us."

"Hmm… Why?"

"Apparently, she didn't know how serious our relationship was before the newspaper articles reported the scandal with Ikechi. The different accounts took a toll on her and since then, she's been acting a tiny bit insecure and pressuring me to step up to a commitment."

"But she knew we were engaged," said Nfudu. "It was front-page news at the time. Are you saying she was completely unaware?"

"Apparently so. Not everyone reads the gossip columns."

It was then that Nfudu realized the reason behind Samantha's sudden change in attitude towards her. The look that transpired earlier on when she talked about the trial wasn't an effort to protect Javier, but rather it was an indication of her frustration over the effect she had on Javier.

"Don't beat yourself up about it," Javier said. "Neither one of us could have controlled what happened with Ikechi. We also can't erase the fact that we had a relationship. I'll talk to her and set things right. My only concern is that the trial could further drag our lives into the public eye. I have been apprehensive about that."

As Nfudu was about to respond, Samantha joined them on the garden bench, where they had been sitting for fifteen minutes. "Dinner is ready," she said. "But it'll take a few minutes for the servers to set the table, so we can take our time."

The three of them walked around the garden one more time, with Javier and Samantha holding hands until they were ready to retreat inside for their meal.

Dinner was a delicious spread of roasted potatoes, chicken, fresh vegetables and cranberry sauce. Nfudu was happy to have a home-cooked meal at her disposal as she hadn't had one since she moved out of Knightsworth Manor. Since her move, she had relied on restaurant food and takeout to keep herself nourished. She never could find time between her work and her troubles to prepare a proper meal. It was at times like this that she missed being home with her parents and siblings.

"That was delicious," said Nfudu as their plates were being cleared by the server.

"Thank you," responded Samantha. "You know, I rarely cooked until I met Javier. Don't get me wrong, I've always known how to, but wouldn't be bothered because of all the travelling I used to do."

"You'll have to give me some of your recipes. I must confess that I only know how to cook Nigerian dishes. I haven't yet mastered the art of English cooking."

"By all means, whenever you're ready. I have a whole folder of recipes I started collecting since I was an experimental teenager."

"Thank you." Nfudu looked at her watch and sprang up. "Wow! It's time to catch my train."

"Oh. That's too bad," said Samantha. "Just as I was beginning to enjoy the only female company I've had in days. Please come again. It was good to see you."

"Thank you for having me and thanks again for dinner. Let me know when you'll be in London so we can get a drink or coffee ...anything."

"No problem. Have a safe ride."

"Goodbye."

Javier drove Nfudu to the train station to catch the six o'clock to London.

"I'm not sure why you're rushing back to London tonight. You could have stayed in Nice. Samantha and I would have taken good care of you. I can see that the events of the past few weeks have worn you down."

"If only you knew how bad things have been for me, you would have put me in a straitjacket and sent me to an asylum," Nfudu thought to herself. She never told him about the *osu* dilemma that had almost kept her and Ikechi apart and taken a big toll on her sanity and family relations. Even though she had been tempted to tell him many times, for some reason, she decided it was none of his business.

Still in her head, she heard Javier say, "Will you consider staying then? It will help you escape the hustle and bustle that has become your life in London."

"No... I have to get back," replied Nfudu, but what she really wanted to say was "I don't think it's a good idea. Have you forgotten that you have a serious girlfriend who adores you and possibly hates me?"

"Maybe next time I'll plan to stay. Please thank Samantha for dinner again. It was delicious."

"No problem."

"I hate to bring this up now, but there was never a chance to really discuss any serious matter in there. What do you think about the attempted murder charge?"

"Well, he did try to kill me..."

"That's right! He could have killed you. It was really scary," replied Nfudu.

There was an uncomfortable pause before Javier said, "But attempted murder? Even though I still get flashbacks about that day and imagine that my life could have easily ended, I'm a little wary about going that route."

"My thoughts exactly," agreed Nfudu. "This whole affair has become so stressful. I'm going out of my mind."

"Give me some time to think about what the next steps should be," said Javier. "In the meantime, I'll ask you to try and keep your mind off it. You can't afford to fall ill from the stress. The problem keeps me up at night as well, but we'll get through it."

Javier and Nfudu arrived at the train station about forty-five minutes before Nfudu's train was scheduled to leave. Nfudu was lucky to have purchased her ticket ahead of time; otherwise, she would have had to stand in the long queue with other last-minute buyers at the station. When she was about to board, Javier held her arms and kissed her forehead, after which he cleared his throat and said with subtle emotion "come again soon."

"I will. Nice is beautiful and I can stare at that garden all day." Nfudu said, trying to control her feelings for the man standing in front of her. She knew even when she said it that the garden wasn't her priority – he was – but how could she tell him that, after the damage she caused.

"I'll try my best to be in London next week. I feel bad leaving you to do all the work alone."

"Take all the time you need to recover. I have been managing fine."

"I know, but that's no reason to leave it all to you. Is it? God bless you and have a good night."

"You too."

From the train station, Nfudu branched to the Carnaby store to pick up some paperwork before going home. When she entered the lobby of her building at around ten o'clock, the doorman gave her a note addressed by Radke Solicitors & Associates. Shuddering as she speculated what the contents of the letter might be, she regretted the day she met the sender – Ikechi. Her father had tried to warn her, but his warning came too late – after she had already fallen hook line and sinker for him. Remembering her father, she felt like a little girl again and wished for his protection. After slipping a note into the doorman's hand, she marched down towards the elevator. She was too exhausted to handle the emotions that scourged through her whole body in that moment. There were thoughts of Javier and then this never-ending issue with Ikechi. When she closed the elevator door, she anxiously tore the envelope open to reveal the contents of the letter. Just as she had guessed, the letter was written by Ikechi's attorney on his behalf.

> *Dear Nfudu,*
>
> *You probably never want to see or hear from me again after all you have been through. I regret the role I played in wrecking our relationship.*
>
> *I know that Javier is the right person to address this letter to, but I realize that it may be an exercise in futility. Please consider pleading with him on my behalf to drop the charges against me and agree for us to settle outside of court.*
>
> *I promise to pay restitution, including covering the cost of his medical bills, cost for time off work, and a punitive amount that he sees fit to cover other costs that cannot be objectively determined. I also promise to the best of my ability to keep to the terms of the protective order taken against me and avoid being within five hundred feet of him and any member of his family.*
>
> *I am truly sorry for my offense and hope he'll consider this plea to enable me move on with my life and my business. If found guilty, I will be subjected to a jail term and classed as a dangerous offender ...*

The contents of the letter were too much for Nfudu to bear. She desperately wished she could run out of the elevator as so many thoughts flashed through her mind about the events leading to her meeting, and falling for Ikechi and his charms. Complying with his request, she thought would be a mistake as he could confuse their kindness for foolishness. If that happened, he would remain a clear and present danger to both her and Javier. The most she was willing to do at that point was help reduce his charge to assault and have him pay as the courts deemed fit. She already had the cross to bear for dropping her first set of charges against him. Had she not dropped them, he could have been in custody for a different murder charge, and Javier would not have suffered assault.

Nfudu kept the letter for days and despite trying her best to forget it and focus on her work, her mind kept returning to it. A few times, she thought about calling Javier to discuss the contents, but convinced herself each time that it was unnecessary.

Within a few days, Nfudu received a call from Ikechi's lawyer.

"Please, I need you to consider Ikechi's plea," he said. "Have you had a chance to speak with Javier about it?"

Nfudu didn't want to be bothered anymore and could only think about unpalatable things to say to the lawyer. However, she held her composure and said, "I have thought a lot in the past few days about the best way to approach the letter, but could not come to a resolution within myself, let alone ask Javier."

"So what information would you like me to pass to him?" asked the lawyer.

"Let him know that I'm still thinking about it. He needs to understand that this is not easy for me. I'll get back to him when I have an answer."

Nfudu felt sorry for Ikechi despite everything he had done to her. She felt obliged to at least hear him out as he had requested in the ending of his letter, but was torn between her compassion and the need to protect herself and the ones she loved.

"Attempted murder is a serious charge," said Javier after Nfudu shared Ikechi's letter with him. "I've had some time to think about this and I think we need to drop all the charges against him. It was a difficult choice for me, but I don't think we need his destruction hanging over our heads for the rest of our lives."

"I agree with you," said Nfudu heaving a huge sigh of relief. "He has his whole life ahead of him and we should not take it away from him. He definitely has some evil in him, but I believe he has learnt his lesson."

"I'm happy he made the first move towards this with his plea. It gives us room to negotiate," said Javier. "But how can we make sure this doesn't happen again? I wonder if I'm making a rational decision."

"The protective order we have against him is enough. It should put him on high alert. Non-compliance will result in another arrest and possible prosecution. But Javier, before you drop the charges don't you think it'll be a good idea to speak with him to see where his head's at?"

"I have no objections to you speaking with him. You probably need to do so for closure. You didn't get it the last time. As for me, I never want to see him again. It's sad that things have to end this way, but I feel like a heavy weight has been lifted off my shoulders."

"That is for sure," stressed Nfudu, "Only problem is that I have the additional burden of visiting him in jail."

—

Nfudu visited Ikechi in detention after she deliberated over and over again with her mother and later decided it was the right thing to do. She had never been in the vicinity of a jail, so she felt very strange in the surroundings. There was a certain air of apprehension, which made her uncomfortable. The uniformed workers looked like they were going to jump at the slightest provocation.

After being ushered into the visiting room, where several prisoners were seated with their guests, she noticed that only some of the prisoners were handcuffed. Ikechi was already seated and waiting for her when she entered. He looked a lot thinner, but still had that confident look in his eyes. He smiled when he said hello to her. He spoke quietly, his words slow and yielding.

"How have you been?"

"I don't know," Nfudu answered, feeling immense pity for him. "You had something to tell me."

"Yes. I've had a lot of time to think about everything since I've been in custody and it's funny how your mind plays tricks on you when you sit around all day with nothing to do. I wanted to apologize for everything, especially about the baby…"

On hearing baby, Nfudu sat upright and became more alert.

"Go on…"

"I lied when I told you that I had nothing to do with it… the miscarriage. I was ashamed and didn't know how to admit what I had done. I went insane when I found out the baby could belong to another man. The fact that you wouldn't consider an abortion further drove me mad. I loved you, still love you… but couldn't imagine raising another man's baby. I now know how shortsighted I have been. I didn't even stop to think that the baby could be mine. I'm sorry…"

Nfudu was sitting on the edge of her seat shocked and enraged by the time Ikechi was done speaking. Looking frantically from side to side, she hoped to get an answer from somewhere, anywhere, but even the walls seemed to be closing in on her. She tried to open her mouth to speak, but all she could deliver was an agape mouth and a pant that could be heard halfway across the room. By the time she recovered from her daze, she found herself yelling.

"You love me? But you killed my baby! Shame on you!" She drifted into a distressing sob, "What did my baby do to you? And Javier, what did he do to you to deserve almost being killed? I think I made a mistake coming here. I should let you rot in jail." She stood up to leave.

While she ranted, Ikechi just sat and looked with the most frightened expression on his face. He grabbed Nfudu's hand to stop her from leaving and she pulled it violently away from him. One of the guards approached their table.

"Is he hurting you, Miss?"

Nfudu looked at him and shook her head, her eyes forlorn and filled with tears.

"No. I'm fine. Thank you."

"You'll let me know if there's any problem, Miss."

"Yes," she nodded.

Ikechi froze when the guard came by and waited till he walked away to speak again.

"I am sorry for everything. Please forgive me." He had his head to one side.

Nfudu thought he looked incredibly pathetic. Her first instinct was to walk away and leave him to rot and die in jail. The thought of it gave her immediate satisfaction, but this lasted for only five seconds. She sat back down and looked at him with utmost disgust.

"I pity you and I've already forgiven you. I knew it was you all along because all the evidence pointed to you, but some part of me still wanted to believe that it was not true especially since you denied over and over again having anything to do with that. At some point, I started wondering if I sleepwalked and administered the drug to myself. I almost went mad. I don't know whether to be happy or sad with the realization that it was you."

Ikechi sat quietly listening to Nfudu with his two hands placed on the table. When she paused for a moment he pleaded, "Please. Don't abandon me here…" He darted his eyes across the room. Nfudu spotted the glint of terror in them when he finally looked at her.

His gaze kept her completely transfixed for almost five minutes before she responded.

"Javier and I will do our best to get you out of the jam you're in. He's willing to drop the charges if you'll promise to comply with the terms of the protective order."

"I have no choice…" Ikechi said, shaking his head, now with a somber look on his face.

"I don't think he'll appreciate that answer. He'll need to know that you'll comply, even if you had a choice. You know what I mean?"

"I understand. What I meant to say was that I'm grateful. Let him know that I'm really sorry for what I did to him. I'll seek help to make myself a better person. As for you, please find space in your heart to forgive me."

Nfudu ignored his last statement and beckoned to the guards to notify them that she was ready to leave. One of them accompanied her out of the room, while another took Ikechi in a different direction. When she got outside, she took a deep breath of fresh air and imagined how Ikechi felt being locked in there all day. He somehow deserved it, she thought. She didn't think he was a bad person. He had merely been too obsessed with her and been too possessed by his own insecurities that he didn't know how to act in an acceptable manner. When they were together, he had gotten along well enough with Javier, as much as the circumstances allowed. The recent turn of events, including the investigation and final break up, drove him insane. She hoped he had realized there was something worse than losing one's pride – losing one's freedom.

Immediately she got to her flat, she called Javier to brief him about her encounter with Ikechi.

"What an immense relief," he said. "You don't know how happy this makes me. It removes the mystery surrounding the poisoning incident it. Thinking about it sometimes almost drives me crazy. You don't want to know how far I take it in my mind."

"I can only imagine. I have thought sometimes that I may have done it to myself without knowing," Nfudu confessed.

"It was definitely torture to live with, especially when I remember that the evidence we had against him was circumstantial at best. I shudder to think what the court appearances for that case would have been like."

Ikechi was released two days after Javier dropped the charges against him. The night of his release, Nfudu got a call from his mother, who had been in London since she heard of her son's plight.

"Hello," Nfudu said when she picked the phone.

"This is Mrs. Ifejaku, Ikechi's mother."

"Oh," Nfudu said, surprised to be receiving a call from her. "Good evening Ma."

"My dear, please I'm just calling to ask for your forgiveness for what Ikechi did to your friend. Is there anything that can be done to retrieve your relationship?"

"No, ma. So much has been destroyed and the things that happened in the past make this situation more tragic for me than the issue of what happened between him and my friend."

"What past?" Ikechi's mother asked with a perplexed tone in her voice.

It was then that Nfudu realized that Ikechi's mother was completely in the dark about the depth of her son's transgressions. Even though Nfudu did not feel it was her place to reveal the details to Ikechi's mother, her persistent pleas left Nfudu no choice but to tell her the whole story. When she was done, Ikechi's mother seemed frozen at the other end, but within a few seconds, Nfudu heard a loud, "*Ogini bu ife a* o o – What is this? Why didn't anybody tell me this before now? '*Chimooo* – Oh my God'."

Her outburst lasted only a few seconds before she continued, "My daughter, please forgive him in any way you can. You know forgiveness is not for the other person, but for your own benefit."

Nfudu rolled her eyes at that epigram and thought that if she ever heard it again for as long as she lived she would give herself ten slaps. She thought of saying something sarcastic but instead settled for, "I have forgiven him already."

"From woman to woman, is there any way you can get back together with him? He really loves you. Jealousy must have driven him to commit these crimes."

"No, Ma. We've both given this relationship our best shot. It's time for me to move on."

"My daughter, please try. I am on my knees begging you. I promise that he won't stoop so low again. ...I promise."

Mrs. Ifejaku continued to plead with Nfudu, until Nfudu convinced her that under no circumstance would she consider getting back with Ikechi again. When she hung up, Nfudu pondered for a long time, what it was about some mothers and their sons that made them – the mothers – believe infinitely in their sons, even when they have committed the most hideous of crimes.

26

JAVIER came to London every other week for business. During those trips, he visited the stores to lend a hand wherever he could. Nfudu looked forward to his visits. Of recent, she had begun to nurse hopes of getting back with him. It had taken her inexplicable misguided desire for Ikechi and the destruction it brought along its way for her to realize that Javier was her one true love.

Someday in mid-July, Javier came by and gave a warm hello in the general direction of the cashiers in the Carnaby store and walked straight to Nfudu's office. She was expecting him, but could not understand why he appeared exceptionally happy that day. When he approached her, she got a feeling of déjà vu. He had a bounce in his steps and a warm smile slowly spread across his lips. He bent towards her and kissed her left cheek. "You look so happy," she said.

"Does it show?"

"Oh, it definitely does show," responded Nfudu nodding her head in successive movements.

Javier ran his hand down his right cheek in his typical fashion.

"Well, I am happy."

Suddenly, they heard the deep voice of a radio announcer reporting the removal of Asian non-citizens by Idi-Amin from Uganda and a confiscation of their businesses. Nfudu turned off the radio and shook her head.

"This brings back bad memories," she said.

"Of what?" inquired Javier, unable to understand her sudden change in mood.

"The war..." she said sullenly.

"I get it," said Javier. "This is why I hate listening to the news. Something always creeps up on you when you least expect it. Are you free for lunch this afternoon? ...Our favorite spot?"

"Sure." Nfudu was happy for an opportunity to hang out with Javier. "We can leave whenever you're ready."

They walked to their favorite restaurant on the ground floor of Harrods and quickly made a dash for the only available window seat they could find. They wanted to fulfill their favorite pastime of watching and commenting on passersby on the busy Knightsbridge Street, while they dined. As usual, they ordered lunch for each other and sipped on their drinks as each waited for the other to break the silence.

"The reason," started Javier, but paused when he realized Nfudu was speaking also. "Go ahead my dear," he said.

"I was about to say how much I love days like this. It makes me feel so lucky to be alive."

During their meal, they discussed exciting topics and commented on passersby on the street. They guessed which couples were married and which were simply dating or worse still sleeping together. Forgetting at times that they were in a public setting, they laughed like old times. Midway through their meal, Javier assumed a serious stance.

"Nfudu ...there's something I feel I need to tell you."

"Go on!" Nfudu said wishing he would get to it without first arousing her suspense.

"Samantha and I have decided to get married."

Nfudu dropped her cutlery gently on her plate and looked at him intently. "When did you this happen?" she asked, a sullen look spreading across her face.

"We got engaged last weekend in a private ceremony in Nice."

"Congratulations!" Nfudu managed to say at the same time trying to mask the fact that her blood was boiling.

"She's a great girl and really meets every criterion I want in a wife."

"Does Vanessa know about this?"

"Yes, she was there at the proposal."

"When is the wedding?"

"I'm not sure yet, but Sammy loves everything spring, so I'm assuming it'll be then."

"I'm speechless…" Nfudu said as she stood up to give Javier a lackluster hug. When she sat down, she gently pushed her half-eaten lunch away as a feeling of isolation consumed her. Javier noticed the pain in her eyes.

"What is it?" he asked.

Nfudu struggled for the right words to say to him. "Nothing," she lied. "I'm just so happy for you. …It's getting so hot in here. I think we better leave now for our one o'clock."

The rest of the day was a blur to Nfudu as she found it difficult to wrap her head around the news that Javier was getting married. Following their meeting, she feigned a headache and returned to her flat. She poured herself a glass of red wine and drew up a hot bath, where she soaked for an hour hoping to melt her sadness away. Unfortunately, the bath did nothing to ease her pain, but the wine made her so hazy that she soon fell asleep. She woke up as early as four o'clock, but felt lethargic and confused as to her whereabouts. The moment she remembered the events of the day before, she broke down into tears and crawled back into bed for another hour.

At work, her responsibilities gave her enough to occupy her mind, but as the day wore on she realized they didn't do enough to cure the heaviness in her heart. She felt as though she was carrying a heavy load around and no matter how much she tried, her thoughts consisted only of Javier. By the end of the day, she concluded that she still loved and wanted him back. She had known this for a long time but had refused to admit it to herself because she imagined he would always be there for her. It had not occurred to her that he could actually move on with someone else.

In the weeks that followed, Nfudu directed her focus on completing her fall collection – the most talked about of all her collections. It was an extremely creative one, conceptualized during a painful phase in her life, which caused her to be radical with the concept. She strayed from the typical fall colors of orange, green and browns and dared to incorporate black and purples and grays. These bold overtures gave the collection a gothic but classy look such as had never been seen before in the world of fashion. The collection included bell-bottomed power suits for the working girl as well as evening dresses and maxis to match the taste of the hard to please socialite. The resulting creation had enough flair to push Nfudu to the next level of her career. Although the collection was yet to be made available to the public, it already received critical acclaim from the fashion editors of Aller and Vintage fashion magazines, who were allowed a sneak peek during a promotion exercise for the fall collection. The Aller wrote:

"Never in your lifetime will you see another collection like this. It captures the very essence of the modern woman. It is unique, classy, upbeat and breathtakingly beautiful. Every woman would want an Nfudu in their closet. From their pantsuits to their evening dresses, to their haute couture, the collection breaks every barrier that has been set for modern fashion. It needs to be seen to be believed."

The collection was set to debut at the London Fashion Show and the Paris Couture Show, both in September. The success of those events would directly impact the success of the international stores when they opened their doors to the public. Any good publicity derived from the shows had the potential to expand Nfudu's customer base – mostly comprised of working women over twenty as well as society women, amongst who her evening and haute couture dresses were already a hit. Preparing for the shows was no easy feat and as the time approached, Nfudu found herself in a bind, with so much work to do and too little time to accomplish everything. Like she did whenever she found herself in similar situations, she called Vanessa to help her out.

Vanessa, who was pregnant with her first baby with David, was happy to lend a helping hand. She and David had been trying for a baby for a while and since she was in her second trimester, he forbade her from working too long on any task and Nfudu was no exception. Nfudu had been very supportive to both of them during their struggle to get pregnant. Even though she didn't have any children of her own she always knew the right thing to say to Vanessa to get her to relax.

"Nfudu my love." Vanessa cooed as she waddled into the room with her protruded stomach and with David walking in behind her. Vanessa's stomach was the biggest Nfudu had ever seen on a pregnant woman. She was only five months pregnant but looked as though she was about to deliver in one month. Nfudu had thought she was carrying twins, until an ultrasound, which she accompanied her to revealed it was a single birth.

"Hi, Darling. Hi, David," said Nfudu. "David, are you staying or will you pick her up later?"

"I'll pick her later," responded David. "I have a few places to go. See you both around eight."

"Eight it is then."

David left as the two women settled down to work, and the latest gossip. Nfudu hadn't seen Vanessa since Javier gave her news of his engagement to Samantha. She desperately wanted to ask Vanessa some questions about that affair, but was too embarrassed to broach the subject. Luckily for her, Vanessa brought it up.

"Have you heard about Dad and Samantha?" Vanessa asked.

"Yeah, I have," responded Nfudu. "He told me about it."

Vanessa stood up to pour herself some tea that Nfudu had left brewing for a while on the kitchen counter. "So what are your thoughts?"

"I'm happy for him. But then when I remember what we had I miss him…" Nfudu said, her voice trailing off as her emotions got the better of her.

Vanessa was in awe about her comment and stood, mouth agape, for a minute. "Have you told him that you miss him?" she asked. "I thought you had moved on when you left him for Ikechi."

Nfudu glanced at her, relieved that she hadn't treated her like she was off her bonkers for missing Javier. She took a sip from her cup before she responded.

"No. I haven't told him yet and I don't think I can tell him anymore. Not now that he's engaged to Samantha. We already had our shot and I blew it."

"Hmm!" exclaimed Vanessa. "If you still miss him, You should tell him. I know the timing sucks but c'mon. You were engaged to him and you never know if he still has feelings for you. You never know. He may still be in love with you."

"If he were, he wouldn't have asked Samantha to marry him."

"Well …I think you should speak with him. That's the only way to find out."

"Forget it," said Nfudu shaking her head. "He's moved on and so should I. Promise me you won't discuss this with anyone."

"I promise," said Vanessa, crossing her heart. "It's a personal matter between you and him, so I'll keep my mouth shut. Before I forget… David and I are hosting a baby shower next weekend. So please clear your calendar."

"Great! Are you hiring an event planner?"

"No, it's going to be a small one, with close friends and family. We're dressing up though."

"I wouldn't miss it for the world," Nfudu said as she rubbed Vanessa's big belly. "Do you know the sex of the baby?"

"I do, but I'm keeping it from David because I want it to be a surprise for him. Do you want me to burden you with a secret?"

"No. I'll pass," said Nfudu waving both hands in the air. I want to be surprised too."

David arrived just in time to pick up Vanessa, but with the loud music playing in the background he was left at the door for nearly fifteen minutes before Nfudu finally let him in.

"Did you two forget about me? I've been knocking."

"We're so sorry," Vanessa said. "I should have looked at the time."

"I see you girls did more than just work," said David looking at the mess they made with a box of chocolates and a tray of half-eaten macaroons. Fashion magazines were strewn all over the floor. "If I didn't know any better I would have thought you had ten other friends over for a party." Nfudu and Vanessa smiled mischievously at each other, and they burst into laughter when they caught David looking at them like they were a couple of juveniles. Vanessa helped pick up the magazines and hugged Nfudu before heading out the door with David.

"We'll see you at the shower," David said.

"Definitely," responded Nfudu. "I'll be there."

She was exhausted by the time they left and slept almost as soon as her body touched her bed. When she dreamt, she saw only Javier. It seemed as though nothing had occurred between them to sever their relationship. Like old times, they were together and happy, doing things that lovers would normally do. At some point, they were walking down a stream and stopped to kiss near some rose bushes. Kissing turned into lovemaking and when he laid her down, the thorny bushes mysteriously made way for plush white linen. While she was underneath him, she squealed with delight and curled her toes upwards to bring every ripple to the center. In the throes of passion, her alarm rang. She woke up and tried to move, but her muscles were tense. With a million emotions coursing through her body, she lay down and tried to recall every single detail of her dream. Slowly, she induced herself into a reverie – that, unlike her dream, she could control – and it was all up to her to either stay in or out of it.

27

VANESSA'S baby shower was nothing like Nfudu had expected. Vanessa had told her that it would be a small affair, with only their closest friends and family members, but the turnout seemed to indicate otherwise. There were at least one hundred guests at the lodge by the time Nfudu arrived and more were still on their way. Furniture was moved to strategic positions to accommodate all the guests in the large Victorian living room. The hallways, Verandas and garden were converted into sitting areas and a bar was strategically positioned where the television previously stood. Beautiful summer flowers were placed in tall vases in every corner. String lights, lanterns and chandeliers, all working together to create an exotic ambience were used to illuminate the entire space. The venue took Nfudu's breath away. She tried to fathom how Vanessa could have pulled off such impressive results without the help of a professional.

Vanessa looked beautiful in a multicolored maxi, one of Nfudu's designs, and David, who always had a great sense of style, looked handsome in a sleek pair of trousers, matching vest and a silk buttoned down shirt. Javier and Samantha were both dressed in black. Samantha was in a long evening dress that revealed her model figure and beautiful complexion, while Javier had on a pant and a satin shirt. His shirt sleeves were rolled up to reveal his perfectly toned arms and some buttons were left open to show a glimpse of his chest. Nfudu gasped silently when she saw him. He had never looked more handsome. She was glad she had paid particular attention to her own appearance; otherwise, she would have felt out of a place.

Nfudu recognized only a handful of the guests, but quite a lot knew who she was. They engaged her in conversation on different topics ranging from what was going on in America with the human rights movement to John Hicks Nobel prize for Economics. Several of the topics and a great number of the guests didn't interest her. One of them, a tall handsome gentleman, who introduced himself as Charles, insisted on an answer from her with regards to the fate of the Ugandan Asians expelled by Idi Amin. In an elevated voice that seemed to mask a slight cockney accent, he asked a group of five, "What do you think will become of those people?" When he didn't receive an answer immediately, he gestured in Nfudu's direction to prompt her for an answer.

"I don't know," Nfudu said, spreading her hands out and frowning unapologetically.

"Why not?" insisted the gentleman, "They're your people."

Nfudu was offended by his inference and obvious ignorance about geography, race and bias. At first, she did not want to accord his foolishness with another response, but on second thought, she decided to educate him a little bit.

"Firstly," she said, counting with her right index and left pinky finger. "None of 'them' are anymore my people than they are yours. Secondly," she said holding on to her left ring finger, "If you mean the 'Black Ugandans' they're from a place called Uganda and I am from Nigeria. These are two totally different countries and I can bet you will be able to find more of your relatives there than I can find mine."

"I'm sorry," muttered Charles while the rest of their company laughed at Nfudu's analysis of the issue. His ears became slightly reddened as he made a lame attempt to redeem himself. "I actually was referring to the Asians. Just concerned they'll storm Britain and create a refugee crisis."

"What?" retorted Nfudu, bending her head and looking at him in astonishment. "Does that make the issue any better?" Nfudu was glad to see Stanley in that moment. She excused herself from the group as

Stanley led her away. "I wasn't expecting you," she said. "I was so sure you'd be in Australia by now."

"My Australian trip is not until the end of the year. How are you?"

"I'm doing great now that you've rescued me yet again. How are you?"

"I'm doing great also. I've been watching you from across the room. You look more beautiful than the last time I saw you."

"Hmm…" purred Nfudu with a smile. She was used to getting compliments about her appearance from Stanley, but this time, there was something different about the way he delivered it. It actually made her feel warm and cozy. It didn't help that he looked well toned in his gray suit and matching tie. She cherished their friendship and quickly dismissed thoughts that were cropping up in her head about what it might be like to kiss him. When he spoke, she was awoken from her daydream.

"I'll like to take you to dinner sometime next week. Do you think you'll be able to spare some time?"

"Do you mean this coming week?"

"Yes," answered Stanley with a nod.

"I will be swamped next week. We have a fashion show the week after. Can we try to squeeze something in the following week?"

"I sure can. Have your assistant tell me which evenings you're free, so we can schedule something."

Their conversation was cut short when Vanessa announced her name over the microphone and invited her to make an opening speech. Stanley guided her to the center of the room, where she was handed a small microphone with a rounded tip. After she cleared her throat and took a quick glance around the room, she noticed that all eyes were on her – admiring glances – but nonetheless intimidating.

"Ladies and Gentlemen," she began. "It gives me great pleasure to extend a warm welcome to each and every one of you that made it out today to witness such a happy occasion. Many of you know me as the Lead Designer of Nfudu's Couture and the owner of Nfudu Stores. Vanessa and I have been friends for over seven years since we met at the International Institute of Fashion and have remained friends ever since.

"As students at the institute, Vanessa and I often discussed what our lives would be like when we were married. We both agreed that marriage and babies sounded like a lot of fun, but that the baby making aspect would have been more fun if the task was relegated to the guys." Laughter reverberated around the room as Nfudu gained more confidence speaking in front of the crowd.

"Once, I remember Vanessa saying to a group of guys that we hung out with, 'I wish roles could be reversed so that guys could carry the babies. If that was the case, I would impregnate my husband every year, have twelve children within twelve years, buy a football field and then hire a coach'" More laughter filled the room as Nfudu organized her thoughts.

"I bet she doesn't feel the same way anymore. Judging by the ease with which she is carrying this pregnancy and the glow in her eyes, I'm sure she's going to be a wonderful mother to this child and the remaining eleven she and David are going to have." There was more laughter.

"Prepare yourself to be wined, dined and entertained. Thank you all for coming and I hope you'll all have a fabulous time."

The guests clapped and cheered for Nfudu as Stanley ran to her side and exclaimed, "Wow! I didn't know you were such a great speech writer."

"I didn't write it," responded Nfudu, still out of breath from the challenge. "I was never even told I'll be making a speech."

In that instant, Vanessa came from behind and hugged Nfudu from the back. "That was awesome! I hadn't planned for a welcome speech but was informed by my aunt that one was necessary just minutes before I called you to take the floor. I knew you could do it!"

"What if I fell flat on my face?" asked Nfudu, agitated. "I was so nervous. It's a wonder I was able to pull that off."

"Well you did," said Vanessa. "Stanley will take care of you. I have to run to attend to other guests."

A live band started to play a favorite tune as the guests sipped their cocktails and socialized with one another. Nfudu spotted Javier looking at her from one end of the room. He winked at her when he caught her eye and she smiled slowly at him. Her heart beat uncontrollably again in that familiar pattern. While she contemplated walking up to him, Samantha appeared by his side and whispered something in his ears. Nfudu turned her back to him to look for a suitable pastime. The luxuriously set buffet table, filled with a variety of seafood – clams, lobsters, crabs and sushi, as well as roasted lamb and turkey, salads and hors-d'oeuvres of every kind provided just that. She helped herself to the delicious food and mingled with the crowd.

Halfway through the event, after the guests had been treated to the luxurious buffet feast, the Master of Ceremony announced that the hosts had an important announcement to make. Immediately, Javier took the floor with Samantha on his arms and addressed the guests.

"Good evening everyone. Thank you for making it out today. It has been such an amazing event – I honestly don't know how to thank everyone who had a hand in organizing this. Other than the baby shower, there's another reason for asking all of you here today. It's no news to most of you that Samantha and I have been dating for close to a year now. Samantha is an amazing woman, who came into my life at a time when I didn't know that love was possible for me. She stood by my side through some very difficult times…" He paused a little and you could hear a pin drop while the guests looked on in anticipation. "I love this woman," he said, looking at Samantha. Raising her hand, he placed it on his chest, then leaned sideways and gave her a kiss on the lips. "That is why I have asked her to marry me. And it may surprise some of you to know that she said yes."

The crowd was stunned at first, but when Samantha raised her left hand to show off her ring they cheered and surrounded the newly engaged couple to congratulate them. Nfudu stood transfixed to a spot after Javier's speech. She was crushed to a million pieces. The prior warning Javier gave her about his engagement did nothing to alleviate the hurt she felt over the surprise public announcement. Trying hard to maintain her composure, she toasted with the rest of the guests amidst chants of "congratulations." She wanted so desperately to leave, but couldn't find any escape route, so she walked aimlessly to the direction of the bedrooms. Vanessa saw her from a distance and rushed to her side.

"Are you ok?"

"No" responded Nfudu. "I'm not ok. I feel betrayed by everyone."

"How?" asked Vanessa, taking her hands and guiding her away from the chattering crowd to one of the guest bedrooms.

Nfudu looked at her.

"I really wish you had warned me."

"But Dad told you. You told me so the other night," said Vanessa, defensively.

"It's one thing to be aware they're getting married and another to witness it being announced to the whole world. It's so embarrassing to think that I just stood there in front of everybody and made a fool of myself with that speech."

"Don't say that," chided Vanessa. "You didn't make a fool of yourself. Your speech was amazing and neither has anything to do with the other."

"I thought I was just attending your baby shower but…" Nfudu's voice trailed off as she sniffed and wiped the tears from her eyes.

"I know. So did everybody else. I'm so sorry love. Dad thought it would be a good idea to combine the baby shower with an engagement announcement only a few days ago. It did not occur to me to inform you since you already knew about their engagement. It's my fault, I of all people should have known you would be offended. I have been so overwhelmed with work and planning for the shower I missed that."

"That's ok," responded Nfudu, wiping the last of her tears. "I'm such a mess. I should leave."

"You don't look a mess to me, but I'll perfectly understand if you leave." replied Vanessa. "But at least stay for the cake and then you can sneak out afterwards."

Nfudu powdered her nose and went right behind Vanessa to the living room where some of the guests were dancing and others were conversing at the top of their voices, some in a half-drunken state. She felt better instantly as the joyful air in the room infected her spirit to the point that she found herself smiling again. When she started to get into the groove, she saw Javier coming towards her. She smiled when he took her hand and led her to the dance floor. While they danced, she congratulated him as if nothing had happened to upset her. His masculine scent made her heady and she laughed at a corny joke he told her, until Samantha interrupted their dance to invite him to meet some of her friends. Nfudu took that as her cue to leave.

-

Several days after the shower, Nfudu fought hard with her emotions to get back to feeling as normal as she could. No matter how hard she tried, nothing seemed to work in helping her forget about Javier. She felt extremely lonely and thought of speaking with Vanessa again about the issue, but cautioned herself against it because she didn't want to seem too needy. As time passed, she agonized too much to function properly, so she did the only thing she could imagine when she had nowhere else to turn – call the person she trusted the most in this world, her mother. She was the only person she knew who would not judge her no matter how foolish she seemed – her go-to person, whenever her life became unbearable.

"What is it again Nfudu?" Mrs. Ibe asked when she heard her breathing heavily after a protracted silence.

"It's Javier. He's getting married."

"But you left him for Ikechi. Did you not expect him to move on with his life *ehn*?"

Nfudu felt foolish but nevertheless felt in charge of her own feelings. "Yes, Mama. I blame myself for leaving Javier for Ikechi, causing both of them so much pain and leaving a disastrous trail behind. But don't forget the stress Papa gave me when I wanted to marry Javier. If not for that, I would never have fallen for Ikechi."

"Ah!" exclaimed Mrs. Ibe. "So you're blaming your father now. That's all right. He probably deserves some of the blame. What I would like you to do now is to stop this pity party and try to answer one important question for me. Do you still love Javier?"

"Yes!" responded Nfudu. "I have never stopped loving him. I had merely fallen for Ikechi's dangerous charm at the expense of what I now know to be true love."

"I'm not surprised."

"What do you mean?" Nfudu asked.

"Where do I begin? …I knew how much you loved this man the first time you came home right after the war, which was why I stuck out my head to try and convince your father to let you marry him. Your father's stubbornness did not allow him to see beyond his white skin. His age was a different matter, but that didn't bother me. I knew he would be able to take care of you."

"Why didn't you insist then? Why did you let me follow Ikechi?" Nfudu said in an exasperated tone.

"Well, Ikechi seemed like a good choice at the time – an Igbo boy, from a well-to-do family, who seemed to love you immensely. It's nobody's fault that it ended the way it did. No one could have predicted that he could commit those atrocities. Call it bad luck or bad choice; I strongly believe your gut feeling must have told you that you were making the wrong decision."

"I mistook Mister 'wrong' for Mister 'right'…"

"Quite possibly, but don't beat yourself up about it. The notion that there's only one right person for everyone is a little bit antiquated. You're a very beautiful girl and still very young. You can still meet someone great to marry. Besides, Javier has not married this girl yet…what is her name again?"

"Samantha."

"Yes. Samantha!" exclaimed Mrs. Ibe. "Have you told him how you feel? Chances are that he feels the same way too."

"Really? Can I do that?"

"I see no harm in it," replied Mrs. Ibe.

Nfudu took her mother's words to heart. Most importantly, she felt so much better after their discussion and was again able to carry on as normal. She pondered how much of the good advice she received from her mother she was going to take and which ones she was going to toss, but later resolved that she was going to try to win Javier back.

She knew she could never love anyone as much as she loved him. He was her first love and in her mind, they were meant for each other.

-

The London fashion show was another huge success for Nfudu's Couture. It was attended by designers, celebrities, magazine editors and buyers from all over Europe. The team had anticipated a good turnout but had not planned for the huge crowd that showed up at the Roadhouse Arena – the venue of the event. Javier had to quickly round up additional help to cater to the large crowd. Twelve designers featured their designs on that day, and since seats were too limited to accommodate most of the guests, a great number of them stood during the show.

The activities that followed the show were every bit as significant as the main event. Representatives of retailers, boutiques, established designers and emerging designers all wanted a piece of Nfudu and her designs. The press that followed corroborated earlier press on the exquisiteness of the new collection.

"I am so proud of our team," said Javier to Nfudu. "But I'm mostly proud of you. You're a genius."

"Thank you so much," responded Nfudu excitedly.

"Honestly, your creativity and business sense both merge together in a perfect formula to merit you that title."

Nfudu did not really consider herself a genius. The only things she felt any ingenuity about, was her ability to put together a great team. That required being a good judge of character. Also, the fact that she was always willing and able to learn new things gave her the opportunity to leverage the skills of each and every one in her team.

"The team worked so hard for months to make this happen. I can't take all the glory."

"They need to work even harder for the Paris Couture show," added Javier. "That's the one that keeps me up at night. It can either make or break our ambition to conquer the international scene."

"I agree. We need to get to work right away. Tonight though, I'm going to take a break," she said, letting out a small yawn.

"You look exhausted. Let me take you to dinner tomorrow to celebrate. ...What do you say?"

Nfudu accepted the invitation but felt guilty for not accepting Stanley's offer the week before.

Javier took her to dinner the following day.

"Get your dancing shoes," he said. "We're going to the Mastid for an a la carte and some dancing afterwards."

"Are you sure about that?" Nfudu protested. "My body still aches from working non-stop."

"It will help loosen your muscles and relieve the pain. C'mon, I'll pick you up at nine o'clock on the dot."

On the ride to the restaurant, Nfudu felt the urge to lean sideways and kiss him as the blues playing on the radio toyed with her senses. However, she restrained herself from fear that she might make a fool of herself.

She was still lost in her daydream when Javier asked her a question.

"Other than work, what else are you up to these days?"

"Nothing much..."

"Seeing anyone?"

Nfudu mustered all the strength she could to avoid baring her heart to him. "No. ...Not at all."

"I find that hard to believe. I saw all the eligible bachelors and even the married men gawking at you during the baby shower. Don't worry you won't be single for long."

"Dating is the least of my priorities now. I'd rather wait for the right person," Nfudu lied. She wondered what he might think if he knew she would rather not have anyone if she couldn't have him.

Javier continued to tease her.

"Stanley, Vanessa's friend was all over you. I know you're all friends, but every time I saw him at the shower, he was either with you or staring at you from a distance. One time, he even asked me if I knew where you were and I told him that you may have left. He looked disappointed when I gave him that piece of information. By the way, why did you leave without telling anyone?"

"I told Vanessa."

He leaned over her, and she held her breath. For a moment, she thought he was bending towards her for a kiss, but was disappointed when she realized he was just leaning over to pull out her door latch. On getting over her disappointment, a sudden impulse hit her. She wondered if that was the right moment to tell him how she felt about him but quickly decided against it. It was better to wait until the Paris Couture show, she thought, to avoid distractions from the important work ahead of them. Moreover, he had not shown any real interest in her since he started seeing Samantha. All that could be left between them might be a great friendship and she did not want to destroy that by acting on the spur of the moment.

Dinner was different from what she had expected. They were seated across a long table with a number of other guests and the food was prepared right before them. The guests got an opportunity to converse with each other and build rapport with one another. Nfudu learned from the waiter that this was considered necessary since they were to dance together afterwards.

"Do you like the look of it?" Javier asked after her plate was placed in front of her.

"I think so. It smells delicious and is made with all fresh ingredients. I'm sure it'll be great."

Their conversation was interrupted by a Chinese couple sitting next to them.

"Are you two married?" the man asked, while his partner looked on.

"No." responded Javier. "We're close friends."

"Oh, ok." nodded the man. "My wife and I were debating if you were husband and wife or boyfriend and girlfriend. You look good together, though."

Javier and Nfudu looked at each other and giggled.

After their meal, they danced for a couple of hours. Javier stared at Nfudu as she put her hands above her head and wriggled her hips in every direction while she smiled seductively at him.

Javier admired how carefree she was and thought to himself how sexy she looked at twenty-eight. A far cry from the twenty-year-old he once knew.

When the night was over, he took her back to her flat and gave her a kiss on her left cheek. Nfudu was disappointed as this was less than their customary one kiss on each of her cheeks and then a third one on the forehead.

"I'll see you in Paris." He said.

"Paris it is." Responded Nfudu, hoping she would have better luck with love in the city of light.

28

THE Paris Couture Show was a huge success. The weeklong event showcased eighteen old designers and four new ones. Once again, Nfudu's ready to wear collection was a hit amongst the buyers for major department stores and boutiques. Her haute couture collection left show attendees wanting more as they watched in amazement when her models walked down the runway. The demand for the brand and the designer skyrocketed. Press was daunting, but with the help of her publicist, Nfudu was able to prioritize requests for interviews, which reduced the demands on her time.

The joy Nfudu felt at the success of her outing was marred by her sadness over Javier's last minute cancellation. The day before they were to leave for Paris, he sent apologies in order to attend to a pressing business matter. Nfudu, who had become accustomed to having him by her side at such events, felt too exposed without him. This was a trap she often found herself falling into over and over again – as a result of her excessive dependency on him. Often times, she had cautioned herself over the need to learn to stand on her own, but his absence in Paris bothered her in particular because she had planned to tell him how she felt about him on the trip.

When she returned to London, she called him, not so much out of curiosity for why he cancelled at the last minute but out of the love she felt for him.

"Hey how did it go?" asked Javier.

"It went really well. Better than expected," responded Nfudu. "I was wondering why you couldn't make it, though. I missed you."

"I was terribly occupied. I'm so sorry. I had to help Sammy out with something. I hope it wasn't so much of an inconvenience."

"No. Not really. There were a couple of events I would have liked to attend with you by my side, but I guess it is what it is."

"I'm sorry dear. I promise. I'll try and make it up to you. I'll be in London next week. See you then."

"Ok. Bye."

Nfudu was livid after she hung up. Javier hadn't provided her with any tangible explanation for abandoning her at such a critical moment. His initial excuse – having an urgent business matter was much more acceptable to her than his second – canceling because Samantha needed help with 'something'. She felt betrayed and like she did whenever she felt sorry for herself, she buried herself in her work. Luckily for her, the week after the Paris show was a very busy one for her, so it gave her the escape she needed. Buyers streamed in and out of their showroom to review the collection and place their orders. She and her team reconciled the orders – another uphill task – with many moving parts, and finalized the numbers to be transferred to the production team. Also on her plate were the Milan, Paris and Athens stores, which were due to begin operations in a matter of months. Customer's interest in the stores spiked after the Paris Couture Show – which further propelled Nfudu's Couture to a new level of recognition – an international status.

Nfudu's trip to Lagos was imminent. Her partners in Nigeria worked fervently to make the launching of the Lagos Fashion School a success. The pioneer class of students was already enrolled and attending lessons. Except for the flooding experienced with the heavy rains in July which threatened the staff block, most of the feedback Nfudu received from Fibi indicated that things were going in the right direction.

The past year was not only physically exhausting for Nfudu, but had also been emotionally and psychologically draining. Nfudu hoped to use her coming visit to Nigeria as an opportunity for a much needed vacation. She prayed the trip would be nothing like her last one, which had been highly emotional, because of the devastation left by the war, her father's objection to Javier and her illicit love affair with Ikechi. When she phoned to remind her parents about her visit, her father was thrilled.

"We can't wait to see you again my dear. Is there any particular purpose for this trip or you're just coming to visit us?"

"Papa, did you forget?" asked Nfudu. "I told you a few weeks ago that I'd be coming for the opening of the Lagos Fashion School."

Nfudu could hear her mother in the background.

"What kind of question is that Papa Nfudu? Don't you want her to return to her father's house? How many times have I told you that she's coming to open the new school in Lagos?"

"You don't mean it!" exclaimed Chief Ibe.

"Congratulations, my dear!"

"Thank you, Papa."

Mrs. Ibe took the phone from him. "My dear, we're really looking forward to seeing you. Some of us will attend the event but we'll know for sure when it gets closer to the time."

"No problem Mama. Please greet everyone."

"I will my dear. Take good care of yourself."

"Yes Ma," responded Nfudu. She wondered about her father's health as he seemed so forgetful the last few times she spoke with him, but decided to discuss it with her mother the next time she called.

-

Stanley met Nfudu for their long awaited dinner date at a hip new restaurant in Chelsea, Ricardo's – Stanley's suggestion. Nfudu had heard about the restaurant as being frequented by the royals. Stanley was already seated by the time she arrived. He looked lost in thought when she walked up to him.

"Hi Stan," she said.

"Hello," said Stanley, as pleasantly as ever. He got up to give her a hug. "I didn't see you walk in. How are you?"

"I'm fine. Feeling a little overworked though. When did you come into London?"

"Yesterday. How did your shows go?"

"Very well. Thank you."

"Congratulations on a job well done."

"Oh. Thanks!"

"I'll like to go straight to the point about why I've been trying to meet with you," said Stanley, placing his elbows on the table, and clasping his hands in front of him while he looked directly at Nfudu. He looked up for a second to signal to the waiter approaching their table to return later, before he said matter-of-factly, "It's pretty obvious what I feel about you and I was wondering if by any chance you feel the same way about me. Don't want to scare you off, but I need to know where your head is at."

"Hmm...," hummed Nfudu. "I remember that day during our second year in Paris when you told me you'd come and marry me after you become a senator in the Italian Parliament." She eyed Stanley in amusement and waited for him to respond, but he was chuckling lightly, with one fist covering the right side of his mouth.

"Yes," nodded Stanley. "I remember that. It was the night of Jeremy's birthday party. You have an excellent memory."

"Well, you don't forget something like that, do you? No one has ever said anything that romantic to me and I thought it was very sweet at the time. I still do. By the way, whatever happened to that ambition? Do you still plan to run for a Senate seat?"

"Yes," said Stanley nodding his head. "I haven't completely abandoned the ambition, but for now, I'll rather stay with the firm, till I make partner and that's only a few months away. It'll be fast-tracked with my move to Australia. After I've partnered for a few years then I'll consider running for office."

"Sounds great. Keep the dream alive."

"Back to our discussion. Since I made that statement to you, I've seen you with these other men – Javier and then your ex-husband and I've beaten myself up for not moving fast enough. You're single now, so what do you say we give a relationship a try?"

Nfudu sat wide-eyed. It took her a moment to absorb Stanley's proposal before she replied. "Stan, I really …really like you. It's so easy for anyone to see that you would have been the perfect man for me. We always got along so well and you treat me like a delicate flower. I appreciate all you've done for me. You've rescued me more times than I can count…but …I'm in love with somebody else."

"Who?"

"I'm not sure if it's appropriate for me to say."

"Is it Javier?"

Nfudu was stunned. "How did you know?"

Stanley paused for a moment before responding.

"I was watching you at the baby shower when the engagement was announced. You looked like a ton of bricks had been dumped on your head. I looked for you afterwards, but you were nowhere to be found. I didn't know what to make of the whole incident. I thought you were the one who left Javier… so I couldn't figure out why you were so upset."

"Was I that obvious? Would anyone else have noticed?"

"Probably not. I couldn't take my eyes off you the whole evening. Maybe that's why I noticed."

Nfudu sat there, looking down in embarrassment, unable to speak any longer. Stanley reached over to take her hand. When she looked up, he saw the deep pain in her eyes.

"I'm sorry dear. I didn't mean to upset you. In fact, when I saw what happened I wasn't sure what to make of it. I also didn't want to jump to any conclusions. If it'll make you feel any better, I'll keep our discussion today to myself."

"I'd appreciate that Stan. About how I feel about you, I do care about you. I know we could have a romantic connection and we're super compatible. But with how I feel about Javier, I'll be no good to you or anybody right now, what with all the baggage I'm dragging along with me. Yet, I won't rule out anything between us in the future. Right now, I just have too much to deal with. I hope you understand."

"I understand. Take all the time you need."

"Thank you."

While they dined, they reminisced about old times. They also talked about their upcoming trips – Stanley's to Australia and Nfudu's to Nigeria. Later, Stanley took her to her flat. He came out of the car when he got to her building to get her door. When she stepped out, they exchanged a long hug.

"I'll miss you," he said.

"I'll miss you too," Nfudu said, wondering when their paths would cross again.

"I'll write when I get to Australia. Take good care of your gorgeous self."

"Thank you," she smiled. "Good night."

The next day at work, Nfudu found herself in frequent reverie as she reminisced about her date with Stanley. She thought of calling Vanessa to discuss his request but immediately thought against it to maintain his confidentiality. But, it was no secret to Vanessa and every one of their friends that Stanley had a soft spot for her. She had been teased severally about it in the past and she always had the same reaction to it – laughed it off as wrong because she never knew for certain how he felt about her until now.

Javier did not come to London the following week as promised nor the next. He came in three weeks later when Nfudu had only three weeks left until her trip to Nigeria. Nfudu could not wait any longer to tell him what had been bogging her mind. She decided to go against her better judgment and invite him to her flat on his first night in London under the pretext that she wanted to discuss business. He arrived just as she was taking food out of the oven.

"What's that aroma?"

"It's fish and chips. I made dinner for us."

"Thank you. Can we sit outside on the verandah? I sat indoors in meetings all day. I could do with some fresh air."

"Let's take it outdoors then," said Nfudu. "I love the cool October air. It's warm enough to be outside, but not that cold that you have to be stuck inside."

"I know the perfect spot," said Javier moving the balcony table closer to the railing and pulling two chairs to face each other. Next, he got two glasses from the kitchenette, while Nfudu applied finishing touches to the meal. "There's quite a spread here."

Nfudu laughed.

"I didn't say fish and chips was all there is. The meat pie and lasagna were going to be a surprise."

Javier poured two drinks, while Nfudu put the rest of the dishes on the table.

"This looks delicious," said Javier. "I prefer a home cooked meal to eating out any day."

"How is Samantha?"

"She's in Florence for a photo shoot as the new face of Laurel Cosmetics."

"That's nice!" Nfudu responded nodding. She couldn't help but feel happy that Samantha's photo shoot gave room for the evening.

"Yeah. She was really excited about the opportunity."

It was a beautiful night. The silvery white moon was high up in the sky, giving off enough illumination to replace the light from the candlelight, which died within minutes after Nfudu placed it on the table. The leaves on the trees let out a soft whistle while a gentle breeze blew. Nfudu's heart tugged as she viewed Javier's face in the moonlight. She wondered if he could feel what she was feeling in that moment. Soon it was starting to feel a little chilly. Nfudu shivered from the cold breeze.

"Please excuse me," she said. She walked to her bedroom and came back with a scarf across her shoulders.

"I would have kept you warm," said Javier with a grin after she returned to her seat. He always flirted with her, which never stopped, even after he started seeing Samantha. It was probably impossible for him to stop now.

While they ate, Nfudu searched for the perfect opportunity to broach the subject that had been plaguing her mind for weeks. It was hard since they had so much else to discuss – the Paris Couture Show, the stores, the Lagos Fashion School and her upcoming trip to Nigeria. It didn't help that they hadn't seen each other in almost a month.

"Our plates are full." He said.

"Oh no… They're empty," responded Nfudu, sarcastically, not realizing he was not talking about the plates in front of them.

"I don't mean the plates in front of us. I'm speaking figuratively."

"I understand."

"What's on your mind?" Javier asked, "You seem lost in thought."

Nfudu was anxious, but took that moment as the perfect opportunity to bare her mind to him. "I need to tell you something."

"Go on. I'm listening."

"I don't know how to put this. The thing is…" She sighed and looked above the horizon at the moon and stars and in doing that forgot her intentions for one minute. When she came to herself, she wondered what he might think of her if she told him what was on her mind.

"Are you in some type of trouble? Talk to me."

"No. I'm not in any trouble. It's something else," said Nfudu shaking her head.

"I'm…I'm still in love with you… I never stopped loving you. I realize that I've been stupid and made many mistakes and I'm so sorry for that. Please forgive me," she paused to dab her nostril with the back of her hand as her voice graduated to a sob. "These past few months, I've been unable to function properly. All I do is think about you day and night. I have this recurrent dream about us and it's driving me crazy."

Javier sat there motionless, with a ghostly expression on his face. He didn't know what to make of her revelation.

"I didn't know you still cared about me, at least not to this extent," he said. "I don't know what to say about this. I mean…I'm speechless right now."

"Is there a chance of us getting back together?"

Javier shook his head and sighed in exasperation. "I love Samantha. Even though what I have with her may not compare with the passion we once shared, I feel at peace with her. She encompasses everything I have ever wanted in a woman. I don't see myself leaving her."

Nfudu felt as though her heart had been ripped out of her chest and shredded into a million pieces. She realized in that moment what it meant to have a broken heart. Here she was pouring her heart out to him and all he could do in response was sing Samantha's praises. She wished she had kept her feelings to herself or better still controlled her urges. It was all too much for her to bear and the more she thought about it, the more she lost control and started to sob uncontrollably. Javier knelt beside her and held her in his hands to try and console her. Amidst her sobs, she whispered to him, "Is there no way we could get back together?" in a final attempt at winning him back.

Javier was firm in his conviction. He shook his head, while he drew her body away from his to get a better look at her.

"No...I can't leave Sammy. That would be unwarranted." He wiped her eyes with his thumb and waited for her to calm down before moving back to his seat. She looked away in embarrassment when she caught him looking at her, and hugged her scarf. For the rest of their meal, she picked at her plate. When Javier tried to cheer her up, she felt he was patronizing, which to her was worse than rejection. For the rest of the evening, they made only small talk. When Javier finally got up to leave, he kissed her on both cheeks and then on her forehead, but she barely looked at him. Before he shut the door behind him, he took her chin in his hands and pulled it gently towards him at a slight angle and said, "You'll be fine my lovely girl. Trust me!"

Nfudu didn't know what to make of his statement and cried herself to sleep that night. She couldn't believe she had lost Javier forever. Her heart sank so deep into her chest; she felt it might burst through. For the first time in so long, she prayed to God that night to take her pain away. Almost instantaneously, she started to feel much lighter and eventually fell asleep.

When she woke up in the morning and looked herself in the mirror, her eyes were red and swollen from sobbing the night before. Wallowing in self-pity, she cancelled all her appointments for the day.

She didn't blame Javier for her predicament, but rather felt guilty for broaching the subject with him. Her biggest concern was the impact her revelation would have on their friendship and working relationship. When she got up to bathe, she felt a sharp pain on the right side of her head. After she took some aspirin, she went back to bed and slept until she heard the sound of her phone ringing. She thought it might be Javier calling to apologize and decided it would be great to let him ring himself into oblivion until he realized the damage he caused. In her mind, that would make him feel guilty enough to stop and realize that he loved her and only her. When she finally picked the phone, she was disappointed when Vanessa's voice greeted her on the other end of the line. Her first instinct was to hang up. The thought that Javier had abandoned her after her state from the night before, overwhelmed and made her angry.

"Hello dear. I went to your office and was told you were ill. How are you feeling?" Vanessa asked.

"Not so well, so I decided to take a sick day."

"Do you want me to come over?"

"No. No... Don't worry. I'll be fine soon. I just need a little rest." Nfudu wasn't sure if Vanessa knew about her meeting with her Dad the night before, and was too embarrassed to bring up the subject with her.

"Are you sure?" Vanessa insisted.

"Yes, I'm sure."

"Ok. Let me know if you need anything."

Javier had called Vanessa that morning to vent and was shocked at how much she already knew about Nfudu's feelings towards him. Feeling distraught himself, he pleaded with Vanessa to discreetly check up on her. Having been in her shoes, he knew how badly it hurt to have ones love unrequited.

When Nfudu broke up with him, he had relied on friends and family to make the healing process easier, but half the time, he felt like a caged lion, whose roar could only be heard in its own head. He shed tears in the presence of his chauffeur the day Nfudu told him about

Ikechi. He shed many more tears when he was by himself and felt the most miserable he had ever been in his life. Having Vanessa and David's support at that time was a saving grace, and he wanted Nfudu to get all the support she needed.

Vanessa wanted to get to the root of the matter, so she visited Javier at the lodge the following day.

"Are you sure Dad?" she asked, referring to his decision on which woman to be with.

"Of course I am. When I met Sammy, my whole outlook on life changed. She was nothing like Nfudu. In fact, she was the opposite of her. She took care of me and always seemed to be able to read my mind. She was all I needed to move on from my hurt. I'm looking forward to spending the rest of my life with her."

"I'm saddened by the situation," said Vanessa, "But I'm glad you've both got the closure you need to move on. I hope Nfudu can move on from this."

"I hope so too," agreed Javier. "My only regret is realizing I may have led her on by the closeness I maintained with her even after we broke up. I should have kept some distance to avoid giving her the wrong impression. Samantha raised the issue many times with me, but I brushed it off as a misconception. It was the only reason I skipped the Paris show."

"I won't say I'm surprised," said Vanessa. "If I was in Samantha's shoes, I wouldn't have let you go to Paris either. A whole week in Paris with your ex-fiancée seems like a recipe for disaster to me. How did Nfudu take it?"

"I didn't tell her the real reason I missed the show. I felt awful for letting her down and then lying about it."

"Don't beat yourself up about it. She should understand. The chemistry between you and her was always apparent to everybody, including Samantha. She must have befriended Nfudu as a coping mechanism knowing that her closeness with you was something neither she nor anyone could change."

Javier shook his head.

"I never saw it that way," he said. "I thought Sammy was just being friendly."

Nfudu tried to pick the pieces of her life up before her trip. Even though she still craved Javier, she learnt to cope by relying on friends and family and most importantly her work. She planned to be back before Vanessa's due date – the last week in November to witness the birth of her baby, being that she held the coveted Godmother role. Vanessa was anxious that Nfudu was leaving at such a crucial time.

29

NFUDU was in a celebratory mood when she stepped into the arrival terminal of the Lagos International Airport. "It's always good to be home," she said to Fibi when she first set eyes on her outside of baggage claims. She had a lovely looking gentleman, who she introduced as her fiancé on her arms. Nfudu recognized him as Fibi's boyfriend from the pictures she sent in one of her letters.

"When did you get engaged?" Nfudu asked.

"Two weeks ago. I wanted to surprise you," Fibi said as she flashed a gold engagement ring, with a diamond in the centre. It was a beautiful ring – basic – but beautiful.

"Hmm. This is really nice. Congratulations! Any wedding date yet?"

"We're planning for sometime next year."

Fibi's Fiancé, Aki, was an attractive young man who ran his father's telecommunications business. Fibi considered herself lucky to have found him because he had all the qualities she needed in a partner.

"How did you two meet?" asked Nfudu.

Fibi and Aki looked at each other and smiled. "Go ahead," Aki said to Fibi.

"Ok. We have you to thank for our meeting."

"How?" Nfudu asked. "I wasn't here."

"We met when Aki came to the school to inquire about admissions for his niece. We went on our first date the following day and since then, we've been inseparable."

"Ohh...!" Nfudu exclaimed. "That's awesome." Their story reminded her of her first meeting with Javier. The circumstances under which they met weren't much different.

Aki was only five years older than Fibi, but seemed a decade older because of his calm nature and caring attitude. Fibi loved and respected him, and he adored her in return.

A Range Rover was waiting to take Nfudu to her hotel. When she got into the backseat, she recognized Tunji at the steering. He greeted her with a wide smile.

"Good evening, Ma."

"Hello, Tunji. How have you been?"

"Fine, Ma. Welcome back."

"Thank you."

Aki joined Tunji in the front seat, while Fibi joined Nfudu at the back. Nfudu thought Fibi and Aki made the perfect match. She caught him looking at her lovingly when the car drove out of the airport, into the crazy Lagos traffic. As they approached the Island, Aki reached behind to hold Fibi's hand and she shyly pulled away. His affection towards Fibi reminded Nfudu of what she was missing. She felt a little melancholic, but soon snapped out of it when the ocean breeze hit her face. She opened her window to get a better view of the evening sky. The island breeze always did wonders for her mood.

"Hmm...I love the island. I missed the ocean, the smells and the lights," she said.

"I wonder how you can live so far away from home," responded Fibi. "You should move back. I for sure need you here..." While Fibi rambled on, Nfudu stuck her head out of the car window for more air.

When Tunji pulled in front of her hotel lobby, Nfudu hesitated a little.

"I am way too hungry to relax and unpack my luggage," she said. "Can you guys take me to the roasted fish joint in Victoria Island?"

"Which one?" Fibi asked, with a quizzical look on her face. "Several have opened since the last time you were here."

"Take me to anyone that is close by."

"We can go to Madam Koko's. I haven't eaten there, but I hear it's the best in town."

"Madam Koko! What a name." Nfudu said with a puzzled look on her face. "She sounds like someone with good roasted fish though."

Dinner was delicious, but a bit too spicy for Nfudu's now British taste buds. She ate voraciously as she had been craving roasted fish for months. By the time she got back to her hotel, she was too tired to get anything done, let alone remove her makeup, so she plopped into her bed. She woke up early the following morning, had breakfast in bed and made a few phone calls. There was so much to do for the school opening ceremony two weeks away and too little time to accomplish everything. She had several meetings booked, presentations to prepare and speeches to write. A chunk of the work was being handled by her team on ground. Even though they had made amazing progress by the time Nfudu arrived, she still needed to verify what was already accomplished to avoid any surprises on opening day.

The days flew by. Nfudu scoped out her new environment whenever she had some free time. So much had changed since the last time she was in Lagos. The new Lagos National Stadium was a sight to behold with its Olympic-sized swimming arena and lawn tennis courts. The facilities provided her with adequate distractions during her stay. Also, Fibi and Aki took her to so many new lounges and clubs she never knew existed. A few were painful reminders of the days she spent gallivanting around Lagos with Ikechi. In her mind, those days were gone forever and she couldn't get them back even if she wanted to. Ikechi was a foregone conclusion – a mistake of sorts. Why it hurt to remember him was something she really couldn't understand.

-

Nfudu planned to visit her parents in Abasi immediately after the school launching, before returning to London. Just before she left London, they informed her they would be unable to attend the ceremony in Lagos but would send Afonwa to represent the entire family. Chief Ibe's health had deteriorated significantly and Mrs. Ibe was wary of leaving his side for a long period. Afonwa arrived the day before the event. Tunji picked her at the airport and drove her straight to Nfudu's hotel. When the two sisters set eyes on each other, they ran and hugged each other tightly.

"Afonwa, you've matured so much!" Nfudu exclaimed. She held her upper arm and moved her in different directions to get a better view of her entire body causing Afonwa to giggle. "I've missed you so much."

"I've missed you too," said Afonwa, clinging onto her big sister as if for dear life.

"How are Mama, Papa, everyone?"

"They're all fine. Papa sends his apologies. I honestly believe he'll start to feel better when he sees you."

"Come in," said Nfudu. "We have so much work to do. Is your outfit ready? What are you wearing?"

"Nothing... Just kidding." Afonwa said giggling mischievously.

"You've not changed Afonwa. You're still as naughty as ever."

"My clothes are ready sis." Afonwa finally admitted. "How about you? Do you need help with anything?"

"Yes! Some last minute items. I'm usually very organized, but this time around, I feel so frazzled. I don't know why. It's probably something to do with my ramshackle private life."

"Don't worry. I'm here to help."

Afonwa helped Nfudu sort out her clothes and accessories, then she helped her review her speech and make a few calls. Fibi came in later to take over where Afonwa had left off. They ordered dinner in the suite and worked till it was close to midnight until Nfudu insisted on getting some rest before the opening ceremony the following day.

The venue of the launching, the South Ikoyi Hotels conference room, was filled to the brim with all kinds of dignitaries – politicians, businessmen and professionals. Some of the guests – the influential political figures – arrived with police escorts, who stood beside them and jumped at the slightest provocation. A good number of them came to honor the invitation extended by D.Y Ibrahim, who was also an influential political figure. They came with their checkbooks ready to impress with donations for the school and the causes it supported. They were all decked out in flamboyant clothes, but the women were the most fascinating. They looked as though they stepped out of the most glamorous fashion magazines in New York or Paris. Their clothes – though made by local designers – merited international acclaim just for their creativity and fit. The details were exquisite and they hugged them in all the right places. All the women felt sexy in their own skin – which showed by the way they rocked their bodies no matter what size they were.

The décor was out of the ordinary. Every inch of the walls and the ceiling was decorated with plush gold and blue satin. The chairs were covered with gold satin and chiffon, while the tables had gold damask table clothes and blue runners. Several chandeliers hung from the ceilings and a massive one rotated in the center of the room, about two feet from where the high table was set up, giving the room a wonderful ambience.

Nfudu could not believe her eyes when she saw the venue. It was reminiscent of the glamour Nigerians were known for. All eyes were on her when she walked in. Photographers scrambled to get a picture of the young woman that took the European fashion world by storm and returned to her country to establish a training ground for budding fashionistas. The lights from their cameras flashed, blinding her temporarily while the ushers helped her maneuver her way to the high table. D.Y. Ibrahim was seated on her left and the Commissioner for Education for Lagos State was seated on her right. They both stood up to shake her hands and exchange pleasantries.

"Congratulations, my dear!" The commissioner said in a rather gruff voice.

"Thank you, sir," Nfudu responded.

"You have really made our country proud. I hope many more young women will follow in your footsteps."

"I'm flattered sir," Nfudu responded, smiling.

The two men waited for Nfudu to take her seat before they sat down.

The event started soon after with an opening prayer by the Master of Ceremony, followed by an opening speech delivered by

Nfudu. In her speech, she welcomed the guests, thanked them for attending and proceeded to describe her motivation for starting the Lagos Fashion School. She talked about the challenges she faced to get the school to the point it was at and the 'Angels' that came to her rescue by delivering on their promises to partner and turn the concept into reality. After thanking her partners, especially D.Y. for their roles, she went on to share that the school's pioneer class had a hundred percent enrollment – which was a great achievement – considering it was the first school of its kind in Nigeria. Finally, she commended her team for their efforts and asked that they continue to do their best to move the school in a positive direction.

There was great applause for her speech. Several speeches followed, including one by D.Y. Ibrahim and the Commissioner for Education – who expressed his pleasure at the interest in vocational careers and the ingenuity shown by the owners by setting up such a fine institution. Nfudu was baffled by the length of some of the speeches. Most of the speakers spoke for an uncomfortably long time that she began to wonder when the event would transition to entertainment and refreshments. When it finally came, entertainment included a performance from a traditional dance group from Badagry, a comedy skit and a musical performance by Sunny Akosa. Food was abundant. The guests were given the option of eating from a buffet table or ordering from a selection of dishes to be served by the uniformed waiters that swarmed the event hall. The food selection was such that it catered to every taste bud. It included a wide variety of seafood, rice dishes, local soups and desserts.

After the food was served, the floor was opened for donations. At first, Nfudu was impressed by the generosity exhibited by some of her guests. However, she was dazed by the competition that followed as the donors tried to outdo each other as though it was a game for which an incredible prize awaited the highest donor. Ultimately, almost ten million naira was raised for the causes Nfudu and her team put forward to support to their shock and amazement. Following donations, a red satin ribbon was set up for a ceremonious cut to represent the official opening of the school. Music coming from the D.J's station reverberated from the speakers placed in strategic positions, all over the event venue. Guests took to the dance floor in response to the remarkable Afro music playing in the background. The party went on until late in the evening. Nfudu got her cue to leave when her heart sank after the couple she saw kissing in a corner reminded her about Javier. Luckily for her, Fibi joined her soon after at her table.

"This was amazing," Nfudu said. "It was hugely successful – like nothing I've ever seen. I'm so proud of you guys for organizing this."

"Thanks," said Fibi. "I'm also surprised by how well it turned out. I'm still speechless. This will be the 'talk of the town' for a while."

When Nfudu got to her room that night, thoughts of Javier filled her mind. She thought of calling him under the guise of discussing the success of the opening, but immediately convinced herself it was a bad idea. Oblivious to Afonwa's chatter in the background, she fell asleep almost immediately, but with a heavy heart despite all the wonderful things that were going on around her.

By the next day, true to Fibi's prediction, all the Lagos entertainment magazines published stories about the event. The Society Magazine published a multi-page spread of the occasion. It showcased the guests and the highlights that made the event successful. The article that followed described Nfudu as:

"...A Paris educated international fashion designer that came to take her homeland by storm and establish the first fashion school of its kind...."

It then went ahead to list her accomplishments and also highlight that she had stores all over the world.

Nfudu was elated by the publicity the event garnered for her business. She immediately directed her team in London to capitalize on the opportunity for their other businesses. The Paris, Milan and Athens stores were already operational before Nfudu stepped into Lagos. However, since their official openings were still slated for a time in the future, Nfudu utilized any available avenue to drive interest in the stores pending the formal opening.

Nfudu was scheduled to return to London in a few days, but not before visiting her parents in Abasi. The night before she was supposed to head to Abasi with Afonwa, she hung out at the Vesmo Lounge with Fibi, Aki and a couple of the staff from the school to celebrate the success of the launching. Everyone in attendance seemed very happy and jovial as they danced the night away and drank to their heart's content. Nfudu was the only exception. She felt lonely even with the excellent company around her. All she could think about was Javier. She made every possible effort to eradicate him from her mind but found it impossible to do so. After lying to her team about an urgent matter she needed to attend to at the hotel, she was able to leave without protest. All she needed was privacy to rest, think and nurse her hurt without the chaos surrounding her.

30

WHEN Nfudu left the Vesmo lounge, she longed desperately to return to her hotel suite, soak in a tub, cuddle up under her sheets and think of nothing, but Javier, until sleep came. Arriving in her suite, she saw the light flicking on her answering machine. When she clicked to listen, she heard David's frantic voice: *"Vanessa delivered a baby boy at eight PM yesterday at St George's hospital in London. Both mother and son are doing great. Call us as soon as you get this..."*

Nfudu was thrilled by the news and tried several times to call David and Vanessa's flat but couldn't reach them. She tried Javier's number but couldn't reach him also. David finally picked around three o'clock.

"David?"

"Yes? Who's this?"

"David, it's Nfudu."

"Oh, hey. Why are you up so late? Did you get my message?"

"I did. I've been trying to call for the past two hours. I even tried to call Javier, but he didn't pick up..."

"We were all at the hospital. I just came home to catch a few hours of sleep. How are you doing?"

"I'm fine. I thought she was due in three weeks."

"That's what we thought, too. I panicked when she went into labor last night. I drove her to the hospital, hoping that the pregnancy could be prolonged to prevent a premature birth. As it turned out, the baby's weight was substantial enough for it to be considered full term. The doctors still felt the need to keep him in a special care unit just as a precaution."

"What a relief. How are they doing?"

"They're doing great. Vanessa wishes you were here. She misses you terribly."

"I'm so happy that both of them are doing fine, but I'm utterly disappointed I wasn't there when the baby arrived. We obviously miscalculated. What I wouldn't have given to be there with her."

"She said the same thing too, but hey, don't worry about it. You're coming back soon aren't you?"

"I'll be back in a week," said Nfudu. "Tomorrow – or today actually – I'll be visiting my hometown. I'll call you guys when I get there."

"Great! See you soon. Give my regards to your family."

"I will. Give my love to Vanessa and the baby."

Nfudu finally slept at the very early hours of the morning and was woken at eight o'clock as Fibi banged on the door of her suite.

"Hurry! I can't believe you're both still sleeping. You're about to miss your flight!" Fibi shrieked after Afonwa let her in. She scurried around picking up pieces of clothing that were left strewn all over the floor from the night before.

"What time is it?" Nfudu asked peeking a little from under the sheets.

"Eight something. There's no time…"

"Oh, that late?" said Nfudu scampering out of bed. "Afonwa…Afonwaaa…hurry we have to leave now."

Afonwa, who was still groggy from one too many drinks, scrambled alongside Nfudu to get their personal items together. After the mad rush, they were able to make it to the airport in time. However, they found out their flight had been delayed for two hours because of inclement weather. While they waited for an announcement on their new flight departure time, they rested in the V.I.P lounge. Nfudu was disappointed by the delay. She was eager to get home and be with the rest of her family, who she missed dearly. She missed her mother the most and wished to collapse in her arms right then, and voiced her anguish to Afonwa.

"I hope this issue with our flight is resolved soon because I can't wait to get home. I'm so exhausted and I miss Mama very much."

"Me too..." Afonwa replied, "I miss Mama too."

"But you see her every day," protested Nfudu, while she adjusted her *gele*, which had started to slip off her head as she leaned on the lounge chairs. "I haven't set eyes on her for three years and I can't wait to eat her *'onugbu soup'*."

Afonwa laughed at Nfudu's juvenile comments and realized that her sister had not lost the attachment she had to their mother even after moving to Paris and becoming an international fashion designer. She loved that Nfudu, irrespective of her great achievements, still managed to maintain a 'down to earth' nature, when other women of her status, especially in high society would have put up airs around themselves. This, Afonwa believed, allowed her to remain likeable and approachable.

By the time their plane touched down in Benin City, a driver was already waiting to take them to Abasi. They rode along beautiful tree-lined roads which provided a familiar feeling of being close to home. As the scenery changed, Nfudu recalled all the events of the past few years, and how they helped her evolve into the person she had now become. She slept during the second hour of their two-hour drive, while Afonwa monitored the driver to make sure he didn't drive at unreasonable speeds. "Slow down!" she said numerous times to the driver whenever he started to pick up speed.

At one point, the driver, tired of Afonwa's paranoia retorted, "Sister, at this rate we may not reach until midnight. I'm rushing to avoid the rush hour traffic at Bridgehead."

"Ok, ok," replied Afonwa, waving her fingers at him. "But please just take it easy."

Nfudu woke up as they were nearing the Niger Bridge and took in the sites. There was a marked improvement from what she saw when she returned just three years back in nineteen seventy. The wreckage brought on by the war had gradually become a thing of the past. It was now replaced by a shiny new bridge and a beautiful constellation of shops – on each side of the river. She was filled with emotion at the sight before her. Her eyes welled up as she grabbed Afonwa's arm.

"Afoo, you didn't tell me…"

"I wanted you to see for yourself," Afonwa replied shrugging her shoulders.

"What about Abasi? Any changes?"

"Hmm…" Afonwa sighed moving her head slowly from one side to the next. "Not substantially, but people have picked up their lives. Aferi market has been reconstructed and a new church building is under construction. Peoples home still have shell holes and a lot still struggle with getting back to where they were before the war."

Nfudu wiped a tear from the corner of her eye.

"I thank God for everything. I know we'll all soon be delivered from our pain."

When they arrived at their father's compound, everywhere seemed more quiet than usual. No one came out to welcome them. Nfudu feared something could be wrong until they noticed the white Peugeot car parked in the visitor's section of their driveway. "I see why," she said. "They have a visitor."

"Even so," retorted Afonwa. "I'm thoroughly disappointed in all of them. They knew we were coming. Whoever came to visit must be 'very important' for them not to care that we've arrived."

Nfudu ignored her tantrums and ran right up the stairs to the huge sitting room, where her family gathered on special occasions. Standing at the centre of the room, all six feet and two inches of him, with a wry smile spread across his face was Javier.

Nfudu was transfixed to the spot.

"What's going on?" she asked looking frantically around, hoping her mother and father, who she spotted at their favorite positions in the room would help provide an answer.

Javier walked up to her. She looked suspiciously at him, her heart pounding furiously in her chest. When he got close enough to her, he held her hand, looked straight into her eyes and declared, "Did you ever think I was going to let you get away…?"

Before Nfudu could respond, Javier slid his hand around her waist and led her to the adjoining balcony for some privacy. Unknown to him, Afonwa and the other siblings crowded the windows in the living room with a view of the balcony to gawk at them.

"Nfudu," Javier called with a sense of urgency and held both her hands. She looked lovingly at him, at a loss for words.

"Yes," she responded, her heart pounding heavily.

"Two nights ago," he continued, "I held my very first grandchild in my arms… It was the most beautiful thing I have ever seen. In that moment, I felt the weirdest combination of love and joy. But, even with my entire family surrounding me, I felt empty when I looked around and saw you weren't there. In that instant, I knew what I needed to do to feel complete. I got my daughter's blessing and here I am …." The emotions in his voice increased the longer he spoke and rendered his words almost inaudible. "Darling I'm amazed by you…. Please marry me my dearest. I love you and will love you till the day I die…"

Distraught by his speech, Nfudu placed her hands on his shoulders to anchor her wobbling frame.

"My heart almost stopped when I first set my eyes on you" Nfudu said choking on her words. "That I could recover… What I have never been able to recover from, is the way I feel about you. Darling …I love you! I love you! I love you…," she ended, sobbing lightly on his shoulders.

Javier held her tight and lifted her into the air, while everyone clapped and cheered in excitement. Nfudu looked in the direction of the doorway, where her entire family was now gathered and was mortified when she realized they may have overheard her entire exchange with Javier. When she caught her father's eye, the glow in it told her everything she needed to know – Javier had his approval. Afonwa was standing behind him, stunned. The whole episode had been as much a surprise to her as it was to Nfudu.

Javier put Nfudu down and presented her with the red diamond engagement ring.

"I kept it all this while because it was too painful to return it," he confessed to Nfudu. "Frankly, I'm glad I didn't because it would have been hard to find something this rare in seventy-three." Nfudu's mouth was agape when she saw her old ring glistening in the shiny black box it came in. She glanced at it and looked up at Javier before stretching her left hand for him to place the ring in its rightful position.

"I never thought I'd ever set eyes on this beauty again." She said shaking her head gently from side to side. "Thank God you saved it. It's the most exquisite thing I've ever seen."

Everyone surrounded her to view the ring. They marveled at its beauty.

"A rare gem! ...You deserve it, my child." Chief Ibe exclaimed.

"Thank you, Papa," she said before she turned to Javier. "I'm so glad we get another chance. I promise I'll never mess us up again."

"I know you won't my darling. I know."

He pulled her close for a lengthy kiss, creating excitement for her siblings – her parents, not so much.

–

The festivities that followed, although only hours in the making since Javier arrived that morning was worthy of an engagement party made in Chief Ibe's household. A feast was set in the formal dining room, with delicious entrees – most Javier had never seen before. It included goat meat pepper soup, *ugba*, roasted fish, *nkwobi* and *jollof* rice. Friends and neighbors were invited to join the party. Many, who were able to attend at short notice stayed for hours on end. They marveled at how Nfudu and Javier were able to succeed against all odds. Even though Javier loved meeting all the guests, he couldn't wait for them to leave so he could spend alone time with his fiancée.

They headed back to Lagos two days later and then to London the following day. Javier broke up his engagement with Samantha as soon as he arrived in London. Samantha felt betrayed, but confessed that she knew Javier still loved Nfudu the whole time they were together. She always knew she couldn't compete with their undying love for each other. In a matter of days, she moved her belongings out of Javier's homes in Nice and London.

Vanessa and David's baby was named Jorge after Javier's father. He was a handsome little thing, who had David's fair hair and blue eyes. With proper scrutiny, one could see that he had Vanessa's well-defined features. He acquired the best physical qualities of both his parents. His christening took place on the first of December at St Martin's church in Trafalgar. Nfudu looked beautiful in a white dress that she designed many months before for the occasion. After church, the guests were invited for an intimate lunch at the lodge. Everyone marveled at how beautiful the baby was. Nfudu considered him her miracle baby for reuniting her and Javier.

They said "I do" in a beautiful private ceremony, six months after the Milan stores formal opening. It was an outdoor wedding at Javier's home in Nice. Jorge was already a year old and looked adorable in his ring bearer attire – a black tuxedo and red bow tie. Vanessa, who was two months pregnant with her second child, was the 'Maid of Honor', while Javier's friend Mark was the 'Best Man'. Chief Ibe, his wife, Afonwa and Chineme were in attendance from Nigeria. Dike and Emeka were also there to honor the event. Nfudu's family looked spectacular in their matching *aso-ebi* made from a silvery purple silk *aso-oke* fabric.

Javier wanted to surprise his bride, so he kept the location of their honeymoon a secret until they arrived at their destination in the private jet he rented for their trip. When they landed on the beautiful Island of Tahiti, Nfudu's expression convinced him that she was thrilled by his choice. It was everything she had imagined and more. On landing, they were welcomed by two brawny males in raffia skirts and nothing to cover their glistening chests, who handed them coconut water in their shells. A chauffeur drove them to an exclusive resort, where a honeymoon suite was set aside to provide them an experience of a lifetime.

For two weeks, they ate, slept, swam, toured the island, hung out with the locals, shopped and made love. Nfudu, being a self-acclaimed 'foodie', explored several exotic dishes from Tahiti and its neighboring Islands.

The day before they were to leave, they toured the waterfalls and were both inspired by the beauty and nature that surrounded them. Javier was the perfect husband. He brought her a platter of desserts after they returned to their suite, and massaged her feet to ease any tense spots. Nfudu considered herself lucky and wondered what good she did to deserve him.

The lovebirds returned to Nice the following day, where Nfudu moved all her belongings from her London flat as she resumed her life as Mrs. St Pierre.

THE END

Acknowledgments

First and foremost I would like to thank the Almighty God, with whom everything is possible.

Next, I would like to thank my grandmother, the late Edna Ifeobu who provided the inspiration for this novel. You were an epitome of beauty and your magnanimity was felt by everyone around you.

To Dad, you're my guardian angel. You went to work at the same hour you passed from this earth. I miss you always.

To Mum, you always have a way of putting things into the right perspective. Thank you for always being there for me.

To Dumkele and Nnamdi who reminded me daily to pick up my writing and showed extreme eagerness to read my earlier works. That melted my heart and motivated me to keep writing, at first to please you guys, and then later because I just couldn't stop. Thank you, Dumkele for your first round of edits.

To Ofor, you encouraged me in more ways than one to finish this novel. Your feedback on some of the scenes was invaluable.

To Ogo, thank you for your editorial advice and feedback. Your encouragement helped me work harder at publishing this novel.

To Chichi, Moby and Keke, Thank you for cheering me on and always providing your unwavering support.

Made in the USA
Columbia, SC
03 February 2018